"Last night was num‎‎‏‎‏ ‏‎‎ job interview. I shared r‎‎ ‏‎‎ ‎‎ ‎‎ ‎‎ ‎‎ ‎‎ ‎‎ while she kept me company by phone. School was out, and I'd caught her prepping in her classroom.

"You've reduced your meets to numbers?"

"What's the point in names? I'm not seeing any of these guys again, and you just get confused." I pulled into the Waffle Cone parking lot and unhooked my seat belt.

"True. But you're turning into a cynic."

"As soon as I find my someone special, I'll tell you his name."

"Sounds good. So what about your number nine?"

"We traded tales from the trenches and he—"

"Trenches? What trenches?"

"Dating trenches, what other kinds of trenches do you think? He met eight women, all in one day. In a coffee shop in Hartford. Two coffee shops. Back to back appointments."

"You are joking."

"He ran from one coffee shop to the other. Had it all timed—half an hour in one coffee shop, and then he'd run a block to the second, and so forth."

"People do these things?" Isabel asked.

"Oh, lots of weird behavior. I thought it was bold. In fact, I can't believe what some guys tell me. And do."

## Praise for *MIDDLE AGE*ISH

"A delightful read! Jump in the deep end of online dating and starting over with Sunny Chanel in this debut Rom-Com adventure."

*~Jean M Grant, Author*

~

"This clever romantic comedy turns middle-aged dating into a lighthearted, entertaining guessing game."

*~Patti Cavaliere, Author*

~

"...Bridget Jones rides again, only she's older, knows more, and still is just as funny."

*~Constance Wilson, ARC Reader*

~

"...a feel-good read about love and friendship, with a sharp-witted heroine starting over and loving it."

*~Nora Wigley, ARC Reader*

~

"An engagingly told story illustrating that no matter what the medium is in romance, words still matter."

*~Peter Menta, ARC Reader*

~

"A delightful glimpse into the world of online dating. You'll chuckle at the characters you meet and the situations they find themselves in. The online dating struggle is real!"

*~ Mered Lawson, ARC Reader*

~

"This charged romantic novel illuminates the joyous yet scary fun of middle-aged dating and sends the reader on a powerful roller coaster of an experience."

*~ Tom Malchodi, ARC Reader*

# Middle Age*ish*

by

## Shirley Goldberg

*Starting Over, Book 1*

**Middle Age*ish***

*The Dynamics of Chaos* from collected poems has been reprinted with the permission of the author © Francesca Androulaki

Cover Art by *The Wild Rose Press, Inc.*
Contact Information: info@thewildrosepress.com
The Wild Rose Press, Inc.
PO Box 708
Adams Basin, NY 14410-0708
Visit us at www.thewildrosepress.com

Publishing History
First Champagne Rose Edition, 2020
Trade Paperback ISBN 978-1-5092-3250-5
Digital ISBN 978-1-5092-3251-2

*Starting Over, Book 1*
Published in the United States of America

## Dedication

This book is dedicated to all my writerly friends IRL and online. And to all the women with the guts to get out there and look for that special someone, no matter where you find yourself in life.

# Acknowledgments

I especially want to thank the very talented poet Francesca Sweeney-Androulaki for permitting me to use her poem *"The Dynamics of Chaos"* in my story.

A word for my family: thanks for always accepting me, even when I'm ornery—Annie, Sandi, Barb, and Davey. Thank you to my friends on four continents for listening to me rattle on about my characters, real and fictional. Patti and again my sister Barb for reading and commenting bluntly. Mr. Tom for his patience and understanding. My TARA writer friends who are an inspiration and share their knowledge. And all my new Wild Rose Press fellow authors because you are the best. My Unitarian friends, especially Pidgie, my beta reader. My Wedgewood friends and Welcome Club members for rooting me on. And my fellow dancers at Sara Dance who kept asking, "When's the book coming out?"

Thanks to Mark Mathes for his writing and marketing expertise. And a special thanks to Maureen Sevilla, my editor, for recognizing the qualities in Sunny that shine on these pages. And Tom for reading all the drafts. And my fellow Inky Links writers—how I love our little group. Rob, Teri, Marisa, Jim, Pam, Lizzie, and Teresa.

Chapter One
Paris—This ain't decaf…

"Morning." I poured coffee into my dog mug with the tail handle and glanced at the calendar on the bulletin board by the fridge. *Will he remember today is our anniversary? Probably not.*

Laurent had highlighted two other much more important dates in green. One for a haircut, another for his colonoscopy. He slouched at the tiny bistro table drinking Italian espresso, eating toast with La Vache qui rit—the plastic cheese—and gazing out the window. Which meant he was working. He's half British, half French, a professor of environmental studies, travels twenty days a month, and proofreads heavy stuff at breakfast.

"I have a tough week," I said. "Subbing plus my regular schedule."

He turned back to his journal and picked up his pencil. The hair at the back of his neck curled. I used to love the hair factor, the idea that *my man* still had hair. I squinted to imagine a balding husband.

Pluto sat and lifted his paw, the signal he wanted his ears ruffled. And a treat. "Good boy," Laurent said, bending and scratching our dog's ear. He slipped Pluto a small chunk of toast with cheese.

Maybe if I were cute like our fox terrier with one floppy ear, I'd get my ears ruffled too. I moved closer with the coffee pot to get into his line of vision.

Laurent's eyes focused on me, traveled up and down. "Nice," he said.

And what was wrong with baggy black sweats and a long black sweatshirt? Disguised the extra ten pounds, didn't it?

His mouth curled in a pseudo-smile, and he tapped his coffee cup. "Warm-up. Please."

Deep in my gut something scraped. I tilted the coffee pot as Laurent raised his cup, his eyes busy scanning the page. Dribbled coffee into the mug before shifting the pot a few inches to the right, where coffee plinked onto the table like spring rain hitting the windshield.

His latest journal, a fat offering by a Berkeley, California environmental group, took the first hit. Circling the table, I kept the pot moving, and lifted it a few inches to create splatter, going for a crime scene effect. Coffee cascaded from the table onto the floor.

"What the bloody hell?" Laurent raised his arms in a protective stance and jerked back, tipping the chair over and sending Pluto whimpering into a corner.

I set the pot on the counter and stepped over the pool of coffee, took my jacket and Pluto's leash from the hook on the wall. "I don't like you anymore."

Pluto and I took the stairs, the dog scampering down the six flights in an eager rush for this unexpected walk. I pulled open the heavy lobby door and stood in front of the building inhaling the odor of gasoline from the buses and trucks, listening to the sounds of honking. Everyone was going places, busy with their lives.

*I don't like you anymore.* He didn't seem to like me either, and backing away was his coping mechanism.

Pluto pulled, and we trotted around the block, my thoughts unspooling in a tangle. The mud-gray day mirrored my mental state and Laurent's mood for the past year, as I remembered how we used to be in the old days. Mornings at breakfast, squeezed together at the kitchen table, reading Le Monde. He'd mention there was jazz around the corner at Le Top or a new Coen Brothers movie.

These days I could eat out of the dog bowl and he wouldn't notice.

At least there was Pluto to mull things over with, partake in one-sided conversations about my students, or share a snack...his favorite activity. These days, I cringed at hearing Laurent's key in the lock, not knowing if he would greet me, ignore me, or give me his creepy nod.

By the time I made it around the block and into the elevator, my jacket was soaked, and my sneakers made little squishing sounds. The doors opened on the fifth-floor penthouse apartment, six rooms, not counting the two bathrooms. Luxembourg Gardens in the sixth arrondissement is a primo location. Laurent's family had owned the place for decades, and we had updated and refurbished it ten years earlier. The kitchen is a techno-steel marvel that suits Laurent's esthetics—not mine.

My hands searched my pockets for keys. Nothing. I knocked. Several minutes went by. I was about to knock again when there were footsteps.

"Who's that?" I asked Pluto, employing my excited voice. Pluto barked, as if on cue, and the door opened. Laurent eyed us before handing me a towel and disappearing into the apartment.

I dried Pluto in the hall, hung my wet jacket over one of Laurent's chic-Frenchie jackets on the hook behind the door, and squish-walked into the bedroom where Laurent was packing for his next trip.

"I've been thinking we've somehow got to..." My voice trailed off as he walked back and forth between the suitcase splayed on the bed, the closet, and his bureau, ignoring me.

He uses the scientific method involving plastic zip baggies and confines his travel wardrobe to gray, beige, and off white. No color. *No color?* So, what was that baby blue item playing peekaboo from a corner of the suitcase? When he turned his back to grab something from the dresser drawer, I copped a feel. Underwear. Definitely silk. *My husband wears man-panties?*

The sour taste of too much black coffee rose in my throat. "I have something important to tell—"

"You're leaving puddles all over the floor with those super-saturated trainers. Take them off. And for God's sake, can this wait? I have to leave in an hour for a meeting."

"This can't wait." If I didn't get it out now, I'd barf into his carefully packed suitcase. "You can't ignore me forever." *Like you are ignoring our twenty-third wedding anniversary.*

I turned as he moved, sliding as if I were dancing. "We need some kind of...maybe we need counseling?"

He didn't stop and instead increased his speed as if he were fast-forwarding.

"We need to talk. This is serious."

"What? *Marriage* counseling? I heard you. Don't talk bloody rubbish." He stopped and stared at me. His mouth went slack, the lines across his forehead

4

deepening. "Crap. If you won't clean this mess up, I'll—"

I reached behind him with both hands, seized a few of the straight-from-the-cleaner dress shirts, and whatever else I could grab, and pitched them on the floor. Pluto dove on the scattered pile and came up with—a pair of forest green man-panties. He huffed and growled, whipping them from side to side.

"Here, boy, here—bloody crap." Laurent dived for his underwear, but Pluto tunneled under the bed. "Here, boy, give, give." Laurent kneeled and lifted the quilt to peer underneath, but smarty-pants Pluto was already out the other side. Laurent never was any good at disciplining our dog, and I was feeling way too ornery to heel.

He got to his feet, staring at the wet marks on his pants and back at me. "Now I've got to change. What's got into you today? You're acting juvenile. *Tu m'énerve.*"

As he scrabbled around on hands and knees, it came to me, how unhappy we'd been for a long while. Laurent doesn't talk because he has nothing to say. Not to me anyway.

He gathered underwear and shirts from the floor.

"Sunny, how can I take you seriously when you act crazy? And I could have been burnt this morning. Damn lucky I jumped out of your way—"

"I'm sorry," I yelled, embarrassed and at the same time, fiercely proud I'd taken a stand. "I was *diligent* in pouring that coffee, but there was no intent to cause harm."

"You planned it?"

"What the hell?" *Is he serious?* "Of course not." I

headed for the hall closet, came back with the sponge mop, and ran it over the floor. "I snapped."

"Snapped?" He looked genuinely confused. "What is it with—"

"You piss me off. In fact, you've been pissing me off for a while now. Ignoring me. Ignoring our anniversary. Refusing to talk." I approached him, my finger in the air, the better to make my point. He backed up. "You have to talk to me." My voice came out in a croak. "You have to."

I scanned the bedroom for a sharp object to throw at him, even though this made no sense, and I wasn't a thrower. The single item on the bureau was a bottle of Chanel, last year's anniversary gift, and it had no sharp edges.

"Excuse me," and he left the room. Typical Laurent behavior. I'd give him a few minutes.

Pluto jumped on the bed, and I flopped down next to him. He rolled from side to side on his back, displaying his balls and making a snuffling sound.

I scratched his head. How long had Laurent been pulling back? And how long had I been pretending it wasn't happening?" I leaned over and rubbed my forehead against Pluto's neck, and he licked my ear. Laurent moved around the kitchen, opening cupboards, slamming the refrigerator door, clanking a pot on the stove. Was he cooking? Now? Didn't he have a meeting? Then I heard him on his mobile phone. I closed my eyes.

After a while, Laurent's voice called out from the kitchen. "Sunny?"

"Are you talking to me from another room?" An old joke from back when we liked each other.

He appeared in the doorway clutching a bottle of wine. "I've opened this, need to let it breathe."

Pluto sat up, and so did I. *Wine? I hadn't even had breakfast.* Seconds went by, Laurent looking at the two of us.

"You're right," he said. "We need to talk."

****

In the kitchen, Pluto and I joined Laurent at the stove, where deliciousness percolated, and Pluto could get in on the action. He sat on his pillow in the corner and licked his lips in anticipation.

"I moved my meeting to another day, and I'm making lunch. Brunch, actually."

The mouth-watering aroma of olive oil and onions sizzling in the pan hit me, and I salivated. He turned down the flame and wiped his hands on his birthday apron, the one that said *Frenchmen do it with an Accent.*

"Not much, but I've got asparagus to go in the omelet. And a baguette. With butter, if you like."

"I like butter on my baguette, and so does Pluto." *You have no business liking butter with that extra ten pounds,* my brain said in the middle of all this.

Laurent poured the wine and handed me a glass. "This is a nice Beaujolais. Picked it up a few months ago in Lyon." He raised his glass. "To us."

Toasting to *us*? I lifted my glass. *Isn't it a bit late to be making nice?*

We sipped, and he poured the eggs into the pan and sliced the asparagus into bites. I wondered where all this was leading, this lunch togetherness, and when we'd get to the talking part. Laurent tilted the pan, so the uncooked portion of the omelet flowed and settled evenly.

"Uh…" and my gut did its familiar twist. I couldn't force him to talk, and what I wanted was impossible. I wanted the old Laurent, the funny, talky, arrogant-but-not-with-me Laurent. I wanted our romantic dinners at Chez Louis, or around the corner at Indonesia, holidays spent for the last twenty-two years with his friends. What had happened?

I eased my butt onto the kitchen chair, thinking hard. When had we last gone out with our good friends Jean-Paul and Marie? Over a year ago. How was it possible I hadn't noticed?

"What do you want to talk about?" Laurent said over his shoulder.

As my mind was busy shouting, *What the hell do you think I want to talk about?* I couldn't respond right away. The silence ticked on, the aroma of onions and omelet permeating the kitchen. Laurent folded the omelet, tilted the pan again. "Ready in two minutes," he said.

"For starters, be honest," I said so loudly I surprised myself. "Why don't we ever do anything together anymore?"

He stood facing me, spatula raised over the frying pan, bits of egg clinging. "You want me to spend more time with you? You've got to be kidding. We've gone over this." His words must have sounded harsh even to his ears because he softened his voice and shifted into patient mode. "You know what my schedule is like." He turned back to the stove, lifted a piece of omelet onto a plate, and flourished it in front of me along with a chunk of baguette and the butter. "You keep busy enough, don't you? You've got your students and such.

Your friends."

"That's not how marriage works."

He sat opposite. "I'm sorry."

"Sorry?" I said, surprised. Laurent never apologized.

He leaned forward, his eyes shifting to the right as if avoiding eye contact eased the impact of his message. "I want a separation."

Crazy that I had the urge to laugh. The twisty thing in my gut that had bothered me all morning dissolved, and I forked a bite of the omelet, stuffed it in my mouth. Perfect. A hint of butter, not too much. Chewed more slowly. Why rush after all? We weren't going anywhere.

In fact, we were going nowhere.

Before taking the next bite, I inhaled, enjoying the scent of the slightly caramelized onions. I put down the fork, grabbed my wine glass, and shoved it toward Laurent. "Fill it up."

What a dick. The worst was happening. Now I knew where I stood, and it wasn't a surprise. He'd ignored me for months and months because he didn't dare tell me he wanted a separation?

*Separation or divorce? Which is it?*

He filled my glass and took a slug from his own. "I lost interest. I don't know. I got so tired of it all. The same people, the same old restaurants. One bloody boring play after another, and if I never see— I'm sorry, I shouldn't say that." He sucked in a deep breath. "Your friends. I've got nothing to say to them anymore." He held up his hand, knowing I would call him on this one. "Look, I'm not blaming anyone. Not your friends. Not you. Truth is I don't know what I

9

want. I don't know, but I want something different."
His fingers drummed on the table. "Sometimes, I feel
so angry. And I know I take it out on you. It's not
right." He looked at me as if expecting a response or an
argument. "Let's not blame ourselves."

"Oh." I felt nothing, not much anyway. Relief
mostly. All my backing off had come to this. Our
anniversary didn't count. Twenty-three years didn't
count. I took another bite of omelet. Where would I go?
Could I get custody of Pluto? And who got the
apartment?

Maybe Laurent should move out.

"So, where will you live?" I said, chewing. *Why
should I be the one to leave?*

"Can you afford the upkeep on this place?" he
asked.

I took a piece of bread and piled egg on top to
create a little sandwich. *He has a point about the
upkeep.* Laurent had been living here—one of Paris'
most pricey neighborhoods—when we met. *Who am I
kidding?* The apartment belongs to his family, and it's
where he'll live until he dies.

My brain seemed to be on holiday, and despite the
separation news, my body was relaxing, helped by the
wine. I'd need a nap soon. "Afford the upkeep?
Probably not," I said, unworried.

Laurent watched me, secretly astounded, no doubt,
by the cool way I reacted to this whole thing. "Look.
We'll find you a place. Smaller than this, of course,"
and his eyes swept the rooms as if calculating the size
of the space I'd require. Our living room and dining
rooms combined were spacious enough to host thirty,
although it had been years since our last party.

Instantly, I saw myself in a sixth-floor classic au pair one-roomer, the size of a walk-in closet. Which is where I'd started when I came to Paris, twenty-five years ago. I took French language and literature courses at the Sorbonne, and five and a half days a week I cared for an eight-year-old and a ten-year-old in exchange for that little room and meals with the family. I'd been, unbelievably, twenty-five?

"Laurent?" I tilted the glass, felt the warmth as the wine trickled down my throat. A glass and a half so far, with no sign of stopping.

"We'll still see one another," he said. "I know this will be a big change for us both. I need space right now, that's all. I've been thinking about this for a long time—"

"Wait. What?"

Laurent looked at me as if I'd caught him with his hand up our neighbor's dress.

"No way. I can't stay here." I broke off the heel of the baguette, my favorite part. He wouldn't talk to me, but he'd been thinking about moving me out for a long time.

"We'll figure it out," he said. "I'll ask around. This—"

"I'm going back to the States." I buttered the heel and bit in.

"Are you crazy?" Laurent said. "Have you thought this through?"

I swallowed the last bit of bread and wiped my hand on the napkin. "Hey, you did me a favor, backing away all these months. Of course, I freakin' well knew things were down the crapper, but I couldn't admit it to myself. So, no shock here. Thanks for brunch, by the

11

way. The asparagus was a nice touch." My voice reeked of sarcasm. "Right now, I have a lot of thinking to do."

*And I need a nap to clear my mind.* I reached for my wine and drained it. Might as well finish the bottle. I poured the remaining inch into my glass.

"We need to decide what—" Laurent began, but I cut him off.

"I'm going back to school," I said. "I'll live with my parents and earn my certification so I can support myself. Teaching makes sense. It's what I do."

Making things up on the spot, and they shot out of my mouth, each one a tiny surprise. "Remember, I've been taking those certification courses."

Thank God for the head start—since I visited my parents in Connecticut for a month every summer. "Honey, why don't you take a course at Southern? You never know," my mother said. *A brilliant idea.*

I'd dig out my transcripts, add up the credits.

"Why not?" Laurent managed a shaky smile. This was turning into a logical plan, and Laurent, being French, was a logical man. He had grown up on Descartes, even though over the past year, he'd modified the famous *I think, therefore I am* to...*I yell, therefore I am.*

My eyes closed for a couple of seconds. "I have so much to research. Courses. Registration. Calls to make."

My friends, I had to tell my friends, who've been listening to me bitching about Laurent all these months.

"Can't think now." I wobbled to my feet, and when Laurent extended an arm to support me, I grabbed it. He walked me to the bedroom, heaved off the suitcase, and helped me onto the bed. Pluto jumped up and curled into my side.

"Look, I'm sorry about—"

"I'll need money," I said, closing my eyes, not wanting to hear any lame apologizing. "…to start over."

****

It was almost two in the afternoon when I woke, surprised to find Laurent still home.

"Coffee." I leaned an elbow on the table to support my throbbing head.

"I made a pot when I heard you get up." Laurent poured me a cup of coffee and sat opposite me at the little bistro table. "You're making some calls today?"

"After." I gave him a weak smile. "Will you make me some toast?" Getting up and going over to the toaster would be too much. I gulped my coffee and closed my eyes. "Could you close those blinds, please?"

"Sure," he said, and the room darkened. "Better?" All cheery, as if the wine hadn't made a dent in his day. Of course, I'd consumed most of the bottle. I chugged my coffee and heard the bread go in the toaster. After a few moments, it popped up, under-toasted, the way I like it.

"Butter?" said Laurent.

"Just jelly."

"Give your parents my regards when you talk to them," he said, handing me the toast, his voice soft.

"Sure."

"Take some aspirin. And lock in those courses, whatever you can manage to nail down. You can matriculate later. Let me know how it goes tonight? I won't be home late. I leave for Brussels tomorrow."

After Laurent left, I sprawled on the couch and called Isabel, my best friend.

Two rings.

I surveyed the living room, each piece familiar, chosen with care, from the multi-hued area rug in shades of gray to the coffee table. An abstract, painted by an artist friend of Laurent's, hung over the fireplace. My gaze shifted to the hand-blown lamps lazing happily on metal end tables we purchased on a trip to Crete.

I'd need everything. From forks and spoons to a bed.

Five rings. *Be home. Be home.* It was around 9:00 a.m. in the States.

The call went to voicemail, so I left a message. My life in two sentences, details to follow. Then I dialed my parents, imagining myself in my old bedroom in Connecticut with the slanted ceilings. I wondered if my mother would make cornflake chicken for my homecoming, the way she did when I was in college.

Living at home with my parents, I would feel safe, a comforting thought, like meatloaf with mashed potatoes for dinner in the winter.

"Hello."

"Hi, Mom."

"Sunny? Is that you? I'm so glad you called." There was a pause, and I heard whispering. "Your father wants to tell you something." A click as my father got on the extension.

"What? What's going on?"

"We have news." My father cleared his throat. "It happened yesterday. We never expected the house to sell so fast. Never expected it. We're packing. Moving to Scottsdale. We'll be near Sarah. We'll get to see the kids."

What in hell was he talking about? And then he was explaining how it was all so sudden, and every once in a while my mind tuned in, and through the rush of steamy, wet air to my brain, the air that impeded my ability to reason, I heard stuff that made sense and didn't make sense. My sister Sarah...the kids...teenagers are so busy...the warm weather, no shoveling, no winter clothes, the tennis, and the kids.

The kids he was talking about were in college, but that wasn't the point. I swallowed. No place to stay, and where was the bosom of my family now?

"We're thinking of leaving you some things," my mother said. "But since you don't live here...."

"Maybe Isabel would store it," my father said. "The items. Meanwhile."

"Maybe."

"Of course, there is no humidity in the desert." My mother intoned. "It's hot, but it's a dry heat, you know."

"Yes, I've heard that," I said. "That's good." Silence. And then I told them I was leaving Laurent, moving back to New Haven. Going back to school.

"You're leaving Laurent?"

"Yes."

"That's what I thought you said." She hesitated. "It's about time. He's a tad lacking in the support and warmth departments. Both departments."

Funny, this observation coming from my mom.

I sighed, dug my ass deeper into the leathery cushion of the sofa. This was my favorite spot to read, and I'd miss it, miss my life here. All Laurent's little lacks added together made a pretty big negative. For a few seconds, I sat holding the phone, my thoughts untidy with the realization that my own mother had known all along that I was married to a cold French-Brit trout.

And they'd be in the desert when I arrived. Somehow, the Arizona desert seemed the exact opposite of Paris.

"Mom?"

"Yes, honey?"

"Well, I haven't been...I haven't been happy in a while now." I sank deeper into the couch. I'd said it aloud, the unhappy thing.

"Honey, I'm sorry."

"I'll be fine." *I will be fine.*

"Wait, when are you coming?"

"Well, as soon as I can organize everything. Six weeks? This was all just decided, and I haven't made the reservation yet—"

"We can't go, Moe, we can't go. Sunny's coming. She's moving back. We'll have to...We can't just up and leave, not now." A frantic element in my mom's voice, the same degree of frantic she used the day my sister let go of the carriage handle and ran in front of a car in the supermarket parking lot. It stopped the driver, who luckily had her window open and could hear the screech of a mother saving her child's life.

"Calm down, sweetie. The house is sold," my father said in his temperate-climate voice designed to soothe my mom at such moments. "There's not much we can do about that."

"What are you saying? Houses can be unsold. People do it all the time." How my mother knew this, I had no idea. "I'm sure we can rent it from them. We'll ask, and I'm sure we can work out something. Our

Sunny is dumping her husband, and we need to be here to support her. What's another month in the scheme of things? Sunny?" she said as if realizing I was still there, live on the phone. Don't worry about—"

"Stop, you guys. I'm not worried. It's a surprise to me, sure, but you need to go ahead with whatever you planned. It's ridiculous to think of screwing your plans up because I decide to leave my husband."

*Because he wants a divorce and tells me on our anniversary then pretends it's a separation.*

"It's hard to think of you alone with nowhere to go," my mother said.

"Isabel will put me up," I assured her. "I *know* I can stay with Isabel." Putting real vigor and a no-nonsense tone into this reassurance. "Don't you dare change any plans. I'm fifty years old, and I can take care of myself." There, I'd convinced them, I was certain of it. Maybe I'd even convinced myself.

My mother let out a big breath of air, so big, it snaked through the phone lines long distance from Hamden, Connecticut to Paris, and I felt the residual heat as it smacked my cheek.

"See, Annie, she'll be fine," my father said. "She's a big girl."

"Honey, we'll call you again," my mother said. "To see how you're doing. I know you'll do well in your courses. You're never too old to learn." My mother loved the concept of lifelong learning.

"So what's going on there?" Best change the subject right about now.

"Hilda and Philly are coming," my father said. "Your mother made dinner."

"I made a turkey breast. They were on sale at Stop

and Shop."

"Tell them I said hello and give them hugs." I loved the idea that my parents were hanging out with their friends, and that all was normal. *A turkey breast.*

After hanging up, I researched courses online, scribbling notes. Then I made a few calls about shipping my things. It would take two months by boat, so I'd be there before my belongings. I needed to pack, call my Paris friends, and…my boss at the Institute. My students. Oh, well, there was that, telling my students, some I'd known for years, hung with at the movies, or gone clubbing with, even mentoring a few who'd applied to colleges in the States.

Chocolate. I wanted a jumbo bar of chocolate packed with nuts, but I'd cleaned out the kitchen cabinets, and thrown away a half-eaten candy bar that had somehow gotten behind the lentils. One of my recent changes, eliminating junk food.

"Yup, Pluto. I'm starting over," I said in my singsong voice, the voice that jumpstarted him every time. He snuffled, bounced over to his basket of toys, and grabbed his stuffed dog, named after my friend Isabel's bull terrier. Really her boyfriend's dog, but they were living together. Holding Gertie in his jaws, he batted his tennis ball with his paw. Funny how it was always the right paw. He has his habits, like everyone.

Right there I almost lost it, fought back the sob, pinching my nose, letting loose a wheezing sound that made Pluto stare before he went back to swiping his ball.

I would miss my dog…more than I'd miss my husband.

****

Of course my goodbye party was at Chez Lulu. Two months had passed in a tsunami of work, hanging out with friends and packing, and now, here we were. Lulu's has that Fifties diner look—clean, spare and edgy like an Edward Hopper painting minus the feeling of isolation. It's always packed, and the music is Buddy Holly, early Elvis, Patsy Cline, the Everly Brothers—a mix of rock and roll and country.

"Dinner's here," announced Dulcie, waving her beer glass before taking a long pull. "Everyone let them through!"

"Hey, ain't this a swell party?" said Bertrand, arriving at our noisy table with an armload of gourmet burgers. "Who's got the Marilyn Monroe with Mickey Mantles?"

Have I mentioned all the waiters are imitation James Deans, white T-shirts and jeans with rolled cuffs? Bertrand and Albert—they both speak perfect, slangy English—are our favorites. Bertrand is flirty in a sweet way and working his way through the Institute d'Etudes Politiques de Paris. A future politician with class.

"And the Robert Mitchum with Buddy Holly fries?" Lulu's boasts seven varieties of American fries, named for baseball players, or French and American pop stars.

"Two Jane Russells with Joe DiMaggio fries?" Albert, at Lulu's between acting jobs, shouted, and everyone quieted for a moment, shuffling plates and passing them across the table. Movie star burgers with caramelized onions on miniature baguette buns. My mouth was so ready.

*My going-away party…and I am not going to cry*

*on my presents.*

Next to me, Natalie held out *The Middle-Aged Idiot's Guide to Online Dating.*

"For when you start dating," she yelled over the roar that is Lulu's. "This book helped—"

"Dating? Seriously?" I grabbed two curly fries, the Joe DiMaggios, and popped them in my mouth. Picked up the burger, took a bite. Camembert oozed around the edges. Orgasmic. "Like dating is on my list of things to do?" I said around the burger. "Right below sticking a rusty fork in my eye."

"Hey," Natalie said, grabbing my hand and squeezing. "Not the time for joking. What you're doing is not easy. I know. I've been through it, the cheater husband—not that yours was cheating. The jury's out on that one, isn't it? But the moving, starting over." She patted my shoulder. "My move was a short distance, across the Seine, but still."

The burger lodged in my throat, and I spit it into the napkin.

*What am I doing? Am I mad?* Everything was changing. My little world, my happy little speck in the universe—I pushed away from the table. *Happy? Not happy at all.*

Spitting out Jane Russell must have rattled Natalie, because she leaned in and hugged me, crushing my chest against hers.

Before I met Laurent, I'd known Natalie, through her marriage and eventual separation and divorce. During her turbo-dating period Natalie sent texts and emails by the dozen. I'm talking daily dozen, here. Meeting Bertrand—her thirty-eighth date? A thrill for Natalie. A relief for me.

"Camembert. On your chin." Natalie dabbed at the spot.

*I am leaving my friends. This is unreal.*

While everyone yelled across the table, voices blending into a solid block of sound, Natalie leaned close to whisper. "You'll be fine. You will. I know you will. And you'll want to have sex again. For sure." Her head bobbed up and down as if confirming what came out of her mouth. "This is a good thing, wanting to date, wanting to have sex. It's healthy."

"Well, I guess. I haven't thought that far ahead," I said. "Thanks."

Her hand shot out to grab mine. "The online dating? I'll help you. We'll Skype." She lifted her glass, tipped it in my direction. "Here's to your first online meet."

We clinked glasses. "I'm not even divorced."

"Don't let that stop you. I met Bertrand before my divorce—"

"Yes, yes, but I've got to find a place to live. I'll be studying—"

"Listen to me. You think I sat around waiting for my divorce papers? I went online the day after my husband moved out."

Opening my presents, I should have been in the moment, but somehow I was *unthere*. I could barely focus on a sleek black agenda from Dulcie, my lunch and shopping buddy, the only chubby Parisienne I knew. My three British friends from the Institute chipped in for a first-class, slouchy leather backpack, personalized with my initials.

I shook my head. Gradually the voices grew dimmer, swirled around me. It was beyond strange, this…business of leaving. I leaned back, feeling my gut twist like someone had grabbed the layer of fat on my stomach from the inside and squeezed.

Hugs all around after dinner as we gathered for goodbyes, promises to Facebook daily, never let go of one another.

Sailing down St-Germain-des-Prés in the taxi home, I stared out at the stores, bistros, and old hangouts my friends and I rarely frequented nowadays, like the Brasserie Lipp, more a spot for tourists, now.

My thoughts rambled over the evening. Natalie with the online dating. She'd mentioned it once before, and I'd laughed in her face.

But I hadn't counted all the ways I was starting over. I could feel the weight of them—a mudslide of changes—moving, finding a place to live, taking courses. I hadn't thought past the obvious, not until Natalie presented me with her dumb online dating book.

*And you'll want to have sex again.*

How does online dating work? Do I give out my home telephone number? Research the guy online before meeting? How to protect myself from weirdos? And, if I didn't shave my legs, was that a guarantee I wouldn't sleep with the guy on a first meet? The leg-shaving thing wasn't original. A woman on a podcast advised that was her way of controlling her inner slut.

Imagine having an inner slut.

****

*New Haven, Isabel's house*

"Did you get a lawyer?" Isabel asked. "You know you need one. Don't wait." She carried the cups to the sink.

The aroma of grilled chicken mixed with lemon and garlic hung in the air as we cleaned up after dinner. Chatting, grabbing plastic containers for the leftovers, wiping the table. Together. The opposite of my living arrangement, which I viewed as a special kind of made-to-order hell for the mature woman. A second adolescence, rife with the sort of stimulation you get from scrubbing out the toilet bowl because no one else will, subsisting on ramen-boring-noodles, and awakening in the wee hours to moans of pleasure coming from bedrooms…not your own.

"It's under control." I was rinsing and stacking the dishes in the dishwasher. "This is Laurent we're talking about here. Promised me at the airport I wouldn't have financial worries."

"Your Laurent? I never could warm up to him. Roberto is my best friend. Laurent was never yours. Even early on, you used to call me and complain about him. Said he was selfish and full of—"

"Hey, lighten up. My mother already informed me he was a tad lacking in the warmth department. And now you and Natalie want to get the divorce rolling. She sends me nagging reminders on Facebook. Enough already."

"Remember, I was married with young children and no job while I was being philandered upon," Isabel said. "I thought I knew my husband, and he'd never do anything to hurt me and the kids." Her way of reminding me she'd been dragged into court twenty-four times in sixteen months and still managed to finish her master's in spite of no financial support. "I was driving that fifteen-year-old Honda."

"He had his first Porsche," I chimed in.

At the final hearing, the hand of God intervened in the person of His Honorableness, the judge who awarded her a handsome settlement.

Isabel smiled and poured liquid soap into the slot in the dishwasher door. "Hey, living happy is the best revenge."

"That's no lie."

"I know he'll take good care of your dog."

"Yeah." Pluto was on my mind a lot, but I didn't want to tell Isabel. I wrapped up the leftover chicken and threw out two pieces of garlic bread. Then I slid into one of the high-backed stools and leaned an elbow on the counter. "I'm paying $500 a month for a room in a dilapidated house, facing a gray wall. I've got to get a job."

"At least your parents left you the truck."

"And a big fat gift certificate to Best Buy. They must have felt guilty. I'm not complaining. Laurent will come through. He's working out the money thing, I'm sure."

"I don't think you're a big worrier, but you want some control here."

"Hey." Roberto swung around in his computer chair. "You know, Sunny, you ought to try a Meetup. Great way to make friends. Pick an interest. Wine tasting is a good one." He swiveled back. I glanced in his direction, but he was typing, his eyes intent on the screen. *What is he doing?*

Isabel put her hands on her hips, the dishtowel hanging at her side. "Didn't he agree to support you for a while?"

"He promised to send money until we work out the settlement."

"You're talking about your husband, the guest lecturer who frequents five-star restaurants, and has an expense account? God knows *I* know what you're going through. And it's your money too. You know that, don't you?" She had the laundry basket up on the counter. "You've been here like what? Six weeks? Already you've got angst." She pulled Roberto's boxers out of the basket and folded them in half. "That's a man you can trust?"

Isabel had dated too, strictly online, where she met older, bossy Paul; Bob the Bland, her words; and Lionel, all the way from Baltimore in barbecue-stained white shorts, as if he had his period.

Now she looked at me and cleared her throat. "Even though you don't talk about it much, you and Laurent had been leading separate lives for a long time. Am I right?"

I stared at a dime-sized splotch of butter on the counter.

"You were in deep denial," Isabel said.

It was true. I was one of those people who can't get in touch with their feelings. A stinking cliché. I smudged the butter splotch with my thumb and glanced at Roberto, still lost in cyberspace.

"I thought separate was good as long as you came together," I said. "We stopped coming together."

"You didn't realize it for a long time, did you?"

So true. I saw it all now. The backing off, the disappearances. So obvious.

Roberto swiveled around, motioning me over. "I've messaged someone. As you."

"Wait." I tapped his shoulder. "How the hell—"

"Look, a one-sentence profile, on a site called

InstaDate. You post a photo and a sentence, and it goes up. Instantly. No vetting. Come on, what's your handle?"

"No vetting? What does that mean?"

"The site doesn't check your photos or your info," Isabel said. "Roberto will give you the password."

I couldn't think, wanted Roberto to stop. "I'm not ready—"

"Calm down," Isabel said. "You'll never have to see these people again."

"Very funny." All I could think about was the linguistics paper due in two days. Tuition was due in three weeks. And my lack of friends. Roberto was right. *Meetup* was a possibility. Over the years, I'd lost touch with many of my friends, in spite of Facebook. Plus everything overwhelmed me, but I didn't want to complain to Isabel, who'd survived tough times and done it while caring for her kids.

"You're Smilingnow39," said Roberto. I stood behind him, peering at the screen, reading over his shoulder.

"Welcome Smilingnow39," said Mark4U. "Where are you from, Smilingnow39?"

I tapped Roberto on the head. "Don't answer that guy."

"From CT," typed Roberto.

"I'm in CT, too," said Mark4U. "Hartford."

"Hey, Mark," Roberto typed. "Can you send me a picture?"

"Three words and you're asking this guy for his photo? What if he asks for my photo?"

"Took care of that," said Roberto.

"Where did you get my photo?" I glanced at Isabel.

She held up a pair of Roberto's boxers and made a great show of folding them in half behind a huge grin.

"And here it is." Roberto opened the file attached to the Mark4U email. There sat Mark on his Harley in what looked like a navy blue fog, wearing a huge smile. "Sorry this photo is so dark, haven't taken any pictures recently," Roberto read out loud.

I felt powerless against the relentless energy Roberto put out on my behalf as if his kindness and sweet intention would be wasted.

"We don't care if his picture is dark, do we?" He glanced at me. I'm asking Mark4U if he wants to meet."

"Don't," I said. "I'm not ready to meet anyone." I turned my back on Roberto.

"He'll contact you directly. On your new, anonymous, aardvarkmail.com addy."

Chapter Two
Raining a few good men...

That night, I awoke in a jerk of apprehension, my heart beating as if I'd been galloping in my sleep. Despite the whir of the fan, the air floated heavy with moisture. Nothing in the dark but the hulking shadow of the stationary bike. Sweat leaked down my neck and between my breasts. I flicked on the reading light. Three o'clock. Crap.

In the downstairs bathroom, I dipped my head under the faucet, soaked my hair, and wrapped it in a towel. The money Laurent had sent a week earlier was spent. The rent, $1,000 for two months. Car insurance, $1,100. Tuition, one semester including university fees, came to over $6,000. No surprise, since Laurent and I had studied the tuition and fees together the very afternoon he'd cooked and asked for the separation.

With mind newsreels waking me at two, three, and four in the morning, I could no longer put Laurent on ignore.

Laurent checked his email no matter where he was in the world.

*To: Laurent Chanel*
*From: Sunny Chanel*
*Subject: Laurent, we need to talk.*
*I am stressed out with all this uncertainty about when you're sending me money. Is there a money*

*problem? I thought we had an agreement. You're doling out the funds like they are yours, and NOT MINE TOO. Remember, we both agreed you'd support me until I got my teaching certification.*

Were the caps and the word doling too strong? I peered at the monitor, squeezing the keyboard in both hands, imitating one of those "I must, I must, I must increase my bust," exercises we used to chant in the seventh-grade locker room after gym.

"Not strong enough," I said aloud and felt a frisson of tension leave my back as I added a couple more sentences to the email. The word lawyer now appeared at the end. Where he'd notice. I clicked send. Slouched, staring at the screen. Strong was good. I flexed my biceps and consulted the sticky note from Roberto. Time to bring up my shiny new aardvark email account.

There was an email from Mark4U asking to meet.

\*\*\*\*

Forest Road is a winding, tree-lined street with snazzy, expansive homes, the kind with an endless rolling driveway leading to a three-car garage. I drove with the windows open, Ella singing about how birds do it. Before getting out, I checked my lipstick in the rearview mirror.

According to his email, Mark4U liked to read, mostly nonfiction. That was fine. Not everyone could share my Ed McBain police procedural or literary or romance or thriller or historical fetish. When it came to reading habits, I was all over the place.

I picked my way through the parking lot past three over-filled trash cans. Wouldn't it be funny if I started dating the first guy I met? And would he like my outfit? Despite living in Paris, a spot on the chic-map where women dress to be noticed, I wasn't used to wearing anything fitted. For my first date in twenty-three years, I wore a red-ribbed sweater. Ribbed like a condom. Sleeveless. Plus, I was thin*nish*. A saleswoman told me when I tried on the ribbed sweater. As in, "You're so thin. You can wear anything."

Of course, I bought the sweater.

At the door to the restaurant, I sucked in a breath and turned the handle. A guy in a pink shirt at the bar swiveled around to face me, eyebrows raised. Three other guys swiveled around too.

"Sunny?" said the pink-shirt guy.

"Mark?" I stepped up to the bar and stood at the empty stool beside him.

The bartender leaned against the sink, absentmindedly drying a glass, gazing at a soundless black and white movie on the television mounted over the bar. A quick peek. Bette Davis and Joan Crawford silently yelling at each other, their lipstick thick and dark, extending over the natural lip line.

Mark grinned. "So how are you?"

My throat contracted. Nothing came out.

"Did you have trouble finding this place?"

Shook my head.

"Well, you're here," he said.

There was a splotch of grease on the cuff of the pink shirt.

"This morning, I recycled some bottles," he said.

My eyes traveled down to the two nickel-size stains on his trouser leg.

"Went to Sears for light bulbs. Stocked up."

Down to the sneakers. Something on the toe. I sniffed. Shit for sure.

"I go to CVS for my paper goods. Buy in bulk on sale."

"Ah."

"And then it was time to meet you." He lifted his arm to adjust his glasses. "Funny how chores eat up the day."

A ring of wet at his armpit and the aroma of stale man-sweat floated up. I stepped back.

Well, I'd showered, exfoliated, slathered cream, and spritzed Cabochard. Modeled two pairs of pants, two sweaters, and a skirt in the mirror, examining each outfit through narrowed eyes, trying for tastefully sexy.

"So." He drew out the word as if it had deep meaning.

*Please, quick, think of something. Ask about his reading habits. A mystery writer.*

"I'm a little nervous. You're my first date. You know, first online date." Shifting from one foot to the other.

"Relax." Mark motioned for me to sit. "Drink?"

"Club soda, please." I climbed onto the stool, as relaxed as a squirrel. It cheered me to hear laughter from a small group in the corner, people whose mental processes were in working order.

"So, you're just starting to date?" Mark's thigh grazed mine.

"Yeah, er, yes." There was a little press and release. I stirred my club soda with the little swizzle stick and squeezed the lime into the drink, my eyes on the glass as if I'd discover a topic in the ice.

"So, what do you think?" I could feel him studying me. Weird since I was facing the row of bottles lined up on the opposite side of the counter.

"Think about what?" My nose hairs stood on end.

"Do you like the way I look? Think we might hit it off?"

My eyes on the glass, I began stirring the ice around, listening to the clinking of the cubes. "You look just fine, Mark." I tilted to the right, away from Mark's body parts. "Do you think we can move to a table? My back." Once we were seated, I asked him why he divorced.

He slid his chair next to mine, as if we were one of those European couples, all cozy on one side of the table, and propped an elbow under his chin. "I've been divorced four times, you know. I told you that, didn't I?" He cleared his throat and took a sip of his drink. "My last wife left without telling me. I came home from work and found the house empty. Said she didn't want to be married anymore."

"That's awful." I felt at a loss. We'd gone from bulk-buying to heartbreak in ten minutes. "How long were you married?"

"Two years. That time."

"Oh."

"Yeah. Met my first wife in college, my second wife in a bar, and three and four online."

"How very enterprising." Pause. "And you've got this dating thing down, don't you? What do you look for when you advertise? I mean—"

"You can say advertising. It's sort of like that." Mark relaxed his shoulders and turned to face me.

"Well, I am very demanding, you know." He dipped a finger into his glass, fingered a small chunk of ice. "First of all, a woman who isn't bigger than me. That's a given." Mark gestured toward his body like a game show hostess. "Also, someone who's about my own age. You can tell when a gal lies."

"Can you?" I hadn't heard the word gal since 1979.

"It comes out in little things. They get caught, you know."

"And you've experienced women lying to you?" I had lied to Paul Donovan, a boy who liked me in the second grade. When he wasn't looking, I switched my used box of crayons for his brand new, pointy ones. He stopped liking me.

"Not that I'm trying to catch anyone..."

"Does it make that big a difference?"

"Suppose not." He scraped his chair back and crossed his legs. "Where was I? So, the third thing is that the woman should like sex." Mark jangled the ice in his empty glass and asked me if I wanted another drink. "How about some stuffed mushrooms? And those potato skins. With the cheese stuffing? I'm starving."

"Just the soda for me, thanks."

He waved at the waiter for more drinks and ordered the appetizers.

"You're not in an eating mood? That's too bad. Where was I? Oh, yes. Sex. That's important."

"You didn't tell me anything about your work," I said.

Unfortunately, it turned out that the pharmaceutical company he worked for manufactured the latest drug for impotence.

"Yes, that was our biggest success. Still selling hard, if you know what I mean."

A peek at my watch. "Wow." My voice rose like Doris Day spying Rock Hudson's bare ass for the first time. "It's four-fifteen already. I need to get going." My jaw felt wired open with all the fake smiling.

"Oh." Mark abandoned his drink, leaned closer, his voice low. "I thought you'd stay for a mushroom." He looked across the room. "Here they come." He held his hands together, and I expected him to clap.

"One mushie. I'll stay for one mushroom." *To make nice.* "I'll keep you company."

When the waiter set the steaming platter on the table, Mark forked the largest of the mushrooms, propelling it mouth-ward, lips puckered like a horse. He held it aloft and blew before inserting it. I felt my stomach twist, and then I turned toward the bar where the waiter stood facing the mirror, finger-combing his hair.

"Ahh," yelled Mark. "Oww." I jerked my head around in time to see the mushroom fly out of his mouth, bounce on the table, and roll onto his trousers. There it sat, looking like a large brown growth.

"Friggin' waiter." Saliva dribbled down Mark's chin. "He should have warned me." He reached for a napkin and wiped. "Hey. You." He caught the mushroom rolling off his pants as he stood.

"Yes, sir?" The waiter stared in the mirror at Mark.

"Hey, you. I almost burned myself. These crappy mushrooms are hot."

"Sir, please."

"This is very bad service."

"Sir, I must warn you. Please lower your voice." The waiter faced us, a towel draped over his arm. Too late. Everyone in the bar was interested. A woman reached for her cell phone.

"I am not paying for such...such *abdominal*

service." Mark sputtered, and I looked away toward the door.

*Abdominal? Really?* My hand crept to my bag on the back of the chair.

Mark's mushroom hand rose in the air. "I ordered in good faith." His voice cracked. He glanced at me. "My date can back me up on this one."

The waiter jerked his head toward the kitchen door. "Sir. I'll get someone to speak with you."

"You think I am in a *speaking* mood?" Mark was in full shout now, his face fuchsia. His hand went back for the wind-up, and Mark pitched the mushroom, not at the waiter but at the mirror, hitting a tall, red bottle. The red bottle tilted onto its neighbor and...

That's when I grabbed my bag, and sprinted for the door. No reason to see what hell might break loose, especially since I'd worn flats suitable for the running gal.

****

Dana, my study buddy, and I *slounged,* a combination of studying and lounging, and we did it two or three nights a week at Dana's condo off Whitney Avenue. I'm talking hardwood floors, windows that rose almost to the ceiling, and a tasteful bareness that was soothing.

"I am the gnat, and you're the praying mantis," I said to her the first time we crammed at her place. Tall as Uma Thurman with olive skin, she wore fitted shirts and skinny jeans, dangling earrings, and pushed her hair behind her ears.

She burst out laughing. "You mean the large insect that eats the head off her mate after copulating?"

"Forgot that little detail," I said, and relaxed into

our study sessions. We'd met in the linguistics course, gone for coffee, and started studying at her house. Nothing mattered but passing the Praxis exam, the requirement for state certification in French. Actors, movies—which the French take seriously—who's the Lady of Chaillot, the use of the historical past, Monet, Manet, even how to order a rental car. Anything could pop up.

It was getting late. I shuffled through an art history book, came to a Rodin, and peered at the defined thigh muscle, the curved perfection of buttocks.

"Actually, I would go out with him," Dana said over my shoulder.

"Who wouldn't?" I shoved books and papers into my farewell satchel from Paris and cat-stretched on the thick rug. "I should get going."

"Do you date?"

"Well, not exactly."

"Sorry, didn't mean to pry," Dana said.

"No, it's not that. Last week I had an online meet—you know, awkward. First meets are worse than blind dates. It was—well, it was funky."

"Funky?"

"The guy burned his mouth on a mushroom and got so pissed he pitched it across the bar," I said.

Dana, who'd just gulped down her water, choked, her face turning crimson. "What?"

Pausing while she recovered. "He seemed normal, you know, normal and a little boring. He was so upset he used the word *abdominal* for abominable. Referring to the service…which it wasn't, by the way."

"Imagine what he'd do if you ever said you didn't want sex or—"

"Stop, please, stop." I held out my hand, laughing.

"Seriously, I do not have the nerve for the online slog, and it's hard meeting someone the organic way." Dana headed for the kitchen. "I'm opening a very nice Chardonnay."

"Wait. You taught kindergarten for ten years. You can do anything."

"Funny. We have done three hours of cramming, and we deserve it." She stood at the kitchen island, doing a little dance, peeling away the seal on the wine. "I want to take salsa lessons." She yanked the opener over the bottle. "Let's take dance lessons. When we're done with Praxis."

"Sure. Laurent, my ex never wanted to dance. Ever."

She poured two glasses of wine, came over, and handed me one. "To our success on the exam." We toasted. "Wait. I have an addendum toast." She lifted her glass higher. "Here is to forgiving ourselves for all our man mistakes."

She sat on the rug. "I have been divorced long enough that even my daughter is getting on my case to go online." She focused somewhere across the room. "She says beating myself up about the divorce is keeping me from moving on." She took a sip of wine. "The best friend and lover thing? Do you think it's a fantasy? I want to believe it's possible. Don't you want that?" She gazed at me over her glass.

"Yes, but I think it's hard in a long-term marriage. You get too used to one another, and then…you're not enough." The Chardonnay slid down so very nicely. "Until last week, I hadn't had a date in twenty years. Plus, we're not even divorced."

"Your divorce is in the works?" Dana asked. I nodded. "And it seems your marriage ran out of steam a long time ago, like mine. Actually, by the time we agreed to a divorce, I'd done all my crying. Then the self-flagellation began."

"Yeah. Another divorce statistic."

"Let me get this straight," said Dana. "You leave your husband of twenty-plus years, travel an ocean away, find a place to live with roommates half your age, no less, and go back to school." She smiled at me as if I'd done something weird but praiseworthy, like a hike up Kilimanjaro in stilettos. "You've got guts, and I think you could do anything." Dana set her glass on the table. "Could you help me? With the internet dating?"

"Help you? How? I don't know anything."

"Well, sooner or later you'll want to date. Let's try it together. Brainstorm, whatever. I am thinking out loud here. Wouldn't it be fun if, say, you go on a few dates and coach me? I need a push."

"Who doesn't need a push?" I took another sip of wine, appreciating the glow, the girl friendliness of the occasion. *I miss my friends.* "Nice Chardonnay, by the way."

"Glad you like it. So." She was looking at me, as if afraid to ask a question.

"What?"

"What would it take? A bribe? A reward? To get you to meet guys? Go on a bunch of dates?"

"What's a bunch? Seven?"

"Twenty-five."

"Twenty-five? Are you serious?" My mind turned back to Lulu's, Natalie urging me to date at my going-away party, "Twenty-eight men before my Bertrand came into my life." Isabel reminding me Roberto was her best friend, "Living happily is the best revenge."

"You are changing your whole life, starting over," she said. "You're bailing out of a long-term marriage, and this is another piece of the experience." Dana was on a roll, gaining momentum as she outlined a plan. A plan for me? "Number one is the mushroom guy, so you've already started. Keep notes."

"Meet men and keep notes?" Downed my wine in two slugs, held out the glass. "Another please, Miss," in a fake-pleading voice. "Even if I have to Uber home."

"Coming right up." Dana filled my glass, gestured toward the kitchen. "Come on, I'm hungry, and I have these to-die-for English crackers. Tomato and basil hummus, homemade. Goat cheese."

I slipped onto a bar stool, thinking how much I enjoyed studying at her place, so much more soothing than three roommates, a communal kitchen, and one bathroom.

Dana dipped her knife into the goat cheese and spread it on a cracker, handed it to me. "Twenty-five guys in six months—four guys a month—that's doable. Don't you think?"

"Maybe," I hedged. *Twenty-five guys?*

This was a side of Dana I'd never suspected, and I liked it. Liked it so much my chest expanded with the joy of discovering a single girlfriend, someone to confide in. Weren't we doing a little confiding right now? Confiding and drinking Chardonnay, what girlfriends did.

Crap, I missed my friends.

"Look…after the exam, or whenever, let's get away for the weekend," Dana said. "I'll get my friend

Tony's key to his place on the Upper East Side. He's seldom there. We'll go clubbing. Eat Thai. Deal? Will you help me with the online hump part?"

"Are you bribing me?"

"Sort of."

"What is the hump part exactly?" I said.

She reached over and sank a cracker into the hummus. "My husband—never mind. I can't talk about it." For a moment her eyes glistened. "Me. Insecurities. Rampant."

"No more than anyone else. Me included." I held up a finger. "First rule. Meet in a public place. Text each other after every date. No canceling our study sessions. So little time until the exam."

"And we have to spend one hour with the guy for it to count," added Dana. "Agreed?"

"The first to reach twenty-five dates pays for dinner in New York?" I said.

Dana put down the cracker. "Oh. We're doing this?"

"Isn't that what you wanted?"

"So soon? I'm not quite ready."

"What's with you? This is our project. We're in it together." I surveyed the counter of goodies and slid off the stool. "I should get going."

"No, no, don't go. Look, did I mention the added bonus of sticking it to your soon-to-be-ex? Show him you are moving on."

"Never mind your so-called bonus." That sounded harsh. I stood and swayed. Tipsy, definitely tipsy. And seeing the bonus from a different angle, I sat back on the stool. "I know someone who can help us."

Dana leaned forward, her expression serious. "I

40

will try, but promise you will not get on my case if—"

"I'll get on your case. I'll be all over you like— *whatever*—" And we both burst out laughing. I finished off my wine, and we cleaned up, stacked dishes in the dishwasher then sat on the couch. After flipping around Netflix, I must have dozed off. All I know is right before Dana guided me upstairs to the guest room and tucked me in, *Laurent is a dickhead* floated through my brain.

"We can do it," Dana said as she closed the door.

*We?* Didn't she mean me?

****

"So, how do we start?" I whined into the phone to Isabel. "I've never done this before." Dana and Isabel and I were on a three-way conversation with a twenty-minute window, as Dana had to make her gym class.

On the floor by the desk, I'd arranged the contents of my personalized dating package, Isabel's gift. A box of miniature chocolates, a how-to internet dating guide written by a much-married psychologist, and a card Isabel told me to prop up on my desk. The word "RELAX" was printed in ten-inch neon pink capital letters.

"Here's the scoop," Isabel said. "Get onto letsclick.com and fill everything out. You'll like that part. You get to be creative. Be yourselves."

"Actually, that's the part I'm not good at," said Dana. "Being myself with strangers."

"But we'll do our best," I said.

"Don't give any guy your real email address," Isabel said. "Until you know something about him."

"Tell them not to give out any personal information," Roberto said in the background.

"You hear that?" Isabel said.

"Yup, but—"

"Tell them not to get stuck in email land," Roberto said. "And get his full name before meeting anyone."

"You hear that?"

"Full name." I switched phone ears, afraid I'd miss a nuance of how the thing worked. "Email land...what's email land?"

"Type of job is always good for conversation. You want to move it to the phone as soon as you can. Don't keep emailing forever is what Roberto is saying."

"Phone sounds good," said Dana.

"Get the basics. Divorced or widowed. Offspring. That kind of thing."

"Slow down, please." We were taking notes, and I could hear the click of Dana's keyboard.

"Don't ask if he owns or rents. Or if he has credit card debt. You don't want to grill the guy 'cause that's a turnoff."

"Are you joking?" I said. "Who asks a stranger about debt?"

"Well, it could be handy. If you want to eliminate a certain financially-challenged element," Dana said.

That's your choice then." Isabel was all business. "And get the phone app. It saves a lot of time. Swipe and delete while you're in line at the supermarket.

"What about Tinder?" I asked.

"I don't do Tinder, but feel free to try it out," Isabel said.

"So. What's next?" I said.

Wife's name."

"What?" said Dana.

"Kidding. If he asks for your number, make sure

you get his. Put it into your phone so you can track who's calling you."

"Good idea," said Dana.

Too much, too soon. I went quiet. Too soon after Laurent and Mark and his mushroom meltdown. It would be nice, so nice, to sit on my bed, the spot to watch *Friends* or *Everybody Loves Raymond* reruns. Sitcoms served a purpose. The whole point of watching them was to experience someone *else's* relationship.

"Piece of cake," Dana said. "Thank you for the info. I'd better run." We said our goodbyes.

"The letsclick.com site is where I met Roberto," said Isabel when Dana disconnected.

"Is it fun? Internet dating?" I asked.

There was silence, then a snort of laughter. "It's like dipping your eyeballs in hot wax and putting them back in your head," she said. "Remember. Nothing counts until the meet, and I don't care how cute he comes off in email." In her voice, that unsubtle tone of superiority veteran daters adopt with those who haven't got a clue.

After talking, I changed into my home clothes, threadbare shorts with tiny blue bears, and an old gray T-shirt with the sleeves cut off. Hell, studying was on hold tonight. I couldn't wait to hear the new playlist Isabel had put together especially for me.

Thunder cracked on the soundtrack as the home page splattered onto the screen. A couple of plastic kissy-face dolls with magnetic pursed lips sailed into focus.

The letsclick.com icon advertised a free week, and I went for it. That's when the raining men song exploded in a crescendo of enthusiasm and celebration.

Scrunching over the keyboard, shoulder-twitching to the beat, reading the header out loud—such fun. "The Let's Click Brazen Questionnaire for the Mature Man." Interesting. Why not take a quick look?

"As far as favorite women's body parts go, I would characterize myself as a leg man. Breast man. A nice tush turns me on." Skipped down a few categories to questions about how often the guy changes his sheets. Once a week was one of the choices. Was Isabel out of her mind or was this one freaky dating site?

Over at the women's questionnaire, I skimmed a few items and turned down the music. Dialed Isabel. She picked up after four rings.

"You met Roberto on this site?" Accusatory.

"Why? What's wrong?"

"These questions are bizarre."

"Oh, I forgot. It's been a while since…come on, loosen up."

"First question is about men's body parts. Butts, a hairy chest, a guy with a big—"

"Where's your sense of humor?"

In the background I could hear voices. She and Roberto enjoying a lovely evening of Netflix while I labored over this dumb dating site.

"How often I change boyfriends? What kind of algorithm do these people use? And I'm not divorced. How do I answer that question? And I have to write a profile." As if it were her fault.

"You're getting worked up over nothing."

"It's not nothing."

"You left your husband and moved a continent away. Believe me, this is nothing."

Neither one of us said anything for a long moment.

"Sunny? You all right?"

"Yes." I cleared my throat. "I'm getting a glass of wine. Thanks for talking me down."

"Anytime," and she hung up.

Twenty-five questions and a glass of pinot grigio later, I had most of my profile written. In the profile, I failed to mention bingeing on old sitcoms or my potato chip and ice cream habit. Didn't say a word about Pluto and how much I missed him or my Paris friends.

Next came proofing and downloading a photo. I glanced at the clock. Where would I find a photo? My back felt like someone bent me in half the wrong way.

Maybe by now, Laurent had transferred a few dollars to my account. Once I'd logged into my bank though, that familiar ragged brick lodged in my chest. The total balance read $413.78. At least slouching at the computer, reading the life stories of strangers, took my mind off the unkind reality. I was broke. Which I would have to tackle soon. Very soon.

My phone whistled. A message from Dana asking how many guys I'd written. I told her none.

—*Me either. Working on profile*—

—*Me too*—

Time for a snack. I pounded downstairs to the kitchen, borrowed a vanilla yogurt, opened my can of peaches, drained the syrup, and scooped the yogurt over the peaches.

Back at the computer, I ate and typed. Yogurt dribbled onto the mouse, and I reached down with my tongue to lick it off. Clicked *Super Duper Search*, and gripped my hands together.

A row of profiles illuminated the screen. I clicked on *sophisticatedguy52*.

*I am Ready to Please. I know how to TREAT a lady well. I am LOOKING for someone I CAN discover LIFE with. My activities match my Mood, whether it's the movies, museums, theater, Sports, or just a WALK. I like reading in FRONT of the fireplace, too, ESPECIALLY with my HEAD on that someone special's LAP. If you agree, Write Me—*

Despite his misuse of caps, I emailed this man. He didn't express himself badly, after all. Well, he expressed himself badly, but I didn't care. Everyone was into phony press here. Baloney could be read between the lines and in the handles, headlines, and the warnings about game playing. I answered.

*From: Sunny*
*To: sophisticatedguy52*
*Subject: Greetings*
*Dear Sophisticate,*

*Several things struck me about your profile. First, you seem like an active guy, and I am looking for someone who's got a sense of humor and who doesn't "couch-it" all the time. I am totally new to this online dating thing, but here I am jumping in, so if you'd like to write, drop me a line. What's your name, btw?*

Next was putty man: *puttyinyourhandsXYZ*
*Squish me silly*

*I'm Brandon. Great sense of humor, and yes, I said so myself, wasted at the gas station, in line at the supermarket, and on those tele*marketing *robots. I've been told I'm personable and cute enough not to embarrass my date. If the world is divided into givers and takers, I'm a giver. Since I'm very religious, and my knowledge of religion comes from the movies, I constantly battle over issues such as exactly how much* *plastic surgery this or that movie star has had.*

Clever, especially after *Mark4U*, the mushroom man. This man I definitely wanted to meet.

"Hallelujah," I twanged out loud, rocking forward in the chair. This was almost fun. Maybe Dana had good instincts. Maybe this was a healthy way of amping up my life a few notches by getting out of my comfort zone. I read two more profiles that I dismissed because of extreme spelling. Then I put the playlist on replay and read on and on and on.

*—I suppose an ideal woman for me would be beautiful, slim and in shape, a college grad although I prefer a PhD, and financially independent preferably with a six-figure income...*

*—I am a handsome, good looking man, 55, with all my hair and eyes...*

*—I have a job. I am careful about my apearance...*

*—I almost always wear colone...*

By the time I finished reading what seemed like 8,337 profiles and responded to sixteen more, it was 2:30 in the morning, way too late to text Dana. All I could think was it was too bad I had an early class the next day...and I wondered how long it would take before they wrote back?

\*\*\*\*

Later that week after my kickboxing class, I microwaved a high salt, fatless frozen dinner and checked my bank account. Crap and double crap. Laurent had deposited enough cash to pay one stinkin' month's rent, eat a little Kraft macaroni and cheese with an iceberg lettuce chaser, and contribute to the common toilet paper fund. He was pissing me off.

I jotted down a few notes about *MARK4U*, the

mushroom tosser, in my notebook.

First date in over twenty years and the notes said nothing about how I'd gone home and straight to bed with the shakes. A wave of bile rose in my throat. I shoved the notebook into the top drawer and slammed it twice, the ancient dresser rocking back on its hind legs. Then I checked my parents' last few posts on Facebook, and messaged them about the prof's positive comments on my classroom diversity paper.

Now for the fun stuff. I logged onto the dating site.

*To: Sunny*

*From: extheaterman1*

*Dear Sunny,*

*Looked for your photo but I guess you haven't posted one yet. I used to work in the theater. You can see a photo of me from when I played in The Fantastics. Now my work takes me many places. Have you travelled?*

*Ps Like you even without a photo.*

On his profile, Andrew had one headshot and one black and white. The black and white showed a chunky guy in a straw bowler and baggy trousers with suspenders, standing on a stage. Cute.

I wedged my back into the chair and closed my eyes. The proof I was compliment-starved was the almost heady feeling I got from the throw-away line, *Like you without a photo,* from a man I'd never met.

Thanks, Andrew, for reminding me about needing a mugshot. There was the one Dulcie and Natalie took of me posing in front of the Tour Eiffel. Me with the balloon seller, the two of us smiling into the camera, my sunglasses hiding my sad eyes. I located it and loaded it onto my profile.

That day, months before I confronted Laurent, I'd had a food hangover.

The previous night, Laurent and I had a fight, and he left the apartment without dinner. As soon as the door closed, I glommed down a giant chocolate bar, a mammoth chocolate pretzel, a pale-yellow marzipan duck, an airplane bag of pretzels, two slivers of yellow cake with freezer burn, and a three-month-old hollow Easter egg. Then, standing over the sink, a slice of toast with butter. The buttered toast always came at the end. Isabel called this the Buttered Noodle Syndrome. Craving salt after too much sweetness.

And I'd itemized that binge because it scared me, and because I was gray-tired of feeling crummy about myself. I had lost more than control. I had lost my sense of well-being.

So even that unsatisfying first meet with *Mark4U* was better than pushing down my feelings with food. Uncertainty took guts.

My insides churned as I spied with my little eye the email responses loading on the website. The icky sensation, like eating three tablespoons of peanut butter with Marshmallow Fluff, disappeared as I read.

Whom to email first? Andrew, the theatre guy, or Brandon? Pick one out and ask to talk on the phone? What about sophisticated guy? Wait, hadn't I emailed him? Cruising down the list, I was confused when a new email landed in my mailbox. *Bluesky.* Had I written this guy? I couldn't remember, and didn't find anything in my notes. Silly that a small thrill shot through me, simply because this man had studied a slew of stamp-sized photos and picked me. Of course, he could be writing multiple women like I was writing multiple men.

Dana would want to know about my progress so I quick-texted her, and scrolled down to his profile.

*Bluesky I fly*

*Soul mates?*

*I am looking for my elusive soul mate. Someone who enjoys the same things I do: hiking, cooking, biographies and fiction, going into the city—lots of things. I'd like a cute, silly at times, other times serious, devoted to me woman unafraid to show me who she really is and accepts me with all my warts and old baggage. I am Luke.*

His photo? Big smile, sun-bleached hair falling over his forehead. I clicked on his profile for more photos. A full-length beach shot in rolled-up jeans, ankle-deep in water. Oh, no shirt. And lookin' good. Oh, oh, oh, this was more fun than humans should be allowed.

*To: Bluesky/Luke*

*From: Sunny*

*Hey there, Mr. Blue Sky,*

*I've always wondered how you know when you've met your soulmate. Is there a soulmate test? If so, please pass on a copy cuz I'd like to use it. I like your profile name, btw. Do you fly?*

*Sunny*

*PS Do you have warts? Oh, no, did I get too personal?*

He responded in twenty seconds.

*Dear dear Sunny,*

*I fly down the mountain and over the fields on Cornrow, the horse I ride any weekend I can manage the time. And I like your name. Are you always in a good mood? Unfortunately, there is no soul mate test. I wish one existed. My life would be an easy one.*

*By the way, are you of this world? Earth girl or woman from another galaxy? I'd like to see your photo, but it doesn't matter. I await your next communication. My heart beats quicker.*

I read Luke's email twice and slid his photo onto my desktop. "My heart beats quicker." See, that was my problem. Words. A few sweet words, and I already was crushing on a guy I hadn't even talked to on the phone. I wrote him back, knowing I might never hear from him again because that was how the online cookie crumbled.

But at least he'd see my new Tour Eiffel photo on my profile.

He'd write again. Maybe.

\*\*\*\*

Tymes is sprawling and noisy, with hardwood floors and a bar that snakes around the dining area. The good smells of steak and racks of ribs, American classics, drifted into the lobby. I wore a shortish-but-not-too-short skirt, my geometric fool-the-eye sweater from the Paris flea market, and a spritz of Chanel. The classic. No. 5.

Ahead, a podium for the official greeter, but I veered off to the right to hit the restroom, check my lipstick. The distasteful memory of the *Mark4U* date lingered, even after several weeks, and if anyone could erase it, that person would be Andrew, I was certain. Why? We'd talked for over an hour and some things you just know.

On the phone, Andrew's voice had a resonant, Barry White quality that sent tingles down under. He was articulate and funny, told stories about growing up in a family of five brothers, two sisters, and professor parents. So yeah, I'd carried Barry White's voice around all week, building expectations.

"Sunny?"

At the entrance to the dining room, a large man waited. Smiling as if he knew me.

No way *he* was Andrew. That man was colossal.

Sure, the photo posted on his profile showed a chubby guy. The black and white photo of Andrew on stage, from his theater days. Was he still in the theater or were those photos from—

"Excuse me, are you Sunny?"

"Andrew?" The jolt of surprise in my voice was all too obvious.

"Hi, how are you?" He shook my hand, and I felt him watching, measuring my reaction. He knew. Irritation stabbed my insides. Didn't he feel embarrassed, posting such a misleading photo? I felt mean for even thinking this.

We followed the waiter to a table by the window. I held my breath as Andrew eased himself into his seat and smiled. His sides stuck out of the chair, and he couldn't get close to the table.

"Would you like something to drink?" he asked. "They have a nice pinot noir on the menu. I know because I checked online."

"Nice, that would be very nice," I nodded. After he ordered, I asked about his work. Andrew supervised the manufacturing of clothes for the larger man, a company called Big But Regal. When he told me the name, I flashed on Big *Butt* Regal and held back a gust of nervous laughter.

The wine arrived, and the waiter poured. "Let me order a few appetizers. We'll share."

"So, you were in *The Fantastics*?"

"Broadway, off-Broadway, supporting roles in sixteen movies in my twenties and thirties. *Grease*, *Pippin*, a play with Meryl Streep. Bernadette Peters and I were in two musicals," he said in that wonderful Barry White voice. I sipped my wine, imagined a slim, singing, dancing Andrew in *A Chorus Line*.

Barry White, almost 375 pounds, died in 2003 of kidney failure, according to Wikipedia. Yup, I'd researched Barry after our phone conversation, when my expectations first soared.

Andrew dropped his voice to a Marlon Brando monotone. "I coulda been a contenda," he joked. His voice trailed off, and he gazed to his right as if Bernadette Peters herself sat at a nearby table. "But I guess I've always liked food too damn much."

Imagine liking food more than your work, more than living. Imagine not being able to stop eating. I could scarcely breathe when he said that, I felt so sorry for him. I stared at Andrew and then looked away, embarrassed, afraid he could tell I pitied him.

We talked for two hours, what Laurent and I used to call a slow dine. Sharing seafood pasta and lamb chops with parsley pesto. For dessert, he ordered one chocolate mousse triple-decker, individual pie with real crème fraîche and two forks. The evening ended with Andrew straining to get out of his chair and me averting my gaze, hoping to give him some privacy, even here in public.

In the lobby, Andrew reached for my hand and kissed it, a dry, gentle brush of his lips. "Would you have come out with me if I told you I was so fat?"

"Absolutely." It popped out like a jack in the box, but without the musical wind up. Did he believe me? I wanted him to believe me. "You're a lovely person, and I enjoyed getting to know you." True. But I didn't want another date.

On the drive home, there was a sadness I couldn't shake off, and the Everly Brothers on the oldies station sank me deeper into a nameless funk. Not ready to go back to my cramped room, I veered off onto the highway toward the shoreline. Isabel had to be home, although the closer I got, the more certain I was that Isabel and Roberto were in their PJs under the duvet, deep into their favorite creepy sci-fi series. Or having hot, prolonged sex on a school night.

No matter. I'd *interruptus* them, make them play with me.

Chapter Three
Lawyering up…

The reassuring sound of the waves lifted my mood as I slid out of the truck and stood, breathing in the sea air. Always a pleasure dropping by The Estate, as I called their beach home in Guilford.

"Hey." Roberto's face poked out the door. "What a surprise."

"Hi." I slowed as I approached. "I should have called."

"Come in. You're just in time." Roberto opened the door wider, blocking Gertie, his sweetheart of a bull terrier, with his knee. I stepped into the huge foyer, and Gertie, fifty polite pounds of pure muscle, who would never think of jumping on a guest, nudged me with her muzzle. "Isabel will be right back. What's up?"

"I'm coming from an online meet." I looked past Roberto, and out the huge windows to the expanse of lawn leading down to their little dock, illuminated by the outdoor lighting, the silhouettes of a few boats tethered in the harbor visible.

The door opened, and Isabel came in carrying a bag. "Saw your car. Perfect timing. The pie is hot, still in the oven. Come on guys, pie and vanilla for Roberto, who's a classicist when it comes to ice cream. Chocolate with nuts and fudge bits for us two."

The kitchen had that American pie scent of apple,

cinnamon, and just-baked deliciousness I hadn't smelled in a long while…maybe years.

Isabel opened the oven and nudged the pie out, placing it on a wood board in the middle of the island. "Roberto, you'll do the honors?"

"Of course. By the way, Sunny came here from her date." He cut generous pieces, and I didn't stop him, or ask for a smaller portion, in spite of my full meal. Gertie sat at Roberto's feet, head on her paws, waiting for a tidbit. It was great slouching at the counter, being with my friends. I filled them in on Andrew.

Isabel licked the ice cream scoop and put it in the sink. "You just started dating," she said. "If you don't like this one, move on."

"Don't talk like he's not a person."

Isabel, always so clinical. "Apparently he's not *your* person."

"Maybe not, but he has a lot going for him, except…he weighs three hundred pounds, well, that's my guess. He used to be an actor, and he asked questions, wanted to know about Paris, my friends, and if I miss them. Such a nice man. I decided right then, while we were talking, that I'll go back for a few weeks in the summer."

"So that's a good thing."

I sneaked a look at Roberto, who chewed thoughtfully but probably didn't plan on entering the discussion.

"Well, I asked him about his acting. He isn't acting now, but why couldn't he do community theatre? He'd be in demand." My voice gathered momentum as my idea for Andrew's future expanded. "If he followed his passion, he'd be less interested in eating. I've lost weight. I'm thinking I could keep in touch with him, you know, sort of help him out. Not out of pity or anything but—"

Isabel laid a calming hand on my arm. "You can't fix him."

"I'm not trying to fix him. I'm trying to help him. He wants to meet someone. I know because…well, didn't you meet guys you felt sorry for when you did all that dating?"

"You did a lot of dating?" Roberto said, squinting at Isabel.

"Who can remember? I may have felt sorry for a few, but that didn't make me want to see them again, much less adopt them. And I never liked dating more than one person at a time." She gave his cheek a little squeeze. "You're so cute when you're pretending to be jealous." A goofy smile from Roberto.

"With all the whiny texts I got about your online dating agony? Who are you kidding?"

"Look," said Isabel, "we've all got issues. But his stuff isn't fixable, at least not by you. Never mind Andrew, deal with your husband, get a settlement rolling. You need a lawyer."

My hands went to my forehead in frustration. "I hate calling him."

"It wasn't much fun when I went through all that crap, let me tell you," said Isabel. "And my lawyer got some kind of an academic position in New Mexico, or I'd give you his name."

"Can I take my pie home?" I spooned up the rest of the chocolate ice cream. Two desserts in one night, even if this was half a dessert. "Dana might have a lawyer."

"Text her. Right now. Then, enough of this lawyer shit." She dumped the dishes in the sink. "You and me against Roberto," Isabel said. "I found my old Yahtzee, and it's game time." Gertie, stirred by the excitement, looked up from her doggie bed and barked.

"Gertie, girl," said Roberto, "you can play, too."

\*\*\*\*

It was past noon the next day when I shuffled downstairs with a three-aspirin hangover. Too much Yahtzee along with two of Roberto's special apple martinis. Two. What possessed me? They were lethal, especially after sharing the bottle of pinot noir at dinner with Andrew.

A squirrel outside the window crunched an apple core, enjoying the hell out of it by the way her tail twitched. I reached into the freezer for an ice cube, applied it to my forehead, and leaned on the counter while the coffee machine dripped and growled.

Upstairs, the sound of the shower, a reminder one of the roomies was still home.

After two gigantic cups of life-restoring coffee, I located the text Dana had sent with her lawyer's number. Calling a lawyer while under the influence of a serious hangover wasn't the plan for today, but I wanted to get the whole mess over and done with. Still holding the ice cube to my head, I dialed, surprised when lawyer Duke picked up. Sam Duke, cool name. He sounded expensive.

"Prepare your husband for what's coming," Duke warned. "Try to get him on board." Well, that was laughable. I made an appointment, then rinsed my coffee cup and set it in the drain.

It was time.

My insides roiling from coffee mixed with dread, I made the call. According to Sam Duke, everything hinged on our ability as a couple to reach an agreement. As the phone buzzed, I imagined the apartment, the sliders, the dark oak chest in the hallway, pictured Pluto following Laurent to answer it, looking up at him as he talked. Did Pluto miss me?

"*Allo, oui?*"

By some miracle, I had caught Laurent on the way out, taking Pluto for an afternoon walk, so we small-talked for a minute or two.

Then I told him what lawyer Duke had said about the do-it-yourself divorce packet, the perfect solution if Laurent and I could reach an agreement about finances. "If we can work out the finances, I'll probably file for some kind of no-fault divorce." *I'm a sweetheart, aren't I?*

He grunted. Which meant he was back to the old distant Laurent, the one who backed away from meaningful conversation. And because he was in Paris, I couldn't reach out and slap him on the back of his head. Which I should have done when I had the chance.

"Having no children makes our case simple," I said.

"It does?"

"Well, relatively simple."

"This apartment has been in my family for generations," he reminded me.

His apartment hadn't entered my mind. "I wouldn't dream of having you sell the apartment."

"Thank God."

"Unless it becomes absolutely necessary." This popped out, surprising me.

Silence.

"By the way," I said. "I've got to tell you something." Another grunt. "I want to buy a house." As soon as I blurted out the house thing, I knew it was true. It had been at the edge of my mind, waiting. Waiting for the right time to break it to Laurent? There was no right time, not with the newly permanent distant Laurent. "Or maybe a condo. Very soon."

More silence. The longer I subsisted in one room among roommates, the more I resented Laurent. In fact, there was a whole hell of a lot of resenting going on this very minute, and I meant to put a stop to it. Resentment is bad for the soul.

And what my new evolving personhood needed was a mortgage.

"You haven't finished your program, and you want a house?"

"Yes, I do." My voice was firm, even a tad loud.

"We'll talk," he said.

I told him to kiss Pluto for me, hung up, sat, and stared at the phone. Why so wishy-washy with Laurent? We'll talk?

Yes, we'd talk. A pointy thing in my chest turned over as I redialed. He picked up on the first ring. "The house thing? We talked about it. Look, I hate asking for money when it's our money." My stomach gurgled, as if urging me on. "Ours, not yours. I had a job too."

"We'll work this out."

Now it was my turn to go silent and think about how I'd gotten myself into this financial pickle. Or maybe it was more than a pickle, but calling it a pickle gave me hope. It wasn't as if we had a formal separation agreement. I had nothing in writing. First mistake. The second was worse.

Because I'd made a big blooper not getting myself to a lawyer in Paris, not informing myself better about French divorce laws when it came to a long-term marriage. Trusting Laurent. Well, the trust honeymoon had ended.

Laurent broke the silence this time. "Give me a few weeks."

"Three weeks exactly."

"Is that an ultimatum? Don't give me an ultimatum. I don't respond well to ultimatums."

"Of course not." I took a breath to steady myself. "I don't respond well to worrying if I can buy groceries or eat out."

Silence.

"You eat out," I said, louder this time. "All over the world. You eat well."

Silence.

"I'm too old to live like this." My chest expanded as if the air inside my lungs had reached a boil.

Silence.

"It's degrading. I don't deserve to be treated like this."

"You're exaggerating, of course," he said. His voice cracked as if I'd finally gotten to him.

"Am I? That's not the point. The point was we had an agreement. And I thought I could trust you."

"You can trust me. It's just—"

"I'm living with *roommates*."

"This is what you wanted."

"This is what we *both* wanted," I said in a flat voice. "Remember?"

He cleared his throat.

"Are you punishing me?" I asked.

"Don't be ridiculous."

"You're punishing me. For leaving. A complete joke because you didn't want me."

"I never said that."

"You said it when you didn't spend time with me. That alone says it all. Look, I don't want this. I don't want to argue." What I needed was to kick something very hard. "Meanwhile, I might like to buy a pair of jeans or a sweater. Two sweaters."

"Buy yourself the jeans or whatever you need. You're not a spendthrift."

"No, I'm not. I'll charge it—should have done that in the first place." My hand went to my hair, ruffling it so it stood in clumps. Why hadn't I thought of this sooner instead of stressing? Because I didn't like the idea of credit card debt. I paid my bill in full every month.

"Look, this isn't about buying jeans and groceries." I was thinking much more clearly now. "This is about you being in control of our finances." I sighed a loud sigh, the sort of sigh I hoped would irritate Laurent— the sort of sigh that used to irritate him.

"But you're talking about buying a house. It's not that simple," he said. "You're not working yet. Let me think about this."

"Three weeks," I said. "Starting today."

"Let me see what I can do. Three weeks isn't much time."

"It's long enough." I gripped the phone, the pointy thing in my gut doing a little thrust and twist. "I have to tell you I called a lawyer. I need one. For my own protection."

"So," he said, "this will be an adversarial relationship. Is that what you want?"

"What do you think?"

"It looks that way." He grunted goodbye.

After hanging up, I shrugged into gym pants and grabbed my boxing gloves. In kickboxing class, when I slammed my knee into that bag at about scrotum level, guess who I'd be picturing?

****

Cutting through side streets toward Whalley Avenue, I hung a left, heading for Star Tree. Vegetarian takeout. Frittatas sounded inviting or maybe the ginger salad with noodles. Or the shepherd's pie.

Queen launched into "Bohemian Rhapsody" as a black, low-slung junker burst out of a side street aimed straight at me. For a moment I couldn't breathe, yet managed to turn the wheel, just not before the junker swiped the front of my truck on the passenger side.

My foot slid off the gas pedal as the momentum propelled the truck across the road onto the curb. A whirring noise—the guy slamming on his brakes—and the pop of the airbag as it exploded on my chest, pinning me to the seat. I gripped the wheel, nails digging into skin, my heart sloshing in my chest so hard it seemed the airbag would rupture. Several hours passed, or maybe it was minutes. I breathed in, then out, big chunks of air.

"Miss, miss, you all right?" A big-eyed kid with longish hair gaped through the cracked passenger window. "I'm sorry—oh God, a lady's coming." His whole body twitched, his hands clutching his chest. "The lady. She'll help you."

The kid retreated as I wrestled to unbuckle the seat

belt. Then came the slam of a car door, and I twisted around in time to catch sight of a snaggle-toothed front fender before the kid sped away. One of those teenagers whose daddy pays several thousand in car insurance. The almost uninsurable. I sat blinking at the wonder of the modern airbag, my first- ever close observation of its life-saving work. Wondering if my breasts would be sore or bruised.

*He probably has no insurance.*

"Are you all right?" A woman peered in the window.

When I opened my mouth, nothing happened, so I sat back and breathed in and out again. I had no idea of the make or model and hadn't even thought of getting the plate number. I pressed the button, slid the window down, and turned off the smoking motor.

"Do you need help?"

Probably. I opened the door and stuck my foot out, put both feet on the ground, and hobbled around the front. The half-dented door gave the SUV a sunken-cheek look, like a plastic surgery gone bad. This made me want to cry. My poor vehicle didn't deserve this.

"I'm Mrs. Walters. You…you look very pale."

I did feel a little woozy.

"Don't worry, I'll call for a tow." She was right. The damaged fender made the truck undrivable.

Mrs. Walters led me across the lawn, and we climbed the cement steps leading to the wooden porch. In the living room, which smelled of mothballs and lemon, I folded myself onto her floral couch and closed my eyes. She reappeared with hot tea and oatmeal cookies.

"Relax. No rush," she said. "Do you feel up to

calling road service?"

"Yes." I felt like hugging her.

After making the call to the towing service, I slid onto the couch, eyes closed. Mrs. Walters reminded me of my grandmother Mimi. On Saturday sleepover nights, she toasted cinnamon bread and spread it with sour cream for our bedtime snack. She told me growing-up stories, like the one where my mother jumped on a big kid who bullied my uncle.

And what I should do with my life.

Well, it wasn't that she told me what to do. More how she came to America at the age of eleven to live with cousins and aunts and uncles, and how she worked in a neighborhood store with a real pickle barrel you could dip your hands into. I never tired of her stories.

No doubt there'd be a black and blue mark on my knee and maybe my chest. I probed the knee with a finger. For the first time since my parents moved to Phoenix, I felt vulnerable and old, thinking how my head could have slammed into the steering wheel, how I could have landed in the ER at Yale New Haven Hospital. Alone.

Outside, the tow guy hoisted my vehicle, butt backwards. Thank God my father was in Arizona where he couldn't see his truck in that embarrassing position.

\*\*\*\*

When I woke, a vague memory floated somewhere in the distance. Isabel and Roberto fetching me at Mrs. Walter's house. My legs were stiff, as if they had been tied to wooden boards. Light poured into the room, and I blinked, scratching my mind to remember...the lab at Southern where Dana and I took the Praxis exam, and the drive on the back roads to Star Tree for takeout vegetarian, thrilled when the exam was finally over. The black junker, the whirling, high-pitched sound of braking and skidding before impact. The kid peering in at me. *A lady's coming. She'll help you.*

The kid hauling ass. Unforgivable.

When I pulled off the sheet to check my knee, a red bruise the size of Cleveland winked back at me, shiny and puffy, an angry reminder that the little shit who'd done this was still at large. If I ever saw him again, I'd...

At least my chest didn't hurt. I turned my neck slowly to locate the clock, noticed a carton of soup, along with a bowl and a spoon on a tray. It was almost noon. Fourteen hours I had slept. Thanks to Isabel and Roberto, I was back in my bedroom with no memory of how I got here.

With a few pillows shoved against the wall, I shifted my legs under the sheet. No more feeling sorry for myself. There are plenty of women without husbands who worry about important things like a job, rent, clothes, food, and all the extras their kids think are essentials.

This was a blip.

With the phone cradled on the pillow near my ear, I dialed my parents. No answer. Next, I called the high school in Seyford, and begged them to let me start student teaching the following Monday because of the accident.

What was with the feeling lonely? As if the accident would have been easier with Laurent in my life. We're talking about a man who lacked the bedside manner gene, lacked the soothing gene entirely. I reached for a tissue, wiped my face, and took a swig of water from the bottle on the little nightstand.

Even if I had to live alone for the rest of my life, eat beans four times a week, and bag groceries, I'd still have left him.

****

That Friday, before Isabel took me to pick up my truck, I tacked a note on the fridge, nine neon bus-yellow stickies taped together with lettering in black marker:

*Monster stationary bike for sale*
*See Sunny*

Isabel dropped me off at the body shop. I stepped into the tiny office, breathing in the smell of grease, oil, and heavy metal—thank God for mandatory uninsured motorist coverage—and admired the truck's new fender before setting off for my appointment.

Mr. Duke, Dana's lawyer, had an office in Hamden, a suburb of New Haven, in one of those modern, square buildings housing mostly doctor types. His office was three doors down from the elevator, clearly marked: Samuel Duke, Attorney at Law

The place smelled of wood and pine, reminiscent of an upscale cleanser. Or was it the smell of money? Did he teach? "Yes, yes," I imagined Mr. Duke saying, "Divorce has been very, very good to me."

In a moment, a woman who looked about sixty opened a side door and poked her head out. "Be right with you." I stood in the middle of the reception area, immersed in Old World shabbiness, the stuff you see in those black and white movies—worn leather sofas and paintings of hunting dogs above the couch. Stuff I normally catch at the British Museum downtown.

The woman reappeared, strode to her desk, and

consulted a huge calendar that lay across it. The calendar was covered with neon-colored stickies and gel pen notations.

"Yes?" She had a blotch of dark pink lipstick on her chin.

I looked up from the calendar. "Your stickies look so enticing."

"Mr. Duke is ready for you," she said, pointing to a door to the right of the desk.

"Thank you." I hesitated. "Here," I pointed to my chin. "Lipstick."

"Oh," and her hand went to the spot. "Thanks."

When I tapped on the door and opened it, Mr. Duke stood and waved me into his office. Crossing the threshold, I confronted an Oriental rug so thick I almost had to step up to walk across it.

He held out his hand. "Sam Duke, Ms. Chanel. Dana told me a little about your situation." Sam Duke had Jeff Bridges hair, plus it looked like he spent time at the gym. Couldn't hide those shoulders, even in a suit jacket. He motioned for me to have a seat. "I have the gist of the problem, but I'd like you to tell me about it briefly so I can get a timeline."

I read from my notes, kept it brief, and covered the highlights—how long we'd been married, the promises, how Laurent didn't share.

"I'll have to research this a bit." He pulled open a desk drawer, closed it. "And I understand you are in graduate school?" I nodded. "Then if we can force the issue, you might actually be able to use the forms in the pamphlet."

He motioned for the Quickie Divorce packet in my hands, a result of Dana's insistence I visit the courthouse before seeing lawyer Duke. I handed it over.

"Avoiding a lawyer. Costly," he said shaking his head. "Let's take a look at this. Don't see these often." He scanned the pages. "The terms are simple. No children if I recall?"

"No." Reality biting my ass. Did I look as shattered as I felt? Cutting Laurent out of my life was for real.

"A cash settlement is what makes sense in this case. I'm quite sure it's doable. The thing is to offer an incentive."

"An incentive?"

"An incentive to get your husband to act quickly. Save money. A lot of money, frankly. Avoid my services with that Quickie Divorce route. No quibbling. So you can get on with your life." He was looking at me, perhaps measuring my courage factor.

"He's a quibbler."

"I'm not surprised. The key here is financial disclosure. As much as possible. How much do you know about his assets?" He paused, scratching his chin. "I should say your communal assets." He picked up a piece of paper. "Did he own anything significant before you were married?"

"I should say so." The words popped out of my mouth before I could stop them. Lawyer Duke did a double-take. It was subtle, a professional double take. The man had control. All I could think of was a Lucy episode where Lucy says *I should say so* to Ricky. Except Lucy is funny. "Sorry, didn't mean it to come out like that. You see he has an apartment. A valuable apartment. In a posh part of Paris."

"That's a consideration. I'm glad you mentioned that at the outset." He put the paper down.

"I know some things. I should know more. I mean about the assets," I mumbled, hardly trusting myself to speak. This was where you were supposed to be in the know about your money. Women don't take an interest in the financial end of the marriage until it's too late. Some women, anyway. Me.

"It is essential to inform yourself about the assets. This is your future, the basis for your future. Do you have someone who can help? In Paris? Someone who can do some research?" He was groping in the top drawer of his desk, and his hand came out with a single cigarette. "I'd apologize for smoking, but I never light them," he said with a grin.

"Still no excuse," and I grinned back. "How often do you pseudo-smoke?"

"Two or three times a day." He was looking at me. "So?"

"So?"

"Who can help you? Assets. With the assets."

Who the hell could help me look at Laurent's bank accounts? With a sudden jolt, I realized Laurent had kept his accounts, if not exactly secret, low profile. So low profile I hadn't noticed.

"I have someone who can help. I'm almost positive. Yes." Dulcie. Dulcie knew. Dulcie would help me nail the stingy little bastard.

****

It was still early that night when I heard a rap on my door. There stood the two Patties, sometimes called Patti One and Patti Two. I stared, almost unable to comprehend the concept of visitors. The two Patties were both short and chubby, with straight, limp, dirty blonde hair. I'd asked if they were sisters when I first met them. "No," one of them answered. "But we get that question a lot."

What were these young women doing here, and why were they disturbing my lovely habit of sitting and staring at the gray wall outside the window?

"Hi. We saw your note."

"So, that's it," one Patti said, peering over my shoulder. I turned around to look, mildly surprised at the stationary bicycle with two pairs of gym pants, a bra, and three shirts hanging from the handle. And an apple on the seat.

"That's it." I moved so they could see the monster. "It's new, works great. My mother left it for me..." Did they care about the life story of the bike?

They nodded in unison. "How much are you asking?"

Good question. "A half month's rent," popped out of my mouth. They nodded again, heads together. "Talk it over if you want." I was cool, so cool I side-stepped over to the computer to check my email.

"What is it? Your rent. You pay what?"

This was a surprise. Didn't we all pay the same? I wheeled around. "Six hundred."

They blinked at me. "Six hundred a month?" They stared.

"That's a lot." There was throat clearing. "You're getting ripped off." They looked out the window at my favorite gray wall.

A prickle of irritation hit me realizing that I wouldn't get as much for the bike as I'd thought.

"Maybe you should speak to Melissa. The lease is in her name."

*You're being taken for a fool, a fool, a fool*

repeated inside my head until I thought the Patties could hear it. Aware they were watching my face change, a sort of Mrs. Hyde thing, the way Spencer Tracy did it, without makeup.

They shifted from one leg to the other as if everything they did, they did ensemble. "Hey, we'd definitely like the bike. We're sharing it. What about two hundred?"

"Sold." I wanted this whole thing over. Like my marriage.

"No problem. Can we Venmo you?"

"Venmo? Is that your bank?"

They looked at each other, and I detected a little smile as if I'd said something funny.

"Uh, no," said Patti One, dragging out the *no*, so that I knew it wasn't a bank.

"It's no problem," Patti Two jumped in. "We'll pay cash. We can pay right away, maybe tonight even?"

"Sure. I'll be here." I stuck out my hand, feeling like a participant on *Flea Market Flip*, and I shook on it with both Patties. "What do you each pay for rent anyway?"

"Four hundred." They backed toward the door, looking at one another. "That Melissa is something else."

"Making a profit on this dump."

Once they'd gone, I yanked at the gym shorts and watched the apple tumble to the floor, then grabbed the shirts and the bra, and threw them on the bed. I jogged downstairs to Melissa's room and rapped. Waited and put my ear to the door. Melissa wasn't home. Well, I'd deal with her later.

Upstairs in my room, I surveyed the contents of the

closet, phone in hand. Black shirts and pants, charcoal gray trousers, jackets and shirts in several shades of gray. As if my clothes still thought we were in Paris, the black capital of the world. My single red sweater stood out like a foreigner. Never mind. For student teaching, this would do, this serious look.

I closed the closet door and pressed the Siri button on my phone. The screen lit up.

"What is Venmo?" I asked, loudly and clearly, so Siri wouldn't think I wanted to research venom.

"Here's what I found," said Siri. *Mobile payment service owned by PayPal.* So that's what they were laughing about. I gave a little hoot, remembering the way they'd exchanged glances.

Did they even know what a check was?

****

It was after six and, in the last fifteen minutes, I'd checked my watch three times, holding my wrist at lap level so Donald, my latest meet, wouldn't notice. Nope, too busy texting.

On my second glass of wine—we'd hit the early bird special, Donald's suggestion—at a new fish place on the water, The Fin and Tater. The air surrounding us held the briny scent of fresh tuna and their specialty, fifteen potato dishes, from sweet mashed to curly and deep fried in olive oil.

"One minute, almost done here," his thumbs operating at warp speed on his phone, an oversize smart phone.

Would Donald ever get off his phone? I salivated. An appetizer, however small, would do the trick.

"Sorry about that," he said. "Don't like to be unavailable to Johnny. So. Where was I? Oh, did I tell you he just turned twelve?"

"Um—"

"And I asked him…we're going on a father-son trip," he explained. "I may be an older father, but I've got enthusiasm."

Enthusiasm for your screen, an irritating voice in my head piped up.

His phone dinged, signaling another text. "Sorry, one second."

The urge to gulp the wine was almost overwhelming, but I forced myself to sip slowly, realizing my whole face was clenched. No use telling Donald about my new student teaching gig. Third day and I was still observing, although I read and corrected papers and helped in small group work. Soon I'd graduate to the big leagues, do actual teaching.

And here I was in the shortish red skirt to my red suit, feeling pretty jazzed because I'd worn it with the red sleeveless sweater, showing a little arm definition and for what? So Donald could text-date his son on my time?

Plus, there was the hunger factor.

My phone pinged with a chat alert from the dating site. Since it was easier to text, and I was twiddling away here with a few popovers for company, I sent José my phone number. Twenty seconds later, I had a text.

—*Hi, I'm intrigued. I am doing this and watching three news channels, so please excuse me if I am not seamless. Anyway, I work at U. of Connecticut in the psychology department. Still new to this dating and match-up stuff. I have talked to a couple women. One wanted to know if I was ready for a serious commitment. After one email. Is this normal? I am thinking you have more online match-type experience than I have but I do not want to presume.*

*PS I hope you don't mind my talking about dating here—*

Dinner wasn't materializing, as our menus sat in the middle of the table where Donald had left them when he got his latest text. Yup, the other early-birders were chomping away. I breathed in the unmistakable, mouthwatering aroma of freshly-delivered garlic potatoes at the next table. If I could catch Donald between texts, I'd lobby for a potato appetizer, plenty of garlic, since there wouldn't be any kissing.

A glance over at Donald, confirmed he was still texting in a corner of the lobby. At the moment I texted José my phone number, our server appeared with a basket of rolls wrapped in cloth.

"Did you get a chance to look at the menu?" she asked. The early bird deadline was upon us.

"Not yet," I said, afraid she'd disappear with the rolls. I peeled back the napkin, inhaled the scent, the warm goodness radiating from the basket. Before the rolls, I'd considered leaving, but I was now twenty-seven minutes into the date. Plus, the rolls weren't crappy, white doughy rolls.

"I'll be back to check on you."

Nope. They were dark and seeded, three different kinds, scones and crisp crusts, a couple with raisins, or were those cranberries? I grabbed a seedy, raisiny one, tore it in half and smeared it with butter, top and bottom. Took a generous bite, geez. It was heaven. I took a healthy glug of wine. That second glass was going to my head in a good way.

Donald set his phone aside. "Sorry. I can't help

myself when it comes to my son. Do you have kids?"

Donald's phone rang as I started to answer, and he excused himself, getting up and moving toward the little alcove in the lobby where he babysat his son on the phone.

This was turning out to be a great dinner. I finished my roll and grabbed a popover, tore off a piece and chewed, savoring the buttery smoothness. I pulled my phone out of my bag, figuring to get some business done while Donald was busy being rude.

I logged on to check my bank account. The balance was down to $989.56. Nothing new there. Texted Dana to snark about Donald and munched on the popover. My phone rang with a caller ID I didn't recognize.

"Hello?"

"Hi. Sunny? This is José. Figured talking was better than texting. You don't fool around, do you? Fearless, I'll call you fearless."

"Well I—"

"You gave me your number. Right away. That was awesome." His voice was a purr, and my whole body reacted in a jumpy, jittery, adrenaline mini-rush. I grabbed my bag and headed for the door, waving and pointing so Donald would know I was stepping outside for my own phone call. His head bobbed, and he gave me a thumbs up. Apt.

The restaurant is known for its location at the end of a small street that dead ends at a boatyard and hosts a sailing club. Boats of all sizes and types, from Sunfish to two-motor jobs were docked along the jetty, but it was too dark to walk the wooden plank surrounding the parking lot. I stood listening to the slap of the waves as José waxed on about a meet that turned out to be a bust, and his history of short relationships.

"I yearn for normal," he said.

"You didn't have normal?" I was fascinated by his word choice. *Normal*. Normal was for the very young when you met one another in school or at a party. Normal was mostly over at our age, or was I wrong?

"Well, it depends on your definition." He paused. "I know this sounds dumb. I feel I can talk to you." His voice lowered. "Lots of sex early on. And then if there's nothing else, it all fades away. You get bored. And you start the next one. And the next."

"Well," I hesitated, "I have this naïve idea that as we mature, we realize that sex is important, yes, but not the most important element in a relationship. Unless it's missing." *I feel I can talk to you.* José was better company than Donald, my so-called date.

"Shouldn't it be that way?" he said. "When you get older, well, you look for more."

José talked the talk, but it irked me that he might be feeding me a line. For that reason, I tried to truly listen to the voice, the breaks and pauses. Listen for the sincerity.

"Do you look for chemistry?" I asked, knowing the answer before he said it.

"Of course. That's essential. Absolutely essential."

"Gotta go," I said, turning back to the restaurant. The smell of rotting fish from somewhere on the docks overpowered me. "I'm on this lousy date," I blurted. "A first meet. You're better company than—"

"He doesn't deserve you. Leave him and don't bother with goodbyes. You're too polite. Seriously. Don't put up with that shit."

"Yeah, I am a polite person." Sweet that José had

no boundaries when it came to offering advice to strangers.

"Nice talking to you. I'll call you again."

Inside the restaurant, Donald was bent over his phone in a classic text-neck posture. I wandered back to our table and plucked the remaining half of my popover, wrapped it in a napkin, and stuck it in my bag. I didn't bother sitting. Our time was up, and according to Dana's rules, I'd spent the required hour with Donald.

"Hey, I've got to get going." I hitched my bag across my shoulder. For a second, I contemplated offering to pay for the wine. I'd consumed two glasses. Donald looked up as if not sure what was happening. A wave of irritation mixed with impatience washed over me, but I pushed it away. Not my place to tell Donald how to date or what women want.

"Good luck, Donald." I gave a little two-fingered wave, and headed out.

Later, in my comfy pajamas and an old sweater, I went online, determined to start over, be more positive. I was no longer the neophyte, and I didn't *need* to date just for the experience. No writing random guys. I would scrutinize profiles before agreeing to meet.

After writing a couple of guys from my "favorites" folder—which contained a dozen guys—an email from José hit my inbox, then another and another. I skimmed the first two, and read the third email three times.

*To: Sunny*
*From: José*
*I hope my telephone persona did not come across as too serious. So what do you dream about? What do you hope for? I feel I have one life to live, and while I*

78

*want great sex, it is also important to have great romance and a sense of closeness. Let's meet soon.*

I crawled into bed, smiling. Great sex, huh? Does anyone want crappy sex?

Chapter Four
Ups and downs…

Marvelous, the restaurant José picked, sat at the
end of a cul de sac, an old, converted mansion on the
Quinnipiac River. I stood for a moment to get my
bearings, hearing Isabel's voice inside my head
lecturing about the dangers of expectations. "No matter
how great he is on the phone, it doesn't count.
Remember, nothing counts until you meet the man." I'd
gone silent after her little speech. "You already have
expectations, don't you?" she said.

"Not exactly," I lied. "A few. One or two."

I couldn't help thinking we'd hit it off. Click
because José and I were both communicators, and were
on a site called *letsclick.com*. How could it not be? Our
talks on the phone were fluid and fun and sometimes
profound. We'd talked five nights in a row, counting
the night I'd met and discarded Donald.

The best thing about the Donald meet had been
talking with José on the phone.

To the left, I glimpsed tables with fresh white
cloths, the silverware winking, as if beckoning diners.
There were booths in the dimly lit bar, and I grabbed
one toward the front by the window so José could easily
find me. I'd told him I was wearing blue and a smile. It
was safe to be flirty in email. My hair was freshly
washed, and it smelled of whatever that shampoo is

where the women in the old commercial work up a lather and had to have orgasms. And I wore a shortish skirt with a pale blue sweater that hugged me in a sexy but tasteful manner.

Looking around as if you're not looking around is tricky. You want to appear confident as if no one in his right mind would keep you waiting, or worse, stand you up. José stand me up? No way. I could talk with him about things I hadn't been able to talk to Laurent about.

After a few minutes, I went to the ladies' room, certain he'd be standing at the bar when I got back. But it was still the same couples and three guys on bar stools. I slid into the booth, ordered a glass of the house cabernet, and checked out the three guys for something to do. An older guy, haunches hanging off the sides of the stool, and two very young men. My good friend José was now officially late. I took a sip, contemplated the decor, sort of late fifties chrome and pleather.

A movement outside the window caught my attention. A man peered in at me and waved, his bald head illuminated in the terrace lights outside. He pointed to me and then to himself, mouthing something. I looked away, stared at the sagging butt on the bar stool. Was that José outside?

The door swung open, and he was at my booth—a beefy man on the short side, hands in his pockets. He made eye contact.

"Are you Sunny?"

"What were you doing out there?" I glanced at his worn sneakers, the bottoms of his frayed jeans, hemmed a tad too long and dragging on the floor. He slid into the booth and sat opposite me for a few moments before answering.

"Looking you over, I guess," he said. His eyes dropped to my breasts, back to my face, then to my breasts again. I instantly regretted wearing my provocative sweater, the one with the button that looked like it was coming undone but never would because I had *smallened* the button hole. *Smallen* was another word Isabel and I made up when we were kids. I'd liked the sweater too much to take it back to the store.

"I watched you come in from a booth in the back."

At some point, he'd gotten up from his back perch and gone outside. A calculated move. Maybe when I'd gone to the ladies' room? I took another sip of wine to digest this information, pictured José in the back, watching me, enjoying being invisible. "Are you mad at me?" He stared at my hand, gripping the wine. "You have nice hands. You turn me on. Here, put your hand on my chest, feel my tit." He made a grab for my hand, but I jerked it away.

"You're nuts."

"But you didn't leave, did you?"

"The night is young," I said, taking a sip of wine. I squeezed the stem of the glass. I could throw it in his face, like in the movies. No, that wasn't me.

I flashed on Dana. Dana wouldn't put up with this crap. Dana would squash him like a bug, or aim a knee to the groin, and it wasn't because she was tall and imposing. It was because she had a strong sense of herself. It was because she'd never stay with a husband who ignored her and refused to have sex with her yet wasn't adverse to still sleep in the same bed. Well, actually, I didn't know anything about Dana's marriage or her husband. Except she wouldn't talk about him. What was up with that?

And why wasn't she texting me about her meets? She'd sure as shit hear about this one. *Feel my tit?*

This was the man without boundaries, who'd told me a few days ago on the phone to dump Donald. *He doesn't deserve you. Leave him, and don't bother with goodbyes.*

If I walked out now, I wouldn't make my one-hour minimum for the stupid contest. It wasn't even a contest, and Dana and I were both in our fifties. Too old for this crap.

The waiter arrived and moved us to a table in the dining room. I clutched the wine glass for emotional support, a little warning voice urging me not to drink too much.

"I've been staring at your sweater all night. Waiting for that button to come undone," he smirked as we sat.

"It won't." I unfolded the napkin and put it in my lap.

"You seem sure."

"Absolutely certain."

He talked about the work he did for a homeless women's group, for battered women, and for teens. The waiter appeared, and we ordered. Several seconds passed, and he looked around the dining room, fixed me with an intense look. "I'm very attracted to you. You have a body made for sin."

"So now you're quoting *Working Girl*? And what was with you standing outside to get my attention?"

"Oh, well I…" He picked up the breadbasket, set it down.

"That was rather rude."

"Yes, it was. Will you forgive me?"

"It depends on how well you can suck up." Uh oh, big mistake using the word *suck.* I wanted to take it back.

"Sucking up is my specialty. Starting at your toes and going from there." He leaned across the table. "Is that the outline of your nipple through your sweater? I like pink nipples, but not big ones."

My nipples clenched as if they'd heard him.

"But good for you, calling me on my shit." He seemed to settle in his seat as he talked as if I had boosted his confidence by not leaving. "I like it all," he said. "Do you walk around nude? I hope so. I hope you like it on top." He glanced at my breasts. "I hope you like to be licked and kissed all over."

His mouth opened, a smile spreading slowly across the cheeks, the mustache so long bits of the ends caught in the corners of his mouth. He glanced again at my sweater. "You know, you've got to like going down—"

The waiter arrived with our salads. Was it my imagination, or did he give José a funny look? "Vinaigrette?" José indicated me with a nod of his head.

Enough already. I ground my molars together, the way my mother did when we were kids and had pushed her to her limit. "Excuse me a second," and I grabbed my bag, avoiding his gaze.

"Don't be too long, I'll miss you."

In the ladies' room, I stood in one of the stalls. The evening stretched before me. Endless sparring. Cheesy. I should have left. I should have left at *I had a back booth. I watched you come in.*

Taken in by the long phone calls, the sweet, caring José. But part of me, the adventurous part, had wanted to see how this would play out.

I washed my hands, put on lipstick, and walked out of the ladies' room then straight out the front door of the restaurant.

"Hey, honey, going so soon?" shouted some guy at the bar.

When I reached my car, I locked the doors with a flick of the switch, and sat a minute. *Damn.* I'd left my coat over the chair in the restaurant.

By the time I got back to the table, the entrees had arrived. "Our dinners are getting cold," he said. "I waited for you."

Ignoring him, I grabbed my coat.

"Now, you're going? Are you serious?" He looked genuinely disappointed, and a rush of satisfaction shot through me. So. I'd finally succeeded in irritating *him*.

My hand stretched toward the glass of water—an almost-full glass, chocked with ice cubes—by his plate. It wouldn't take much more than a gentle push to urge it onto its side. I imagined the subzero contents spilling over José's crotch and thighs, an instant flashback to the coffee spatter and Laurent leaping out of the way.

Except I didn't want to be that person.

For the first time all evening, as I headed out, I was smiling.

So what if this meet didn't count according to Dana's rules?

\*\*\*\*

Was early a good thing, or did it scream insecurity in a job candidate? Forty-five minutes in advance of my interview, I was stashed in the conference room next to the front office, and desperate for another cup of coffee. The aroma from the fresh coffee machine three feet away was so inviting I almost helped myself.

Isabel and my parents said they'd be thinking of me. I had dragged myself out of bed after a night of little sleep to make the 6:00 a.m. aerobics class. I scanned texts from Dulcie and Natalie, and three friends from the Institute where I'd worked in Paris. Everyone wished me luck. And there was a break-a-leg text from Dana.

*—You'll ace it on your first interview.—*

Finally, that wonderful fresh coffee smell was too much to resist. I slid off the chair and reached for one of the paper cups beside the coffee maker.

"Sunny Chanel?"

The sound of my name hurled from the doorway startled me, and I dropped the cup. A man, short, bony, and wearing a dark, overlarge suit stood waiting. Lack of affect came to mind.

"Yes," I said, bent to retrieve the cup, but couldn't decide whether to discard it or replace it on the coffee stand. The man hiked his shoulders as if encouraging his suit to fit better, and I shoved the cup into my bag.

"Please come with me."

I followed him down the corridor. This was the first day of my new life, the day I would get a position teaching French in Walford, a school district with an excellent reputation. Attitude. It was all in the attitude.

One thing, though. I shouldn't have worn my red suit. This was not a red suit kind of place.

The red suit was an accident, tucked away among the size fourteens at a place called Revisit on Dixwell Avenue. I'd found it when trolling the consignment shops on the off-chance I'd find a jacket I could slap on with a black skirt to create an interview suit. No question you can fake it if you've got seven black skirts—all different shapes and lengths—in your closet. I'd peered at the suit, wishing it smaller. But the short jacket fit, just curved enough to hug the waist, and I could have the skirt altered. I bought it and had worn the skirt on a few dates already.

The man in the big suit took me into the inner sanctum where there was a floating chair, *my designated chair*, twenty feet away from three women in almost identical navy blue suits. The phrase sanctum sanctorum, *holy of holies,* came to mind. I couldn't place it, and there it sat in my brain ready for a word search. I sat on the edge of the oversized chair, my arms rigid on the rests. I'd have to shout to be heard.

Suit man introduced the three women as teachers in the foreign language department. They weren't wearing suits exactly, it was just some combination of navy and white. Was there a school uniform? Maybe the navy was a coincidence. It wasn't as if they'd phoned one another that morning to wear navy for my interview.

"Let's begin, shall we?" said Suit, who sat watching like a spider while the women asked questions. Even far, far away, I could tell he rarely blinked.

One of the navy women sat in the middle chair, her toes peeking out of Birkenstocks under the table. Piggies unpolished.

I tried not to rush my words, looked straight at my interviewers all the way across the room in Norway. Fielded questions about class management, pace, pressure, the curriculum, homework, and parent contact. The Suit rose and left the room. I turned around to see who had beckoned him from the door. No one.

"Do you speak Spanish?" the woman on the right asked just as he returned and, without glancing at anyone, took his seat. He picked up a pamphlet, turned the pages, closed the pamphlet, and picked it up again.

"No, no. I don't." I cleared my throat. "I understood I was interviewing for a position teaching French."

"Oh, yes," the man spoke up for the first time. "True. But Spanish and French—a double certification—well, it is always helpful. After all."

These people were professionals. Without warmth, yes. But I would warm them up, like that delicious seeded bread at the restaurant on the Donald date.

I reached down, grabbed my student teaching portfolio and unzipped it. "Brought my portfolio of work samples." I'd show them my students' *Le Petit Prince* illustrations and the photos showcasing our French luncheon for the seniors. Pictures of my students serving sandwich slivers with the crusts cut off, speaking little *politesses*. I'd wow them.

The first woman whispered in the second woman's ear.

Suit man looked up from the pamphlet. "I wish you had told us that in the beginning."

My fingers lingered on the zipper, and I didn't open the portfolio. Silence. The two women glanced at one another, the third stared straight ahead at me.

Of course. How could I be so naive? They already had someone lined up for the position, most likely a teacher at this school, or a colleague from another school in the district. Advertising and interviewing candidates was mandatory, but they were going through the motions.

I slouched, letting my muscles dissolve into jelly, my mind floating, taking in the details of the room and the conversation, so I could tell Isabel and Roberto and the whole crowd of relatives and kids this coming weekend, on Thanksgiving. And Dana and my parents, and my Paris friends.

"What made you decide to wear a red suit?" the first navy woman asked. She smiled without opening her mouth.

My armpits dampened. I was back in the second grade, standing in line in Miss Ponderoy's class, and Jenny, a chubby girl with blond pigtails, had just announced she didn't like my red sweater, the one my grandmother Mimi had hand-knitted for my birthday. I had stood staring, too polite to react.

"I guess I was all out of navy," I said. My voice bounced off all the navy blue and hung there. The Suit looked at the first woman, and the second woman looked at the first woman.

"Do you have any questions for us?" the man asked.

"No questions," I said.

"Thank you for coming. We will reach a decision in a week." The women nodded.

"My red suit and I thank you for the interview." I plucked the portfolio from the table and zipped it. My mouth rigid, I stood, inclined my head at the group, turned and left.

Outside in the parking lot, I deposited my portfolio and my handbag on the passenger seat and walked around to the driver's side. I stood for a moment, panting by the open door in spite of the cold.

"F-u-u-u-c-k," I brayed. I pulled my red skirt up,

climbed in, and pulled out of the lot.

At the stoplight, I glanced into the car that pulled up beside me. The driver leaned over to the woman sitting beside him, whispered in her ear. She shook her head. The guy leaned over again. The woman turned toward him with a serious expression and shook her head, again and turned away.

Big Suit popped into my head. Big Suit nagging his wife to have sex with him.

"But honey," she said, a sweet smile on her face. "We've already had sex this year. You'll have to be patient. Next year will be here before you know it."

\*\*\*\*

There was an awful ringing. Had I set the alarm? I opened one eye, glanced down. Surprise. I was fully dressed. Hadn't even pulled the covers up.

Now it was coming back. My evening with the insurance executive, the two beers to dull the droning voice on the marvels of payouts, annuities, dividends.

Back home in a pissy mood—which I'd been in ever since the date with José and my tragic interview— I'd trolled online with a glass of wine, and crashed in jeans and my fuchsia sweater, my standard first-meet outfit.

The residual stink of the José experience was messing with my head. Isabel had commented that I wasn't myself on Thanksgiving, and I'd denied it as if denying would make everything go away.

Almost a week already, replaying his comments, wishing I'd walked out the moment he'd uttered, "The best relationships are the ones that naturally evolve." Such pretty words, and I'd liked him so much...before our meet. José was proof I was a bad judge of character, and my ability to pick a good man was doubtful.

My mouth held the sour smell of the beer and wine mix. No doubt I'd neglected to brush before bed. This wasn't like me. I rolled over on my side and squinted at the clock. Ten to six.

The ringing started again, and I squeezed my eyes shut. The phone. I rolled over, reached for it. "Hello."

"Sunny."

"Hi, Laurent," I said with a strained-cheery voice, the better to sound wide awake, as if I'd been vacuuming the living room or cleaning the toilet bowl. A woman who cleans early in the morning cannot be taken lightly.

"Hi."

Nothing more. I willed myself to be quiet. Several seconds passed.

"I got the letter. From your lawyer." His voice was flat.

"Yes. That was the plan." I was sitting up wishing I knew how to record the conversation on my phone.

"What do you hope to accomplish threatening me?"

Fully awake now, I stacked pillows behind me, the better to concentrate, measure my words. "My sweet side wasn't making much of an impression on you, so I got a lawyer. A recommendation from a friend." I breathed into the phone to calm my nerves. This was the call I'd been waiting for, and I'd prepared by taking notes, which were somewhere on the other side of the room. "I want to move on. I want a new start. What we discussed. This isn't news. We talked about my move before I left. If I'd known you weren't going to—"

"Don't blame me," said Laurent. "It seems from

where I sit, you had it pretty damn good. You weren't doing all the traveling, didn't have the responsibility of maintaining a household. It was all on me. And now you want to walk away—"

"You wanted me to walk away. Admit it," I kept my voice low, flat, emotionless—the best way to deal with the new, irrational Laurent.

"That's no excuse to threaten—"

"Admit it," I said, still keeping my voice low. "Admit you shut me out for over a year. Admit it."

He didn't say anything. The silence stretched out between Paris and New Haven for thousands and thousands of miles, a silence that reminded me why I'd left.

"Admit, you shut me out. You backed off. Backing off tells a woman she's not wanted," I said. "It's simple."

"So, that's it? Because I backed off, you got a lawyer? A man has the right to back off, doesn't he?"

"Of course. You back off far enough and long enough, and I have the right to leave, don't I?"

Silence on his side. "You're not fooling around."

"Not at all." My gut clenched in a hard wad of beer residue and angst. "Laurent, this is my life you're talking about. I don't know about you, but I don't want to spend it being unhappy. And you shouldn't either."

Remembering the good times, how I used to look forward to Laurent's key in the lock. He'd bring home scallops and a carton of crème fraîche, or little filets and mushrooms for dinner. Ironic that I'd been thinner when Laurent and I braised, poached, fricasseed, and chatted side-by-side every evening after work. We experimented with recipes, invented, laughed when it all went wrong. Now the idea of laughing at anything...

Breathing on his side of the phone. "I—well." Laurent was rarely at a loss for words. He sighed.

"Talk to me," I said. "Please."

"You left. I didn't like it. I'll admit it. Didn't like that you left. Left Paris. That it was your decision, and you took off."

That stopped me cold. "You resent me for wanting to start over? A separation would have left me in limbo. The way I see it, you're getting what you wanted, so why complain? This is better for us both." I breathed out, trying to calm myself against the powerful current that was Laurent's anger. Oh, crap, what difference did it make? Whatever I said, he'd be pissed, so why hold back?

"About the money? It's my money, too." I said this quietly, but I was squishing my pillow, sick of going over and over the same thing.

"Laurent, I will come to Paris if I have to. I will come there and occupy the corridor outside your office. I swear. Dulcie will help me. She promised, and she has...well, never mind that. I don't have to do this on my own. So make your decision." If I didn't get a cup of coffee inside me right now, I'd lose it on the phone, lose my edge, and all my cool negotiating would have been for naught, as Laurent would say.

"I have an appointment with my lawyer. Later this week," he said.

"Is it Jean-Paul?" So. He had a plan. This was good. Maybe.

"Yes."

"Well, that's a start. Give him my love."

"It's strange, though, isn't it?" His voice sounded

weary, as tired of the bickering and bad blood between us as I was.

"Yes," I said. "It is strange, you having Jean-Paul for your lawyer."

"Well, I'll be in touch."

When we disconnected, I sat on the floor in the lotus position or my version of a lotus position. Laurent was using our old friend, Jean-Paul, for the divorce. We'd known them forever. His wife made the best *couscous*, was partial to Pluto, and we'd hit a movie now and then, just the girls. Over the years, Jean-Paul, a divorce lawyer for thirty years, would tell us stories about his clients, the craziness, the hiding of assets, the lack of sex.

We were about to be one of those tales.

\*\*\*\*

"Last night was number nine," I said, en route to a job interview. I shared recent experiences with Isabel while she kept me company by phone. School was out, and I'd caught her prepping in her classroom

"You've reduced your meets to numbers?"

"What's the point in names? I'm not seeing any of these guys again, and you just get confused." I pulled into the Waffle Cone parking lot and unhooked my seat belt.

"True. But you're turning into a cynic."

"As soon as I find my someone special, I'll tell you his name."

"Sounds good. So what about your number nine?"

"We traded tales from the trenches and he—"

"Trenches? What trenches?"

"Dating trenches, what other kinds of trenches do you think? He met eight women, all in one day. In a coffee shop in Hartford. Two coffee shops. Back to back appointments."

"You are joking."

"He ran from one coffee shop to the other. Had it all timed—half an hour in one coffee shop, and then he'd run a block to the second, and so forth."

"People do these things?" Isabel asked.

"Oh, lots of weird behavior. I thought it was bold. In fact, I can't believe what some guys tell me. And do."

"Like what?"

"Oh, the last guy I met, number eight, said his first wife was a pathological liar, and they got into heavy debt because of it. Now, until he finds the right woman for him, he's sleeping with two women friends. Calls it symbiotic sex. They both know about one another."

"You'll go out with anybody, won't you?" Isabel asked.

"Don't be snotty. It takes time to get to know someone. And after Laurent, it's no wonder I respond to talky men."

"How's Dana doing? What number is she on?

"As far as I know, she hasn't met anyone, yet." This sort of pissed me off, but that I kept to myself.

"Well, don't say more. Please. I don't want to know anything else about numbers eight or nine."

"Then I won't tell you how nine thinks middle-aged women are sexually starved and therefore insatiable."

"Ug. I'm gonna hang up now. I swear I don't know why you want to date in bulk."

"And how they come on to him when he's in line at the—"

She hung up.

*To find my person*, I'd wanted to tell her. *Why else?*

I clicked on Facebook to check for messages. One from Dulcie and Natalie, who would never hang up on me, no matter what I said. When we'd Skyped, they laughed like idiots at my José story, calling him Nasty Man and Mr. Suck Up.

"You're undauntable," Natalie said, and although I wasn't sure it was a word, I loved the sentiment.

A snort from Dulcie. "You should have dumped his ass right at the beginning when he deserved it."

The Skyping was great, as I got to see and hear them laughing and mugging, just like the old days. "Sure, sure," I said, "but then I wouldn't have you peeing in your panties, would I?"

*Peeing in your panties* was an expression I had never used. Which is probably why they'd laughed harder. Geez, I missed all that, and a shiver of longing for my old life racked me as I cracked the door open, and stepped out of the car into the chill.

It was crazy having a vanilla cone lunch in the winter, but that's what I had, shivering with the motor off as the cold shot from teeth to the brain stem. I reapplied my lipstick and drove to the school where the interviewers were normal people sitting in a normal-size room. No one left during the interview, and the panel showed interest in my portfolio. One interviewer spoke French with a southern accent. Not a brochure in sight.

After the interview, I headed back toward New Haven and slowed for a red light at the intersection. Something familiar about the car ahead of me grabbed my attention, a car with a mangled fender. The car turned into Burger King at the intersection.

Signaling, I pulled into the lot, and even though the van in front blocked my view, I caught a glimpse of a young guy getting out of the car and ambling to the entrance. He disappeared inside the restaurant.

On the far end of the lot, I found a spot and turned off the motor. After sitting a few minutes and thinking, I got out and walked over to inspect his vehicle, leaning close to get a better look at the dent. Someone had fooled with it, tried to bend it back into place. An amateur job.

What was with the parents? If the kid was as young as he looked, didn't his parents take an interest? Hadn't they noticed the fender dent? I cracked open my handbag, searching for a pen. Tough luck. Then I noticed the number plate. KS33

How could I have missed that one, so short, so memorable? Well, I'd been pretty shaken up when he slammed into me. KS for kiss and—what to do now? I pulled out my cell and took a few photos, keeping my back to the windows of the restaurant, not wanting the kid to see me crouched down by his car.

The mouth-watering French fry smell hit as I pulled the door open, but for once, it didn't stir my appetite. I surveyed the counter, where a girl of about sixteen, clearly bored, stood hand on hip at the cash register, waiting for a man with a walker to make a decision. His wife, in pants three sizes too large, stood patiently at his side. I squared my shoulders and took a deep breath, then another, as I imagined Isabel whisper quite clearly in my ear, *Go get 'em, girl.*

He was sitting by the window. I stepped over to the

table and stood in front of him. He had his mouth around a hamburger, a bag of fries on his tray along with a milkshake. Vanilla, it looked like. The kid could eat, and he wasn't putting on the pounds. He had one of those skinny frames that keeps on burning.

"Hi."

"Hi." He was chewing. He swallowed, his Adam's apple visible, a scruffy-looking kid with grease blotches on his jeans and a smear on his forehead. His hair hung in his face. "Who are you?"

"Pardon me for interrupting your dinner."

"It's okay." He took another bite. "Who are you?" At this rate, he'd be finished and out the door in a minute. I watched his hands holding the burger, they seemed cleaner than his face. Maybe he'd washed them before eating.

"I'm a friend of your mother's." What if the kid didn't have a mother? I needed to sit. I didn't ask, slid into the chair at the adjoining table.

He took a fistful of French fries, folded them in half, stuffed them in his mouth. If I'd been a friend of his mother's, I would have advised her to clamp down on his table manners. "I don't remember you. You on the bowling team?" He dipped three or four fries in ketchup, tilted his head and suspending the fries, deposited them in his open mouth. "You don't look familiar."

"Bowling. Not exactly." I sat staring at him while he finished chewing the fries, wiped his hands on several napkins, and tossed them on the tray. There was a bite or two of the hamburger left and half the bag of fries. He picked up the milkshake and took a long slug.

"What's that mean?" he asked. "Not exactly?" I

detected a tone, an attitudinal tone. "I don't get that."

"Let me clarify for you." Here goes. "I've been hired by someone to find you." I stopped, wanting to see how he reacted to this.

"Yeah. That's a joke. Who hired you?" The attitude again. But he put down the milkshake and didn't pick up the burger. I could detect a thin line of milkshake mustache. The kid reminded me of a couple of my former students who occasionally felt the need to test the teacher.

"The person wants me to handle this. Not get your parents involved." Hoping he wouldn't simply stand up and leave before I got a chance to scare the shit out of him. I could do this. I'd done it to my own husband.

"My parents?" He picked up the hamburger and put it down. "What do my parents have to do with this?" A slight frown line appeared on his forehead.

"No discussion. I'm laying this out now." Trying to sound like someone who knew what she was talking about, rather than a person speaking off the cuff. The kid had pimples and was most likely still in high school. Surely, I could outsmart even a high school senior.

"What do you mean?"

"No. No discussion. Not yet." I said this loudly enough that two other couples at adjoining tables turned to look. He seemed to slither down in his seat.

"Sorr—y, you don't have to yell."

"I'll be the judge of that." I straightened my back, tightened my mouth. His expression, his whole face couldn't hide the shock. The kid was intimidated. Well, I'd mentioned parents. What if he was my kid, how would I feel, what would I say to let him know his callous behavior had been unforgivable? If nothing came of this, if the kid bolted and dived for the door and I never saw him again, this finding him and talking to him would have been worthwhile.

The old teacher trick. I used it. Spoke softly, so he had to lean in slightly to hear me, unaware of what he was doing. "Here it is. You hit a woman who was driving an SUV. Three months ago. Approximately. It's taken me this long to find you. She has hospital bills. You will pay them."

"You're crazy." He sat there looking at me. His eyes twitched, and he looked away. "You're nuts. I never hit nobody."

"Just now, I took a sample of paint. Out there in the parking lot. That's the first thing. Second."

"My parents will get a lawyer."

"Feel free. Inform your parents." My voice was loud. I was embarrassing myself. One of the couples walked toward the door, and the woman glanced over her shoulder in our direction. The kid buried himself lower down in the seat. "Second. We had a partial plate reading. That's why it took so long." I kept eye contact. Geez, now I was using Law and Order reruns to make this stuff up.

He lowered his gaze, stared at his hands. "I didn't know what to do."

"Your parents will be notified. Unless."

He looked up. "My parents will kill me." He paused. "I didn't mean it about the lawyer. Is she—is the woman all right?"

"Actually she's doing all right. The car repair bills. The insurance is covering most of that."

"Most?"

"Are you ready for what you can do?"

"I guess."

"What grade are you in?" I asked out of the blue to get some kind of a perspective on this kid.

"Not in a grade. I graduated. Last year."

"Where do you work?"

"Tony's. Tony's Auto Body Works." He pointed over his shoulder out the window. "Up on Whalley." He coughed, put his hand up to wipe his forehead. "But I live at home. With my parents."

"That's good."

"My insurance. It's this tremendous—well, it's a lot. A whole lot to pay."

"We can keep this quiet if you can pay her back."

"My insurance will go up. If I report it." He paused. "If I report the accident."

"So the point is not to make waves here. To pay her back."

"Yeah, I guess so." He stopped. "That's why I ran."

"You ran?" I asked, not understanding.

"I ran. I mean, I drove away. I was scared."

I forced myself not to say anything.

"How much? How much do I gotta pay her? I have a little saved."

Had I come this far? So close and it was too bad. I was about to mess it up entirely, since I'd left my pen and pad in my briefcase after the interview. Hoping to buy a little time, I opened my handbag. My phone. Of course.

"Give me your phone number and address."

He did, and I punched in his number, relieved when his phone, sitting on the table, rang.

"Sorry, had to be sure." I added the kid to my contacts.

An idea formed. "I want to make this easy for you and my…client. I'm texting you her address."

His phone dinged. "You've got some savings? To start paying her?"

"About sixty. Sixty bucks."

I'll admit it, I blinked. *So the kid has no savings.* "That's a start. A good start." I cleared my throat. Reminded myself not to go soft that he'd bashed into me. "You're expected to pay a hundred. Every two weeks. You get paid every two weeks?"

He nodded.

"Without fail. Or your parents get notified."

He nodded. "Every two weeks," he repeated.

"Good. You have a checking account?"

"Hardly ever use it." He wanted this to be over and me to disappear.

*Keep it simple. No complicated instructions.* "Your first payment?" I was figuring in my head.

"The fifteenth. It's the fifteenth," he said. "I'm good at math stuff."

The total was $500, enough to cover the deductible.

"Can I go now?" he asked.

"Tony's Auto Body on Whalley, right?"

He nodded, jumped out of his seat, stood for a moment. "Well, thank you for not telling my parents."

He turned and headed for the door, leaving behind the cold burger and fries. The good thing? I knew where to find him if he tried disappearing.

\*\*\*\*

When I called Big Doc, my latest meet, to tell him

I was stuck in traffic on the Merritt Parkway, he told me to take my time. "I'm looking forward to meeting you, no worries, I'll wait for you," he said. A sense of humor, *I'll wait for you*, and a bedside manner that soothed.

The next exit was mine, and at the stoplight, I thumbed the app open to reread his profile.

*bigdoc5685 Ready for Intimacy*

*My friends often comment on the dichotomy between my work and play. I'm a pill pusher otherwise known as a pharmacist, and a master of the game of chess. Then there is the inevitable question of my physique. In fact, I strike a rather imposing figure, even for a man half my age. I'm not modest, you remark. I am, however, thoughtful, kind, fun-loving, and warm. Warmth is very different from charm, which can be seductive and cold at the same time.*

Oddly formal profile. I turned right, following my GPS. My phone rang the frog ribbit, Dana's special ring.

"Hey, I have two minutes. Waiting for my date." She sounded breathless, and I had trouble hearing her with the background noise of restaurant chatter. "Drinks and we'll see about dinner. Actually, I don't want to have dinner if he's boring, so I'm checking him out over a glass of wine. I wore my jeans with heels, but low heels, and sleeveless, but I have a cardigan. I don't like being this nervous. Can you tell?"

"No, but—"

"Wait, is that him? Gotta go, he's here, and he looks exactly like his profile photo. Cute and he has hair. Later," and she hung up as I pulled into the lot, sat a moment waiting for the anxiety of a first meet to fade away. I don't like being this nervous. I'd wanted to tell her I got nervous, too.

The place was packed, couples, businessmen and groups of women in their luncheon outfits, the restaurant a medley of red bows, with a huge fireplace at one end and a Christmas tree in the corner. I spotted Frank Steiner, Big Doc, at the bar. His smile broadened as I approached.

"Frank? There was an accident."

He took my hand in his large one. "Relax, no worries. You're on school vacation, aren't you?" A gesture that made me feel as if I'd just had a glass of wine. "Come, sit, drink something festive."

We sat, and Frank told me a bit about the menu and why he often came here. I listened, purring way inside where he couldn't hear.

Frank was hunkier than his picture, brown curly hair and plenty of it, on the short side. He had a strong chin, sort of a hero cartoon character Superman look. His eyes were brown with brows that arched as if plucked—not at all an effeminate look on Frank. And his body. Well, I could almost feel the women at the next table leaning closer.

We had no trouble making conversation over lunch, beginning, of course, with pleasantries and going on to mini life stories, skimming over marriage, kids, divorce. Everything proper, no spousal bad-mouthing.

Over the next two hours, Frank told tales about pharmaceutical sales reps he had known and loved, how much he enjoyed reading my amusing emails and asked about my student teaching.

"I have to get back to the store. May I call you again please, Sunny? What would you like to do? The art museum? Think about it and let me know. I can be free occasionally during the day." He smiled.

Frank walked me to my car and, ignoring the hand I offered—well, not exactly ignoring it, using it to pull me closer—kissed me on the cheek in broad daylight. I jerked away, astonished at my own reaction.

He shrugged and laughed. "Take it easy. I'll never go beyond your level of comfort." He looked at me with an intent, focused expression. "Come to dinner with me. Next Saturday, will that work for you?"

The formality worked for me, the reserved way he asked me out, unassuming. Pretty much the whole Frank package.

Well, the pharmacy talk was a little boring.

****

That evening, I slogged through the job listings in Milford and Hamden, two nearby districts. The process for applying online was tedious, and any openings would be freakish good luck several months into the school year. Still, I had to look. Sure enough, Milford listed three teaching jobs. Wait, those were substitute positions. Of course, why hadn't I thought about sub jobs sooner? The money wasn't much, but every bit helped. Plus, it was a way to gain some experience. Meet the principals at different schools. Learn.

The site invited candidates to apply for non-permanent positions, and I whipped through applications for the two districts, feeling a sense of well-being and productivity, a lethal combination. High on myself and using my noggin, as my father would say.

By that time the oven beeped, signaling it was up to temperature, and I salivated, looking forward to my

classic TV dinner. I read the directions and bent down
the plastic wrap on the top corner of the tray, exposing
something that resembled a potato, yellowish and
dented. I slid the tray into the oven.

Back at the computer, I clicked over to the dating
site and joined for three months, and since I was there
anyway, checked out a few guys for Dana. Guys with
height and a touch of clever in their profiles. One
teacher, one architect, and a guy with a ten-word profile
that made me laugh. His photo showed him holding his
pug dog, ugly-adorable. I mailed her the links.

An alert sounded. Yup, a little numbered box in the
right-hand corner indicated twenty-eight new emails.
*Too much*, another of my father's expressions. And
eleven *ding dongs*, short little blurbs indicating a guy
wanted to meet but didn't care to expend any effort
emailing. I ignored the *ding dongs*.

The first email in the lineup was from Luke,
Soulmate Guy, I called him, because he was the first
who'd talked about it—even though there were 7,000
other guys online clamoring for a soulmate.

The oven pinged and I shut off the timer, pulled the
plastic off, and carried the TV dinner over on a tray, so
I could eat and wade through all the emails. I plunged
my fork into the potato-like substance, took a bite.
Bland. A bite of chicken. Edible. I ate mechanically,
checking the emails, one by one, my gut twisting.
Twenty-eight emails were doable, but twenty-five
meets? Too much. I couldn't do it. Well, I could do it,
but I didn't want to do it. What would it get me?
Another nasty man? Well, there was Frank. He was
nice.

Luke's email? Saved for last.

Luke wrote about a vacation he took every summer on an island in Canada, and how the island was so small that at high tide it almost disappeared. He went there alone, and although this surprised me, I could understand the appeal of digging my toes into the sand and talking out loud to myself on the beach.

Luke, the *Bluesky* guy, popped up in a cartoon bubble: Would you like to chat with Luke?

I hit, *yes*. Chat was the site's version of texting, and this was my first time.

—LUKE: Hey, got a few minutes? This messaging is friendlier than old school emails. How goes it? Back from vacation. Went to the island. So different there in the winter. Beautiful in a different way. Just came home from doing a little bar dancing. I stayed about an hour. Every once in a while, I do that on a tense night. This was my tense night.

—SUNNY: Tense, *shmense*. What's wrong?

—LUKE: One of those old girlfriend things. We have a lot in common—biking, riding, skiing, and some total madness thrown in, but she doesn't give me space. It's complicated.

—SUNNY: What's with the old girlfriend thing? If you'll be so kind as to be my dating mentor, I have a question. Dating mentor, is it wise to re-date old girl/boy friends?

—LUKE: Absolutely not, are you nuts? My prob is I don't like being alone. I like sharing things with someone.

—SUNNY: So what is it you look for in a woman? I'm serious, no fooling around here.

—LUKE: I know you're not. I'm taking your question seriously. Well, I'm past craving the 30-year olds with zero body fat and total flawless skin. That is a truly good thing since I'm 54 and they wouldn't want me anyhow. But our bodies are important, so I can't pretend I don't care about the shape a woman is in. I like smiles, legs, arms, necks. You get the picture. Oh, can't forget that erotic zone called the mind. That's most of it.

—SUNNY: Wow.

—LUKE: I can't stand it anymore. I'm signing off here so I can call you. Give me your phone number. Please. Now.

I sat on the bed with a big fat smile. One ring. Two rings. This is a guy who has a thing going with an old girlfriend. Three rings. Yet he's on a dating site. Four rings. Answer, for crap sake.

"Hello. I'm here," I said.

"This is nice."

"Oh, good."

His voice was relaxed, mellow, as if he put people at ease on a daily, professional basis. I asked him more about his island vacation. "What do you do there?"

"Hm. Well, picture this. No cars. No bars, no phones. Most people go around in golf carts. Or they walk."

"Actually walk to get somewhere?"

"Way cool. Walking. So, look. Here's my own definition of nothin'. Doin' nothin'. You get up when the sun comes up. Go out on the deck with your coffee. A book maybe. Watch the sun rising up. Watch the gulls, listen to the waves. Surf—listen to the surf."

I heard him drinking something. "What are you sipping?" I said.

"Tea. Want some?"

"Mmm, maybe later."

"Say it's low tide. You go to the next island to go clam hunting or mussel hunting. Depends on what you feel like having. Also if it's summer."

"It's not summer."

"I know." He laughed. "But I'm giving you the summer rundown."

"You know at seven in the morning what you'll want for dinner?" His routine sounded so great.

"Sorta. See, it's the hunt."

"I see," I said in a way that mocked him slightly, let him know I didn't see. I wanted him to keep talking, liked the sound of his voice.

"You're playing with me." So, he caught it immediately. "But it's true. They're tricky little buggers. You've gotta be real-real quiet. Serenade them or sing a lullaby so you can sneak up and grab 'em."

"How long does it take to hunt dinner?"

"Say, well—an hour or more."

"And after that?"

"You sit around and read, and soak up a few of those harmful rays." He told me more about his days on the island, and as he talked, I was thinking how this guy sounded like he was good looking. Is it possible that a guy can sound *really* good looking? I wanted to pass this theory by Dana and Isabel, and besides, I'd get to do the research.

Luke, Island Boy, asked me out.

Chapter Five
Mr. Sounds Good-Looking...

My first errand after school was the grocery store, a quick stop for a few items, apples, and maybe some chicken for sandwiches. I parked and shuffled into the store, heading for the produce section, not quite feeling myself.

Grape tomatoes. Those tiny oblong, sweet little tomatoes that taste like candy when you crush them with your teeth. I plucked a basket from the stack as a strange, out-of-place floaty feeling rose in my head. I leaned against the tomato display counter as dizziness overtook me. Oh, no, it was happening again.

In slow-motion, I slid to the floor. There I sat quietly, head against the counter, eyes closed as if I could block out the world simply by shutting my eyes. Minutes passed before the scuffling started. I opened my eyes. Feet, legs. A face peered down. The mouth moved. I heard a gushing inside my head, and then it went away. *I must be sitting in something truly yucky.*

Someone touched my arm. "Miss, are you all right?" Two men in black trousers and white shirts with name tags.

"Been better," I mumbled.

"When you're ready, we'll help you to your feet, if that's all right."

"Thank you." Were people staring? Was I a

spectacle yet?

"Are you dizzy?"

"A bit." Words couldn't describe my sense of detachment from myself, the floaty feeling that had taken me down still present.

"You sit for a minute. We'll help you up when you're ready." They crouched, affording me emotional support, identical looks of concern on their faces. Minutes passed. I couldn't stand it much longer, the staring.

"Ah, I'm ready."

"Good. Miss, we'll help you up now." When I nodded, they slid their hands under my arms, and put me on my feet. I stood a moment, testing my balance. "I'm not dizzy." One on each side of me, they piloted me to a bench by the restrooms.

"Rest a few minutes. We're calling the manager."

A woman with two toddlers loaded her groceries onto the belt in front of where I perched. Boxes of cereal, bottles of juice, the little girl pulling on her arm. If we'd had a kid, maybe Laurent and I would still be married. There I sat watching shoppers, imagining their lives for what seemed like hours, and was maybe four minutes. No, that couldn't be true. Like so many others with kids, we'd be divorced. Kids didn't fix a marriage.

The store manager approached. His expression was wary as if he were sizing me up. "How are you feeling? I brought you a glass of water."

I stretched out my hand, took the glass, and drank it down, every drop. "Thanks."

He held out a bag. "Are these yours?"

I peered inside. There was one item in the bag: a box of grape tomatoes. I shook my head.

He sat beside me. "They're yours," he prodded. "Please take them. How are you feeling? Do you need me to call anyone? I'd be happy to do that."

Three more days of student teaching. I'd miss my students, miss them badly.

"We can have someone accompany you to your car."

I shook my head. "I'll sit a bit."

"Shouldn't you call someone?"

"I have this vasovagal thing that runs in my family. I'll be fine."

I clutched the tomatoes to my chest. "Oh, it's not a big deal, the body's reaction to stress," I quoted from my doctor. "Not serious."

Not serious, passing out at the tomato counter? Well, it wasn't a pleasant way to spend the afternoon, but it wasn't life-threatening either. The last time I'd had vasovagal syncope was at my friend Natalie's house. I'd stayed over to keep her company the night her husband moved out. Years earlier, I remembered I'd once grown lightheaded on the toilet, slid off when I realized what was happening, and banged my cheek on the tile floor.

Why had I passed out? My doctor couldn't provide any concrete reasons other than the family stress thing.

It had never happened again. Until now.

I squatted there for ten minutes before exiting the store with the bag of tomatoes and driving home. In the bedroom, I toed off my sneakers and plopped across the bed, eyes closed.

Maybe it was Laurent and worrying about money. Maybe stress over the move and living in one room with roommates or stress from the job search. Or the man search. Everything was too much.

Maybe I slept for a bit. Later, awake with a little drool sliding down my chin, I rolled off the bed, threw on a jacket and hat, and slammed out the door, heading up the street. The sky was darkening to a dirty bronze, and the slight breeze at my back prodded me to break into a canter. Everything became clear as I jogged, then slowed to a walk, jogged again for a minute letting my body find its rhythm.

I pulled out my phone and called Dana.

"Hey," I said when she answered. "I'm trying to get a sub job, and I'm meeting guys, and some of them try so hard, like Nelson, who drove up in his monster mobile, as he called it." I stopped at the red light and pushed the walk button. "His wife kicked him out of the house. So sad. And I texted you about the guy who—"

"Slow down. Are you on a caffeine high?"

"I went shopping, and I passed out in the supermarket, landed in some gook, and before you get all excited, I'm fine. It's a family thing, I'll explain another time, but it's caused by stress, and I guess I'm stressed."

"Wait. Stop. You passed out—"

"I'm fine." I crossed the street, filling Dana in on the details of the supermarket episode. "Friday is my last day of student teaching. What am I going to do all day?"

Dana cackled. "Um, look for a job? Besides, you need some time off. You're pressuring yourself."

"I need to handle my stress better. I know that. How's your meeting men going? You don't tell me anything," I said, my voice sounding like my jealous six-year-old self when my best friend wouldn't share her new Barbie.

"Not much going on. Two meets." I waited for more information. Nothing.

"Hold on," I said. "You didn't even tell me if he had *negative* stomach. You always notice the guy's belly mass. Or if he's shorter than what's listed on his profile. Or...or anything." Oversharing every detail of my accumulating roster of dates made me feel foolish, especially when Dana was so tight-lipped about hers.

"Hey, calm down. It's not a big deal. I like him, but who knows? It's a jungle out there. Actually, right now I'm mired in the job search thing, so we should compare notes. Districts and such. And you shouldn't invest so much in each person you meet. That's draining."

"I suppose." My sneakers pounded the sidewalk. Peculiar that Dana didn't want to talk about her date.

We chatted a bit more about districts and who we could talk with for job leads. When we hung up, I race walked the few blocks home, admiring the huge houses that bordered the park, imagining which one I'd choose if I could afford one of them.

At the computer, I filled my glass with ice water and stared at the screen in frustration. Who was Doug2Bee? Who were Heartfelt, SmartSo, and Mad Max? Maybe Dana and Isabel were right, and I needed to slow down, not pressure myself. The phone rang. My mother.

"Are you using your new computer?"

"Of course," I said. "I use it all the time."

"You're on the computer that much? What are you doing? Research?"

A pause. "I'm internet dating."

Silence. I counted. One, two, three, four, five—I heard someone sniffling, no snorting—my mother was laughing great donkey hee-haws. "I'm sorry," she managed to choke out. "Did you say mating?" I heard more snorts.

"Dating, not mating." Then I thought about mating, how my own mother said *mating*, and it made me laugh. I couldn't speak, even to tell her I was laughing, but she could hear me, so it didn't matter that I couldn't talk. The receiver, squirming and slippery with tears, fell out of my hand. I leaned over, scooped it off the floor, and grabbed a tissue to wipe my eyes.

"I miss you so much. I can't believe I didn't get to see you and Dad," I said. "Coming back here. When I got back." Now my eyes filled. I slapped the tissue to my face, blotting. "I forgot how we used to laugh like this."

"We always have fun, and we laugh a lot. You'll come out here. When you get a break. Our treat. It'll be a treat for me, for both of us."

"Great, I'd love that." I didn't want to think about it, too far away. I had too much to get through before I could relax, take time off.

"So, you're online dating? Good for you."

I waited for her to tell me to be careful, to meet in a public place, to tell someone where I was going, leave a name.

"Have you met anyone sexy?"

*Luke. Luke on the phone, telling me about his island routine, clamming, the little buggers.*

"Well, I...not yet."

\*\*\*\*

Luke picked three restaurants and texted the names

and menus on a digital card, personalized with side-by-side photos from our profiles.

—*Choose, please. Luke is smiling and looking forward to meeting you—*

Vibrato, in Woodmont on the water, no contest. Instantly activating childhood memories of the house on the beach owned by my mother's best friend, Florence. The house faced the sea and was protected by a fifteen-foot wall. At high tide, you could jump in from the fourth stair, but you had to be careful not to scrape your legs on the rocks.

It was a beautiful evening, and I'd eaten very little all day, unlike my usual food-loving self. An older couple held the door open, and I paused in the entryway. Ahh, Vibrato. The aroma of garlic, oregano, and tomato sauce—the made from scratch and simmered for hours kind—made my mouth water. The hostess smiled, and I asked for Mr. Munroe. No point in mentioning we'd never met.

"A Mr. Monroe said he was waiting for someone he doesn't know," said the hostess. She pointed. "He's seated at the bar."

So Mr. Monroe wasn't scared to let people know he was on a blind date, huh? I paused and eyeballed the bar. The guy at the end raised his wine glass in a mini-toast. Mr. Monroe, the guy who sounded good looking on the phone? Well, he was lookin' good from across the room, smiling a big one. I danced on over.

"Have a seat right here next to me." He tilted his head and patted the bar stool.

"Hi." A tiny, hard thread of anticipation had formed in my stomach. I climbed onto the stool, and we looked at each other.

"Well, here we are," he said.

"Uh-oh." I tried to look fake-worried. "We're not gonna have trouble talking now are we?"

A three-octave bump laugh. "Yes we are, and we're gonna have fun doing it."

When he asked what I wanted to drink, I told him I'd try whatever red he was enjoying.

"Zinfandel," and he signaled to the bartender. "A mellifluous, funky flavor, redolent of the vineyards of Sicily."

"Oh. I've never been able to pronounce that word."

"Flavor?"

"Yes, flavor." I made a face, shifted on my seat as the bartender placed the wine on the counter in front of me. I sipped. "Nice, very nice. Redol..."

"Redolent," he said, drawing it out ever so slightly. "Redolent, redolent."

"Got it."

"Shall we order an appetizer or something?" I glanced down. His foot rested on the crossbar of my stool, the pants leg pulled tight around his thigh. I swallowed.

"Sure." I cleared my throat, hoping he wasn't one of those guys who notices every little thing. "So, are you over your heartache or shouldn't I ask? Sorry but it sounded as if you two have been over that ground before." He had mentioned breaking up with his girlfriend in a recent email.

"You're right, it's getting to be a pattern."

"A pattern?"

"Well, it seems we get together, and things are all right for a while."

"Oh." *So the on-again, off-again girlfriend is still*

*around.*

"And when I need some alone time or travel time—I have to attend conferences, give talks—she wants to come along. I hate to hurt her feelings, but she requires a lot of attention. There's more to it." His hand went to mine.

"Oh." What else could I say? She seemed present and problematic, and I wondered what Luke was doing here.

He motioned for the bartender. "Let's see what's on for an appetizer."

A couple in the far corner shared a big dessert covered in whipped cream. The man held his spoon under the woman's mouth. I could almost taste that first bite.

"It isn't working, and I haven't seen her for a few weeks. I very much need this break-up to be final." He shook his head. "I'm so sorry. I shouldn't be telling you this stuff. I'm here with you. It's where I want to be."

The waiter came to tell us our table was ready. I could already feel the wine and was glad for it. *Enjoy the evening and cross Luke off your list,* my internal monitor warned. The man was unavailable.

We were seated at a corner table, and Luke made a little ceremony of pulling the chair out for me. Sweet. I always look at the other diners—there was a smattering of women in cocktail-ish dresses, men in suits or jackets. Most people were dressed casually, but no one was wearing jeans. I had worn gray trousers with a gray, sleeveless, fitted sweater, and it wasn't just the happy wine feeling. I knew I looked good.

He told me more about his secret island vacation. It was an island he and his wife had discovered years before, the one he'd talked about on the phone. I sipped a little more wine. The waiter appeared, recited the specials, and retreated.

"What would you like?" Luke asked.

"Blackened salmon with mango salsa. I love what they do with salmon these days." We spent the next hour talking about bar dancing, film noir, digging for clams, and our idea of a dream vacation. Between drunk and me was the salad, and when the waiter brought my salmon and his tuna, I sat back and sighed.

"That's a good sigh?" he asked.

"It's just that..."

"Go on," he urged. "Take the first bite."

"Well, everything is so great." I chunked a sliver of salmon and slid it onto my tongue where it melted. "But, it's as if the food is unimportant." *Shut up, shut up*, I told myself even as I forked an asparagus spear. *Not available. Not not not.*

He smiled. "I'm having a great time, a great time."

He talked about his daughter, how she'd been up all night with her friends and come home around five in the morning to wake him up and tell him the details. I watched as he talked, gesturing with his hands. Above his left eye, I could see the half-inch scar he'd told me about on the phone before our meet, a joke so I could recognize him at the restaurant. Someone had come around the corner on a huge motorcycle, and he'd had to dive for the side of the road. No warning.

I dipped the salmon in mango salsa, chewed. *He's more handsome than Frank.* I jerked my hand to my mouth, thinking for a second I had spoken out loud. Luke took a sip of wine, a bite of his salad, oblivious I was busy comparing him to another date.

"How long have we been emailing?" I asked. I was attracted, very attracted, a different attraction than the pull I felt toward Frank. "I just wondered."

"Well, let's see." He touched my hand. "We began writing...I lost track of you, then contacted you again. Awhile."

"Two months?"

"Seems like I've known you longer."

"Yes, it does," I agreed.

"My daughter...well, they're a trip at that age. Girls and the stuff they're concerned about. Or should I say obsessed with, yeah, obsessed is more like it." He reached over and touched my arm, and a little heat spread to my neck. "Well, you know, you work with adolescents." He smiled, and the heat moved to my face. We chatted children, the exes, and reasons for the split, without getting too personal. His wife hadn't wanted the divorce. Theirs was a civil, mature relationship. "I suspect she'd take me back." He didn't seem to be bragging.

You can tell when you're hitting it off with someone, when you both seem to be on the same station, flirting to be sure, but you're discovering and would like to know more. And something else. Warmth. That was it. Frank was handsome and smart, but despite what he said in his profile—warmth was a special quality he desired above all others—Frank wasn't a super-warm guy.

"Enough of that. Just reach out and slap me when I go off on one of my tangents."

I smirked. "Right, like that's what I'll do."

"There's just so much I want to tell you. You know I loved your profile, I told you that. Twice already probably, yeah. And we were writing back and forth, and I had to call you. More fun than I've had in a long time."

*Yes, me too.* I wanted to tell him, but I didn't. Luke had been divorced for ten years, and I couldn't help thinking he had a lot of dating experience.

"So, does it get any easier? I mean meeting. Trying to get to know someone. Is it fun, or is it tedious?" He put his fork down as if considering the question before answering.

"It's the part I like the least." He settled back in his chair. "You meet someone, you fall in love for a while, and then you discover something bothers you about that person. You can't get over it, so you break up, and then you start all over again." A little red flag went up inside my head.

Later on, when the waiter brought the bill and Luke took out his credit card, I felt deflated. I'd been on a high all evening. He looked at me after handing over the card. "Would you like to go somewhere else, somewhere for coffee?"

"Are you sure? You're the one who has to work tomorrow."

"Maybe you're right. We'll save it for another time. Let me walk you to your car."

The night sky was clear, the air clean with the smell of the sea, and I could hear the movement of the waves, soothing and reassuring. I pointed to the truck, and Luke took my hand.

"Such a great time," he said. And pulled me close, put his hand under my chin, and bent to kiss me, a brush of his lips, intimate without being pushy. Then he did it again, this time lingering a little longer. Nice, very nice.

He didn't say he'd call, but I knew he would.

That night, in bed in my purple flannel pajamas, I texted him, thanked him for the great evening.

Luke. Funny, nice, warm. Cute.

Cute, hell. I wanted to brush my mouth over the scar above his eye and then let my lips travel down his cheek to the side of his mouth, and then slowly, slowly, to his neck.

**\*\*\*\***

Facebook, the great time-suck. I spent an hour reading posts, messages, notifications, and a few blogs before checking out The Doggist on Instagram. Read about Pancho the French bulldog, Alistair the Border Collie, Lola the Bernedoodle, and a pack of other dogs from Rhode Island to Puerto Rico. Three minutes on Twitter. On the Huffington Post, I came across an article written by a woman who'd met a thousand men in one year. Did she have a book contract beforehand? Who would do that for the fun of it?

The ribbit ring startled me. Dana.

"Hi, checking in," she said. "I've had two interviews this past week. You?"

"One. I can't remember when. The days are blending together. And I miss my students."

"That's a good thing. Oh, got your text about the Luke guy. You *like*, yes?"

"Yeah." I didn't want to get started, put it out there for discussion. Anyway, there was nothing to discuss. "You?"

"That one meet? I think it broke the ice. But I could never do what you're doing."

"What do you mean?" A little ping of irritation.

"This dating thing? I don't have your patience. The way you're throwing yourself into it…I need to go slower."

"Well, what about our little contest? Is that still on?"

A moment of silence before she answered, "Sure, if you want it to be on, it's on."

"If I want it? I thought we were in this together." My irritation pinged up a notch. Two notches.

"This is difficult. It's hard for me—" Dana, who was never at a loss for words, was having a tough time forming her thoughts. "It's hard for me to trust men," came out in a rush. "But, we *are* in this together. I wanted us to do this, and I want to continue." A horn blared. "Look. This is awkward, and I'm hitting traffic. Let's compare notes…you'll come over. Or I'll call you when I'm home and can concentrate."

"Good," I said. "What's his name?"

"His name?"

"Yeah, your first meet."

"Jerry," she said. "We have chemistry and that scares me. I should date other guys, shouldn't I? No, don't answer that."

"Remember we're supposed to be having fun."

"Fun it is," she said, and I hit the red disconnect button. I was taking this way too personally. Dana and I were two different people with our own way of doing things.

From down the hall came the telltale clank of the mail slot, followed by the thud of mail hitting the floor. I wandered over, scooped it up, and separated my mail from the roomies'. Mostly junk, but a blue envelope with no return address caught my eye. I tore it open to find my first check from The Kid, who'd stuffed it inside a get-well card.

Back on Facebook, there was a new message from my mother, asking how the *mating* was going. According to her, her friend Martha was very happy dating a gentleman she'd met online. Six months now. *And your father says he would get online to find someone if I passed away unexpectedly. Bless his soul.*

My mom wrote that: *Bless his soul.* Her reaction was like a shoulder shrug, not at all bothered by my dad's matter of fact attitude toward her passing away unexpectedly. What was with my father? Was he insensitive? Or oblivious? Probably both.

Men in general were insensitive. I clicked off Facebook, glowered at the screen. Every stinkin' one. Luke was insensitive. Talking about his not-quite ex-girlfriend.

Texting him last night was a mistake. Too soon after our meet, it reeked of overeager. What if he never wrote back? Worse than checking my email every minute was avoiding it altogether. I logged onto the dating site.

*To: Sunny*
*From: Luke*
*Re: dinner*
*You're welcome, I had a very nice time too. You are so much fun to be with. I haven't been to that restaurant before. I'd go again.*

Read it three times, got up, and peered out the window overlooking the neighbor's yard. Back at the computer, I scanned the inbox as if I'd missed something. Emailing rather than texting seemed less intimate, as if we'd gone backward, even though we exchanged a few texts before our meet. Was this a subtle way of saying he wasn't interested?

I replied to one new guy on the dating site, but my heart wasn't into trolling, not tonight. Something about Luke's email. I reread it. Short, polite but nothing concrete, not even a coffee invitation.

In the closet, I bent to retrieve the purple plastic basket where I kept all my pedicure stuff. *You and Luke are past the coffee invitation phase,* my mind chided. I sat on the bed and read the label on the cuticle cream.

Luke popped into my mind newsreel, his elbow raised. What was it he'd toasted? "A mellifluous funky flavor, redolent of the vineyards of Sicily."

This was the age-old why didn't he call question. I knew we'd hit it off. I uncapped the cuticle cream, heard Isabel's voice of reason in my head. "Sometimes they do it for entertainment."

"A guy will be all charming and impressive just to prove to himself he still has the stuff." This time, the voice in my head was Dana's.

For crap's sake, he has a girlfriend I reminded myself as I tucked a towel under my feet and applied the cream. He talked about her in his messages, offering, "It's complicated" as his explanation. He talked about her at dinner. He talked about her, talked about her, talked…

I sat staring at my toes, my head resting on my knees. "I still have Frank," I told the room.

****

Frank and I were keeping company, as my mother joked when she talked about dating in the olden days. A comedy club in Stamford, a Japanese restaurant, the Peabody Museum in New Haven, a movie. Now we were at Bespoke, plenty trendy.

I wore the red crepe dress and kitten heels. "Rayon crepe reveals," the saleswoman had said. "But you can carry it off because you're slim."

Frank's eyes widened when I opened the door to greet him. "You look very nice," he said in his low-key Frank way. To celebrate the end of my student teaching, Frank had called Bespoke ten days ahead to reserve, and was told to telephone again the day of the reservation. He told me this as he scanned the menu, laughed at the absurdity of it.

"They had to repeat everything, I swear I didn't get it." His eyes traveled over the menu, and he looked up, hesitated. "Interesting menu."

Frank laid the menu on the table. "Have you met anyone else online? I mean if you don't mind talking about it. Parsing it out. The dating. It truly is difficult to make a connection."

"Parsing it out?" Buying a few seconds, even though I knew what he meant.

"Reading people and what they desire, such a challenge."

"Yes, I've gone on a few meets, but nothing clicked." What could I tell him? That all those *man meets* were a bust? That I'd gone out with a very large man, a man with no verbal boundaries, and a man whose neck I'd wanted to run my tongue up and down, but that man hadn't called. I gulped my wine.

"That's usually how it is, you meet someone but nothing happens," he said. "No spark."

"True." I scanned the appetizers; the mixed greens with goat cheese sounded delicious. This was fun. This expensive, noisy place. This going out with Frank. How many times had we seen each other? Several. Several times and no moves. Frank was taking it slow. And I had decided to concentrate on Frank, give him a chance, another Isabel-ism. Isabel's measurement was the three-date rule, just like Dana's. By the third date, the guy is himself. He stops the tiptoe routine, and you find out if he's a good kisser.

Closing the menu, I waited for Frank to look up.

"Let's skip the appetizer," Frank said. "It will be too much food, I think. How about the fresh tuna or the chicken?"

"Oh, sure," I nodded. *Gee, there goes the starter. Will he be limiting my wine intake as well?* Perhaps Frank was a fusion of Mr. Control and Mr. Cheapo. I pushed away this thought. We were headed in the direction of physical contact, and if Frank turned out to be as touch-stingy as he was stingy in the appetizer department, that could carry over to arenas of even greater importance, such as the sexual department.

After dinner, we walked to his car. When he unlocked it, the chirp of the alarm sounded particularly loud, and we both laughed. Then he put an arm around me, pulled me close, and bent to kiss me. It was a nice kiss, not pushy. He let me go, opened the door. The red dress, which I had begun thinking of as The Red Dress, was rather revealing, having a great time hiking up, displaying my thighs. Frank closed the car door and walked around to his side and got in. Then he put the key in the ignition.

"Would you do that again, please? The kiss." *Um. Did I say that?*

"Be glad to." And he did it again, this time a bit longer. "Let's go for a drive—take a look at the beach."

We drove in silence. Frank headed toward West Haven and slowed as we neared Chick's, the old fast-food joint. "So sad," I said. "They closed. After sixty-five years in business."

Frank didn't comment. "Shall we try here?" He parked on the edge of the water opposite the deserted restaurant.

"Look, the moon," I said, pointing to a wedge through the windshield. Frank lowered the windows, and the briny smell of the sea rushed inside the car, the salty air so strong I could almost taste it.

I murmured his name as he pulled me close. Smiling like a salesman.

His kisses were long and leisurely, and eventually, we kissed with our mouths open, and then he was kissing my neck and sliding his hand over my breast outside my dress. He ran his hand up and down my arm. "You've got such smooth skin, it makes me want to touch it." His hand was on the back of my neck, and he was kissing me. The hand slid up my legs—very slowly. I pushed it away. He ignored the hint and kept kissing, and every so often the hand would creep up the leg again...until I asked him to stop.

"Relax, I won't push you past your comfort zone. You're experiencing new feelings. I know it's been a long time for you. I know it has."

Whether he was the right man for me, I needed to be kissed and kissed well. Frank was the obvious candidate for at least the short term.

That night, I couldn't stop thinking about the making out. It was like high school all over again—the good part of high school. I leafed through the relationship books from Isabel, books that said if a man wanted to kiss you, he probably wanted to sleep with you. Which wasn't bad, it was a normal testosterone-talking thing. Did I feel comfortable enough yet to sleep with Frank? I needed to build some kind of trust, and that meant knowing him longer than a few weeks and a few meals.

I checked my email several times the next day, expecting to hear from Frank. No phone messages either.

And nothing from Luke. A nudge was in order.

One little nudge wouldn't hurt. As long as I kept it light, breezy, and lots of other clichés. Easy in text.

—*Let's not have another G-A-P here. I like our repartee or however it's spelled. You're my dating mentor, after all. And you tell good island clam-hunting stories*—

Reread it twice. Was this a nudge, or more like a shoulder shove? It had been a couple of days since we met.

In my head, Isabel groaned. Give the guy some space and a chance to miss you. I slid the mouse to send and clicked. Then I checked the sent box.

My stomach was in a knot over a guy I'd met once. Once. *Scar over his eye.* Oh crap.

\*\*\*\*

"Well, I thought you were insensitive, Frank. Not calling me after…afterward." Hunched on a stool in Frank's kitchen, keeping him company while he cooked. *After we made out, and you felt me up, at least a lousy phone call, huh?* This I didn't voice out loud.

He unwrapped a container of Brussels sprouts, emptied half into a pot, rewrapped the container, and secured it with elastic. Yup, he decanted and labeled his vegetables. Well, organization was Frank's middle name, and neatness was not a bad habit.

"You're probably right," he said. "I'm sorry about that. I tend to forget that you haven't got much dating experience. That was a big deal for you."

"Wasn't it for you?" I blurted, instantly sorry. It was ridiculous to think that feeling me up and down was a big deal for Frankie boy. He rinsed the sprouts and put them to the side. Maybe he kept mentioning my dating inexperience to provide an excuse for not contacting me after we'd gotten physical. Maybe women of experience didn't need to be reassured.

"Of course. But it was a milestone of sorts for you. I see that now. It is a transition for you, from your husband, that is. I plan to make it up to you."

He was smooth, I had to give him that. Meaning I couldn't quite read him. The making dinner part was nice. Frank had been traveling, had some big deal in the works.

"I have some quite nice port," he said. "After dinner." He sighed. "If I had to eat out tonight..." he opened the oven door, peeked in, closed it.

"What if you had to eat out tonight?" I prompted.

"Just a few minutes and we can sit. Do you want bread?"

"Sure."

"If I had to eat out tonight, I'd skip dinner. Enough eating out during the week. No. I couldn't face another restaurant meal. I couldn't."

Frank lived in a huge modern, free-standing condo. Funny. I had pictured Frank in a house with sprawling lawns he'd have mowed by professionals who killed weeds and left little signs with a warning that chemicals had been applied. His place was—manly. Leather couches and tastefully framed oils, nothing you'd remember, nothing like Duke, my attorney with taste. A large bar ran across the dining room. There was no dining room table.

"So, Frank." I had to ask, even as I wondered if he'd take offense. "How come you're not still with the woman you were seeing? The one you told me about, you know, last summer? Why didn't it work out?" Fascinating how people connected and disconnected.

He pulled plates from the cabinet over the counter. "I need the closeness more than the act. She disappeared into the bathroom after our lovemaking." He shrugged. "Then she left. Said she had a heavy workload." He shrugged again. "Heavy workload." He sighed. "I know from heavy workloads."

Later, after dinner, he cleared the table, refusing my offer of help. I stood in the living room and surveyed his bookshelves, along with a small collection of CDs, nine or ten, old stuff, classics, a few groups I didn't know. I plopped on the rug, tugged one of the CDs open, and pulled out the liner notes. From the kitchen came the sound of running water, the clack of dishes.

"So you've found my extensive collection." Frank stood in the doorway. He held two tiny glasses, one in each hand. "This port is excellent. Come." I replaced the liner notes and got up. "You'll have to help me buy some new music. Come shopping with me. I need advice." He moved closer, bent, kissed my neck, a quick peck, and handed me the port. "Do you like jazz?"

"Yes. I love jazz." I took a sip, then another, and

held out my glass for a refill.

"Hey, slow down," Frank laughed. "I'll get the bottle." When he came back, he kissed me again on the neck, then my shoulders, and pulled my sweater to the side. I felt as if I'd purr if I could. I sucked in my breath, shivered. It had been too long. I stopped, felt my whole body stiffen as Laurent popped into my head. Laurent had been stingy in the lovemaking department for a long time. I squeezed my eyes shut. Laurent. I hated him, despised Laurent for a second. Two seconds.

"You're tense. Relax, let me rub your shoulders," and he was kneading my shoulders, my neck, his fingers at my waist, kissing my back and running his tongue up to my neck until there were no more Laurent thoughts, nothing but warm skin. He moved toward the bedroom, guiding me forward with a hand on my back, whispering, "I want to see your body. I want to suck your breasts." But I refused to take off my bra, held on to my skirt. "Don't be afraid." He began stroking my legs, and I relaxed. His fingers went under the waistband of my panties, and he was pulling them off. "Shh."

"No, Frank. I'm not ready." He paused, surprised.

"Then let me go down on you, would you like that?"

"I don't know." Well, that was dumb. Big fat chance I'd refuse an offer like that. I giggled.

"Do you like that? Hmm?" Frank mistook my giggle for a moan. "Do you want more? My baby wants more." Frank was down there working, and I was up inside my head thinking way too much to be able to lose control.

He stopped. "I'll learn to make you come, you'll

relax." He wore that salesman smile again, and then he toddled off to the bathroom. When he returned, he kissed me on the cheek and seemed to fall asleep when his ear hit the pillow. I lay awake. *In bed with a man, in bed with a man, in bed with a man.* Even if he wasn't a spooner-in-bed man.

Sometime in the middle of the night he woke me up and we did it. For real. So Holden Caulfield was right when he said girls lose their brains when they kiss. Maybe he meant girls get stupid wanting to please men and it's plain stupid not telling the man what you want. Oh, Frankie did all the right things—touching, yeah, plenty of touching—but what I felt was Frank had his little orgasm agenda. And something else.

You know that old episode of *Sex and the City* when Samantha gets slipped the gherkin? The guy is so small, Samantha compares his penis to a gherkin. Anyway, Big Boy Frankie had a gherkin, and when he finally slipped it in, I asked myself the old gherkin question: *Is it in? Is the gherkin in?* I never thought I'd give a damn about penis size. But maybe it's different if you've got a few complaints in the lovemaking department. Like the guy isn't trying hard enough to make you come.

In the morning, Frank had another orgasm all for himself. Then he went out for bagels, and I sat in his living room, thinking this was a big one for me, but a small one for him. I snorted just as the handle turned.

Later, after bagels and cream cheese, he drove me home, stopped in front of the house, and turned off the motor.

He smiled. "This was so nice, spending time with you."

"But I still need to date." I opened the car door, climbed out, and looked back at him. "I didn't mean it that way. It didn't come out so great."

*How* did I mean it then? Should I have said something about exploring my options? Nah, that was worse. All I knew was that I didn't want to pretend that Frank and I had a big, important *thing* going on. How I knew this, I wasn't sure, but I was certain something was off. All the mocking little jokes at Frank's expense, popping and crackling inside my head, were a big clue.

He blinked. "I fully understand. It's quite all right." Calm, unruffled. Nothing to discuss here. We'd each go about our business.

Everything was so confusing, the kissing and the sex and the inside-my-head snarky comments. If you liked a person, did you make snarky comments?

Which was worse? Telling him, I still needed to date or having him say, *I fully understand. It's quite all right.*

**\*\*\*\***

Later, I lay on the bed talking to Isabel on the phone. Told her about the party my students threw me on the last day of student teaching, the cards, the class video, the speeches in French, the brownies and apple juice.

"It's great to be loved and appreciated," Isabel said.

"Plus, I have a real estate agent." I was on a high. "Looked at two condos today."

"That sounds like fun, but I want to hear about Frank."

"What about him? Good looking. Muscles. And hair. He has hair."

"Have you checked out his financials?" she deadpanned. "How about butt?"

"The butt part. A great butt. Small, tight—"

"I was joking. Is it a screwing-only sort of thing? Is that why you stay in every weekend?"

"Well, he took me out in the beginning. The first month. But now he's beat from extensive—his word—traveling for his consulting job. Selling his stores."

"That explains it then?" Isabel said, her voice rising. "Exhaustion?"

"Yup. He enjoys staying in and cooking. Other than Laurent, I've never had a guy cook for me."

"Have you asked him to take you anywhere? A day trip?"

"Well, we were going to New York."

"What happened?"

"Who knows," I said, irritated with all the questions. "Some work crisis."

"So you used to go out and now you don't," Isabel said. "Is that what I'm hearing?"

"Well, he makes a full dinner."

"A full dinner? Is he cheap?"

"He has businesses. He has money." I had to get off the phone. Isabel was bringing up things I needed to think about on my own, in my quiet space.

"You're standing still."

"What do you mean, standing still?" I said.

"The relationship. You're not moving forward. Remember what Woody Allen said. A relationship is like a shark. It has to move forward."

"I never understood that old cliché anyway."

"Or it *dies*."

"Oh. I forgot that part."

135

"You should meet other guys."

I ignored her advice, didn't feel like telling her I was meeting a new guy on Friday.

"I've got to get going. Anyway, Frank is busy this weekend. He has a family thing on Saturday."

"Fine, he has a family get-together. Why didn't he invite you? Did you tell him it's your birthday?"

"Uh. A week ago.

"Well?"

"Well what? You're interrogating me." Irritation crawled up my backbone, but Isabel didn't hesitate, kept pecking away.

"Let me start over. Did he *hear* you? I'm coming over there and thumping you. *Hear* you, hear you. You know what I mean."

"Apparently not, since he isn't available on my birthday. Are you satisfied? Uh, it's not as if I've been seeing him so very long."

"That's not the point. He could mark the occasion in a small way. You're making excuses for him."

"I'm not making—"

My cell buzzed with an incoming call, the one person I wanted to talk to. And dreaded talking to.

"It's Laurent. Gotta go." I pressed the button to drop Isabel's call, relief washing over me, and I prepared myself to confront my husband.

"Laurent?" I said, to make sure it was Laurent, in person, there on the phone, hardly believing he'd followed the time table set up by lawyer Duke in the letter.

"Good evening. All well with you? Tell me how your courses are going and the student teaching."

And just like that, we were chitchatting like normal

people, like a couple who'd known and appreciated one another, even if it was a while ago. It was a relief knowing we weren't *that* couple, the couple who failed and then became enemies. I told him about classes and studying with Dana, but I didn't mention the online dating. After ten minutes of back and forth, our chat slowed and stopped.

"You saw Jean-Paul?" I said.

"Did I have a choice? I could tell you were bloody angry at me for my bad behavior." I thought I heard him gulp, and his voice was mellow, surprising since the conversation had turned dead serious. I nearly fell off the bed. Laurent wasn't laying blame, and he'd sort of admitted to being wrong, all in two sentences.

"A share so I could get started? That's fair."

"I know. I know," and I could almost feel him nodding. "So we met, went over the papers. To be honest, it took a few weeks for me to digest everything. In the end, we ironed things out. Jean-Paul is of the opinion that your request is reasonable, and I trust him. Which is important. I guess you'll need to go over the terms with your lawyer. You can call Jean-Paul if you have questions." There was a pause. "I had dinner over there. He wanted me to give you his best, they both...they miss you."

Jean-Paul and Marie, his wife. Sending hugs and thoughts and memories of my former life by way of Laurent who sounded regretful delivering the bittersweet message.

"That's the story," said Laurent.

"Oh." What could I say? It was happening, we were getting a divorce and hereafter, I'd be on my own. I lay back on the pillows, let my head sink into the softness, let my gut tighten and took a breath and then another, in and out. Some mental shifting would be required, but I would get used to being a divorced woman.

"Hey, are you there? Are you all right?" The concern in Laurent's voice was real and true, and I rushed to reassure him.

"I'm fine, needed a moment there." I took another breath. "We're doing it, Laurent."

"Yes. I suppose we have come to the end of our marriage." I heard his footsteps and then, "Pluto, come here Pluto. Come here and say hello."

"Pluto, hey boy," I said in a singsong voice.

"He's wagging his tail, he's happy to hear your voice."

"Thanks." I didn't want to spoil the mood by asking him about the actual divorce agreement, but he said Jean-Paul would FedEx the papers in a week or less.

"By the way, you bought that plane ticket, didn't you?"

"Well I—not yet."

He laughed, and I joined in. "You haven't lost your sense of humor. When you visit, I'll take you to dinner, and you can walk Pluto. Whenever you want. Let me know ahead so I'm not traveling."

I hung up, rolled off the bed, and did a little jog around the room. What now? Call my friends?

Best to wait for a signed agreement before celebrating. I decided to tell no one—well, maybe Isabel. And Dana. My parents would want the news, too. And Dulcie and Natalie in Paris.

## Chapter Six
### Faraway Guy...

I couldn't resist calling Isabel back to tell her Laurent was *nice,* we talked, we joked a little, and I said hello to Pluto. "You know I threatened him, don't you? He isn't holding a grudge."

"Excellent. I'll bet he respects you more because you stood up for yourself. It worked out. Best news I've heard all week. And how is your friend Dana doing with her online meets?"

"Other than the occasional text, I haven't heard much." I basked in the knowledge that my life was moving forward, that I'd be visiting my friends in Paris—oh, it was nice to know I wouldn't be enemies with my soon-to-be-ex, to have a plan for the future—and then I heard Frank's name.

"What?"

"This Frank person? I don't like him," Isabel said. "Selfish. Not a nice man. I don't think he's right for you."

"Who knows at this point—"

"You can tell. There are signs, even early on. His family thing and your birthday. It doesn't matter. You're coming here on your birthday anyway."

"Are you baking me a cake?"

"Of course. Either bake or buy."

"I hate this," I said.

"It isn't always easy. Why didn't you ask him?"

"What? Nag about my birthday? I couldn't."

"No, the family thing," she said. "Ask him to take you."

"Is that polite?"

"Is that what you want to be? Polite?"

"I don't know…it didn't occur to me to ask. That's like inviting myself."

"Sometimes you've got to be direct," she said. "Ask the right question to get an answer."

"If he wanted to invite me, I guess he would have."

"That means he doesn't see you as special in his life."

I thought about this.

"He wouldn't pass the airport test," said Isabel.

"The airport test? There's no airport test." I could hear myself sputtering in frustration. "You're just trying to make a point."

"If a man goes out of his way to pick you up from the airport, it shows he thinks you're special."

"I'm not going to the airport, yet." *Lame joke. I know what she's talking about.*

"Look, I'm not trying to be mean. It's just better if you see things clearly, isn't it?"

"Maybe I'm just beginning to see things." And trying to convince myself.

"Do you have a crush on this man?"

"Sort of. I did. I think now it's, um, evaporated." It was true. As soon as I said it, I realized that what I felt for Frank was *meh*. It had been fun for a while, but the thrill was gone.

"Look, this is your first sexual experience. Since Laurent."

"Meaning?"

"Time will tell," she said. "I'm guessing you'll move on. He's a cold fish."

"He's busy Saturday, and I told him I'm not free Friday." Weekends, Frank and I would have dinner together. Dinner and a little hanky-panky. I swallowed hard. "Crap, I just realized we have a routine. Double crap," I yelled to Isabel. "It's too early for a *routine*."

"Too true. You're like a prematurely old, married couple," and she burst out laughing.

"Not funny." *Why hang on to Frank?*

"It's very funny."

"Frank-wise, things are getting boring. Didn't know until we started the analyzation process."

"Yes, the great analyzer. Me." She sighed into the phone, as if apologizing. "It's too soon in the relationship to be bored. Did he ask what you're doing?

"Doing?"

"Why you're not free on Friday?"

"No," I said."

"What are you doing?"

"I'm meeting someone."

"Good."

"Frank compartmentalizes me in his life. The sex was exciting at first. Now it's like brushing my teeth."

"He doesn't make you come first, does he?"

"Gotta go."

"You don't care to talk about it?" Isabel said, always eager to push.

"Bye," and I hung up. Swiveled over to the computer, and got on the dating site.

It took less than an hour to scrub my old profile and write a new*ish* one, cutting and pasting from the old. New headline, photo to follow as soon as I located a good one. I didn't think Frank would notice the disappearance of my profile, and if he did, he wouldn't comment. One thing for certain, Frank was non-confrontational.

Underground on the dating site, I was reborn as AmandaX. *So, life is tough, get a helmet,* read the header for my profile.

Saturday morning, I celebrated my birthday by dressing up to go condo hunting with Nell, my real estate agent, a referral from Dana. The temperature was in the low sixties, sunny and spectacular, and I felt I'd burst out of my skin with the possibility of owning my own place.

On a whim, I left a message on Frank's machine, curious about how he'd react to an invitation to come along. "It's my birthday, Frank," I added before hanging up. "Come celebrate with me. We can go somewhere for a drink after." A chance for Frank to go out of his way for me, show I was special in his life.

He called back to say he was tied up. "Oh, that sounds fascinating."

"Being tied up is something that's never interested me," he replied.

How was it that I had never before noticed he had no sense of humor? Not that it was his fault for having a meeting, or whatever It wasn't that. It was Isabel's words, "I don't think he's good for you" niggling inside my head. They colored my opinion about Frank because…they were true.

Nell met me in front of the complex dressed in winter white, boots included, and guided me up the walk, chatting about the history of Whitney Moss. She was the good witch, Glinda, and I was the Wicked Witch of the West, all in black.

"Some of the condos have fireplaces," she said. "Including this one. And all the condos in the Whitney Moss Association used to be one-family residences."

We stepped inside the foyer with its high ceilings and worn hardwood floors, the look of an old, classic home. It smelled of history, the quaint odor of bygone meals, a hundred years of roasts, boiled potatoes, and apple pies. There was a second fireplace in the master bedroom, and floor-to-ceiling shelves in the kitchen and pantry so I could buy in bulk at Costco. As for the peeling paint and food-splattered cabinet doors sagging open, they were charming.

There was a bonus, unusual for New Haven, a parking space in the underground garage. "I want the place. Bad," I told Nell, hoping it was all right to be upfront with your real estate agent. "But I still want to see the others." Almost the same thing I'd said to Frank after sex the first time.

The second apartment, on the first floor of a huge complex, had dark paneling in the den and off-white wall to wall carpeting. I wrinkled my nose. At the last condo, three bicycles and piles of books littered the floor, and the carpeting would have to be ripped up and replaced by anyone but *moi*.

When I told Nell I had to think about Whitney Moss, she eyed me, eyebrows raised.

"Your eyebrows are eloquent."

"Damn straight."

"Nell, I'm taking this seriously."

"Call me," she said and took out her cell phone. "Real soon."

Back home, I grabbed an iced tea from the fridge, trudged up the stairs, and popped it while logging on to check my email on the dating site. I ran my tongue around the rim of the can, thinking of Frank and how he wasn't meeting my needs.

How I wanted to be someone's special.

Laurent wasn't home when I called, so I left a message, telling him it was important. And then I showered and took my Wicked Witch self over to Isabel's to celebrate my birthday.

Ours was a party of three. We chowed down on fish tacos and spicy roasted vegetables and two beer choices, a pumpkin-flavored brew and Stella Artois, my favorite classic. I tasted the pumpkin because I was in a party mood and Roberto was a sweetie, he'd picked it out. I told them about my new profile, and on my third beer, how the sex with Frank was ho-hum. Which is when Isabel cut me off at my own birthday party.

She drove my truck home with Roberto following. On the sidewalk I hugged them both, thanked them for a lovely time, and staggered a little up the stairs. They waited until I was inside, the door locked, before leaving.

After throwing my clothes on the chair, I pulled on my home clothes and brushed my teeth. The third beer was beginning to wear off. I didn't want to go to bed, I wanted to play.

The first email slid into my inbox while I was trolling for profiles, looking for a man who made me laugh. "One man," I said aloud, "one man with my sense of humor. One." Well, maybe I was still a little beer-happy. That pumpkin beer packed quite a kick.

*To:AX*

*From:Noah*

*Hi AmandaX,*

*What a mystery your name is. It makes me smile. And what happens when four skewed angles come together? Do they make a parallelogram? I loved what you said in your profile. I like to believe I live in the moment, but I know I am not always IN the moment. I could be thinking of a moment in the future, for example, the getting out of work moment. I think this is what you may be talking about. Tell me more.*

*To:Noah*

*From:AX*

*Yes, I am mysterious, provocative. And so are you, apparently. Where is your profile? You read mine and hid yours. Who are you anyway?*

*A. the Imperfect*

*Real name is Sunny*

I got a response a half hour later as I was paying bills online, working even though it was my birthday.

*To: AX*

*From: N*

*Dear Sun Sun Sunny,*

*I apologize for not writing a profile. I'd rather tell you myself. For example, been divorced over 5 years. I haven't been going out much. I did date a woman for over a year but it didn't work out. I'm an animal lover, into self-help, spiritual stuff. My job is NOC. Network Operation Center. I work lots of nights and weekends on a rotating basis. I'm on Long Island. It's in the state of New York.*

*Did you have ice cream eaten from the carton with two spoons in mind for cooking with someone? I jolly well hope so.*

I logged off and went back to paying bills. If I didn't log off, I'd get those instant messages from guys who had nothing better to do than chat with chicks. I wasn't in the chick category, no more, no more, and those instant messages weren't my thing.

It was my birthday. On your birthday, you do what you want. I clicked on iTunes and chose random play. "Quit Playing Games (With My Heart)," the old Backstreet Boys tune, perfect for a walk down ole Memory Lane. Yes, that pumpkin beer was potent. Potent pumpkin. I'd have to ask Roberto where he'd acquired it. *Acquire.* Good word. I was on letsclick.com to acquire a man.

And a place of my own. I flipped to my notes about the condo, wondered if I could swing the purchase. Everything depended on when the settlement from Laurent became final. Otherwise, I needed his help. "Get back to me, Laurent," I said aloud. Oh, he could be anywhere, Budapest, for example, well not likely. London or Helsinki.

I emailed him twice, the second email a sort of plaintive plea for help.

\*\*\*\*

My Friday meet was in love with his Harley. We chatted over coffee about his daughter, my student teaching, his Harley, my job quest, his Harley, my friends in Paris.

No chemistry, unfortunately. I drove home thinking about Dana, wondering if she had chemistry with any of her meets. Ahh, chemistry. Like I had with Luke. Well, not quite accurate. The chemistry was lopsided.

The house was quiet, the roomies either studying or

out doing what grad students did on Friday night. I went into the bathroom, grateful for the privacy, ran the water until it was hot, wet a washcloth, and held it over my eyes and face, getting off the grime from the Harley ride.

In the rolling desk chair, I swiveled around the room, surveying my possessions, calculating how much was stored in Isabel's basement. Boxes of books, posters and pictures, clothing, I listed everything, which took thirty seconds.

The first thing I'd do at Whitney Moss? Build a fire in the large master bedroom—no sweat—I used to be a Girl Scout. I pictured the Property Brothers cheering me on as I crouched down to clean my new-to-me toilet with a new toilet brush. My cell rang and I flipped it over. Laurent.

"Hello."

"They're calling my plane. What do you need?"

"Money for a down payment on a place of my own." Nothing like the blunt truth when you were in a hurry. "Plus there's underground parking and—"

"Three weeks...and you'll get the settlement. You can't wait three weeks?"

My stomach did a twist and shout. "I'll lose it. I'll lose the condo."

The terminal announcements rattled in the background as Laurent spoke in a rush. "I've got to go. I'll call and have Jean-Paul expedite it. You should get the money in two days. Enough for a down payment. Good?"

"Yes, yes." And that was it. I celebrated by cranking up Sinatra on my laptop, the younger, better Frank, the Sinatra with a sense of humor in his choice of songs. I hit play and foxtrotted over to look out the window. Nothing much happening on the street. I wondered about street life in my new neighborhood, not that far from this one.

That night I dreamed of Whitney Moss. The fireplace, the spacious, high ceilings, the pantry. My own pantry. At around four in the morning, I got up to pee and couldn't go back to sleep, turned on the TV but I wasn't in the mood to watch other people's lives.

My laptop was charged and ready to go when I brought it back to bed to check my email. There were a few guys on the dating site. A few random emails greeted me, along with a string of emails from Noah, the guy without a profile. The time stamps on the emails began at around midnight and continued throughout the night.

*To: Sunny*

*From: Noah*

*I wanted to call you but thought I should email first since I don't have your number. I would like to meet you, hope the distance is not too much. I will make it easy and offer to do all the driving. I am off for a few days, would you have time to meet? We could perhaps take a long walk?*

*En Francais: Il n'y a aucun déguisement qui peut pour long cacher l'amour où il existe ou le simule where it ain't.*

*To: Soleil*

*From: Le Noah*

*Le plaisir de l'amour est en aimant. Nous sommes plus heureux dans la passion que nous nous sentons que du fait nous réveillons.*

*To: Sunny*

*From: Noah*

*Wherefore art YOU? Have you cast me away?*

I took pity on him, and anyway, he was funny—I wrote him.

*To: Noah*

*From: Sunny*

*Very funny French. What the heck was that? Are you alone all night at your job? Do you get lonely?*

*To: Sunny*

*From: Noah*

*I fooled you good. I know French like two words of French. It's a website that translates. The Frenchie thing is a quote by La Rochefoucauld that says:*

*#1 Il n'y a aucun déguisement qui peut pour long cacher l'amour où il existe ou le simule where it ain't.*

*There is no disguise which can for long conceal love where it exists or simulate it where it does not.*

*#2 Le plaisir de l'amour est en aimant. Nous sommes plus heureux dans la passion que nous nous sentons que in the passion we arouse.*

*The pleasure of love is in loving. We are happier in the passion we feel than in that we arouse. Which would you rather be, AmandaX? The lover or the loved one? You are right, I am a solitary person. I study a lot about personal goal setting stuff. Then, there's the computer and a tad too much TV. Need a woman to be passionate about though, don't you agree?*

*Later, Sunny*

*To: Noah*

*From: Sunny*

*Had a great weekend, went riding on a Harley. Thank God we haven't had snow or I'd be a dead girl. Admit it was a date. Are you jealous? You can't be, we don't even know one another. Besides, you might as well know, I've been seeing someone. He's very involved in his work. I just realized he doesn't make me laugh.*

*To: Sunny*
*From: Noah*
*The ride is a rough one and that is why they are known as hogs and I hope your ride was rough. Yes. I am jealous and no, we don't even know one another. I was sick this week and the image of you riding that hog with some strange dude just made me sicker. BTW, who's the other dude, the one who loves his work?*

*Ps*
*Are you free for the weekend?*

*To: Noah*
*From: Sunny*
*Noah, honey, you may know a "hog" but my ride weren't no rough one, of that I am certain. Did you say you were sick in bed this week? Honey, (I know I am repeating myself) don't you have anyone to bring you chicken soup?*

*I don't think I am busy all weekend. Why do you ask?*

*Ps The work-loving dude I see mostly weekends, he travels a lot for his business. Haven't been seeing him long term. He has hair.*

*To: Sunny*
*From: Noah*
*my ride weren't no rough one*
*And you teach? Sweetie? It's my ride warn't no rough one*

*I don't think I am busy all weekend. Why do you ask?*

*I must find a canal alongside which I may walk Saturday morning about 10:30 in New England. Preferably in CT. Please assistance.*

*ps*

*How is your Hairy Boyfriend the work-loving dude?*

*Psps*

*I too have hair.*

So I exaggerated about the Harley ride, and calling Frank the work-loving dude—even mentioning Frank—was a mistake. Tacky.

The thing was this Noah guy made me laugh, especially when he mentioned the Harley guy and the Hairy Boyfriend, as he called Frank in his emails. And those French emails, so poetic. He lived far away, Long Island, but he'd do all the driving.

My eyes flickered over Noah's profile. His photo showed a smiling guy, red hair with some gray threaded in, and a lanky body.

Hardy har, there I go again with the expectations. I pushed back from the desk and closed the laptop. Hadn't José, Frank, and Luke—especially my Luke crush—taught me anything?

****

My Real Boyfriend, Frank, who was no boyfriend at all, called later in the week. "Congratulations, you've moved. Big news."

"I wish." How could he be so out of touch? "I got the condo, but the closing is six weeks away. I need to go shopping for everything. Bed and mattress, desk, dishes—"

"You can get some favorable deals when you buy several items at one time," said Frank.

For half a second, I imagined shopping with Frank, rolling around in a mattress store for kicks.

That wouldn't happen.

He talked about how the sale of the two pharmacies was taking on a life of its own. "The company wants me to stay on as a consultant, manage my stores and five of their own. Basically, they are trying to blah blah blah...existing stores...twelve of blah blah blah...Midwest."

Was my yawning audible? I put Frank on speaker, reached into my portfolio bag, and pulled out folders.

"This is not something I countenanced," he said as my attention snapped back. "When all this is behind me, we'll go away. Someplace warm."

The idea of being with Frank for a whole weekend made me a little nauseated. It would be like eating hard-boiled eggs for breakfast, lunch, and dinner. I glanced at the clock, yawned again. "So we won't be getting together," I said.

"It looks that way, unfortunately. As I said, it's not blah, blah, blah surprise to use this weekend to..." Frank's voice took on an uneven chirp, like a dying smoke alarm.

Crouching on the floor, I fanned out the brochures on appliances from furniture and mattress stores, Home Depot and Lowe's.

"So, I'll be in touch," I heard him say. "Take care. We'll work something out."

"Fine," I said. "You too."

Promises. Words. *When all this is behind me, we'll go away. Someplace warm.* Little promises were expedient, a way to divert.

I opened the Mattress City brochure as my phone

whistled. A text from my mom.

—*I keep making jokes about the mating. Hope you are having FUN*—

Mattress City carried hundreds of mattresses, and buying a mattress wasn't a big deal. Who needed Frank? In truth, I felt relieved we wouldn't be getting together.

Besides, emailing Noah was more fun than having sex with Frank.

*To: Sun Sun*

*From: Noah*

*May I please have your most honuorable presence to enlarge by far the companionment of my pleasurelyness on Saturday the eighth of December MCMXXVVIIMZQX at 1030 hrs under the auspiciscisable weather conditions of shine or no shine or falling snow or sleat yes, even that for the purpose of our fffirst date in the way of a nice slow freaky amble on the Canal of my dreams. Boat optional.*

*My warmest thoughts, hopes*

*Respect. Fully. Noah*

*Ps Leave the Hairy Worker Boyfriend at home. His home.*

I sat on my bed waiting for the phone to ring, and all I could think of was Luke, the day we emailed back and forth until he said *I can't stand it anymore*, and I'd sent him my phone number.

Well, Noah wasn't Luke.

The phone rang.

"Hello."

"Hello, this is Noah—your blind date."

"Aren't we being polite?"

"Yes, should we be something else?"

"Well, I'm nervous, and you claim to be shy." I picked at my toenail polish.

"You don't believe I'm shy?"

"No, I don't. You're definitely not shy in email."

"No. But I have the chance to think about what I'm writing."

"Yes, that's an advantage." *This guy has a great voice. I wonder if he knows it.* "But it can be a problem because then you have to live up to your email potential." Plus, he was fun to tease.

"My email potential?" He sounded worried. "Now you've got me scared. Running scared."

"So," I said, "should we walk and then meet?"

He laughed, a friendly, reassuring laugh. "I liked it when you said that. Made fun of you, too. Did I get you mad?"

"Absolutely. Did I make you jealous when I went on that Harley date?"

"Definitely."

"Is that why you wanted to meet me?" I asked.

"I wanted to meet you from the beginning."

"What beginning?" *This is fun.*

"Oh, I think it was when you called me "honey" in your email."

"You liked that?"

"I did," he said. "It sorta broke the ice."

"Oh. You have a New York accent. I hear something there, especially when you say "becawze.""

"That's because I live in New York and grew up there, too."

"Of course."

"So, let me tell you something, but I don't want to scare you."

"You're scaring me. Do you have a record or something?" What a waste. That's all I could think. All those lovely emails, the funny French translations, the great voice. The man was hiding something.

"No, it's not that kind of scared." His voice became faint, as if he'd turned his head away.

"Just say it then."

A long pause before he spoke. "I was thinking, just in case we fall madly in love, well, I rented a room there."

"Where?"

"There."

"Here?" I said, bewildered.

"Holy crap, yes. There. Look, I thought if we hit it off, I could stay over and see you tomorrow. That's my idea."

"Oh."

"Oh? Is that all?" He sounded genuinely hurt."

"Well, I feel pressured, and I haven't even met you."

"Don't feel pressured."

After a long pause, I told him I felt pressured.

"Forget it. It was a bad idea. I shouldn't have said anything."

"Yes, you should have." *He shouldn't have.*

"Well, I did and look where it got me."

"Where did you want it to get you?" I asked.

"Seeing you the day after, nothing more. Honest."

"I believe you."

"Will you meet me tomorrow at eleven?"

After we hung up, I sat stewing, my brain tumbling here and there. He wanted to rent a room? What was that all about? What would I wear for a long walk? I needed new sneakers. No, I could wear my comfy boots with jeans. What difference did it make what I wore because, well, there was no way I was going to hit it off with this man, great voice notwithstanding.

To keep the monkey thoughts away, I logged on to check the job listings. Nothing new. I cracked open my email.

*To: Sunny*
*From: Noah*
*You have a sweet voice.*

I felt my whole face smile. And Noah made me laugh, too. He was fun and sort of a Byronesque guy, a romantic. Wanting to stay over so he could spend time with me the next day? That was romantic, not creepy. He wanted to get to know me. This was a man who was looking for a relationship. This was a man who—

My cell whistled from somewhere in my bed, disturbing the rather pleasant path my imagination was leading me. I walked over and lifted the blankets, thumbed it open. Luke.

Luke? My stomach lurched. Too late, Luke, you little pisser. But of course, I had to read the text, there was never a question of not reading it, even though my stomach quavered. I hated that my body responded in this way to a stinking text from a man I'd met once.

*—Sunny, hello. I am writing to apologize for not calling you after our meet. You're probably dating someone else by now, which is my loss. I wanted to tell you that I enjoyed myself so very much. I didn't call because I've been going through some tough times. I'll leave it at that. It's not a health issue, although it is a health issue in a way. I can't explain now, but maybe one day I will be able to see you and make amends in*

*person. Thank you for your understanding.*—

Thank you for your understanding? The man had colossal nerve. Did he expect a response? Well, he wasn't getting one.

Because I had a life, and it didn't include Luke.

\*\*\*\*

I pulled into the lot fifteen minutes late and caught a glimpse of Noah in the car with the door ajar, head bent, reading. It was another one of those freakish warm days, and the lot was already crammed with cars.

He smiled and fiddled for a moment inside the car. Then the door fully opened and he slid out, ambled toward me in no hurry, all bony shoulders that stuck up like coat hangers, dark red hair the color of iodine, trim beard. He slouched by the window.

My face was at his stomach level. No pouch. Another of Dana's observations, that men over forty have a pouch.

"Hi."

"Hi," I said. How tall was this guy anyway? He backed away as I opened my door and stepped out. "So you found it. Easily."

"Easily." He looked down at me. "You're pretty small."

"Am I?"

"I'm Noah. How do you do?"

"Nice to meet you."

We looked at one another. "One minute." He walked back to his car, motioned to me, holding up a small cooler. I walked over to see what it was about.

"Brought you a present. You want some now?" He opened the cooler and handed me a bottle of water.

"Thanks." I twisted the cap, took a swig. Would we

find things to talk about?

There was a hint of a breeze and the sun warmed the canal path, already crowded with walkers, skaters, and runners. It was obvious he slowed his pace for me. My mistake was wearing the vanity boots, not liking the look of sneakers with jeans.

"I don't have a clue about your network thing. What is it?" He had told me in emails about his work, so I thought I'd ask questions. Getting a man to talk about himself was a trick girls learn in seventh grade. In the locker room after gym class, we used to discuss how to formulate questions that required more than a yes or no answer, the sure way to spark a boy's interest. Mary Ryan had read an article about drawing boys out in *Seventeen* magazine, so she was the expert and we all believed everything that appeared in *Seventeen* magazine. "Is it using other languages?" I asked Noah. "And why at night?"

"NOC. Network Operation Center."

"Yeah, that."

"The worst part is after working a few nights, sleeping through most of the first day off. And usually up all night again."

"So, let me get this straight. You work from six in the evening until six in the morning and that's the night shift?" I was walking hard and talking, working up a sweat. I paused to tie my second sweater around my waist, hoping the effect wasn't hippo hips.

"Right," from behind the sunglasses.

"So you are there every night. Alone. With a bunch of computers. No one else is there."

"Well, there are other people who seldom come into my area. I'm alone. Almost always. Exclusively.

Alone."

"You have a job with no stress, don't you?"

"Pretty much. Maybe stress with the occasional electrical storm, but I don't have to fix anything. There are guys who do that."

"Unbelievable." I said this almost to myself. "You've got it made. But aren't you bored?" I picked up the pace.

"I've got stuff I do to keep me busy, mostly my own stuff on the computer."

We kept on this way, me asking questions. Noah asking questions, me telling him about finishing the student teaching, and looking for a long-term sub job. When I finally looked at my watch, we had been going at a satisfying trot for an hour. "Have we met yet?" I asked.

"What?"

"Have you checked me out enough?" Noah clearly didn't remember his joke about walking first and then meeting. "Anyway, it doesn't matter, we've got an hour's walk back, whether you like it or not."

We stopped. He ran his hand through his hair, and I noticed in the sunlight a glint of gray and silver around the temples. "I've got the whole hour going back to make up my mind. Keep walking." He glanced down. "Do your feet hurt in those high heels?"

"They're not high heels." My winter shoe boots were close to flat. In my opinion.

"Mm-hmm."

"Well, they're not the most comfortable for two hours of walking. Little did I know…but it's important to look good when you're meeting someone for the first time." I stared pointedly at his well-worn sneakers.

"You're right. I did hesitate about wearing these."

"Mm-hmm."

"And then I put them on." He smirked, reached down and squeezed my arm.

"Oh, you must be feeling comfortable with me," I said, and he squeezed again. I grinned up at him. *This isn't so bad.*

He began talking, telling me about a woman he'd met online. He had known almost instantly that he wasn't interested, but she persisted.

"How did you know?" I was fascinated by the whole concept of instant chemistry, the idea that he could make up his mind in minutes. "How long were you with her?"

"I knew," he answered. "She wanted to go for coffee."

"Did you?"

"Yes. I had to be polite so we talked for half an hour. But I knew."

When we reached the parking lot, he pointed to a rock in the clearing by the car. "There. Let's rest. Decide what to do next." He headed toward the car, called over his shoulder to tell me he was grabbing the water bottles from the cooler.

Feet aching, I eased down onto the boulder. The boots had been a mistake, two hours of a mistake. Noah slid beside me.

"How are the feet?" Was the man a reader of my mind?

"Fine. Tired but fine."

He handed over my water bottle present. "Good. That's good." He twisted off the cap, took a swig, then another. "I'm hungry. Are you?"

"Starving. Now that you mention it."

We sat for a while watching the walkers and runners until a man glided past us on rollerblades.

"That," I said, "is what I'd like to do. Be an instant gazelle, with no learning curve." I took another water swig. "And that guy is no spring chicken, by the way."

"Me too," Noah said, stood and pulled me up. He squeezed my shoulder. "Let's head out. Tell me where we'll go to eat. If it's all right to leave your car here."

"Fine," I said. "Just keep in mind that those dear to me know of my whereabouts. As I climb into your strange car."

"Oh, don't worry about my car. *I'm* the strange one."

Noah steered down Whitney Avenue, all the way downtown to the small Indian restaurant I'd been to with the oldest guy I'd dated so far, the wobbly one who'd tried for a kiss.

My mouth watered at the thought of yellow rice with pineapple and nuts, all pungent with cinnamon and cumin and turmeric.

In the restaurant, I couldn't decide on a drink.

"Go ahead, try a Brandy Alexander," Noah urged. "I'm here in an Indian restaurant. *My* first time." He looked around as if to check that it was truly Indian. "So, *you* try something new too. A Brandy, Alexander style."

"Growing up in New York, you've never done Indian? Really?" I didn't want to torture the man with my questions, but I thought this highly peculiar.

"Well, we had plain food mostly in my family." He lifted the napkin on the bread basket, peered at the contents. "Looks good. What's it called?"

"It's Naan bread. A classic. Try a piece." I broke off a piece of the bread, handed it to him, and popped a chunk in my mouth. "My mother liked when I cooked," I said. "You know, experimented."

He ate slowly, pausing to listen. Unlike Frank, he looked me in the eye when I spoke. Yup. I'd never realized what a space-looker Frankie was, as if looking directly at me was too intense. Come to think of it, the only time Frank fastened his eyes on mine was when we were having sex. His way of convincing himself he was capable of closeness?

"Don't do much cooking," Noah said, standing up. "Will you excuse me?"

He headed to the back of the restaurant while I thought about the evening I'd stayed over in Dana's guest room. She had confided that she knew things were changing in her marriage when her husband started making excuses, and fobbing off what he'd always considered to be his jobs, like cutting up vegetables, the equivalent of doing a little cooking, servicing the car, and going to the butcher's when they had a dinner party.

"Then one night we were making love," she had said, staring across the room at the abstract above the fireplace. He wouldn't look at me. At first, I thought it was my imagination, but it happened the next time. And I started noticing other changes. He dressed better, fitted shirts and skinny trousers—and it pissed me off that he looked good in them—a trendy haircut. A gym membership, of course. Now that was a tip-off. He always hated gyms."

"Yeah," I said. "There's always something. Laurent couldn't decide what he wanted either, and he dumped me slowly, so it hurt more."

"When it comes to dumping," Dana said, "quicker is better.

And now here I was, in the middle of my new life, introducing Noah to chicken tikka masala, chickpea curry, and the naan bread. If Laurent and I hadn't separated, I wouldn't have met Dana, or any of the guys on the dating site, wouldn't have gone back to school. And the irony was, I'd loved our life together, our little routines and the occasional trips, the whole *couplesness* of marriage, when it was good.

Noah was on his way back to our table and I needed to change the subject in my head. So I asked him a question.

"What was your favorite thing, you know, the thing your mother cooked best, the family favorite?"

He pondered this for an instant before sitting down. "I don't remember," he said.

"No family favorite?"

He shook his head. "I pretty much left home at an early age." His thumb poked at his beard. "Never looked back."

If he'd asked me the same question, I could have answered instantly, "My mother's lasagna."

****

Shivering, I held my coat tucked around my neck as I waited for the car to warm. Short December days were usually a downer, but not this one. We'd languished in the Indian restaurant for three hours, and when we exited, the chilliness of the night air surprised me.

Noah tooled up Whitney, slowed, turned right, and pulled over, stopping on a side street near a church, where he parked. I put my hand on the door handle. *Now isn't this a bit pushy, parking without even asking?* My coat collar covered my chin, although I could feel the heat. Noah left the motor running and slid with his back to the door so he faced me.

"Hope you don't mind," he shrugged. "…thought we could relax and talk a bit. Away from others." He squinted at me. "Are you gripping your coat?"

I relaxed my hand, let it fall in my lap. The car was warm, cozy. Noah reached over and turned the fan to a faint hum. I peered outside at the church lawn, covered in a glaze that gave it the look of a huge frosted loaf cake, much like the church a few blocks away from Laurent's apartment. It was around three in the morning in Paris, and I wondered if my students missed me.

Then I heard myself telling him about my first year teaching in Paris long ago, and how I didn't know all my students. I had so many overcrowded classes I'd even misplaced a few.

"It was difficult to connect with so many kids. I didn't get to know them. A parent came in one day asking about her daughter. Her daughter's grade, you know. For the class." I hadn't thought about this in years. "Said her daughter loved my class."

"That's a good thing."

"It's a good thing she said her daughter's name when she introduced herself." I hesitated.

He smiled, encouraging me to continue.

"The daughter. I had no idea who she was. So I faked it. The grade, the daughter's grade in my class." I slid down in the seat, looking out the front window. "I had to fake it. When the mother told me her daughter didn't get a grade, I told her it was some kind of an oversight. Then I looked her name up in my grade book." I opened my hands in front of me, pretend-holding a grade book, eyeballing the columns. My finger traced the names, stopped. "Oh, here it is. Yes, yes, she has an A-minus. Works very hard." I slammed shut the grade book. "Sounds funny, but it's a good thing she bought it. My act."

"Did she actually have an A-minus?"

"She could have had an A-minus."

"Didn't you keep track? I mean give tests and all?"

"Oh, yes, I did." My grading system at the time had been scatty at best. I barely coped with the overload of students that first year. "I tried to give the students who spoke up in class extra credit. You know, it's scary learning a foreign language. She didn't speak up much. Oh, I can't remember the details."

"Learning a foreign language is scary?" He peered at me in the dark. "Tell me more about living in Paris."

"Like what?"

"Like. Like was learning the language difficult?"

"Not super hard." I considered this question. "I lived there quite a while. I was married there, had French friends. Learning a language, you reach plateaus. Language plateaus. Humps."

"Language humps?"

"Yes, language humps."

"I like listening to you."

The entire front lawn of the house across the street was suddenly illuminated. Daylight streaked into the interior of the car. A man stood peering across at us from the stoop, shielding his eyes with a hand across his forehead.

"Whew," Noah looked over his shoulder. "Does

that guy like floodlights or what?" He shook his head. "He's not subtle, is he? Uptight residential neighborhood." He put his hand on the wheel. "On the other hand, here we sit with the motor running. Probably looks peculiar." He looked at me. "What do you think?"

"You mean if he'll come over?"

"We'll see."

I shifted around in the seat. "Probably I should go home."

"We're going." He looked out again at the man retreating toward his house. "There. He's going in to call the police."

"You think so?" Was Noah serious?

"I'm ninety percent sure."

"Very funny." I looked at him. "How can you be so sure?"

"I'm ninety percent sure I want to see you again."

I looked at him. "I'm chilly again." I yanked my coat up, tucked it under my chin.

"I'm sorry, Madame, please allow me to warm the cockles of your heart." He adjusted the heat. "It'll take a few minutes."

"Is it on a scale of 100?" I asked him.

"No, it's a scale of 90, so that means 100 percent." He paused and I could see him smiling in the dark. "I'm all sure I want to see you again." He pulled out, headed back up Whitney to my car. "Doing pretty well, aren't I? Finding my way around."

"Very well," I said. He pulled into the lot, parked next to my Jeep, and left the motor running. "Except for the cockles part."

"What are cockles?"

"I've always wondered," I said.

"I'll try and look it up," he said. "Online."

"That's settled. Now. Maybe you should ask if I'll be wanting to see you."

"Let's put it this way," he said leaning back. "Do you mind if I give you a peck goodnight?"

A novel approach. He had his back against the car door, a long way off to reach me.

"Do you always ask?"

"Not always. Do you always ask?"

"No." I tried to keep a straight face. "I've just met you. There's no always. Not yet."

"I see. So?"

*Goody. I'll see how he smooches. See if he's a better smoocher than...*

I wasn't prepared for the kiss. It was slow as if he had all the time in the world, and gentle, a series of light, butterfly touches around my mouth. He put his hand on my cheek, hesitant, but he knew how to kiss. No probing tongue. The kiss lasted what seemed like twenty minutes.

"Wow that was some peck." No fuss, no muss. Then he did it again and again until finally he stopped, leaned away from me.

"But you have to go," he said. "I was thinking I'd get a room and stay over."

"What will you do tomorrow?" I didn't know if I wanted to see him again, so soon...for the whole day.

"I could stick around, do stuff during the day. Watch television."

"It doesn't sound so good. I don't think you should. I would feel pressured." What was I getting myself into? We'd discussed this before.

He was looking at me. "I understand. But, I want to kiss you some more."

"Oh. One hundred percent or less?"

"One hundred. Exactly." No smile. "Since I'm not staying overnight, can you stay out later? Please."

"I'd say so."

Chapter Seven
Pancakes...

"Holden Caulfield. The main character. You know. He said sex makes girls lose their brains. Or maybe it was kissing. I don't think he ever had sex. In the book."

It was around ten-thirty Saturday morning in Dana's kitchen, sunlight pouring in through the skylight, giving the whole space a cheery look. I sat on one of the comfy high stools feeling pretty cheery myself—maybe from last night's make out session— enjoying the warmth from the enormous restaurant stove. Dana was mixing up pancake batter.

"What was the big deal with that novel? I never understood it."

"You're kidding. *Catcher in the Rye?*"

"Don't think less of me." She dumped fresh blueberries into the batter, mixed it, and poured it into the pan. In a few seconds, the delicious scent filled the room.

"You're making blueberry pancakes especially for me, so you are forgiven."

She shot me a look. "What's he catching anyway?"

Holden Caufield and his sensibilities, who could explain that? I laughed and made a mental note to get Dana a copy. "Reread it. You'll see for yourself. And what's with your huge stove? Are you a professional?"

"Hardly. Treated myself after the divorce." Dana

wiped her hands on her apron, grabbed the pot of coffee, and filled our cups. "My husband was playing the holding-out game with me," she said. "My lawyer called his bluff. He'd started in banking, advanced rapidly into investing, and started his own consulting firm. So, he had money, but he required prodding to share. A story for another time."

"I gotta ask," I said. "What made you leave?"

"How do you know I left?" Dana placed the serving dish on the table along with a pitcher of syrup, hot.

"Just guessed."

"The syrup is the real Vermont stuff. Dig in. I'm in the mood for this." We chomped for a while, the joy of not thinking about calories evident as the pancakes disappeared. "You are fascinated by this leaving thing, aren't you?" Dana said, looking up from her plate.

"Is he still around?"

"Michael?" She shook her head. "Moved away. And here I am divorced. Never thought it would happen to me." Dana stared at a splotch of syrup on the table. "He didn't want to spend any time with me. Spent time with people who were unimportant. Unimportant in our lives, I mean. I was *spousey*, rhymes with mousey, a good, compliant wife.

"Until the evening..." Dana slumped in the chair. "I've never told anyone this..."

She stopped talking and stared at the blotch of syrup. All I could do was wait, and finally she began again.

"We were at our friends' house. We were a foursome, our kids had grown up together, we took vacations, went to ball games. We'd been to their house hundreds of times for barbecues.

"There was a full moon. I remember the moon because I went out to the deck to get a look, check on the steaks. My husband wasn't doing any grilling." Dana's voice caught. "My best friend and my husband were in... in the hot tub, kissing." She cleared her throat and took a slug of coffee.

"You don't have to—"

"Her husband came right up behind me, bumped into me when he saw them. He made this other-worldly sound, so odd. I thought he'd explode and drag Michael out of the hot tub, but he didn't say a word. Turned around and left the house."

What could I say? My heart turned over for Dana. At least Laurent hadn't humiliated me.

"I went home," Dana said, "and called a locksmith. You should have heard the swearing when the key didn't work." Dana doubled over in her chair. "It was hysterical. The clincher was me dropping a load of his clothes out the second-story window."

"You're joking." A little thrill shot through me. "For real?"

"A handful of his best suits. I almost got him on the head." Dana breathed in and out, both hands on her stomach. "The closest I've come to a scene in a movie. Oh, he took me seriously. Especially when I threatened to call the police."

"Yeah." I didn't know what to say. "Wow," was all that came out. Weird that a man would not be grateful to be with Dana, would not appreciate all that was original, the very *Dananess* of her. We sat like that for a bit, not talking.

"Excuse me a minute." She left the room and I

heard her footsteps on the stairs. I put the dishes in the sink and got my phone to check email. There was one from Noah, and as soon as I wrote him back, another appeared.

*To: Sunny*

*From: Noah*

*I got hungry on the drive home, realized I didn't suggest getting a midnight snack. Sorry about that. You had me occupied.*

*To: Noah*

*From: Sunny*

*Is that all you can tell me, you were thinkin' of my friggin' tummy?*—

*To: Sunny*

*From: Noah*

*Is that all you can tell me, you were thinkin' of my friggin' tummy?*

*Not your tummy—little honey. My tummy—*

My ears tingled reading his emails... Making out in the car with a near-stranger? What was I thinking? My phone whistled with a text alert from Nell.

*—Please let me know by 5:00 pm if you are willing to do an earlier closing time approximate TWO WEEKS from today! Exact date to follow when we speak. Rebate/incentive at closing of $2,000.00 cash from seller. I suggest accept. Call if you have questions—*

Dana thumped down the stairs and barreled around the corner into the kitchen, turned the water on at the sink and pulled open the dishwasher. She'd put on a little makeup, composed herself.

"You all right?"

"Fine." She pulled on rubber gloves.

"Wait." She leaned on the edge of the counter,

shaking.

I led her over to the couch, sat beside her.

"It's true I've never told anyone that story." She swallowed with the effort of explaining. "I came off as a hard ass throwing out his clothes and changing the locks, but he did a job on me, my husband."

I pulled her into a hug, "I know you're a softie at heart." The tremors had stopped.

She managed a watered-down smile. "That linguistics class was torture…except for meeting you."

"Golly." I smirked. "Thanks."

"I have stuff to tell you," said Dana, as we wandered back into the kitchen. "First, what's your news?"

"Well, listen to this—I heard from my agent," I said, then read the text to her, unable to contain my excitement, my gut pounding in a good way. "What should I do? I don't have the money yet, but I should get it in time and—"

"Do it. You love that place. You have to do it." She gripped my hands with her gloved ones, water running onto the floor. "We'll be neighbors. You'll be what? A couple blocks away?"

"Yes. It's perfect. I don't have that much stuff, and even if I have to forfeit my rental deposit, well, I don't care. It's worth it." And then I blurted out, "Oh, and last night, I met someone and we made out in the car for hours. It was fun, and I don't care if I seem like a babbling overgrown teenager."

"Good on you. A real old-fashioned make-out session, how great is that." Dana ran the hot water. "Hey, I've got this. Grab that serving dish for me and go call your agent right now." She waved her hand.

"Go."

My call to Nell went to voicemail, of course, since Nell lived her life on the phone. "Yes," I said into the phone, "to the earlier closing time, call me please. This is Sunny."

Dana was spraying Windex on the stovetop with one hand and wiping with the other as I stood in the middle of her kitchen and announced, "I'm sleeping with one guy and making out with another." I felt my face heating up. "Well, I haven't seen Frank in weeks. So technically, I'm not sleeping with him."

"Shame on you anyway. Shame," squirt, "shame," squirt, squirt. "Come closer and I'll Windex you, make you *real clean*," and she made *real clean* sound evil in a sexy way.

Dana's kitchen was the kitchen of an adult who knows who she is. It reflected Dana, from the professional-grade stove to the oversize oddly-shaped metal clock on the wall.

"Maybe I can't connect," I said. "Maybe I'm abnormal going out with so many men. I don't know anyone else who's doing it. You're not doing it."

Dana put the window cleaner under the sink and slammed the cabinet door. She leaned against the counter, looked at the floor and back up at me. "I've been meaning to talk to you about that."

"You're not meeting anyone?" I said. "If you don't want to meet…if online dating isn't your thing…I'll probably be toning it down anyway, what with moving and working. I'm finding not as many guys contact me anyway, now that I've been on the site a while. You know how it is, well, maybe you don't."

Dana was watching me, probably waiting for me to

stop babbling. "Actually, I'm not sure how it is." She shifted her elbows behind her. "I've met two guys. Two meets. The second one was a very nice individual, but there was no click."

"Oh, you can't stop there, not with two guys." I plunged in, determined to convince Dana, change her attitude. "Two guys is a beginning. It's a numbers game. Have I taught you nothing?" I flicked Dana's arm with my finger, like I used to do to my sister, irritating and satisfying all in one. But Dana didn't take the bait and join in. She didn't laugh, and her serious expression didn't change.

"Come on," I nagged. Let's check out a few profiles, see who's new this week. There're one or two new guys every week. It'll be fun. I have time, and I'm here." I was starting to feel silly. Dana had gone quiet.

"Actually, I met someone."

"Oh, in real life? Where did you meet?" This was turning out to be a great, great day, the day after my best make-out session in a long time, yes, and the day I decided to buy a house. Plus Dana had met someone.

"Online," she said. "The first guy I met." Her voice changed, became more animated the more she talked. "His name is Jerry, and I've been seeing him since...well, you remember. We talked that day. You were meeting—"

"Frank," I said. Frank, who wasn't working out, and I barely heard from these days.

"Yes. What can I say? We hit it off and started dating and doing stuff together. He's a teacher, and he's even helping me in my job search because he knows a few people."

I wanted to be happy for her. I was happy for her.

She was my friend. "Wow, that's great," I managed, but it didn't sound real and sincere, it sounded forced. "You beat the odds. You met someone on the first meet. Fantastic."

"Sorry I didn't tell you," she said. "I should have. I didn't know how. It happened so quickly. My first meet ever, and you were so gung ho about the dating, and you seemed to be having...actually having fun."

Until that moment, I didn't realize how often Dana used the word *actually*.

"Actually, you could have told me, I would have been happy for you." I paused and took a breath. "Now I feel a bit dumb. Texting you about my meets, urging you on like an idiot, when you'd already met someone."

I made myself smile, hoping it didn't come out looking like a grimace and scare the crap out of Dana. On second thought, I hoped it would scare her, so she'd know how I felt.

"You can't say you didn't know how to tell me. Seriously? Text. You could have texted me." I was making this into a big deal.

"You're right." She grabbed me by the shoulders and squeezed. "Please don't be pissed." She let go, and I took a step back. "I handled it badly, and it turned into a bigger thing than it is. Come on, don't pout. You've met someone, too. And neither of us knows if these dudes will work out. They could ghost, and it could turn into a...load of noodles next week."

It was the "don't pout" along with the "noodles" that got me. She was right. I needed to get over myself. Dana deserved a break after the shit she'd gone through with her husband. And she had trusted me, confided in me. I was acting like an adolescent instead of being happy for her. This time when I smiled, it came from the right place.

"A 'load of noodles'? Tsk, tsk. And you took that linguistics course?"

\*\*\*\*

*—Sunny, isn't this the big day? You are moving. So I am wishing you a Happy Moving Day. I certainly hope it all goes smoothly. We shall get together soon to catch up on everything. Regards, Frank Steiner—*

Regards? Signing his full name to a text? For crap sake, we'd slept together, and he couldn't get a little personal? Besides, who'd ever heard of a happy moving day?

Well, on the other hand, we hadn't had much contact, not in the past three or four weeks. So why did the man bother?

I logged off, grabbed my spiral note pad, wrote the date, and made a few notes about Frank and a few other recent meets. There was the chef who said there was nothing he couldn't cure with good food, the out-of-work guy looking for a good woman to move in with, and a police officer with a desk job.

Where was all this hustling getting me? Better to turn up at Home Depot at six in the morning when men were purchasing faucets and toilet seats and screws. "Handy guys are competent in so many departments," Isabel had said last week while we chatted and watched Roberto hang the new floating shelves in the living room. Was there anything the man couldn't do?

I snapped the spiral shut. Now that I'd received the funds from Laurent, there were papers to sign for Mendel Abramowitz, real estate attorney.

Twenty minutes later, I stood in his office and

looked around. Abramowitz was no Duke. "Come on in, be right there," he said from the far room and waved. Mendel had a two-roomer crammed with all the law books he'd owned since law school. Yale, Class of 1901. Kidding. Every space, including chairs, held papers. There was a stainless steel sink off to the side crammed with files.

Mendel hung up the phone, told me to sit, and handed me a sheet of paper. He launched into an explanation of the loan origination fee, followed with a joke about a priest, a chicken, and a real estate agent, then explained the recording fee. He told me a joke about two clients and a lockbox, explained underwriting fees and adjustments for this tax and that deposit. He blew his nose, left the room, returned, and went down the row of figures from the top. Then we were done. I limped out, trying to remember the one about the lawyer and the donkey. I needed a shot of bourbon.

Bruegger's was next, the place for rosemary-olive oil bagels, tuna on a plain bagel in case anyone was fussy, three vegetable soups, three brownies, bottles of water, orange juice, cranberry juice, and then home to meet my moving staff, Dana and Isabel. This translated to packing cars and lugging stuff I was borrowing from everyone I knew.

As soon as they arrived, I introduced everyone, and we got to work carrying everything out to the cars—a fourteen-minute job. I ran inside to make a quick check of the kitchen and left a goodbye card on the fridge for my roommates. My room looked sad and empty. Then, we were off.

Dana's car and Isabel's truck, borrowed from Roberto, were crammed with a card table, borrowed folding chairs, borrowed dishes, borrowed pots and pans, an extra borrowed folding table, three borrowed pillows, my television, my computer, and an assortment of boxes.

Isabel and Dana followed me to the new place and pulled up behind me. We all got out and stared up at the building, four apartments carved from an old mansion.

"Nice," said Isabel. "Can't wait to see inside."

"Hey, thanks, you guys," I said. "Bagel sandwiches. Let's set up the card table. You hungry?"

"You don't have that much stuff," Isabel said. "Let's get it inside. I was going to have Roberto help us if we needed it. He's on call."

"Yeah," said Dana. "When I told Jerry I was helping a friend move this afternoon, he offered to help."

"Oh, thanks." So Jerry and Dana have moved to the help-a-friend-move stage already. And I'm at the nowhere stage, where I started. "I think we're fine. We're just carrying it into the house."

"Easy peasy," said Isabel. She threw me a funny look.

Everything in the three cars would fit in one room, a sorry state of affairs at my age.

And Isabel, my best friend, knew I was feeling a little sorry for myself.

They left after a thorough tour of the echoing rooms. They loved the pantry, the fading sunlight through the skylight…said I could do great things with the kitchen. They loved-loved the fireplace in the bedroom. I closed the door and pulled out my phone.

Noah and I hadn't seen one another since our kissy-face meet. He'd taken on extra shifts, and I'd been busy packing and meeting guys whose names I didn't remember.

A text blew in from Noah.

—*Sunny, I'm a programmer and an analyst, and I figure our date was three hundred dates in one (1) and so the next will be #301. Here are the stats:*

*Canalathon: 6.0 hrs.*

*Eating: 2.5*

*Spot decisions: 0.3*

*Communication: 3.4*

*Navigation i.e. you: 2.5*

*Good night peck: 0.1, 0.1, 0.1, 0.1*

*Final peck: 9.0*

*I had a very pleasant time on our date to see if we should date.*

*May I accompany you to the theater Friday night?*

*Yes, dear. Our seats are side-by-side*

*Sweet sleeps—*

—*The theater? Thank you, Noah. Such a delight.—*

—*Btw, Sun Sun, if I emailed instead of texting, I wouldn't be half as funny as I think I am—*

I logged off and sat looking at my half-eaten tuna sandwich. Noah made me laugh. I was having fun for the first time in a very long time. There was an upside to getting closer to Noah, concentrating on Noah, letting it go wherever it would take me, whether it finished in a dead-end or a long-term relationship. I took a bite of the sandwich. It was tuna with mayo on rye bread. I didn't have lettuce or sprouts in the house. No sprouts in the house…the phrase tinkled in my head. Noah would like that. As short a time as I'd known him, I knew he'd like that.

My phone whistled, and I reached for it, figuring

Isabel was texting me. It wasn't. Good thing I hadn't deleted Luke from my contacts. Not because I was still mooning, more that I liked knowing who was at the other end, calling or texting.

—*Hi. It's Luke. I know I've been less than communicative, and you've probably deleted me from your phone long ago. Would like to explain a few things and thought texting is better than emailing. Talking would be even better. I would like to call you—*

\*\*\*\*

"Attraction is a scary mystery," I intoned into the bathroom mirror while holding the tweezers suspended in the air, training them on a stray chin hair. My phone whistled. Noah? I thumbed it open.

Frank, who didn't like texting, was texting again.

—*Sunny, I am going out of town for two or three days, sorry. I will call upon my return. Regards, Frank—*

"Again with the regards," I said to the mirror. "Upon my return, I shall call. Ain't that swell."

Speaking of swell, I'd been staying up late watching a few of those old black and whites featuring Carole Lombard, sometimes opposite Clark Gable. Sure, I liked Clark all right, but it was Carole, that feisty broad, who had the patter and the clever repartee.

Here I was going on my first date with someone I liked swell, and allowing myself to be irritated by someone I didn't much like. I deleted Frank's text message, then swiped on two layers of mascara and added a hint of blush to my cheeks.

Frank and I were done; I just hadn't informed him officially. I peered into the magnifying mirror and made a face. "Maybe he'll fade away," I said aloud. Imagined my girlfriend, Carole Lombard and I getting ready for our dates. Hers was Clark, of course.

"So, Carole, speaking of *done*, WTF is with Luke? That text last night and the one from before, apologizing after a couple months of no contact. Luke wants to call? What's with that?"

Well, my imaginary Carole said she didn't know what a text message was, but she sure as hell knew a mixed message when she heard one, and that's what Luke was sending.

The doorbell rang. I had emailed Noah directions to my place. A feeling of anticipation—that stomach-crunching jolt. Lust and make-out fever...Oh, shit, I had it bad.

After a peephole confirmation that Noah was indeed on the other side, I opened the door. A breeze wafted in, carrying with it the scent of the neighbors grilling on their deck, reminding me it would be good to make an effort, meet a few folks on the block.

He stood there smiling. I could feel us looking one another over, measuring the attraction, making sure it was still there.

"May I enter, Madame?"

I nodded and stepped aside.

Noah was looking good in a gray sports coat, shirt, and gray slacks. It contrasted with the red iodine of his hair. "Last week you were a roomie. Now you're a homeowner," he said.

An awkward moment until he bent and gently kissed my cheek. "You look wonderful. Beautiful. And so is the red dress." He stood smiling. "Beautiful on you."

I swear I shivered when he said this, a symptom of

being compliment-starved. The problem was the red dress reminded me of Frank. When I riffled through my closet looking for what to wear, the red dress, my special dress seemed to reproach, scolding me for poor judgment. *If I'm so special,* it taunted, *why did you wear me with Frank?* So, I'd wear it to the theatre with Noah. Cancel Frank right out of the dress.

"There's an item on the stoop." He backed toward the door. "May I go out again?"

He reappeared with a four-foot bamboo plant, made a great show of placing it in front of the window. "Your first houseplant I see," he said, gazing around the place. "You'll give me a tour—a quickie. I'm afraid we've got to make haste as they say."

"Absolutely—and thanks for my first houseplant. You replanted it, didn't you?" I turned to look at it again. Plant stores don't supply a gray ceramic planter and matching dish.

"Glad you noticed," he said. "You like the color?"

"Sure do. Now, where the plant is—that's the living room. It leads into the dining room," and I played television game-show hostess, gestured with my hand, sweeping stroke in the air, palm up. I took special care to highlight the fireplace, taking him next into the kitchen, where there was nothing but newspapers and my can of paint. The paintbrush stood in a pail of water in the sink.

"Looking good, pale gray works."

"Foggy Mist, it's called."

He looked at the brush in the pail. "I see you're taking care of your materials."

"Yup, I'm impatient but I try. I may get the floor done. The crappy linoleum look isn't doing it for me."

"Hmm, I see." He looked at his watch. "Let's save the rest. We've got a reservation at Hot Orchids. Next to the theatre, I think."

Yes. And I did the internal jump-up-and-down thing. Hot Orchid—even if Noah preferred the plural—with its spectacular winding staircase, used to be a hotel. It may have even been the dorm when the Culinary Institute of America was located in New Haven. Now it was one of the hottest restaurants in the city.

There was time enough at dinner for him to tell me about his previous life, the twenty-year marriage—divorced seven years—an adult son living in Santa Fe. It was one of those dinners where you can't talk enough, can't fit in all the questions, and yet you don't want to appear downright nosy. I asked lots of questions and mostly he answered them.

Noah fell asleep forty minutes into the ballet. He woke just as the lights popped on for intermission.

Afterward, we walked slowly back to the car. He held the door open, and I climbed in trying to look as agile as possible, like a ballerina. He went around to the other side, got in, and started the motor.

"It was special," I said. "Thanks for taking me to the ballet."

"You're very welcome," he said formally, bowing his head in my direction. "My pleasure."

"And dinner at the Hot Orchid. What a great place."

"Well, you're very welcome, I'm sure."

"I'm sure, too." I giggled. "You did it for me."

"Did what?"

"Took me to the ballet. I know because you fell

asleep."

He sat looking at me. "I had to rest my eyes. Such pressure at work. I hope you'll forgive me."

"I'll think about it." I'd thought it was funny, Noah and hundreds of men before him, thousands, silly clichés falling asleep at the ballet or the opera. "I brought one of my mixes." I pulled a CD from my bag. "Old stuff. It's got some Pointers, some blues, and other movie soundtracks. I can't remember."

He took the CD from my hand, put it in the slot, and turned up the volume.

"Garth," he said smiling, making no move to pull it out. "Garth Brooks. Shall we find a place to go now?"

"Go?"

"Well, I—er—I want to give you a peck."

"One peck?" Parking and pecking.

"One long peck. One very long peck." I directed him up Whitney Avenue toward Hamden, past the huge houses on the New Haven side of Whitney.

"Maybe a feel or two," he added.

"You have your nerve. This is the first date, you know." I thought of my house, an actual place we could go to smooch. Three chairs, wood with straight backs. Sit in one of those, and all the romantic stuff would be up the chimney.

"Well, you'd better count better."

I held out my hand, counted fingers. "Ten hours was it? Our date."

"Look. The last one was twelve hours long. Doesn't that count?" He took my hand and my flesh pingled.

We found a quiet spot several streets off Whitney, and Noah killed the lights. It was a warm evening, almost as if this particular December night had been planned for me, little me, so I could make out in the car with Noah.

"Shall I leave on the heat?" he asked me. I shook my head.

He bent over and kissed me a gentle one, no hurry. He kissed me all around my mouth, forehead, and neck. Do men have any idea what a turn-on it is to be kissed like this? Probably not. Otherwise, they'd all be great kissers, and there'd be no barge-pole-tongue-thrusters, no guys in a hurry.

"Can I come over there?" he asked after a while, indicating my seat.

"What do you mean?" Did he want to sit beside me? He did and it wasn't awkward, in spite of his length. He pulled my seat back. First, he was beside me, and then he was on top. It went like that for what seemed like a short time, kissing and a little massage.

"I love doing this. I love how you feel." He ran his hand up my arm. "You have nice arms and..." he put his hand on my thigh, rubbing gently. "I love your legs. I knew you had beautiful legs."

"How did you know? I mean I've never exposed them."

"I saw them."

"What do you mean, you saw them?"

"I saw them last time."

"Last time I was wearing jeans."

"And wearing them very nicely, too."

"You could tell?"

"Of course I could tell." He stroked my stomach. This is nice, very nice."

He made no fast moves, did nothing that made me

uncomfortable. No out-of-my-comfort-zone Frank talk. Frank talked a lot, but he pushed in a sly way. I felt more comfortable with Noah than I'd ever felt with Frank.

And talk about sly, when Luke made a guest appearance inside my head—right in the middle of kissing Noah—I slapped him away like the bug he was.

****

Early Sunday morning I woke with that draggy feeling you get with too much making out and too little sleep. Not that there was such a thing as too much making out.

Four cups of coffee later and still in my pajamas, I finished up a few nicks in the painting job I'd noticed during the Noah tour. Then I washed out my paintbrush, put it in the pail, and carried it to the small storage room in the basement. After that, I stared at the phone for a few minutes, got up and paced the room. Better done on an empty stomach.

I dialed, my stomach clenching.

"Hello?"

"Hi, Frank, it's Sunny." *Crap. He's home.*

"Hi Sunny. This is a surprise."

"It is?" I held my spiral notebook and gripped my pen tightly. Yes, I planned to take notes so I could read them over, digest the conversation afterward.

"Well, you don't call me that often."

"Oh." Pause. "Can we talk?"

"Sure, I'm working here, but of course."

*He's working and I'm interrupting. Too bad.* "I don't know if you noticed but, well, we haven't talked much or done much together, uh, lately. The truth is," I hesitated, then plunged in, "I haven't been that thrilled…about how things have been going…for a while." I stopped to let Frank absorb this information. Should I have started with a little small talk? Nah.

"Well, you've been a bit removed. Yes, that is true."

"Oh." I thought about that. Removed, huh? "And you didn't say anything?" If Frank had told me, it would have been a conversation starter. At least.

"Well, I didn't want to put you in a precarious position."

"Oh." Precarious. *What's he talking about?* "You remember what I said when we first started going out? Remember that day? We were walking downtown. How I wasn't sure what I wanted, but I knew what I didn't want?"

"Yes. A somewhat nebulous statement to be sure. I chalked it up to your inexperience with dating."

Was this an insult? Probably not. That day we'd been peering in windows. A shoe store, fine jewelry, a trendy furniture store. Frank had touched my arm as I talked, taken my hand, suggested a glass of wine. "I want to concentrate on what you are saying," he'd said. "So, let's go sit and relax. Get to know one another." *Your call is important to me, please leave a message.* Frank left mixed messages, especially lately.

"Well, now I'm opening up to you. Telling you I've been unhappy." My gut roiled with the need to explain.

"Well, I've been consumed with work," he said.

"There are ways…of communicating," I wanted him to understand why it wasn't working, "even when you're busy."

"I suppose. I suppose you are right."

*Damn tootin'.* One of my mother's expressions. "I don't want to be harsh," I said. "But you're like an iceberg."

"Iceberg?"

"No warmth... It's so strange. In a way...a couple of weeks ago, I felt very close to you and then, nothing." There'd been a night we talked for several hours. In bed. And the next day he'd—well, he'd gotten busy. Used work to be unavailable. Had called when I'd certainly be out. Maybe I was trying too hard to make sense of Frank's lack of effort. Overanalyzing. Even so, wasn't it obvious Frank was backing off? The Woody Allen shark thing. I'd never understood it until now.

Pause. "Are you asking if you're the one for me? I can't answer that."

I squeezed the receiver. "I'm not asking that." I wondered if he missed the point on purpose, if he deflected the conversation in a way that he found familiar, somehow comfortable.

"Oh." Silence. "I thought you wanted reassurances that we have a future. I'm not in a position to offer such an assurance at this juncture."

"For crap sake, a future? I want a *present.* I want someone who, even when he's working, well, he wants my company. Just to be there." I adjusted the angle of the phone at my ear. *I want someone who's interested in me.*

"I didn't enter into this relationship casually," he said.

"That is an interesting comment because I barely see it as a relationship."

"You can't mean that," he said, a hiccup in his voice.

"My birthday. I brought it up. Twice," I said. "The last time in bed. I was feeling close to you." It was after we'd made love, and I felt able to risk telling Frank about my birthday. Hmm. Funny how I'd thought telling Frank about my birthday was a risky deal.

"I don't—I don't remember," Frank said.

For a second I couldn't respond. He couldn't *remember*. "You said you didn't celebrate your own birthday. Was that an excuse to ignore mine?"

Isabel had told me to be direct. Well, *direct* was my new middle name, but now I felt worse than naive. I felt stupid.

"Ah," and his voice lowered. "I am sorry about that." Flat. A pancake voice.

"Well, remember what you say about a relationship being as good as what you put into it? What you tell your daughter?"

"Yes, of course."

"I've had my fill of emotional unavailability. You're not there. Not there for me anyway."

"What can I say?" Frank stopped. "I can't invalidate your feelings. They're your feelings." Nothing he said came from his gut; it was all from the head, smoothed over. Homogenized. He sighed. "My emotional batteries are worn down, and at times I am better off alone, so I am not raining on anyone's parade. Was there a time you wanted to talk, and we didn't?"

"Oh, Frank," I sputtered, then forced myself to speak slowly. "The one time you poured your heart out was when you told me you didn't want to wear a condom."

"I wanted to get to know you better," he said.

"You don't get angry, do you?" That's when I

knew I could say anything to Frank, and he'd go on as if he hadn't heard me. I sighed in frustration.

"I don't believe in anger," he said. "Not between two people who have a close relationship."

"Getting angry is normal. It's a reality of life."

"No, I don't think so."

"And I want to remind you what you said to me when I told you about my birthday."

"Please, Sunny." His voice sounded resigned now, as if he knew I meant business.

"And tell me if this rings a bell." I whispered, embarrassed to be repeating his words out loud. "You were giving me your semen as a gift." Then I said it again, louder, the way Miss Ahern, in the sixth grade, urged us when we read aloud. "You were giving me your *semen* as a *gift*."

This was one I hadn't repeated, not even to Isabel. *Sperm.* His universal donor gift to all the ladies? My stomach twisted, and I stood up, stared out the window down at the brown grass at a man walking out of the building with an umbrella. Funny. I hadn't heard the rain.

"Sunny. I am sorry. Sorry you feel this way." Frank had a clever way of saying he was sorry without sounding the least bit sorry. It pissed me off.

"Well. I am finally opening up to you. These are my feelings." I held my breath.

"This is too—"

"Yes. *Feelings.*" I let the air out in a gust powerful enough to knock Frank over, if he'd been standing beside me. "You can't negate them."

"No, that—"

"Now I know what I need. And want. A best

191

friend. A man who has my back and I have his. *And great sex.*" A giggle escaped when I realized I'd quoted José. *With a man who makes me come,* I added inside my head.

The phone at my ear, I looked around my new place, at the card table, the layer of sophisticated, high-class freakin' Foggy Mist on the walls, the possibilities stretching out like undiscovered gifts.

No use expending any more energy on Frank.

"This is so difficult," he said.

"No, it's very easy," I said. "Take care of yourself. I'm—goodbye."

After hanging up, I sat on the chair shaking. This was what it meant to be with a man who didn't consider you special. My body rattled the card table. I'd tried so hard, hadn't I tried? But everything was so new, and I thought I liked Frank. He'd been attentive when I met him, so interested…my body settled into a gentle hum. The brick lump that came and went in my chest slid away, dissolved.

The pale gray walls, the new plant in its gray pot from Noah, my paintings stacked in the corner. Reminders that Frank had never visited me in my new place. Actually, a bonus since it saved me the trouble of purging him.

Chapter Eight
Detective-ing...

Lunch at the computer while I completed the second application for a long-term substitute teaching job. I chomped on a pumpernickel bagel smeared with hummus and two slices of Lorraine low-fat cheese, an apple on the side. A few seeds splattered onto the keyboard as I leaned closer, scanning as the messages loaded. Nope, not a single response, and I'd been filling out forms—eleven to be exact—for over two weeks. I consulted the list, divided by district, the type of opening, and the date the application closed. At this point, I'd take anything. Except math, I wasn't a math person.

Not going to work was plain weird. In fact, it felt wrong, as if an essential part of my life were missing. Little errands and tasks like finding ten turquoise plates and six charcoal mugs on the deep sale table at IKEA were one thing. Plus a set of flatware with a squared-off, abstract design that I loved because it reminded me of my own life. But no, I wasn't fooling myself, chores were no replacement for a job.

As the emails finished loading I flicked my eyes over them, deleting the junk as I went, careful not to overlook any responses to my applications. Nope, nothing on the job front.

Crap. Two emails from Frank stared at me, sent

two seconds apart. Three days since our little talk, and I'd thought I was Frank-free. I clicked and scanned. Yup, identical. I had a feeling about these emails and whatever was flinging itself around in my stomach told me it wasn't the greatest of feelings.

For a moment, I considered deleting them. Just like that. Presto-Clicko.

Impossible. They pleaded to be read.

*From: Frank*

*To: Sunny*

*Re: Conversation*

*Yesterday when you called I was in the middle of an important project that was due early next week so perhaps I was not myself.*

*Your tone was one I seldom if ever tolerate in another human being and I would like to state that I was not pleased. I consider myself to be a warm person, a person concerned with others' feelings and I generally choose to consort with like persons. It was a shock to discover that particular side of you.*

*Upon reflection, I do recall, albeit piecemeal, our conversation concerning your birthday. I have a vague recollection of this discussion having taken place in bed. That is probably why I had such a memory block.*

*I consider bed to be a place of refuge, and not the venue to talk about a subject that is fretful. It is unfortunate that you think otherwise.*

*In conclusion, I reiterate that I do not seek to negate your feelings, nor to invalidate them. I hope that you find what you are seeking.*

*Regards,*

*Frank*

"I consider bed to be a place of refuge," I said in a

squeaky mouse voice. Then in a deeper tone with rounded edges, as the one and only Bullwinkle, "I can reiterate that I do not seek to invalidate your feelings." I'll admit, I stuck Frank's email in a folder marked History, a reminder to *never consort with such a like person* again.

"So there, Frank," I said through my nose in my best sneer voice.

Then I sent Noah an email telling him I was done with the so-called boyfriend. Even though I wanted to, I didn't say anything mean about Frank.

*To: Sunny*
*From: Noah*
*Subject: upholstery*
*I would like us to make time to climb into the backest part of your truck. The better to touch your rembourrage garniture dans the interior—*

*To: Noah*
*From: Sunny*
*I don't mind the garnished rembourrage portion of the program, but not ready for boinking at this juncture—*

*To: Sunny*
*From: Noah*
*Subject: honey*
*Honey, are you still infatuated? I am—*

Oh, the man was a romantic and his emails made my kidneys squeeze. Maybe that didn't sound sexy, but whatever squeezed, and wherever it was located, it felt pretty nice.

My phone whistled and I pressed the message icon. *A text from Mark.*

*—I sent a check for $50 becaus thats all i caN*

*aford this month do to some serious family problems. I
hope this is not an inconvenense—*

I stared at *inconvense,* noting the kid had done a
decent job spelling *serious.* He still owed me, though. I
asked Siri for the number of Tony's Auto Body on
Whalley Avenue, and the phone was picked up on the
first ring.

"Tony's."

"Hello. Is the young kid, Mark, there?"

"Marky!" The voice was muffled, yelling. I could
hear a pounding, then a clanking. I hung up, grabbed
my bag, keys, and set off for Tony's. Normally I'm not
a fast driver, but this was an exception. I shot over
Whitney to Grove and up Whalley, parked on the street
in front of Tony's, grinding my teeth as I got out of the
truck. I pulled open the door. A bell clanged,
announcing my arrival.

He was in the office, bent over at the desk, writing
on a pad.

"Hello," I said. The kid colored a little as he
recognized me. The office was overheated. Someone
had opened the window in an attempt to freshen the air.
Mostly, I smelled dog.

"You get my text?" he said.

"Thank you. For sending the check to my client." I
decided to try the nice guy approach. After all, he had
paid a chunk of the bill, what he could afford, and he'd
been honest about his financial problems.

"Oh." Pause. "Yeah." Pause. "Look. I'm sorry. I
just couldn't pay more."

"She understands. Would you be willing to do
some jobs?"

"Jobs?" He didn't sound grateful for the

opportunity.

The pounding in the place stopped, and there was the sound of drilling. Mark looked over his shoulder into the garage. A guy was working under the hood of an Escort, and another guy was in the corner. I saw feet.

"I'm on break right now," Mark told me, even though I hadn't asked. The drilling continued, then stopped, began again.

"Jobs, I have a few jobs," I plodded on, fabricating as I went, shouting over the drilling. "If you do the work for me, I'll pay my client. That's the best I can do for you."

In the corner, an enormous beige dog, who weighed perhaps thirty pounds more than I did, gazed up at me. Her tail thumped.

"What jobs?" The drilling stopped and we talked in normal voices.

"Oh, painting." I sniffed, wondering if he'd buy my logic, and hoping he wouldn't realize *I* was my own client. "My house. Can you paint?"

"I done it a few times. The garage for my father."

"Well, then."

"The basement."

"Good."

"Finished the basement. Put in drywall. The floor. Nice tile floor."

"So, you can do a lot."

"Did a nice job. The bathroom, too. New cabinet. Double sinks."

"That's great." So. Mark had boundless talent in the car and home repair and installation departments. "You install cabinets."

"Yeah. Floor came out real cool. Those big tiles. A

grayish color and one wall a off-white with charcoal. Smoke it was called."

"You're hired. Let's shake on it."

He shrugged, held out his greasy hand, and we shook. "Okay, when?"

"You have a pen?" I gave him the details, thought of my ugly kitchen floor, how the Kid was around nineteen and strong, and could probably lift the rear end of a Chrysler with one hand.

From Tony's, I headed up Whalley and onto the Merritt Parkway, fluffed my hair, and sang along with Pizza Man—the Pizzarelli trio. Dana had mentioned a consignment shop on the Post Road, and I had time on my hands and no job. Was I starting to sound bitter? Nah, checking out date-worthy, ensembles would be fun. My cell phone rang. At sixty miles an hour, I could barely make out the number—no way to ID who was phoning.

"Hello?"

A woman's voice boomed out from the speaker, "Is this Sunny Chanel? I'm calling from Green Gardens."

Green Gardens? What was that? And who was this woman? And then I got it. This call was about a job, an interview the previous week.

A trailer loaded with new cars flew by and the Jeep shook, as excited as I was about this phone call. I asked the woman to hang on and pulled off at the next exit, unable to concentrate, or write anything down with a truck on my left and a car tailgating. I eased the Jeep into the Walmart lot and parked. "Yes, I'm back, sorry about that." I listened, afraid I'd miss something, a detail, if I searched for pen and paper. They were offering me a job in one of the middle schools. A teacher on maternity leave. Middle school. Middle school was all about hormones and lip gloss and the cool factor.

The connection was lost for a second, and then I heard, "This is short notice, but would it be possible for you to start next week? We were left high and dry."

"Yeah, I can do it. I mean I would like to accept the position."

Three days away, counting the weekend.

\*\*\*\*

That night while Noah was at work, we celebrated my new job by emailing, picking up where we'd left off. We could have talked on the phone, but he needed to keep personal calls to a minimum and we both loved the emailing, could say things in email that would be difficult on the phone and in person.

*To: Sunny*
*From: Noah*
*Subject: bonkers*
*Look, HONEY, since you are concerned not ready for boinking at this juncture with TO BOINK OR NOT TO BOINK, as you call it. Well, let me state this this way: There will be boinking when you are ready and not before. At this point, I may have you begging to boink. Come to think of it, I seriously doubt that.*

*What would you like to do? Meet? Sup? Boink?*
*Sorry.*

*Chinese? Mandarin? Turkish? Pizza at that Bar place? Whatever your sweet, furry, boinking-pixilated little heart desires, Honey.*

Response went like this—

*To: Noah*
*From: Sunny*

*Subject: Get stuffed*

*I HATE it when you YELL AT ME LIKE THIS by saying HONEY instead of honey. Let's decide what to do together.*

*Sunny*

*PS Will you be stepping inside my house?*

He emailed right back.

*To: Sunny*

*From: Noah*

*Subject: stuff*

*No, no, my little honey, I was not yelling at you. HONEY is a bit teasing and I'm not a ole yeller. I will not be stepping inside your house. Not yet. I am thinking of getting a room. Think motel. I will be the host. You can relax.*

*I LIKE planning two weeks into the future, possibly three.*

Then he followed up with...

*To: Sunny*

*From: Noah*

*Subject: dreamin'*

*Sweets, sweet dreams, jelly beans*

*I remain yours, infatuated.*

Then...

*To: Sunny*

*From: Noah*

*Subject: Standing up*

*Think vertical, more vertical stuff. We need to do it.*

What was he talking about?

*To: Noah*

*From: Sunny*

*Subject: what?*

*What?*

*To: Sunny*
*From: Noah*
*Subject: Stuff*
*Vertical stuff. As in the opposite of horizontal stuff.*
*To: Sunny*
*From: Noah*
*Subject: Things to do*
*Sunny, we didn't talk about the weekend but maybe we should narrow it down to fifty or eighty items on the list. Otherwise, I'll have to purchase a small house and stay until March. I can teach you pool. Sleep well, Saturday is a long way off.*

*Ps I have reserved a room. I trust you know why.*

*PSPs Shooting pool involves money. In some circles it is called wagering.*

*To: Noah*
*From: Sunny*
*Subject: didn't know*
*Shooting pool involves money.*

*No, I didn't know. How much bread should I bring?*

*To: Sunny*
*From: Noah*
*Subject: bread*
*No need to bring no lousy bread, jelly bean, you've got all I'm after.*

*And it ain't no dough of ANY kind.*

The man was worried about the vertical and the horizontal. I logged off the site, and drifted into the kitchen for a glass of water, drank it slowly. I could invite Noah to stay over in the guest room if I went back to the bed place and—not a good idea. He probably wouldn't want to be confined to the guest room anyway.

Besides, there was no time this week for major-purchase shopping. I needed to fill out the paperwork, go through the textbooks someone was dropping off at my house tomorrow, prepare lessons, and...my stomach was doing a number on me.

Noah was coming. When would I find the time to do all this? I poured another glass of water and went into my bedroom to undress and watch a little junk TV.

Visiting Noah in a motel room had a sort of sleazy appeal. After all, motel rooms, with the huge motel bed dominating, were all about the horizontal.

And there was nothing I could do about *that*.

****

Noah unlocked the door and pushed it open. "Come in, make yourself at home. My little place. I'm happy you're here."

I stashed my picnic basket on the floor under the television, and crossed my arms, but no matter which way I turned, *it* was there. The bed. Gigantic...and exactly what I had expected in a motel room anyway.

"Let me show you around." He took me by the hand, led me around the room stopping outside the bathroom. "Yes, we have our own private facility. There is also, as you can see, a king-size bed so my legs don't hang off the edge."

He fiddled with the lights for a few seconds, found the dimmer, and turned off the bright overhead.

He pulled me close. "I need to kiss you," his mouth insistent, his arms pressing me into him, mine wrapping around his neck, pulling him down. We were like that until my legs got wobbly.

"Can we kiss sitting down?" I asked.

"No." He kissed my nose. "What's in that basket you brought?"

"Please?"

"Yes, dear," he breathed, lowering me to the bed. He kissed my neck, my most vulnerable area—well, one of many—and worked his way up to my mouth. My lips parted, and I groaned. "What's in that basket?" he said in between kisses.

"You're getting repetitious and..." I tried holding in a moan, "You think that because I am groaning, you can lure me down a path of no resistance."

He threw back his head and laughed, his Adam's apple sticking out. "I think no such thing. What I think is we should read for a while. I brought a couple books. We both could use a cool down." He saw me glance at his crotch. "What are you looking at?"

"Me?" I smoothed my sweater. "What books have you brought?"

"A few. My self-help books." He pointed to his bag. "In there. And you?"

"I'll read you some stuff from *Catcher*."

"*Catcher*?"

"As in, *The Catcher in the Rye*."

"Of course, in the rye." He stood, turned around to adjust his pants. "I think I read that." I could see him fiddling. "In high school. Or college." He walked over to the desk and opened his wallet, closed it.

"Did you like it?"

"Don't remember much, I guess so."

"Didn't think it was funny? Funny-sad. But very funny in places. How everything's bastard this and that." I reached for a tissue. "I'm rereading it with a friend." Well, we were thinking about reading it. "So you—it wasn't a book you remember fondly?" I got up, took off my cardigan.

He took the sweater out of my hands and held it for me. "I don't remember much," he said. "Sorry." Then Noah eyed the picnic basket on the floor. "Your basket is for real. The picnic. You weren't kidding around."

I nodded, got up and brought the basket over to the bed. I reached in and pulled out the package of figs, tore it open, and gave him one to taste. I'd spent time wandering the aisles of an upscale grocery store on Orange Street, the kind where the owner speaks with a heavy Italian accent and offers hot, home-cooked dishes prepared with love by Mama.

"Ah," he said. "My first fig." He took a small bite, held the fig in his fingers. "Thanks for the fig, honey," he said and pulled me to him. He kissed me. The kissing lasted several minutes. "Maybe now is a good time to dine?" He didn't let go.

"Right." I kissed his cheek and pulled away. Opening the basket, one by one, I began taking out goodies and displaying them on the bed.

"We have a nice French Emmental. Some swiss sliced. And a pungent spread. Fatty but delicious." I gestured, palm up, and took out a container. "Then there's a little potato salad, bought not made. A vegetarian *pâté*. *Crudités* in the form of cucumbers, carrots, peppers. A few slices of roast beef. Medium*ish*. Sliced fruits. Fruit."

I pulled out a round plastic container. "Condiments." A little horseradish and mustard in tiny jars I'd discovered when unpacking my box of spices. I'd cleaned Laurent out spice-wise, lifted those jars with the nifty French labels, shipped them over in half a crate. Souvenirs.

"A nice bottle of white, properly chilled." I'd slipped the wine into a thermos bag. "A baguette. And fat paper plates so you won't spill."

We were living out an old movie scene, Audrey Hepburn and Albert Finney in *Two for the Road*. Poor and starving, they'd smuggled food into their hotel room and hidden it under the covers.

We ate slowly, sipping the wine, sitting side-by-side, touching. Afterward, the food got chocked aside, and there we were, making out again.

The horizontal was wonderful, as I'd imagined. "I can't let myself go," I said.

"Yes, you can. Don't worry. I'm in full control, and I won't do anything you don't want to do." He unbuttoned my blouse. Kissed me.

"You have a nice chest and nice breasts." He pulled down the strap of my bra. I grabbed his hand, preventing him from unhooking it. "But don't trust me."

"You're doing this on purpose, aren't you? Turning me on so I'll lose my brain." He was looking into my face. "What's all this trust stuff about?"

"It's for your own protection not to trust me," he said, slowly kissing my neck, my breasts. "I don't want you to get hurt. I don't want to hurt you."

"*You* could get hurt."

"That's right. I could."

"So the horizontal takes care of itself?" I held his hand still. "Flows along. Horizontal making out is so easy."

"Very easy." He paused. "I'm still infatuated." He looked at me, rolled onto his side, and rested on an elbow. "I'm still infatuated, but I want to be with you because of the other, too." I said nothing. "When I'm with you I'm always thinking about touching you. Well, when I'm not with you, I'm thinking about touching you. That worries me."

"Worries you?" Fascinating that he thought about me at home and at work. I thought about him, too—thought about the kissing and touching—not that I'd tell him. Not yet.

"I don't want to be with you *only* because I want to touch you. I need to have more than that," he said. "I'm afraid it will go away." He didn't look at me.

Unable to respond, I swallowed. My feelings for Frank had diluted, little by little until they evaporated. That could happen with Noah. I rolled over, touched his arm. He cuddled me.

"I like it when you touch me," I said. "Is it wrong? We're just getting to know each other."

"Shhh, I know. I worry too much and sometimes I think too much."

"You're intellectualizing. It's what you accuse *me* of," I told him. He was smiling. "So what date are we up to now? This'll be a long weekend. It should count big."

"It does," he said. "By tomorrow night we'll be at around three hundred and seventy dates."

"Sometimes, I have the feeling I know you," I said. "I've known you for months. I can be myself."

It had never come close to this with Frank. In spite of the world-class body, he was more like an old man. Frank had six pairs of loafers, three brown, three black, all identical. He'd told me he liked to keep things simple.

"That's good." Noah stroked my arm, my neck. "Do you have to go home?"

"Pretty much."

After we ate dinner, he took me home, kissed me goodnight, and promised to call early the next day so we could take a drive to the Mystic Aquarium and see the walrus who patted himself on the back. Monday was my first day of school.

****

*To: Sunny*
*From: Noah*
*Subject: comfortable*

*Honey dear, a radio Advice Lady on the drive home was talking about comfort level. A woman called in asking about her boyfriend. He's pushing for sex. No. Doesn't have anything to do with us. The Advice Lady said if you are not comfortable with it, with ANYTHING then don't do it. Don't get coerced. I agree. Just wanted to say it, ok?*

****

By six in the morning I had knocked off a good thirty minutes on the treadmill and another twenty on weights. All night, my mind played and replayed the first day of school ahead of me.

Greeting the kids at the door, checking how much French they spoke, setting up rules for the classroom, and deciding should I or shouldn't I trust this one to go for a pee break? On and on and on. Until I gave up and hauled my body out of bed while it was still dark, the morning air cold and crisp. There was a single car on the road when I set off for the gym. An hour later, on the return trip, the sun was just rising. I stowed the Jeep in the underground parking and headed to the elevator, glancing around out of habit. Underground parking always gave me a vague creepy feeling, even with the secured gates and locked access of the Whitney Moss Garage.

Back inside my place, I stripped, left my yoga pants and sports bra on the floor, and stepped into the shower. It started again, the mind newsreel. I had to design a dialogue to start them off. Did they have French names? How much could they write? Blah, blah, blah, until I realized I'd been scrubbing the same leg for several minutes. I stepped out of the shower, toweled dry, pulled my flannel PJs back on, and sent Noah a quick text.

*—I love being horizontal* with *you—*

It was nothing dirty, but it was perfect, quick and fun, and I was too anxious to be provocative on my first day of school. Besides, it was time to get dressed.

An hour later I stood in front of the class in black trousers and black sweater, the classic Parisienne— gripping the seating chart to hide my nervousness.

"Class, I'll go over the rules first. In English." There were titters of laughter, and I caught a few comments. "I'm not joking. This is French class. I have a strict French-only rule in class." More titters and a few waving hands. I ignored them.

"You get ten minutes at the beginning of class to speak English and ask questions." If they thought I was crazy, well, I couldn't stop them thinking whatever they wanted. "Come prepared."

One overconfident boy coughed, leaned back in his chair, and turned his head slightly to whisper to the boy behind him. I glanced down at my seating chart where his name was listed as Sara MacGregor. Interesting.

"Sara MacGregor?" I shot him the stare, and he straightened up to laughter from the class. Across the room, the real Sara MacGregor raised a hand and rolled her eyes in his direction.

I'd deal with him later.

Meanwhile, I'd take attendance, establish a routine. The boy-girl, boy-girl pattern could work with a few adjustments. I held the seating chart up, consulting it with a knowing grin, letting the whole class know their sub was no fool. I knew their tricks. *Trickage*, we called it, back in the day. We used trickage on Mrs. Oritewheeler to wangle five minutes more recess, but never on the tough-but-lovable Mrs. Riley, a retired teacher whose mind galloped ahead of us.

My stomach grumbled, and the two kids in the front row looked at me funny.

Oh, and there wasn't much of a lesson plan in the folder marked *Substitute*. Miss Moore, the regular teacher, had a lot of nerve telling me she'd left six weeks of lessons. I'd searched the desk drawers, the shelves and cabinets, and the mailbox in the office. Nothing.

"Stand please." I motioned with my hand. *I have my own lessons, thank you very much.* "Please say *présent* before you sit down." I pronounced it like a Frenchie and asked them to repeat it, first the whole class, then in rows. One word. Then we'd go on to the alphabet. I had a dialog and a song. They'd show me how much they knew. They'd love it.

The day galloped by in a blur.

After school, I slouched at the table in the back of the room, gazing around at the bulletin boards, limp with a sense of wonderment at how teachers held it together daily. Today, eighty-six kids practiced the French alphabet in song, learned a six-line dialogue, and how to ask for help in French. We also played Simon Says (in French) and yes, no matter how elevated their cool factor, these high school kids loved playing.

A whistle from my cell. I grabbed it. A text from Noah.

—*Friday is FOUR days away. Kissy, kisskisskisskisskiss.*—

A stir of excitement in my stomach.

Before exhaustion took me down, I needed to prep lessons, plan homework, and read over tomorrow's schedule. Block scheduling was confusing, at least to me, the newbie.

Where to start? The next lesson was grocery shopping. Nouns, numbers, not easy in French, prices and meal planning. Adrenalin kicking in, I trotted to the cabinets at the back of the classroom and opened each one, eyeballing the contents. In the third, a bin of plastic bananas, apples, pears, and a whole collection of vegetables sat in a bin as if waiting for me. The cucumber looked positively pornographic.

I might be forced to hide the little bugger.

\*\*\*\*

Noah and I were at my place on the bed, my head on his shoulder. I'd spent the week working, learning my students' names, and I gave two detentions.

He scratched his head. "I have a question. It's very awkward, and well, we haven't discussed it much but I was wondering if—if—are you still going out with other…"

I propped myself on an elbow.

"With other guys." He put a finger on my mouth just as I was opening it. "It's not quite what you think." He paused and I could see him swallow. "I think you should go out with others. It's better for you."

"Better? Isn't that a bit peculiar?" I sat up and folded my arms.

"We both should. I should too. But I can't." He stared at the ceiling, his hands laced behind his head.

"You're telling me to go out with other guys even though you're not?" My voice squeaked.

"I don't want to go out with other guys," he said.

"Funny."

"Well, it's just the way I am. When I wrote you, I wrote only you. I can't go out with other women. It seems somehow *dishonest*."

"So, you want me to be dishonest?"

"You have to do what you feel like doing. I can't tell you what to do."

This was strange. "But if you're…"

"Wait. The other thing is to meet them, but no touching. I do the touching." He looked at me.

"What's the point of going out with someone if I can't touch him?"

"Now you're mocking me and I was serious."

"Are you pouting?"

"No," he said.

"Should I pout?"

"I know you don't like it when I say that."

"No, I don't like it. And I don't agree with you. I thought we were exclusive." I stood up. "I need to move around. Let's go for a walk. Around the block. Please?" I wanted to clear my head, stop analyzing, stop everything he had started.

After the walk, we sat down to meatloaf and a salad, which I'd proudly baked earlier that day, having acquired a Pyrex dish and two mixing bowls. I didn't have much appetite. I watched his mouth move slowly as he chewed, and he didn't seem to have much of an appetite either.

He got up from the card table slowly and pulled me into the bedroom. "Relax, lie down." I sat on the bed. "I need a minute here," and he pulled something out of his bag. I closed my eyes and in a minute Ray Charles filled the room. Then I felt him next to me, his mouth tasting of something I couldn't name, like kissing a flower, an edible flower, bland and slightly sweet. It was a long time before he unbuttoned my shirt, one button at a time, more kissing, another button. I had planned what to wear, thinking of him unwrapping me.

"It's all right, babe. See, I called you babe." He kissed my nose. "I want to touch you, make you feel nice." I didn't know if I wanted him to make me feel things like that, shook my head.

"No?" he said. "It's all right." He slid off, wrapped his arms around me and hugged me. I could feel his heart thump. "It's probably the stuff I brought up earlier, isn't it?" He didn't wait for an answer. "We can sleep a bit and then…"

"What?" I must have sounded impatient and tired.

"I might have to wake you up later and start all over again."

\*\*\*\*

A week later, we were sitting at Noah's little table in Noah's little kitchen with Thai takeout. "So the no-English thing isn't working so great," I said. The pungent scent of curry floated above us. "They want to translate everything."

"So, translate. You can do that." Noah scraped his chair back from the table, crossed his legs.

"Not the point. I want to speak French. I want them to speak French." I sat contemplating the tofu and vegetables. "They seem to get a kick out of it when they can speak a few words."

"So it's working." He folded his arms.

"When it works, it's fantastic."

"And when it doesn't, it's like being in a bad marriage," he said with more than a hint of irony. "Game playing, attitude, avoidance." He speared a piece of tofu.

"You can't compare a classroom environment to a marriage."

He looked at me over the rim of his glass, then sat up straight. "I think that the day in the subway, going into Brooklyn, the day I met my wife—well, the woman who became my wife—was the worst day of my life."

"How can you say that?" I stopped eating, put down the fork.

Noah's jaw was working, as if the words wouldn't come. "Because everything came from that. We met, we dated, we got married. That was the day it started." Noah smiled, perhaps to lighten the mood. "You do what's expected, I guess." He chewed, seemed to be thinking about what he'd said. "We had our son. She never wanted any more kids. And after a few years, neither did I."

He shook his head. "We never discussed having more children." He sat back, his fingers on his chin smoothing the hairs of his beard. "Maybe I thought it would just happen. Another kid. Like the first time."

So many questions. I took a bite and chewed slowly, imitating Noah's way of answering. I wanted to ask if he was close to his son, or why he and his wife didn't discuss important things. But after my last attempt, I thought it best to let the conversation evolve naturally.

"You're my honey bun who lives so far away. Let's not talk about the past."

And like that, he simply shut down the conversation.

"Another helping? Pad Thai with chicken?" Noah, his hand on the serving spoon, looked at me.

"Not another morsel." I dragged myself away from all the deliciousness, and collapsed on the couch with my third glass of wine. Noah's place was a little like living in a motel room. He'd bought his furniture off the previous tenant, everything matching and crammed into a small square. Two beige couches, end tables with lamps, a rectangular coffee table. A treadmill and bicycle, side-by-side. Four towers of CDs, logged and labeled. "I'm old school anal," he'd said when I arrived and he caught me checking them out.

Noah stood up and went over to the window. "I want to talk to you."

There wasn't much of a view on the third floor, but it was exciting being in a New York City apartment. One of millions, one little gnat in a town of eight million gnats.

"What I'm searching for is hard to explain." He stood looking across at the next building, where lights in the stairwell popped on at night. "Well, I don't know if I'm crazy but it exists. I had it once." He stopped, didn't turn around.

"What?"

"Well...as long as...I'll tell you...but no questions after."

"Fine." He swiveled to look at me. The lights in the building across the way went out.

"All right. It was a couple of years ago. I met this woman at work. I wanted to go out with her but she wasn't interested. I thought about her all the time. At work. At home. I talked to her from time to time. I'd call her, ask her out again. She always said no. She was polite. Always." He paced now, not looking at me, walking between the couches and the CD towers. "Any time she looked at me, there I'd go again. I used any little excuse to talk to her. Keep in touch." He stopped in front of the window again. "Finally, she cut me off. Just like that. The last few times I called her at home, even at night, she never picked up. So I gave up. I was embarrassed."

His hand went to the top of his head, squeezed a handful of hair, and held it in his fist a moment before letting go. When he turned to look at me, I could see his throat moving. "I've never felt like that again." He stood and turned, peering out the window. I could no longer see his face. "I was in love with her."

"You were?" I tried to avoid the croaking toad sound, a dead giveaway to one's feelings. I didn't want Noah to see the surprise jagging around my brain. I wanted to remain neutral. Noah, who'd been married a long time, a sort of shy and quiet guy. Noah—*I was in love with her*—had an adolescent, boyish crush on a woman who wouldn't lift the phone to speak with him.

"It was like I was high." His face filled with a

furtive expression, stiff with the effort to organize his thoughts before he spoke. He walked over to the treadmill and leaned on the front bar. "I won't settle. I want that feeling. I want that again." He stopped and came over to sit beside me. "Do you think I'm crazy? No, you don't have to answer. I said I didn't want to discuss this." He scratched his head, making his hair stand up in the back. "Yes, answer me. Be honest." The stiff look remained on his face, his jaw wired.

His collection of CDs and DVDs, neatly stacked behind him, numbered in the hundreds. He'd told me he tended to hang on to old things. "Noah. That is a heart...heartrending story. Personally...well, you didn't know this woman." *He wants to recapture that feeling again.* "You never went out with her?"

"No, never." Noah bent and pulled out a CD, turned it over and opened it. He pushed it in the player and turned toward me, waiting, his expression naked, vulnerable.

If I didn't choose my words carefully, he might never confide anything important to me again. I swallowed and looked outside into the blackness, the lights. So much I wanted to say, and a little bit of me drew back wanting to ask: *How can you be in love with someone you don't even know?* When it came to love, I was a realist, not a dreamer. How could I compete with the mythical woman of Noah's creation?

"So I am crazy?"

"No," and I moved toward him, laid my head on his chest. "You're a romantic, that's for sure." Lame, so lame, and yet what else could I say, being unable to relate to his definition of love?

I went into the bathroom. Frank would never have

told me such a story, a story that made him vulnerable. I felt like crying, but I peed instead.

We lay on his bed. Noah wrapped his arm around me, stroking my hair. He told me about his colleagues at work, the guys he shared shifts with, who helped him out if he wanted time off. I turned my head slightly, watched his mouth move, his beard hair flecked red and gray. The bedroom was small—a box with a bed, a small closet, tiny bookshelf. I inched away from him, turned onto my stomach, and stared at the floor. He leaned over to knead my neck, squeeze my shoulders.

"What's that?" I asked, pointing with my nose at a blue box.

"You're not still thinking about what I told you, are you?" He stroked my neck, kissed me. "The story. My sad love story." His hands brushed my neck, shoulders, my arms.

I grunted. "What's that box?"

"Well, it's a rather large box of...a box of condoms, actually. On my side of the bed. Where they should be."

"Oh." I thought about that for a moment, slid onto my back and adjusted the pillow. "Aren't you being a little optimistic?"

He stopped touching me, and I glanced at him. He was doubled over, laughing, a little whinny and then a big, loud honk. I wanted to ask him if he was over her, the woman, but I was afraid of the answer.

What can I say? After he stopped laughing, he kissed me. Slow kisses, delicate as a hummingbird's breath, deliberate, until all my thinking dissolved. His hands knew how to touch, how to move, how to melt my skin until it hummed with pleasure and wanting more. It all happened quite naturally, and the undressing was as slow as the kisses, and he talked in a low voice the whole time. I tried not to think, to do nothing but feel. He smelled like grass and honey, fresh and natural.

Afterward, we lay entwined, whisper-talking. I stroked Noah's knobby elbow, remembering Luke, Island Boy, and how he'd babbled about falling in love, and I'd listened with my whole body stretched toward him like a weed seeking the sun. If he'd pursued me, would I be in bed with Luke instead of Noah? Were they interchangeable? I didn't know anything about Noah, not much about his family, what moved him, made him cry.

Except for his crush-woman.

I turned on my side, away from Noah's even, soft breathing, and blinked in the dark, thinking of Laurent. For all his high-class Frenchness, Monsieur Laurent had a peculiar wheezy whistle-snore.

A sliver of light outlined the short hallway and the path to the bathroom. Why did Noah tell me about his dream woman? A warning? He wouldn't settle for less than the infatuation he'd felt with *her*.

Wait a minute.

*I'm still infatuated.* He said it. He told me all the time, as if he loved the idea. So what? Could that mean he was worried? Yes, that was it. Noah was thinking ahead, worried that his infatuation with me might dissolve. Disappear. I shivered.

"Hey. You cold?" I felt his hand on my back, rubbing me warm. Then he babbled, all sorts of nice little nothings.

One I heard before I fell asleep. "I'm glad I found

you. I'm glad I wrote you, and I'm glad you're here."
So maybe that was three things, and they weren't
exactly nothings.

**** 

By the time I got back from the gym, Mark, the
Kid, had pried up all the old linoleum in the bathroom.
"I can help," I said, throwing down my gym bag. "Let
me do something."

Online, I'd read about tiling and planned to work
by his side apprentice-like. After all, it was a small job,
the guest bathroom. The former owner, a lady in her
nineties, had moved in with her daughter, leaving the
work unfinished. The box of tiles sat in the hallway and
Mark had carefully measured and counted. "You should
do the cutting because I'm afraid I'll mess up."

"No tile cutting, Miss," Mark told me,
straightening up. He brandished his pry bar scraper
thing to show he meant business. "Trust me, you'll get
in the way."

The plan was to tile the bathroom and refinish the
hardwood floors in the kitchen and living and dining
rooms. With no furniture, except for the fridge and
stove, Mark figured five days for the job.

"I'll get started on the tile. Tomorrow we start the
sanding, my cousin and me. Might throw on the first
coat of polyurethane 'cause it needs a day to dry."

"Early?"

"Early. After that, we'll have to come afternoons
'cause we both work." He stood staring down at his
hands as if he wanted to say more. I opened my mouth
to speak. "I'm reliable," he said, speaking quickly.
"What I did? I want to make it up to you. You're giving
me a second chance, and I want you to know I'm

219

reliable."

"Okay, then. That's…well, that's a good thing," and I wandered into my bedroom to take a call from Dana.

"This subbing isn't my cup of tea," she said without even a hello. "Two boys in class gave me the finger. The little shits. We're in an upper-class neighborhood. These kids should have better manners."

I sighed. "Their parents will hear. I'm calling at dinnertime."

"Good for you."

"I'll do my best snotty and finish up with a little disappointed and empathetic. I'm a parent too."

Dana made me laugh. "How's it going with Jerry?"

"We're at the hanging out phase." Pause. "We seem to be getting on." Her voice lowered two notches. "Quite well in some areas." Then back to normal volume. "Which reminds me. How's your Noah? Let's go out. The four of us. I want to meet him, and you can meet Jerry. It'll be fun."

"Not *my* Noah," I said. Noah was still making jokes about the future, the horizontal, and the vertical. "But I'll ask him. When I see him."

My phone whistled. Noah texting. *I'll call you.* Oh, so nice, calling me early at my request. Talking when Noah was on his night shift, which we did some nights, despite the rules against it. Our schedules were so different, and he was fresh and going strong at ten p.m. while I faded early, once or twice almost falling asleep in the middle of our conversation.

"What's his problem? Tell him I want to meet him," Dana said. "I want to look him over, pass judgment."

"I've got to pee."

"Take me with you."

"What?"

"Kidding, bye," she said, "Call me tomorrow," and hung up.

The phone rang.

"Hi. See, I called you early," Noah said. "As your loveliness requested."

"Thank you." A shiver of anticipation at the thought of having him here in my house, at my table, in my bed. "I still have to prep lessons and such."

"I'm pretty good with *such*. I'll help you."

"Thanks. Are you definitely coming here early?"

"Yes, bringing breakfast," he said. "Between eight fifteen and nine forty-five. Forty-six."

"That's a really big spread there."

"Later, I'll be doing some spreading."

"What?"

"Spreading out on you. Sorry I was rude. Wanna walk on the Wilbur Canal?"

"Yes, so bring a snowsuit and those ugly sneaks, please, and we should walk both days."

"Remember? About deciding together?"

"Deciding what? Oh, you mean dating others." A twinge of irritation hit me because he brought up the topic. "That again?"

"It's your decision," he said. "I can only ask."

"Are we having a fight?"

"I'm changing the subject, and no, we're not having a fight."

"So you feel better having me still dating a bit, 'cause it takes the pressure off you."

"There's another reason I told you about..." There

was a break of several seconds before he spoke. "This is getting me in deep shit." His low voice went lower and my toes prickled. "I'm still infatuated. So far off, it seems like weeks until I'll see you."

Later, after prepping lessons and a dinner of pea soup, with my e-reader and social media for company, I headed into the bathroom for a shower. Just as I was turning on the water, the front door slammed—my crew of two left for the day. I closed my eyes, let the steam penetrate deep into my pores before reaching for the loofah. Somewhere I'd read that anything sponge-like was riddled with bacteria, and here I was applying hundreds of germs directly to my skin.

Oh, who cared about microorganisms? I'd been seeing Noah for—lost count—over two months. And the three-month mark was a milestone, according to the courtship book that I was reading.

My thoughts snapped back to Noah's love story. For days, my mind had been replaying his words. *I won't settle. I want that feeling. I want that again.* That conversation in his apartment had shifted my perspective, made me question if Noah knew, truly knew what it took to sustain a real relationship. Even in the good old days of being in love with Laurent, there were times I sort of hated his guts. Like the trip to Rocamadour, planned for months, ruined because—

No, I wouldn't relive shitty moments in my marriage. I squirted lotion on my palm and smoothed it over my arms and legs, got into my favorite red plaid flannel pajamas, and settled in bed with a book on my e-reader. The book was about a marriage in jeopardy. The husband, wanting to fill a hole in his life, goes on an interview for a job as a Santa's elf. His wife, no longer infatuated, wants a divorce. He is bereft, but doesn't want to admit it to himself.

I knew how it ended because I'd read the book before.

The ending was satisfactory, the couple reunite.

How often does that occur in real life?

Chapter Nine
Tank theory...

Turned out Mark was right, the job took five days. I wandered through the condo, giddy with the prospect of finally having the place all to myself again.

First, clean up. Mark and his cousin, Stamford, mopped down the floors while I put fresh sheets on the bed, and started in on the dust covering every surface with the hand vac and a wet rag. The empty expanse looked fabulous, the oak floors gleaming in the afternoon sunlight pouring from the huge living room windows and the skylight. They slid the fridge and stove back into place, put the card table and two chairs in the study, and shuffled through the house, inspecting baseboards.

I poured two glasses of water and handed them to the guys. Two wiry young men eager to get going, Mark in a Yankees cap and Stamford in a Red Sox cap, black T-shirts, skinny work jeans, and heavy boots.

"Kitchen came out great," Stamford said, setting his glass on the counter. "Never seen a wood floor in a kitchen before. Works."

"Looks great thanks to you both," I said.

"Yeah, I gotta get goin'," said Stamford. "Pickin' up my girlfriend. We're goin' over to the Cadillac."

"Cadillac? Country dancing?" I said.

"Yup. We pretty much go every Wednesday."

"They're what you call dancing fools," said Mark. "You got a nice place." He drained his glass and looked at me as if he wanted to say more. "We're even."

It took me a few seconds to fill in the blank. I shook my head. "We're not even. You did a lot of work and I owe you. I've written out the check and that's it, no discussion."

"We got an agreement, him and me, and besides you don't owe me nothin'. You been fair. Even if you're *her*. You know."

"Know? What do I know?" He'd caught me. Not a surprise.

"So why'd you pretend? That day when you found me...at Burger King?"

"That day...when you hit my truck?" Stalling, I shifted my feet while Mark waited. Mark could wait as long as it took. He didn't interrupt, didn't get hyper. He had the kind of patience I admired. When I didn't quite get the knack of prying up the baseboards, he'd shown me how to place the crowbar, repeated the process twice. Not that I'd done much, but I liked his approach and his gentleness. Time for me to come clean.

"I honestly didn't know what to do. I didn't have a plan or anything, so I improvised. Did you tell Stamford?"

"Yeah, he knows everything. He knows I was a real asshole." He hung his head and stared at the floor, not looking at me as he spoke. "I would never do that again, not to anybody."

"Good." What else could I say? I hoped he meant it.

We were quiet for a few beats.

"That was pretty cool," said Mark finally, a little

smile playing at the corner of his mouth. "What you said about taking a sample of the paint."

"Is that what I said? Oh, I guess—"

"Those shows? I watch them too. Those police and crime scene investigation shows." Mark gestured with his hand, as animated as he ever got. "Your act? I bought it."

"Well." I cleared my throat. There was a part of me that still didn't believe I'd carried off the whole ruse. "Mostly for me it's reading. You know, police procedurals...." I stopped and looked at him. "I'm sorry I lied to you."

"You did what you had to do at the time." He swayed a little and cracked his knuckles. "I was wrong. What I did. I never apologized to you before now. So I apologize."

"Thank you." I held out my hand. "Let's shake on it." He hesitated, stuck out his arm and we shook.

"Hey, could I borrow one of those police detective books? I'll be sure to return it."

It took me a minute to locate the right book in one of the boxes piled in the guest room. When I came into the hall, they were standing at the door.

"Here, try *this*." I tapped Mark's chest with the book. "Enjoy."

"Thanks, Miss."

"You guys do good work. I can pass your name along to my friends. If you want me to."

"Okay," he said. His cousin nodded. Men of few words. I handed Mark an envelope, but he held up his hands and headed for the door. "You don't owe me nothing. I told you."

"Please take it. It's a fair deal."

His cousin reached over Mark's shoulder for the envelope as my cell rang from somewhere in the house.

"Thank you kindly," Stamford said as they headed down the path toward an old Mustang. I closed the door and made a dash to locate my phone, grabbed it from the bathroom vanity, and put the phone on speaker.

"Hello?" said a male voice I didn't recognize.

"Hello."

"Sunny. It's Luke. Do you remember me?"

Luke. My stomach jolted. Too late. He had me. "I remember you."

"Do you have a minute to talk? Please?"

How I longed to press the button that would shut Luke off, the way he'd shut me off. Put me on Ignore. But the polite gene from my parents prevented that. And his voice stirred a thing in my gut and...well, I was curious. Why call now? Was he going for another ego boost?

"Go ahead." I heard him swallow and wondered if he was drinking for a little courage.

"The reason I didn't contact you again was because I was a mess." He stopped, as if he expected me to interrupt. I didn't. "It wasn't fair to you, and I realized if I talked about her on a date with you, well, it was all wrong.

"Are you making amends?" I didn't like the snotty tone my voice took on, a superior tone I'd recognized in Laurent, particularly toward the end.

"I guess you could say that." Pause. "I'm apologizing. This is an apology."

"Oh." It struck me that this wasn't easy for him. Calling.

"We had such a great time together." Pause, a

pause that stretched. "I think...I know we had a connection. I'd like to see you again."

"Oh." I didn't know what to say.

"Could we start over? There, I said it. I'd like to start over with you. A clean start. Please," and his voice dropped off to almost a whisper. "At least think about it."

I wanted to tell him I was dating someone. A person of interest. And in those few seconds I wondered how long we'd last, Noah and I. And why the sudden doubt when that very afternoon I'd been thinking Noah thoughts. Like how I'd squeeze in painting time for the pantry cabinets later, and how he'd put the squeeze on me when he walked in the door.

"Sunny?" said Luke.

"Yes?"

"Will you? Think about it? I can tell you more, but I'd rather see you. Tell you in person. I know I don't seem dependable, but that was back then, and I'm trying hard to be a better person."

"I'll think about it. Yes." *Is he serious about that better person thing, or is it psychobabble? And does it matter anyway? Because you're seeing someone. You should mention that now. Now is the time. Tell him now.*

"Thank you," he said. "I'll let you go. We'll talk again?"

"Yes. Later. We can talk later."

When later would materialize, I didn't know, and I didn't like Luke intruding on my life at this juncture. *At this juncture* was a joke Laurent and I shared in the old, happy days. "A glass of wine at this juncture?" Laurent would say before pouring, when we were out with friends. It never failed to make me giggle.

Another thing? I didn't like the way my stomach lurched at the sound of Luke's voice.

Two days until Noah, who was still infatuated, and maybe I was infatuated, too, because fifty-year-olds can infatuate, can't we?

****

Friday nights the local bar is usually jamming, but we were lucky and got seats upstairs where there's a view of the whole place, the ever-shifting crowd of townies and Yalies.

"Mashed potatoes as a topping?" Noah asked, scanning the menu. "Are they serious?"

"A classic, here anyway. I've never tried it."

The waiter appeared and we ordered two Toasted Blondes and clinked glasses before taking a good glug.

"You want the mashed?" Noah asked. "On your pizza?"

"Absolutely not, and you're on your own if you order it."

"You'd better do the ordering."

"Thin crust pie with onion, sun-dried tomatoes, eggplant, and sausage," I told the waiter. "And the salad. It's the best. Would you sprinkle on a few extra caramelized walnuts, please?"

"You got it, honey," said the waiter, and I think he winked.

We ate and drank, talking about my friends in Paris, Noah's brother, who was separated and taking dance lessons, and my first day at school. We shared a third beer. Before leaving we stopped in the back room, but the band was dissonant and loud. We didn't stay more than a minute.

Back at my place, I closed the door and we looked at each other. He took my hand and led me into the bedroom, where he eased me onto the bed gently, kissed my neck and pushed my sweater off my shoulders, one shoulder at a time, running his tongue over my skin. "You smell so good," he said, and kissed me for a long time before unbuttoning my cardigan.

Afterward we spooned, his arms wrapped around me. I closed my eyes, drunk on the wine, the caramel-drizzled walnuts, but mostly drunk on Noah in my bed. His voice, so soft, lulled me. "I want to tell you about my tank theory."

"Tell me all about your tank theory." I turned and kissed his bearded chin.

"Here goes. If you're in love with someone, it won't matter if they get squashed by a tank. Maimed. Or disfigured." His hands smoothed my hair. "If two people are—"

My eyes popped open. *Disfigured?* What was he talking about? His voice no longer lulled.

He squeezed me against his chest. "You love them anyway. Even if you no longer have sex with her. Or him. That's my tank theory of love."

His lips on my neck, his hands massaging my back, and I was thinking, thinking way too hard. So that's why he was so bent on doing the vertical. He worried infatuation wasn't enough. *Don't trust me.* An odd thing for a man to say. He was taking the temperature of the relationship, our relationship, because he was looking for what he'd had with *that* woman, the one he told me about, the *I won't settle, I want that feeling* woman.

A few questions about his tank theory rolled

around, but when I opened my mouth, "Next time you come, I'll have a real table and chairs," came out instead. "Unless I need to special order. Special orders take a long time."

"My theories are crazy theories, I know. I'll put on some music. Would you like that?"

"Sure."

Noah was leaving tomorrow morning. He'd be working two weekends in a row, which meant two weeks without Noah. Two weeks would be like two months.

Two months without his touch. I shivered and he squeezed me tight.

****

It had been a slow train into New York, and two weeks without Noah, a long time. His one-bedroom apartment was small, cramped, and the city was all around us, the bus fumes, the fish shop smells two doors down, the souvlaki aromas making my mouth water when we entered his building. That feeling again, the feeling I was just another bump in a city with millions of bumps all living in little boxes.

"I'm a bump," I told Noah, and looked across to the building where a light came on…where I could see bumps going up the stairs. I wanted to go out exploring. Anywhere. "I'm here, let's go somewhere. Take a walk. Look at New York people."

Noah didn't seem to hear me. He shrugged, corkscrewed open a bottle of wine, set it on the table, and sat down. He slouched in his chair, not looking at me, the bottle in front of him.

"Don't you ever get afraid that it'll happen again, that you'll make the same mistake?" He picked up the wine bottle, held it over the glasses, poured half a glass, slowly, as if considering every move before making it. "Like with your ex-husband."

"What mistake?" Where was this going?

"Marrying someone like that. You know." He took a sip of his wine and offered me his glass. I shook my head. "When you know you're not in love, and you still don't get out of it."

How to respond to that?

"But look at the two of us...and them," and he pulled a pad out of the drawer and began to draw rectangles. "Look. I'm doing a flow chart to show you." He drew and I got up and looked over his shoulder. Was it more of the tank theory or more temperature taking? He pointed to a drawing of the four of us, the two ex-couples. "We'll end up like we did before. That's what I'm afraid of." He paused and turned around, grabbed my hand. "I never want to make that mistake again." His voice had a hollow sound.

He let go of my hand and I sat down again at the table. He had a bug up his ass. Yes, the temperature of the relationship thing again. Definitely.

"I've been thinking over the past few weeks," he said. "I haven't wanted to call you as much. I come home and I don't want to message you. That's not good."

Something inside my chest skidded. I had noticed, but didn't think much of it. He was giving me space. It was just a space thing, and he knew I was busy with my new job. "It's not good?" I asked. Where in hell was this going? A prickle crawled up my arm to my shoulder.

"No, I'm..."

"Maybe you have other things in your life that you need to do or think about." I sounded completely logical to myself. "That seems normal to me." But the prickle sat there. It waited.

"But I want to feel it. I want to have that feeling of needing to call you," he said.

That sat there too, the idea that he searched for a particular feeling, like a computer file-searching. "What are you getting at?" I said. "This isn't fantasyland. This is real life. We're still getting to know each other." There was more. I knew there was more and he couldn't say it.

"I was waiting for it to happen, and it didn't happen." He stopped and I just sat looking at him, didn't want to make it easy, *not easy, let him say it, don't fill in the blanks*. The prickle traveled across my shoulder to my backbone and began crawling down, one vertebra at a time. I could feel the progress, as if it had claws, tiny claws that scratched the skin.

"I was waiting to fall in love."

The prickle slid all the way down my back.

*Waiting. To fall. In love.*

"I kept thinking it would happen. I've been thinking about this for a while now."

The claws dug in and hung on. *He is infatuated. He said so. Hadn't he said it just a few weeks ago?*

"Yes, I'm afraid we'll end up like before. You and Laurent, me and Dee. We'll just get used to one another. We'll drift along for years, and we won't be able to stop it.

"No, I don't think that's true." I collapsed into the chair, as if my bones couldn't hold me straight.

"It was when I was watching that old movie,

*Shirley Valentine,* at your house. Remember, she stays. She stays in Greece and you think it's because of him, the guy. But it's not the guy. It's the place. They weren't in love and they were having a good time." He stopped. He'd never before talked this much. "I thought 'I don't have to feel guilty.'"

A sour smell like vomit in the air, in spite of the cinnamon potpourri he simmered on the stove. "How can you compare us to that? She—in the movie—she had a vacation *fling.*"

"I'm not comparing us exactly, of course not." He looked away. "But that's when I thought of it. I've been thinking about it for weeks. It came together." Now he walked around the room, over to the treadmill. He stopped, turned toward me. "Except..." he ran his hand through his beard. "When we are making love. I feel it then. I feel it. I feel love. I feel it every time."

It was like a thwack to my head from a giant finger on high. The reluctance to talk, to make an effort, subtle, very subtle. As if he'd turned off, ever so slightly, never mind the infatuation crap. The infatuation was the sex talking, what he'd been worried about, always analyzing.

"Well, then you've got to date other women," I said. Blurted it out. This was the end, the end of us, here in his little space. He could date one person at a time. *That leaves me out.*

"You must feel the same way. Don't you? I'm sure you aren't in love with me either," he said, a hand on my shoulder. "Are you all right?"

"I'm okay." I turned away. "I'm fine." Besides, why would I want to continue seeing him? He was infatuated when we were horizontal, but it wasn't enough. *I* wasn't enough for Noah.

"Let's leave it. Let's watch a movie and sleep on it, and we'll talk about it tomorrow."

He put on *No Man of Her Own*, with Clark Gable and Carole Lombard, the one movie they were in together, and we sat on the couch, side-by-side, like a real couple. My chest tightened. He reached for my hand, held it, made my skin pringle, even though I didn't want it to. This fake couple thing? It wasn't working.

No, I wasn't in love with him. Love took time, and anyway, love wasn't a falling thing—it was more like a slow and steady increase in warm feelings until…. We were so different. I imagined never seeing him again, and my eyes filled. I wriggled away and escaped into the bathroom, blew my nose, and ran cold water on my face. I came out and stood by the couch with my overnight bag on my shoulder.

"You're going?" he whispered.

"It's better this way," I said. "I need to go." I wanted it to be over, wanted to be home in my own bed.

Outside, he kissed me goodbye, a slow kiss, a kiss that reminded me of the first time, the first kiss, long ago, in his car. He stood watching as I got in, started the motor, got the GPS up on my phone. As if memorizing this moment.

"I'll call you," he said.

He would call. I backed out of the driveway while he waited, and waved me off.

Well, this certainly wasn't the fun part, was it?

****

Monday, Tuesday and Wednesday dragged by like a heavy load. During the day, the eighty-six students who came with my job kept me challenged. Afternoons, after prepping at school, I attached myself to the bed, my special spot to mope and watch TV. And wait.

Thursday evening. I sat in my new ergonomic rolling chair at the crummy card table, holding my breath with the thrill of it. Today I would write him. Three whole stinkin' days I'd delayed, and the self-imposed wait to email Noah had exhausted my psyche. We'd never gone three days with no communication, not since we'd met.

Except we weren't a couple, were we? That thought put a little damper on my thrill.

Well...I would write him. I would write Noah, but I wouldn't send the email. I'd wait for him to contact me. *I'll call you.* A light tone in an email takes time, and my three-liner took an hour. I had to be careful, afraid he'd read between the lines and sense my funk. And my funk would morph into a tangible entity, travel through the ethernet and splatter onto his computer.

Better to err in the direction of doing oh, so well without him.

I hummed and clicked on YouTube, entered a few pertinent keywords, clicked on play. Patience and Prudence's original ditty about getting along without the man in question filled the room, all five rooms, tinkling with forced cheeriness and a chorus of sisterly humming.

After Patience and Prudence finished their song, I clicked send. I'll admit it.

*Were we ever a couple?* That thought struck me right after I sent the email.

Evenings were the worst, filled as they were with swinging monkey thoughts of Noah, a dissection of every recent conversation, all the old funny emails.

Days were so much better. *Thank God for my job.*

Friday afternoon, Dana called. She'd caught me lying on the bed watching *An Affair to Remember*, every woman's favorite tear-jerker. Cary Grant looking for the painting in the last scene? I was prepared to bawl, looked forward to a splendid cry. I paused the movie.

"How was your dirty weekend?" She pronounced *dirty* so it sounded positively filthy with innuendo.

"We're not seeing each other anymore." I held the phone in a death grip, waiting for a comment. It was the fifth straight day for the red plaid pajama bottoms and stained T-shirt, probably mustard or mayonnaise. Maybe both. My new after school home-clothes uniform. Also the fifth straight day I'd skipped the gym. Plus my hair had an all-over grease ball look that I found comforting on the weekend, especially if I pushed it behind my ears. I wasn't going anywhere.

"What? That's sudden. I mean there wasn't any inkling of it?"

"Inkling? Not exactly." I swallowed, determined not to cry. The swallowing helped hold everything in. I swallowed again. "Well, maybe." Not that I wanted to tell Dana.

"It's just that from what you said—" She hesitated, probably didn't know what to say. "It seemed to be going well."

"It was going well, and no way did I see it coming. We were both happy. We had fun together." I bit my bottom lip to keep from bawling. There was no way I was telling her about waking up in the middle of the night, waking up happy and then remembering there was no Noah, not anymore. *He threw us away, just like that. He threw us away.* No, she didn't need to know.

"Am I thick?" I said. "Unperceptive? I thought I was a perceptive person."

"You don't have to talk about it." Her voice softened. The gentle approach.

"He made flow charts." I gulped. "To compare us. Laurent and me. Noah and his ex. To show things. I don't know what the hell he was showing." I sniffed. I wouldn't tell her the only time I didn't think about Noah was while I was teaching.

"Flow charts?"

"He said he's not in love. He was waiting. He was waiting for it to happen and it didn't happen." I stopped. "*It.* That's what he said."

"Interesting." Whispering. She had covered the phone. Then she was back. "He actually said he was waiting for *it* to *happen*?"

"Yeah. So I told him he had to date other people. Sort of blurted it out." Dana didn't interrupt, so I explained how he couldn't date more than one person at a time. "He called it dishonest."

I filled her in on the love of Noah's life, the woman he pined after. "*Perfecta* Woman," I pronounced it with an Italian slant.

"Are you all right?" Her voice dropped to a soft murmur. "You seemed to like this guy."

"Look, I'm fine. I'll be fine. He said he'd call. He won't. I know he won't. It hurts." I squeezed shut my eyes. Good thing she wasn't in the room to witness me crumple like a wet newspaper.

"It happens to us all." Her voice was soothing; this was how she spoke to her daughter. "It means you can feel."

"How could I get so attached after such a short time? Three months." I sniffled, grabbed a tissue. "Hold on, just a sec." I blew my nose, pictured Noah bending over to kiss my neck. Noah rubbing my shoulders, telling me I looked sexy. "I'm ridiculous."

"Question," Dana said.

"Yeah, what?" I picked up the box of tissues and turned it over. Double-ply. What was a ply?

"Here goes. Did you think he was The One? I mean, you were meeting others, you made no bones about it, did you?"

"Bones. No. But, I stopped dating other guys. And I didn't know if he was The One." Where had *The One* concept come from? Frank had said he didn't know if I was The One. "Maybe it was on my mind. A bit. The possibility that we could be important to one another." I remembered an article written by a man who claimed being the dumper could be worse than being the dumpee. I wiped my nose and reached for another tissue. After dumping his girlfriend, he realized he'd made a terrible mistake, and it was too late to get her back.

"Let's get real here," I told Dana. "He said he wasn't in love. When a guy tells you that, it's all over."

"That must have been excruciating for him, a man who's got such a romantic idea of love," Dana said.

"So now you're feeling sorry for him? Because he's on a quest for love, wants to find *looove*." I drew out the word, mocking Noah and the whole concept. *Tell her. Tell her.* "I wrote him."

"Email?"

"Yes. He hasn't written back." I groaned and

mopped my nose.

"He's cutting you off," Dana said. "Sounds like that's his coping mechanism."

"I thought he was a friend."

"Of course."

"That's why it hurts," I said. "Does that sound stupid?"

"Not at all. But I think men have a problem with that. The friend thing. We're open to different kinds of relationships. We handle change better—"

"I'm not handling anything. I'm a stupid mess."

"It's not easy. Lovers as friends." Dana hesitated. "Look. The idea of the perfect love, mooning, thinking of someone all the time. The high. It sounds…adolescent. Unhealthy."

"Yeah, unhealthy." I felt a mass rising from my gut. All this talk about Noah was doing a number on my inner workings.

"Well, you're busy with school and lots of other things, so…."

Dana, in her nice way, was letting me know she'd had enough of grinding on about Noah.

"Yeah, thanks for letting me vent. Plus, I have a ton of work to do." I didn't, but Dana didn't need to know.

The last thing I wanted was Dana feeling sorry for me.

\*\*\*\*

All that week and the next, I left school and headed for the parking lot, imagining *him* standing beside the truck, waiting to tell me he'd made a mistake.

Which wasn't impossible. He had visited me there, once. A Friday after school. The secretary had paged me. I'd skipped down to the main office thinking *Noah, Noah, here in my school.* He'd see the *Le Petit Prince* bulletin boards, the kids' photos, projects, and— everything.

Back in the classroom with him, I'd locked the door. We kissed, pressed against the wall with the lights out, his hand exploring beneath my sweater, my mind racing with the thrill of our little adventure.

Well, today, he was not waiting in the parking lot.

I drove home, hands gripping the steering wheel as if I needed to force the car to the center of the lane. Maybe he'd be waiting on the sidewalk in front of my place, head down, hands in pockets, shivering from the wind that whips across the park. Or he'd be idling in front of the condo complex, motor running, head bent over his reading as I'd first seen him. Our first meet.

Uh, nope.

At home, I pulled off my work clothes, threw them on the chair in the corner, and put on home clothes. Burrowed into the bed, picked up *A Lovely Courtship,* and reread the chapter on the switcheroo. Surely, I must follow the advice of the psychologist, a relationship expert who said the woman must allow the man to back off. She mustn't put pressure on him, must get on with her life. The man *may* return.

I wanted to email this wise woman. I'd have called her, but figured her number was unlisted. What would I say? *Come to my house. Hold my hand. It's the three-month mark. We're pretty much on schedule, like you warned me.*

My fingers gripped the pages as the words became little wriggling tadpoles, diving and jumping.

End of the second week. During lunch, between

tuna bites, I caught myself ruminating. At night I would lie in bed—and this was the worst. I craved him, craved his touch. Imagined his fingers along my arm, his mouth on my neck. It was withdrawal.

Week three. My stash of relationship books were spread out on the bed. Along with a bag of cheese pretzels, a bag of mustard pretzels, a sack of kettle chips, and several slices of cheddar for some much-needed protein. Plus a diet cola.

Propped in the middle of this bounty, I made calls, eager to revisit particular conversations, or pluck special meanings from the odd intimate moment. I called Dana.

"I was thinking about his tank theory and his perfect woman theory. I should have known, but—"

"What?" Hesitation. "I'm disappointed. I thought you were calling about getting facials together."

"Facials?"

"He's neurotic but he was honest with you. Give him that. Look. He's on a quest."

"You mean a quest for the perfect woman?"

"Not the perfect woman so much as a quest for...you said it yourself. A quest for those feelings. That high." Dana's voice turned operatic, sing-songing up and down. "When you can't eat, and you think all the time about the other person."

My belly was starting to grow a pouch. After a week with a few bags of chips, Chinese take-out, and without exercising, I had gained discernible poundage, all in the middle.

"Look, he is not the man for you. Admit it and move forward. You've got to keep busy. Are you busy?"

"Very busy. Being miserable. *J'ai le mal du siècle.*" Those few words invoked a whole cultural and literary *époque* based on the suffering soul in utter despair.

"Don't you throw that French shit at me. One more day to wallow is all you get. I'm calling you after school, and we're going running."

"Running?" I sniffed. "Are you crazy?"

"Dead serious. I don't care if you limp alongside me, so snap out of it. You don't have cancer."

"That's harsh."

"Had to say it. I'm your friend. You need harsh. You need blunt."

"You met Jerry on the first date," I said, as if laying blame. "The *first* date." Yeah, I was jealous.

"What of it? Who knows if it'll work out? Would you actually feel better if Jerry dumped me?"

"Yes. Yes, I would." We both burst out laughing.

"Look, I've got to go prepare for a job interview tomorrow."

"Break a leg. I mean that sincerely."

As soon as Dana disconnected, I speed-dialed Isabel. *Be home, be home, be home.* She picked up on the second ring.

"Bad withdrawal," I said into the phone. "Can't sleep." Gripping the book, my finger on the same old chapter, the switcheroo chapter, prepared to list my symptoms, prepared for sympathy from my best friend. "Remember when I told you about the tank theory?"

"Enough already," she yelled, making me jump, sending the book tumbling off the bed. "Where's my hello? Never mind. So the man dumped you. We've all been there. Get up and get out. You've just gotten divorced, for crap sake. Go out and start dating again. Get your mind off him."

A growing pile of dirty clothes that hadn't made it to the hamper stared at me from the corner. I was alienating my friends. Telling Dana I'd be happy if Jerry dumped her? Not so funny, even if we'd laughed. What was wrong with me?

"There's something you don't realize," Isabel said. "You are whining about a man who stood up for himself. You have to admire his backbone. He could have gone on seeing you, backing off little by little. What most men do. This one didn't. Give him some credit. And the truth, from what I can tell, is you weren't all that sure about him either, with all that tank and horizontal and vertical shit."

She blew a sigh into the phone so hard I swear it smacked me on the cheek. "You're mistaking lust for intimacy. Which is understandable since you've been in an emotional desert for so long." I opened my mouth to speak, but she went on. "Get real about your Mr. Noah. Isn't it ironic that you took no time at all getting rid of your dick of a husband? Once he announced he wanted a separation, you were outta there. Granted he did the whole backing off thing for what? Two years? I know because I still have all those emails with you pouring out your heart to me when he put you on 'ignore'."

"No, it can't be two—"

"Two years. Two. But let me finish while I'm on a therapeutic roll. It's seductive to be treated well by a man. Realize what it is to be cherished. You're learning to have the right kind of expectations." Her voice dropped off. "It took me a while too. You know my history."

Her words slammed me as I lay there, but instead of making me crawl into myself, it was…liberating. She was right. She was right about everything.

"Yeah." That was all I could say.

"Sorry I'm being such a bitch, but I had to get through to you. You know I love you."

"I do," I managed to say. Isabel couldn't see, thank God, as my eyes filled, my nose ran.

"Look, I gotta go. My friend Mickey is in town from Sarasota for a few days, and we're all going to the movies. Come with us?"

"Another time. I'll think about what you said. I promise."

"Good."

After we hung up, I put down the book. Maybe I needed someone to talk to, a professional someone. I blew my nose, ran hot water over a washcloth and applied it to my face. After that, I went on Facebook. I hadn't logged in for weeks, and there'd be flack from Paris. Sure enough, eleven messages from friends—the secretary at the Institute, several of the teachers, and a stack of notifications.

I sent Dulcie and Natalie a short message and sat staring at the desktop, a photo of my old neighborhood taken from our living room window with Luxembourg Gardens in the distance.

Why did I feel this way about him? I couldn't analyze it. All I knew is we'd laughed a lot. And laughing was what I ached for now like a missing limb.

Well, maybe more than that.

*Crap, doo doo, and shit.*

My phone rang, and I glanced at the caller ID. Luke. A part of me wanted to answer, shoot the breeze with Luke, and see if my stomach lurched when I heard his voice. That part of me liked *I'm trying hard to be a better person*. I wanted to accept his apology. The other part shouted *No, it's not the right time*. That's the part that won.

Four rings, five, six, and on seven, voicemail kicked in.

Chapter Ten
Breaking up…

True to her word, Dana dragged me out after
school for a run at Edgerton Park. Or should I say a trot
because I couldn't do more than shuffle as Dana ran
ahead and circled back, urging me not to give up. The
sky was cloudless with a breeze, a classic beautiful day,
the sign of warmer weather coming. Irritating, such
perfection.

"Isn't this better than watching Netflix? Such a
gorgeous day. You'd be inside and—what is it you
were bingeing on? Don't deny it. I caught you more
than once."

"Orange is the New Black," I puffed out,
struggling to talk and trot at the same time. My legs felt
like sticks that could crack any second, and I didn't like
it, hated that in a few short weeks I'd lost my—
whatever it was I'd lost, sitting on the bed, miserable.
"Disturbia," I breathed out and slowed to a walk. "True
dates-from-hell stories. A series." Saying the name out
loud to Dana gave me a fit of the giggles.

"Wow, you're in a weird mood."

I swiped at my eyes, tearing up from the
combination of a slight wind and hysteria. "Reruns are
my pals," I said, as if this were the cleverest thing I'd
uttered in a long while. "That's not the worst." Walking
faster now, putting on some speed.

"Don't tell me you stalked him," Dana said, slowing to a walk and matching my pace.

"How did you know?"

"Oh, I've been there."

"Yeah, I searched for him on the dating site, looked for his profile. I couldn't find it. And then I realized he never posted a profile. He emailed me incognito."

"You didn't write him again, did you?"

"No. I'm not that dumb."

"Come on, we've got another twenty minutes. That'll be an hour. Anyone can do an hour on a flattish surface on a clear afternoon with sunshine and the smell of clean air."

Dana's pep talk worked and I broke into a run, then settled for a trot. Using my muscles felt great and so did hanging out with my friend. We breathed in that special outdoor scent of plants coming alive, stretching.

"So maybe he did me a favor, dumping me."

"Give it a few more weeks, and maybe you'll mean that sincerely."

We headed down Whitney to my house, where Dana had left her car. She glided up the porch steps behind me, and into the kitchen where I poured water for both of us. My laptop sat on the kitchen table.

"Hey, let me take a look, see who's online these days, maybe give you a suggestion. You're on *letsclick*?"

"Yeah. I dredged up the old profile and photo. Wrote a couple guys. The usual boring, 'Hi, liked your profile, check mine out and see if we're a match' generic thing. I'm faking it, you know, the first step to making it."

Dana dragged a chair to the table and sat. "Show

me."

We spent the next half hour trolling, making fun of a couple of guys with lame profiles and selfies that made their features look as if they were buffeted by wind machines.

"Here's one," and she clicked on a dark-haired guy whose profile photo looked like a professional job. "Not bad looking, nice smile. Look, the first sentence. He says he's a wordsmith," Dana said, elbowing my breast. "Your type."

"Ouch. I'm not in the mood."

"Get in the mood. Actually there are a few guys on here you should go for." I raised my elbow in self-protection, and she elbowed me again, this time hitting my funny bone.

"Stop," I yelled. "You want to write them so badly, go ahead," and we traded chairs.

She crouched over the keyboard, typing. "Don't look until I'm done."

When she finished, she tilted the laptop toward me and read out loud. "You're a smart guy with a cute smile. Wanna meet for coffee?"

I got up to refill our water glasses. "Meeting someone for coffee just like that? We haven't even—"

Dana hit send. At least that was what it looked like from the opposite end of the kitchen, where I was pouring water. It splattered on the counter. "Did you send that? I can't believe you did that," I screeched. "I'm not in the mood…" *Not in the mood to have fun?* I was becoming a killjoy, one of my father's words when I was in college and came for visits. My father joked about my mother being the killjoy who wouldn't go out and have a hot fudge sundae *instead* of dinner. Not even once or twice a year.

"I'm not sorry." Dana looked at me. "Let's do a couple more since we're here and online and all that." She grinned, an oversize, exaggerated grin designed to lighten my mood, and it worked. Twenty minutes later we'd contacted three more guys, and then it was time for Dana to go.

"It's after eight. I'm starving." She hugged me hard at the door, and I managed a feeble goodbye smile.

Dinner was half a small can of Bush's baked beans, the kind with brown sugar, because opening a can took no effort. I was finishing up the last bite when my phone whistled. Dana texting.

*—Same time tomorrow. No excuses.—*

I groaned and squinted at the screen. Strange. There was a voicemail I'd never listened to. I pressed speaker and Luke's voice filled the room. "Hi Sunny, Luke here. I'd like to take you to dinner. I've got a great place in mind, and I know you'll love it. You pick the night, but the weekend would be the most relaxing, if that works for you. Looking forward to seeing you."

Hard to believe a few months ago I'd crushed on Luke. His voice didn't sound swoon-worthy, but it sure sounded eager. Like he was interested. And maybe *interested* was what I needed at the moment, and it sure beat writing emails to guys I had little interest in meeting. A little ego boost would be just the thing to lift me out of my...mood.

One ring and he picked up.

"Sunny, hi there. So glad you called, you must be busy, but you got my message?"

"Yeah." My insides squeezed. This was a mistake. The second he greeted me, I knew there would be no mustering of false cheer on my part. Fakery was beyond my ability. With my friends I could be real, with Luke not so much. The gray descended, familiar and unwanted.

"So, I know this great spot on the water—"

"It's not a good time for me, Luke. No offense. I shouldn't have called. I'm not at my best..."

"Oh." There was a moment of silence as we both searched for meaning in *I'm not at my best*. Clearly, I'd surprised him and myself. Why had I called? Why had I blurted out this personal stuff? I barely knew the man.

"Well I'm sorry, Sunny. I didn't—"

"Not your fault. I need some time," and I talked over him because I had to get this straight, the not meeting part. "I broke up with someone," *someone broke up with me*, "and I need some time before..." and my voice trailed off because I had no idea what I needed time for, other than sitting on my bed, mooning over Noah.

Luke cleared his throat. "Of course, you'll need time. Of course. If anyone knows what needing time is like, it's me." There was a crack in his voice, a real break. "I'm here. If you want to talk."

"Thanks. I mean thank you for that." Why would I talk to Luke? I wasn't in a talking mood. I was more in the mood for an old movie or crappy reruns, a few tablespoons of Edy's Double Fudge Brownie, but I'd purged the freezer. Me and my bed and Netflix, thank you very much.

"After I decided not to see...see her again, I gained nine pounds in one month." Luke's voice came out of the phone raspy and low. "My daughter was on my case big time to snap out of my lethargy, as she put it."

There was a longish silence.

"Got addicted to Twinkies and Ding Dongs, of all things. Crazy, right? I don't know what got into me. After work, I'd swing by the grocery store and grab a package, eat them for dinner, finally buy them in bulk. I sat around binge-watching Netflix. My daughter started calling me tubby." He laughed, his voice cracking, and we had a few more seconds of silence until he broke it. "I just want you to know you're not alone."

"How did you get past that? The sitting and watching?"

He told me how he forced himself to go back to the gym, take little walks, and even though he was bad company, he spent more time with his parents. "Had them over three or four times a week. My mother was all for it—said I should break up more often and she'd never cook again. Barbecued chicken with the works, corn on the cob and sweet potatoes, my mom's favorites. Lasagna. Or burgers and dogs. Anything to keep busy at night.

"The truth is I got professional help." A few beats. "Yeah, I'm saying I went to a shrink. To get over myself. It took a few months, but it was worth it, gave me a better understanding of the toxic dynamic between us. Breaking up and then she'd appear at my door."

By the time we stopped talking—he stopped talking—it was eleven. We'd been on the phone for three hours, and my battery was running low. Luke had talked me out of my funk, at least for the moment. And Noah hadn't entered my mind. Not once.

After hanging up, I stuck the leftover beans in the fridge, and retired to my bedroom. Retiring to my bedroom had become my favorite activity these days. I stared at the blank television. For once, the urge to veg out on Netflix held little appeal. I thought about the one-sided Luke conversation, his Twinkie confession. His depression over the break-up. I'd welcomed Luke's monologue, not wanting to spill much of anything about my life.

What did Luke want? Was he interested? Did two or three hours on the phone translate to—wait, he'd already asked me to dinner. Picked out a great place on the water, too.

I'd turned down his invitation.

What was wrong with me? And could I get over it?

\*\*\*\*

My next class rolled in, all cool talking and posing, especially the four seniors, and I took a minute to check the dating app on my phone. Not that anyone noticed, since teachers are invisible during the few social moments before class starts.

There was a message from Billy, the guy Dana had contacted during our flurry of profile writing, at least I thought that was the guy.

—*Lumiere or is it Soleil (Sunny)...Wow, that spells...Well, you are the French Lady teacher...it's French, mon amigo. Since you asked if I want to meet for coffee...yes, please! How about Starbucks? I would be honored. Are you free after school? Around 3:30 or 4:00 pm. My treat—*

Good, a diversion.

—*LOL 4PM works, please confirm—*

Clicked my phone off, tucked it in the top drawer.

Time to get busy, remind the class we spoke French, no English, and start the timer, the signal to get out their homework. It took a few minutes for understanding to blossom, but they got it when I pointed to the schedule on the bulletin board. Soon there was a rustling as everyone yanked papers out of their folders.

"Right on, Ms. Chanel," said Bernie, a heavyset clodhopper on his usual post-lunch high. He turned his head, aiming the next comment at his girlfriend, who sat three rows away. "See, Michelle, isn't this great? We speak French in French class."

Bernie's hilarity was fueled by a double dose of French fries and a juice chaser. I'd made a point, while on lunch duty, of sauntering by his table, drawn by the volume, and caught Bernie shoveling fistfuls of fries in his mouth.

"Disgusting, isn't he?" Michelle said at the time.

"*Je parle français,*" sang Harold from the last row, where I'd isolated him from the others. "French, I speak French," he rapped, jogging his neck and shoulders from side to side.

Which is why the behavior chart came in handy. I scratched a checkmark next to the two boys' names. A warning.

"*Madame, Madame,* excuse *moi,*" said Bernie.

I ignored him and chose other students to write answers to the first five questions on the board.

"Moi, choose moi," yelled Amber, the fourth member of the senior posse. "*S'il* you please," a French-English combo that was praiseworthy. Except for the yelling out part. I glanced around at the faces staring back, gave my students mental credit for enthusiasm and good sportsmanship.

While inside my head, as the lesson continued, a little plan formed.

At the end of the period the other students filed out, and I asked The Fab Four to wait.

"Are we in trouble?" asked Bernie. "What did we do?"

"Why would you be in trouble?" I shrugged and kept my face blank. "I wanted to speak to you about a special project." Smiling, I went over to the windows all casual, pulled the blinds as if we were about to meditate in a darkened room. They blinked. I had their attention.

"Special project?" Bernie asked, hoisting himself onto the supply table near the door.

"I'll tell you about it, but there's a downside." I smiled my pseudo-smile, began erasing the whiteboard, my back to the four students, afraid I'd burst out laughing.

"What downside?" said the girlfriend.

It was difficult to keep a straight face. "The project is an after-school project." I paused and held the eraser high, looking for a reaction, then turned back to finish erasing the board.

Silence. "After school?" asked Howard.

"You wouldn't mind spending time with your teacher after school, would you? Especially if I need your help."

"You need our help? Couldn't we do it during our study period?"

"Don't think you could manage during your study period." I shook my head.

"Is this a detention?" Bernie said.

"Detention?" I shook my head hard enough to slap my earrings against my cheeks. "Who said anything about a detention?"

"I'm thinking this is a detention," Harold said to his buds. They looked uneasy for the first time.

"Well, let me put it this way," I said. "I would never give you a detention. But I *would* ask you to join me after school to work on a special project." They were shifting from one leg to another, looking at each other for support. Funny how they went all polite and quiet.

"How do we know when we have to stay after for this special project?" Bernie asked, worry in his voice.

"Easy. I'll give you a signal. Tell you 'I need help on a special project.' That's it."

"We get it," Harold was nodding. "But if we cool it then and there, we don't have to stay after for detention?"

"Well, I don't get it," said Bernie.

"We're detained." Bernie's girlfriend poked him in the ribs. "But there isn't any detention."

"Nice doing business with you guys. You'd better get to your next class now." I watched them back out the door, closed it and burst out laughing, thought of their expressions as they digested what I was telling them, and laughed harder.

"Oh, I'm loving this job," I said out loud. My phone rang.

"Luke?"

"I hope I'm not bothering you."

"I have a prep period. No bother."

"Just calling to see how you are doing. Nothing more."

"Okay, um, that's nice." *He's keeping in touch.*

"All right if I call you again? When we can talk more? Like last night?"

"Yes, I'd like that."

As soon as we hung up, a message came in from Billy. Confirming our coffee meet. I had an hour to organize the daily folders, go over lesson plans for the next day, and freshen up with a little lipstick. I was almost looking forward to meeting Billy, and that was a good sign.

Another good sign? Luke was a kind man.

\*\*\*\*

"Why are you here?" That's the first thing Magda, my very own shrink, asked. I crossed my legs, thought for a moment. Was bluntness common in the shrink profession?

Her office was one room in an old Victorian in East Rock, my neighborhood. Magda was tall, almost as tall as Dana, with black eyebrows and sleek white hair pulled into a chignon. I liked her face. She wore no makeup, not even lipstick. She sat on a leather sofa and I sat on a chair, my water bottle in my lap.

"Well, this may sound strange, but I've been reading this book." I held up the book I'd picked up at Barnes and Noble. "It made me analyze my relationship."

"Ah, *Sex, Love or Infatuation.* Clever title," she said.

"With infatuation, there's a lot of ups and downs. And sex complicates everything." I shuffled the pages until I came to a graph. "See this? The General Life Spans of Infatuation and Love Compared. The infatuation graph goes up and down, see? But the love graph goes up. The infatuation graph creates, uh, the *illusion* of a profound relationship. According to the author."

Magda didn't say anything. She sat waiting. I fidgeted, wondering if I was boring her. Ten minutes and I was already worried I was putting my therapist to sleep?

"Last night I almost emailed him because, well, he was always saying he was infatuated." *I'm still infatuated.* "If I email him—if I even want to email him, I'm going backward. I know that. But I still wanted to email and explain…because he has all these theories about love and how love works, his tank theory, his…" I stopped talking. My two cups of coffee sloshed around my stomach.

"And who is it we're talking about here?"

It took me a few seconds to realize I hadn't introduced Magda to Noah, so I filled her in. How we'd met, spent time together, and the big dump. It all came out in a monotone, a rote recital of the facts with none of the flavor. *Oh, Magda, I can see your eyelids drooping, you can't fool me.*

"It sounds as if you were attached to this man. Did you want to change his mind? About some of his theories?"

"Maybe…no, I don't think so," I stuttered. *Admit it. You want an excuse to email him. You want Magda's blessing. You'll leave this office and email him two seconds after you hit the sidewalk.* My inner voice cackled knowingly.

"We'll come back to him. Were you married? Can you tell me a little about your background?"

My life in Paris, my friends, missing Pluto, the money fights with Laurent, returning to school, I rattled on about it all before getting back around to Noah, and his story about meeting the woman he loved. The tank theory. "Three months, that's how long we were together."

"And he said he was waiting to fall in love. It didn't happen. Am I correct?" Magda's voice was gentle. "That must have been difficult for you."

I heard myself tell her I wanted to move on, didn't know why I was having such a tough time. "How can I do it faster? I'm dating again. Met one guy for coffee. That's a start, isn't it? Isn't that what I should be doing, you know, that old thing, you fake it till you make it? I'm trying to get him out of my head." *Yes, but am I trying hard enough?* "I miss him. And my friends have been great, but they're losing patience."

Magda waited and listened as I went back over the conversations with Dana. *So, the man dumped you. We've all been there. Get up and get out.* And Isabel. *You're mistaking lust for intimacy.* The attempts to keep up the facade of well-being with Dana during our running forays to Edgerton Park when all I wanted was to be a sloth on my bed. And I knew Dana wasn't talking much about Jerry because of me. Sensitive to what I was going through, how sweet was that? And also unnecessary.

It struck me that the one person who understood what I was going through was Luke.

"I'm faking it with my friends. Pretending I'm moving on."

"How are you feeling now?"

"Well, not great but okay." As soon as I said this, I realized it was true. "I spent a couple weeks wallowing on my bed and I still want...every afternoon it's a battle not to crawl into bed after work." I watched her closely for judgment, which usually showed around the eyes.

But in Magda's case, there was nothing but kindness.

"What is it you miss most about this relationship?"

"Oh, we laughed a lot, even in email. It was a long-distance thing, so we did a lot of emailing."

Magda waited as if expecting more, her expression calm, gazing at me.

"What?"

She waited, still not saying anything.

"What? I answered your question. Laughing is a big deal. In a relationship. Well, it is."

"We have to stop now. Think about my question, and we'll come back to it next time." Magda crossed the room to her desk and suggested I come for another visit. I couldn't believe I'd been droning on for a fifty-minute hour.

I pulled my cell from my bag to make the next appointment.

Magda stood at her desk looking at her calendar. "Next week is available. Same time?"

"Yes, that works for me." I entered the time onto my phone and dropped it into my bag.

"Here's an appointment reminder." Magda held out a card and I crossed the room and took it.

"Thanks." I stood in front of Magda's desk, my mouth open.

"What is it?" Magda said.

"It was the touching," I mumbled, head lowered, focused on the card as the tears formed. One dripped onto my cheek, and I wheeled around. "The touching more than the sex. That's what I miss the most. It's like a craving."

Magda held out a box of tissues, and I took it. She told me we'd discuss whatever I wanted at the next session.

"Not Noah," I said. "Don't let me talk about him. Promise?"

"Not sure I can promise—"

"Promise you'll try to steer me away, at least?"

"Promise."

That was good enough. For now.

\*\*\*\*

"Hi Sunny."

His name popped up on my Caller ID as William Kundel. Billy, the guy I'd met for coffee after school.

"Hi Billy." I was in bed reading a Stephen King novella where the whole town is puking at the pie-eating contest. The mayor's wife has puked on some guy in a suit, and the suit guy lets go all over his own shoes and some middle-aged lady's, maybe the mayor's wife, and on and on.

"What are you doing?" Billy asked.

"Reading 'The Body'." I lifted the book and read from the cover, "*Different Seasons.* A collection. *Stand by Me* was the movie. Have you ever heard of it?"

"Oh, yeah. Great movie. Great song, too."

"Yes, the movie was wonderful," I said. "I can sort of hear the voices of the actors, the boys, while I'm reading."

"There's only one body I'm interested in though."

"What did you say?" I said.

"You heard me."

"I'm digesting what you said, Billy Boy."

"Ooh." A low grunt. "You turn me on when you say my name like that."

"Billy Boy." *Fun. This is fun.*

"But I don't know you well enough to tell you

261

what else you do," he said.

I lay on the bed, squeezed Stephen King in one hand, the phone in the other.

"So, Sunny. You're not going to respond to that one, are you?"

"No. I don't know you well enough to respond to that one."

"Here's one you can respond to," he said. "Dinner and a movie. How does that sound?"

"It has a good sound." *Do I want to go out with Billy and his innuendos?*

"Sunday night?"

"Sunday night. Is that the magic night?"

"Well, I have my kids usually. Over the weekend."

"Oh."

"You're working tomorrow, of course."

"Of course."

"So I'll be thinking of you. Those slim hips of yours. Your T-shirt. Fitted but not too tight. Just right. Your—"

"Stop, please," I pleaded. "My head will explode."

"So will mine."

After hanging up, I lay on the bed smiling at the silliness of our conversation. With Billy there was no pressure, no agenda, and no future. How refreshing was that?

My cell whistled. Luke.

*—Hope I'm not waking you up. Want to say nighty night. Just got home. I'll call you tomorrow.—*

Billy and Luke were opposites because there were no expectations with Billy. Luke was another story. I pictured us at dinner, Luke ordering a special wine— *redolent with the flavors of*—the thought alone made my toes curl. *I'm not ready for dinner and bantering.* I'd be on edge, like at our first dinner. Perfect. And what if our second dinner was wonderful, like the first, and he evaporated again? Would I spend another two weeks mooning?

"That's it," I said aloud, and crawled off the bed, grabbed my phone and texted Billy.

—*Hope we don't have our first fight over which movie to see*—

A reply came instantly, followed by another.

—*I'm a LOVER, no stinkin' fighter. Thinking of you*—

—*Lumiere or Miss Soleil, I'm inspired to spout poetic but I can't get your mouth and those laughing eyes out of my mind. Okay. Movie…not too late. You need your beauteous rest. So as the etoiles rise high up in the sky, I leave you with the words of the divine Hunchback, "Bon soir" lady of my dreams and desires. Have an excellent day with those kids you told me about*—

Ah, Billy of the poetry and corny-corny. Sweet, uncomplicated, and what the doctor would have prescribed if I hadn't self-medicated.

\*\*\*\*

The next day at school, the morning announcements featured our French market. Teachers stopped by all day long—during their prep period or lunch—and we were mobbed. Which is why I didn't immediately notice Mr. Pearson, the head of the foreign language department. Teachers clustered at the turnip, potato, parsley, carrot, and lettuce kiosk.

"*Il y a un estranger dans la classe.*" Too cute, my student's attempt to tell me about a stranger in class.

Mr. Pearson sat under the life-sized poster of French teenagers.

The kids had done most of the work, hauled in everything from apples and nectarines to artichokes, tomatoes, cucumbers, dried figs, and a few exotic items I couldn't identify in the rush to set up. They decorated the five stalls in red, white, and blue, while I ran off euros in three denominations on the color printer in the library. The euros were mainly for show. And souvenirs of the day.

After several minutes of head swiveling, Mr. Pearson got up and headed over to the vendors at the veggie kiosk, and I moved closer, angling myself for a better view. He stopped, nodded a few times as Gerard told him about the freshness of the tomatoes, the crispness of the radishes. We'd practiced adjectives, a solid month of vegetable vocabulary, counting, and polite expressions. Now the kids stuck their lips forward like real French people.

Mr. Pearson plucked a head of lettuce, a tomato, some radishes, and Gerard bagged them. *"D'accord, merci,"* he said and shook Gerard's hand. In that moment, I wanted the job, Miss Charlman's job, along with Miss Charlman's students. Miss Charlman, on maternity leave, would make arrangements for childcare and would be returning to this classroom. Crap and doo doo.

These thoughts yanked at me as I stood watching. Mr. Pearson stayed thirty or forty minutes, wandered the classroom, visited each booth, and spoke French with the students.

He waved me over before leaving. We stood by the door, observing two teachers pluck pears from the pile and hand them over to be weighed.

"Nice lesson," he said. "Real life opportunities for speaking French, and you must have enjoyed high parental involvement with all that shopping."

"Yes, and there are fruit flies involved, too."

He laughed. "Bringing in a scale. Real attention to detail."

I hesitated, wanting to ask questions, wanting to know where I stood. This man hired for ten or fifteen schools, and he knew people. "Was this a formal observation? Because I'm looking for a teaching position."

"Be happy to write it up. Why not? You've done a splendid job. I never know when there'll be an opening, and you'd be a welcome addition to the department." His voice was animated, enthusiastic. "And I did my shopping for a dinner salad. My wife will be thrilled." He hefted the bag.

We stood in the doorway. "Too bad I don't get here too often." He nodded. "Very impressive. They can speak." And he headed off down the hall.

*Hire me.* A wistful sense of longing rose behind my eyes. Six weeks to go. Six weeks, maybe a bit more if Miss Charlman extended her leave.

The hordes were clearing out. "Go to lunch," I said to the kiosk crew. "And take some fruit with you. Come back after your special, and we'll have a sale and clean up." I grabbed a nectarine.

Time to start looking for a permanent position. Once the room cleared out, I grabbed my sandwich from the desk drawer, and hit one of my favorite podcasts. The hosts went on about the agony of relationships. I took a big bite of my sandwich, which was lovely with Boston lettuce, sprouts, and a little sliced pepper on the side. This was good, taking care of myself, eating well.

And I was doing so much better in the *not mooning* department, barely mentioned the name beginning with N during my sessions with Magda these days. I'd lost count. Funny what five or more weeks with a therapist can do for the soul.

The piano riff for the podcast swelled out of my phone greeting me, then the first host told me not to worry, "We're here, the both of us." Why was it that other people's relationship angst was so entertaining and dare I say, amusing, while my own was boring and made my friends want to hang up on me?

After another bite of my sandwich, thoughts of Luke followed. His Twinkie and Ding Dong habit. The confession he'd made one night about how difficult his breakup had been. How he'd tried to make me feel better. Well, I'd text him and let him know the market was a raving success. He knew how I'd worried about market day.

My cell rang interrupting the podcast.

"Hey, Luke." A little happy dance chair performance upon hearing his voice. He never called during the day. Something was up.

"You eating at your desk? I am. Chicken salad on rye."

"Tuna on pumpernickel with red pepper slices." Exchanging little details about our lives, so fun.

"Red pepper slices, nice. Haven't talked much this week, so I thought I'd take a chance." A pause. "How's the job going? Any chance it'll turn into a permanent position?"

"Nah," Tuna bits and sprouts clung to my teeth. "I'm looking around, though. Bad time of the year for anything but sub jobs."

"Yeah, and I'll bet there're more sub jobs in the winter."

"Definitely."

"Colds and other viruses being rampant, you know, in winter," Luke said.

"True. I'll have to waitress if I can't teach. Haven't waitressed in what? Thirty years?" I took a bite of pepper. "Get a job where the food's good. To tide me over." I was babbling, and we were talking about the weather, like boring people. What was up? This wasn't like Luke, not that I knew Luke that well. One date and weeks and weeks of talking on the phone, a nice little *phoneship,* summed up our relationship. Did talking on the phone even count?

My stomach in a wad, I put the tuna sandwich down. Luke and I never ran out of things to say to each other, we joked about *talk, talk, talking.* So what was this?

"I wanted to ask you something."

*Yes, Luke, what is it? Ask me anything.*

Nothing from Luke's side. Then…"Are you there?" I heard his voice on speaker so loud it jolted me.

"Oh, I was waiting for you," I said, chewing fast. "You said you—"

A buzz somewhere in the background on Luke's end, then someone speaking to Luke. I plopped my sandwich on the napkin, aware my toes were curling inside my shoes. This was the moment all our nighttime conversations had led up to. Luke was going to pop the going-to-dinner question. *Yes, yes.*

"Sorry," he said. "I've got a meeting, and I should let you get back to work. Don't you have a class?"

"In eight minutes."

"Talk another time."

He wasn't asking me out. Leaving me in limbo, probably because we had nothing to say to each other. After all those great nights of conversation and learning about his family. And the quirky people he worked with, like Manny the head of the department who was on his third wife, and Alice Ann, who did yoga poses in the corner of her office and brought her toy poodle into work.

*No invite. This is it?*

\*\*\*\*

Late the next afternoon, I lay on Magda's couch. "So, you're seeing this Billy individual and enjoying yourself?"

After multiple Magda sessions, I felt at ease with the occasional silences, freer to take risks, but still hyperaware of holding things in. And when I had trouble phrasing a thought, I stared at the ceiling where a discolored rectangle stood out from the white textured paint job. I shifted on the couch. Magda sat with an elbow resting on her knee, her expression calm.

"Billy says he has enough kids. Well, he has three. Three wives, three kids." Three divorces meant Billy's middle name was baggage, the word invented for serial procreators, men whose actions raced ahead of their common sense. "I'm having fun. He's having fun. I know we won't work out, and I'm all right with that."

I stared at the discolored rectangle, mulling over what I'd just said. "No, it's more like relief, knowing there's no future with Billy. Three kids and a job as a manager at an apartment complex. Some foggy excuse for leaving his previous job. I didn't ask for details."

"That is an indicator," Magda said, "that you are becoming more resilient."

"Resilient. I like that word."

"And you are moving on."

"No, I'm not. I come here and talk about *him* still. How's that moving on?" Something rose in my throat. "You're...That sounds patronizing. You shouldn't baby me and tell me I'm moving on. When I'm not."

"Here are the facts. You haven't talked about mooning..." Pages flapped as she searched. "You mentioned Noah briefly, but in the last three sessions, only in passing. More like a comment."

"That surprises me. I can't believe it."

"That is progress, and it's what you wanted."

She was right. And yet the edginess persisted, as if I wasn't getting my money's worth.

"Our time is almost up, but I have a question. What about the other man? Luke? Still talking with him?"

"Still talking." What was the point in discussing Luke?

"Tell me."

"There's nothing much." I shrugged. "He's the one who didn't call after our first meet. Then he texted—"

"Out of the blue?"

"Yes. And he's still keeping in touch." I sat up to think better. "Calls pretty often. It's cute the way he tells stories about when he was a kid. His college debate team was a big deal for him. His first girlfriend in college, and when his daughter was on the basketball team, how they traveled to games. He loves clamming and cooking. Said he'll cook for me, but that's not gonna happen."

Magda made no comment. She was excellent at getting me to fill in the spaces.

"He could ghost," I said. "Stop calling."

"Trust takes time."

Trust took time. Years. I stood and pulled out my calendar book. I was afraid to tell Magda—it was impossible to admit his voice and sweet words, and the way he checked up on me today—would lull me into thinking ours was a real friendship and not a *phoneship*.

"He called me at school, and I was sort of thinking he might ask me out, but then he got called into a meeting, and it didn't happen. Now I'm not so sure about getting together. My expectations are too high."

"What are you expecting?"

"Too much, way too much." My face warmed under Magda's gaze as she waited me out. Our silence grew to five minutes of discomfort for me that didn't have any effect on Magda. Or so I thought.

"We have a few minutes left. Is there anything else you'd like to tell me?"

"No." We continued sitting, staring into space, my stubbornness an amorphous thing I couldn't control. Magda rose, the signal our session was ending. "I'll see you next week then."

What were my Luke expectations? I closed my eyes to concentrate, collect my thoughts. "I expect a changed man. A better man, like he said. But isn't that way too much?" Did Magda have a response to this?

She was making notes on her desk calendar. "We'll discuss this next time, but I'd say it depends. On the man."

## Chapter Eleven
Depends on the man…

Speaking of the man, early that evening, as I was preparing a salad for dinner, Billy texted. With his address.

—*Maybe now's the moment for us to enjoy…what I got…205 channels of material, who knows what movie fare…Pop on over for a popping good time. I am here all evening. I'll provide the popcorn. YOUR man, Billy Boy—*

It took me fifteen minutes to text him back, chow down a few bites of salad, pull on jeans, and brush a blush of pink on my cheeks, along with a swipe of mascara.

Tooling down Whitney blasting salsa on the radio until I reached the cross street for his building. I pulled into the parking lot of the high rise and found a guest spot. The elevator doors were the only thing between me and the strong scent of cumin in the hallway, mixed with a few more cooking odors I couldn't identify.

Billy let me in wearing a pair of cut-offs and no shirt. Not his best look. Damn how men could let it hang out.

"Whew, Billy." The place was steaming, a taste of Bermuda, as if he'd be slipping me a margarita with a little umbrella. "A little hot in here, don't you think?" I handed him my jacket.

Billy's smile was as fat as his belly. "No problem, I'll turn down the heat. Just trying to encourage you to relax, take a few clothes off."

"Hah." I looked around at the studio with kitchen cubby. Neat. Had to admit Billy did well with one closet. I needed a whole closet for my skirts. Six pairs of shoes were lined up against the wall.

"I'll open a window. Can't turn down the heat, unfortunately." He yanked on the slider leading to the balcony, and with that chubby smile and a firm hand guided me to the couch. "This place is overheated. Like me." His mouth thwacked mine. My teeth and chin went numb. His lips opened, the tongue working like a shovel, digging deep. So different from our movie date, a simple goodbye kiss on the cheek, as if he were trying not to make a wrong move. Now he gripped the back of my head, held it, pressed a little too hard. I put my hands on his chest, bolstered by the belly, and pushed.

"What's the rush? Are we on deadline?"

"Wow." He straightened up. "I wasn't sure you'd come over at the last minute."

"Last minute, yeah, it was," I laughed. "But you said popcorn."

"This is great," he said. He squeezed my arm, bent down to kiss my neck. "The truth? I didn't think you'd come with just a text invite. Hanging out."

"Popcorn gets me every time," I said. "And I knew you wouldn't be too...*demanding*." I knew nothing of the kind.

Billy made a few grunting noises. There came the tongue again. "Too heavy? Am I leaning on you too much?" He drew back keeping his mouth open on mine, tongue moving around, picking up speed. I needed to breathe and shoving him off wasn't going to be easy.

"More of that later," and he stopped the heavy tongue action, heaved himself off, and gestured in the direction of the coffee table. "I got the *Times*. Relax while I make some popcorn."

I sat up and finger-combed my hair, then bent and checked my face in the mirror propped against the wall, brushed away a few specks of black gook. "Sounds great. I want the book section. And the magazine." I began sifting through sports, travel, business. The Sunday paper would be a treat. Billy shuffled around his kitchen cubby, opening cabinets and letting them bang shut. "Billy?"

"Yeah?"

"Where's the magazine? And the book section?"

"Oh." He stood, a bag of microwave popcorn in his hand. "I must have read them." He put his hand to the side of his forehead.

"Maybe you put them someplace?"

"Yeah. I read them. And I took them to the trash room."

"Oh, already?" I studied him. Who dumps the best parts of the newspaper on Sunday? Usually I get rid of the ads and sports and financial. By Tuesday or Wednesday.

"Sorry." I heard the sound of the popcorn bag going into the microwave, the kernels splatching off the sides, the peculiar odor of fake butter and plenty of it.

Interesting, as Isabel would say when she didn't believe someone. Had Billy dumped those primo parts of the paper? More likely, he'd found those sections in the trash room. Why lie about such a small detail?

"Ready?" He'd finally put on a shirt and he stood

at the coffee table pulling the edges of the bag open. "Whew, hot and steamy. Just like you." He plucked a few kernels, popped them in his mouth. "I've got soda. Diet or regular?"

"Diet."

And that's what we did, chomped on popcorn. When I dropped some, Billy tossed a few pieces on the floor and told me not to worry. I threw a few kernels at him and watched them bounce off his belly. One got stuck in the folds of his stomach and he picked it out and flipped it into his mouth. We munched and watched *The Graduate*. Oh, and we smooched a bit, even though Billy's kissing style wasn't a turn on. I sat up around the time Dustin Hoffman crashes the wedding right before the end, and checked my watch.

"Oh, crap. It's past eleven. I've got to go." I stood and looked around. "My jacket."

"Don't panic." He grabbed it out of the closet and walked me to the elevator.

"It's late for me. I never stay out on a school night like this." I pecked him on the cheek. His hand on my back, he guided me into the elevator and stood watching as I pushed the button. The food smell was still there. The elevator doors opened, and I waved goodbye.

It was funny, but descending in that elevator, I had a contented feeling that had been missing for weeks. I didn't want to be anywhere else, doing anything else. Not tonight. Geez, he might be a lousy kisser, but he was playful and took my mind off *things*.

Not every stinkin' relationship had to be with the right man talking the right talk. Wrong-man connections were underrated.

In the lobby, I pulled out my phone, which I'd shut off hours ago. Crap. A missed call from Luke. The voicemail was simply, "Thinking of you."

Well, to figure out if Luke and I had a connection, I needed to see him again. Need and want, two different things.

I wanted to see Luke.

So. What was I going to do about it?

\*\*\*\*

A few nights later, Billy and I were pillow talking—not in the same bed, more like the split-screen movie scene in *When Harry Met Sally*. We were talking on the phone, the bedroom lights dimmed, my head on the pillows stacked behind.

"I think of you every night," Billy said. "You're Sunny Bunny, because, well, you just are. A bunny. All cuddly."

"You're joking." The phone was on speaker, propped on the pillow by my ear.

"Don't make fun of me."

"I can't take you seriously."

"Don't be cruel. My heart is true."

"Oh, dear, you're quoting Elvis."

"I think I love you," he said. "Really. I love you."

My toes made a bump under the sheet. "Gimme a break." I gathered the pillows and shoved them higher behind my back, checked the clock on my dresser, feeling antsy. If Luke called, it was usually about this time. I needed to politely get Billy off the phone. "Does that work? The *faux* love-connection thing."

"Sometimes." He gave a deep-throated laugh. Billy had no problem laughing at himself. "You're the first one who ever called it *faux*. It means fake, right?"

"Right." Billy wasn't afraid to ask for clarification. I liked that, too. "Do you enjoy not very bright women?"

"It depends," he said.

"Well…I've still got prep to do tonight." That was a lie.

"One more question. Do you enjoy…you know."

"It depends," I said.

"On?"

"On the man."

"I'm the man."

"Watch out," I said. "Do you truly want to be the man?"

"It depends."

"Of course it does," I said, and we burst out laughing. Magda knew about Billy, but I hadn't told my friends. He was my dirty little secret, and besides, there was no way to convey the spirit of these silly moments without sounding foolish.

"Come over now," he whispered.

"Is that your seductive voice?"

"Damn straight," he said, in his normal voice. "Baby," he whispered.

"It's too late."

"It's late, but let's play kissy-face."

"Um, not tonight." I wanted to get off the phone.

"When then?"

"I'm not sure. I'm looking for a job now."

"Pizza. You like pizza, don't ya?" The beeping purr of another caller. "Hey, you can trust me. You know that. And tomorrow's Friday, but my kids are doing something else so I'm free. Besides, I like your company. I'll pick you up, no worries."

Luke's name popped up on the Caller ID. "Okay, let me—"

"Remember, you're Sunny Bunny, *my* Sunny Bunny. The one I play kissy-face with."

Five rings and yes, I was counting. I'd lose Luke after two more rings, but excuses weren't rolling off my tongue for some reason, probably because I didn't want to hurt Billy's feelings. He'd propped me up when I needed propping the most, just coming out of my mopey period after the Noah breakup.

"Let me see if I can swing it," I said. The ringing stopped.

I wouldn't swing anything with Billy.

Our conversations, all the brainless repartee that was the core of our so-called relationship the past several weeks, smacked me in the face. I jerked off the bed and crossed the room, pacing as I talked. In a burst of inventive baloney, I told Billy I had to check the job sites. "If there's anything new, I have to apply, and the applications take a long time to fill out. That's my priority right now. You understand, don't you?"

"No *problemo*," his voice sincere, a real sweetie. "Another time. I'll see you around, I hope."

"See you," and I disconnected quickly so I wouldn't have to imagine the look on Billy's face. He had to know I was blowing him off. I was wide awake now, no longer wanting to slouch around and wait for Luke to call again.

What if Luke was calling to chat, nothing but chat, as usual? What if our *phoneship* never progressed beyond all this chatting? Thinking was called for here, and therefore, a little wine. Lucky for me there was a lonely bottle of Malbec in the cupboard, waiting to be opened. I grabbed my cell and strode with purpose into the kitchen.

The bottle was a nifty screw top, and in thirty seconds I was sipping, okay, swallowing a big gulp followed by another—and planning how to invite Luke out on a date. The wine hit me, a reminder I'd had an early dinner, so I was essentially drinking on an empty stomach. I took a smaller sip and reached for the bag of pretzels, the Utz, extra dark sourdough, my favorites.

My phone rang and I checked it. Luke calling back. "Hello."

"I'm jumping right in, and if you're rejecting me, well, go ahead and do it quickly. I want to see you. I want to have dinner with you and relax and get to know you. No more talking on the phone. In person. A real date. This coming Saturday. I'm giving you plenty of notice, and since it's a real date, I'll pick you up at home. You can wear your high heels, and it doesn't matter if they're uncomfortable, because I'll carry you into the restaurant. If you want me to, of course. What do you say?"

From Luke's end came heavy breathing, as if the effort to get it all out had exhausted his resources.

"Carry me into—"

"That was a dumb attempt to be funny, never mind that. What do you say? Say yes," he said. "Spit it out."

"Yes." I raised the wine glass in a silent toast and took a healthy sip.

****

"You've actually gone out with twenty-five men?" Magda leaned forward in her oversize leather chair. "That was your goal, I remember. What did you get out of the experience? Dating so many men in what? Six months?"

From my prone position on the couch, it was easy to avoid looking at Magda, dig my head deeper into the pillow and stare at the crack in the ceiling. Pretend to be the lead character in *Klute,* the old movie where a high-class prostitute wears a mini-skirt and boots, a shag haircut and has a therapist. A hooker in control because that's the single relationship with men she can handle.

"Remember one thing," and my voice took on an all-knowing lecture-like drone. "It's not dating. I *met* a lot of men. You have to understand there's a difference." I drummed on the couch with my fingers going for loud, as loud as the taut leather would play. "A date happens *after* a meet. That's basic to understanding the process."

Magda remained silent, her way of letting me know I hadn't answered her question.

"Where did it get me?" I asked the ceiling. "What's changed? Do I have anyone important in my life now?" I laughed, one of those hollow laughs where the joke's on you. Concentrated all my focus on getting my ideas across to Magda in fifty minutes. I had to make her understand.

"Frank was a cold potato, and now that I'm out of the Noah relationship, I realize we had no real intimacy." Even the hooker in Klute achieved intimacy by the end of the movie.

"All along, I had delusions. Starting with Frank, the iceberg, and José, thinking he was a friend. I should have walked out on him sooner, but I kept thinking he was nice. He used the word *wistful*, for God's sake. What man uses the word *wistful* and then says you've got to like swallowing?"

Could Magda tell I was getting worked up? The words splattered faster and faster, like Lorelai on Gilmore Girls, when she needed to empty the trash bin in her head. "I should've broken up with Frank sooner. And I should have realized Noah was...neurotic." I shook my head. "No, I'm lying. I knew, but I didn't want to admit it to myself that our relationship wasn't working." My throat was tight, and I was mouth breathing. "I had plenty of clues. Plenty."

"It's normal to go through new experiences, make mistakes along the way," said Magda. "Mistakes are not criminal."

"And then there's Luke." I unscrewed the cap and gulped from my water bottle. "He's been calling. I didn't tell you much because I didn't want to analyze everything. He keeps calling and telling me...stuff. About his life. So then, wouldn't you know, the last time he called, he asked me out. And all I can think is— can I trust him? What if we go out and he ghosts again? Ghosting is like the silent treatment, but permanent."

Magda waited. *Again with the waiting?* A couple of minutes slogged by until I couldn't take it. "You're ghosting me. Stop therapy-ghosting me. Please, Magda, talk to me, I can't stand it when—"

"You have a trust issue. You are no different from anyone else, and that is healthy. There should be a trust issue, at least until you get to know an individual."

The simplicity of the idea made me cringe.

"My purpose is not to tell you what to do, but to help you find your way, with a little guidance." Magda's voice cracked. "I'm going to make a suggestion now." She hesitated.

"What?" I felt a flutter somewhere inside, not the

good flutter of anticipation, more on the anxiety side of the flutter spectrum.

"Consider taking a break from the dating. Or slow down."

I lay there focusing again on the crack in the ceiling as Magda talked. I heard random words. "What you have done. Achievement. Resilient. Realizing who is worth your heart. Your trust. Guts to risk getting hurt."

*Resilient.* That damn word again.

"It's a way to gain some clarity and think about your experiences. Get perspective. We'll figure out your goals, set some together. Consider, for example, the possibility of sweet solitude."

*Sweet solitude?* Who the hell was she to feed me this crap? I slid onto the floor in a crouch, heaved myself up, and walked toward the door, swiping at my eyes before I realized I'd left my bag under the couch.

"Please don't leave."

"Why? We're done here, aren't we?" I walked over to the couch and picked up my bag. "You're supposed to be on my side. And all this time you've been listening to my stories and feeling sorry for me. Why? You don't see what I've been doing as..." My voice was a bleat. Just when I'd been so certain I was onto a few clues...that I'd discovered significant truths about myself. "You don't see what I've been doing as worthwhile? The dating was helping me figure things out."

Magda looked up at me with piercing attention. "You're learning as you go. That's all we can do."

My gaze dropped to my feet. "What about Billy? What was that? Harmless? I was in it for the entertainment factor, but wouldn't you think I'd draw the line somewhere? Fifty years old, and I was fooling around with a forty-six-year-old teenager. I humiliated myself."

"Begging your pardon, I disagree. Humiliate? Have you got any idea how many people I talk to in this office who'd give anything to have the guts to do what you've been doing?"

"You expect me to believe that?"

I must have been staring at Magda slack-jawed, because her voice lowered to a soothing purr I'd never heard before.

"Look," she said, standing, taking my hand and squeezing it. "I don't have all the answers. I may not have any of the answers. But you've toughed a few things out and learned a hell of a lot. Think about it. Moving from Paris, completing a degree. So many changes, apart from dating. And you look inside for the answers. Many people are afraid to do that."

"Well, my friend Dana said the same thing."

"She has a point."

"Oh. I'm one of the desperate ones. Always working the room, pushing. Always pushing. I know it shows. Men. They smell that kind of desperation." I couldn't believe I was saying this, even to Magda. Until I'd spoken the words aloud, I didn't recognize what I felt as desperation.

For a moment neither one of us spoke.

"That is fucking ridiculous. You're way too hard on yourself."

Was I beating myself up so badly it showed? I thought about that. "You used unprofessional language."

"The situation called for it."

"What situation?"

"The 'you-beating-yourself-up' situation."

"Oh."

"This isn't about meeting men. It isn't about meeting a special man, and I won't even joke about meeting your soulmate." She stopped and poked me in the arm. "It was never about men. It's about letting go. You need to let go. Forgive yourself for whatever it is you think you should have done better, from your ex-husband to what's his name? Billy? José? It doesn't matter. Forgive yourself and move on."

"Oh." I stood there in front of Magda, my face brightening. "That's it?"

"You're almost there." She grabbed the box of tissues from her desk and handed me one. "If you want to talk more, email me for an appointment."

I wiped my eyes and nose and tossed the tissue into the trash. I opened the door and looked back at Magda.

"Okay."

"All righty then." She smiled. "Have fun. With Luke."

****

Stop and Shop stocked giant shrimp and salmon, and I was in line at the fish counter. Straight from my Wednesday excercise class. Hungry and salivating, as if I could taste the spicy Cajun cocktail sauce already.

Goody, jumbo shrimp were on sale. Someone behind me was talking but the words didn't register, as I was busy list-composing in my mind. Paint the tag sale bookcase I'd picked up two weeks earlier, since my mystery writers, and a bunch of the romance ladies needed more room. Pop over to mall to check out cute little soap dispensers for the guest room. *I have my own guest room.*

"Seriously. How do you pick out a good piece of fish?" Was someone talking to me? I turned around.

"Luke?"

"Hi, I thought it was you."

He looked...cuter than I remembered, jeans and a shirt rolled up at the cuffs, not tucked. He leaned on the handle of his cart, smiling. I blinked with fatigue. I'd stayed up too late watching old movies. *The Thin Man* and half of *After the Thin Man*, William Powell and Myrna Loy drinking martinis, sparring, and fumbling with bad guys.

"You didn't recognize me? I know it's been a while."

"I'm surprised is all. I didn't expect you at my—at this store." I glanced at his cart. "I was daydreaming."

I'll admit to forming an opinion about the lives of strangers based on what they buy at the supermarket, but Luke was a step up from a stranger, so it was more fun. He'd picked about ten items, and they all seemed to be fruits and vegetables.

"It's good to see you." He leaned on the cart looking at me, a slight twitch around the corners of his mouth. "I was thinking of buying fish for dinner. Not quite sure what to get."

"Um, how are you cooking it?"

"Well." He rolled the cart to the side to make room for a woman and an older guy waiting in line. "On the grill. I moved a few months ago, and I just got a new one."

"Okay, let's see. Salmon. Salmon's great. I was thinking of salmon. Salmon's my favorite." At this rate, my middle name could be salmon.

"I remember. To be precise, blackened with mango salsa."

"But not the ones with the bones." I wrinkled my nose. Pretended not to notice his excellent recall of our one and only date. Meet. "I'm no expert. I choose what's on sale. Quite the discerning shopper."

"Sounds good," he said. "Then salmon it is." He nodded. "Thanks. Thanks very much." He started to turn around, affording me the opportunity to check his butt, but the shirttail blocked access.

"Of course, there's also swordfish," I said. "Swordfish steaks are great on the grill." He nodded. "And tuna. Fresh tuna, there's nothing like it. Tuna." I was beginning to sound like a fish ad. Or a fisherman's wife. A fishwife.

He nodded again, this time more enthusiastically. "Wow," he said, smiled and pointed to the enamel fish case. The woman had finished, and the man stepped up. "I'd like to try all of your suggestions. Everything looks so good." He turned to nod at me. "And how about you?'

"Oh. Well, I'm getting the salmon." I touched my hair. "And a couple shrimps." Had I slapped on a little mascara this morning? I brushed a finger under my lashes. Yes, yes, that felt like mascara. My face sported some bronzer to go with my fake tan legs. Luke and I were going to dinner in two days, so that would be another opportunity to talk about salmon. *While dining on salmon?*

"This is such a surprise, bumping into you." He was smiling. "Your help is most appreciated."

"Don't mention it." Yup, he was looking even

better than I remembered. Brown hair with a little gray at the temples and swimmer's shoulders. The blemish above his eye? Still there. Faint and noticeable if you looked for the little scar. I stepped up to the counter and ordered the salmon and four shrimp. I'd enjoy it all later that day with my new book. I knew because I'd already read the first sentence, that important first sentence, the one that grabs the reader. The fishmonger handed over my package of fish goodies.

"See you, Saturday." I rolled my cart away, slowly, feeling awkward, not knowing if I should have stayed to chat while he ordered.

"Looking forward to it," Luke said.

Well, this was a bit clumsy, not major, but even so. Given our lame lunchtime phone conversation on market day, I didn't want to linger. I barely knew the man. *"Yes, you do,"* I sputtered in my head. "We've talked for hours on the phone," I argued with myself while speeding over to the bread section at the opposite end of the store.

Did talking on the phone mean I know him, my argumentative side asked. Who knows?

I grabbed bran muffins and a loaf of French bread, intent on reaching the checkout before Luke, and I almost made it. I was putting my groceries on the checkout counter when I heard his voice behind me.

"So. We meet again." He was here, his cart full of produce, the salmon package and a few others in the little tray on top, a loaf of bread beside it.

"Hi." Was Luke following me? I swiped my credit card and handed over my keys with the Stop and Shop tag. Out of the corner of my eye, I could see him check out the magazine rack, pluck one, leaf through it, and replace it. Everything he did was slow, easy, as if waiting in line were no bother.

"You haven't got any vegetables," he said.

"Oh. I suppose not." I'd rushed through the store. "I'll throw together a salad."

"I have quite a few. All go well with fish."

"Are you criticizing, or donating your vegetables?"

His laugh exploded from his chest, and his head went back as if he needed laugh leverage. The music of it traveled up and slowed to a few bumps before it came to a halt.

"Cash back?" My eyes jerked to the Stop and Shop cashier who had spoken.

"No, no cash. Thanks."

She nodded. "Press the green button."

"Will you wait for me?" he asked.

"Well I—"

"This will take just a minute."

I stood holding my bag by the window until he had paid and pushed his cart to me. "May I?" he asked.

"May I *what*?" I asked.

"No, not you. May *I*?" he smiled. "May I shift your grocery bag? Take two minutes of your time."

I nodded. He lifted my bag, depositing it in the front part of his carriage. He pushed the carriage, headed for the exit, and veered around an older lady in jeans and sneakers, who struggled to pull a shopping cart from the stacks by the door. "I wanted to ask if you would…" He stopped and addressed the lady. "May I help?"

She twisted to look at him, smiled. "These darn things."

"They're tough," he said and yanked the carriage

from the cart convoy.

"Thank you, young man."

I trotted beside him as he shook his head. "Young man. I love it." What was going on here? I felt a bit too much like Luke knew something I didn't.

"Where's your vehicle?"

I pointed. "There." As we headed over, I pressed the remote.

"Mine's in the same row." He looked down at his sneakers, slowing the cart. "Here's the thing. I'm cooking salmon, those handsome salmon filets, and also tuna and swordfish."

"You bought everything?"

"Well, it came highly recommended. I have a source, a new source actually. Seems to have a handle on these things. Oh. And I got the giant shrimp. Or shrimps as you call them. You've got to have an appetizer."

"I—"

"I have a new grill. You know those fancy-shmancy—" He stopped, hit his forehead in mock stupidity.

"Weber?"

"You know grills, too." We watched a woman wheel her cart past, her feet slapping against the rubber of her flip flops. "I'm grilling it up, all of it. I'm not afraid of leftovers. I was thinking..." his voice, which up to this moment had kept up the tone of banter, slowed and died. I put my hand out, touched the plastic bag that held the much-admired salmon, aware that his gaze followed my movements.

We stood at my car. "Well..." He hesitated. "I understand those fish freeze quite well. I mention this, hoping you'll join me in a spectacular fish dinner. Need to prove to you I can cook...that I'm not just another pretty face."

Yes, Luke, island boy and clam hunter could get away with that line, and I relaxed for the first time since we'd bumped into each other.

But, this was all too quick. "Well, I don't think—"

"Think. And while you're contemplating whether you like me enough to come to a private dinner, I'd like to apologize."

I watched as he lifted out my groceries. He reached over, opened the passenger door of the truck, and deposited the bag.

"I'm sorry I didn't call."

My mouth couldn't say anything as it was frozen.

He looked away and shrugged. "I've learned a hell of a lot in the past six months or so," he said and stared straight at me. "Can we talk about that stuff at dinner?" He jangled his keys. "My invitation to dinner is a sincere one. Whether you come over tonight, or I see you Saturday. Your choice."

"Oh."

"Is around six good for you? If you decide to come, that is. No pressure. You might have plans tonight, after all."

"Not much tonight. Reading my Ed McBain." Crawling in bed with him.

"Police procedurals, right? Haven't read him in a long time."

The guy reads Ed? A good sign. I didn't want any more good signs.

He pulled out his wallet, took out a card. "Here's my address."

"Well," I hedged. "A man cooking for me. Sounds like a bribe." *Go with it, my inner voice urged. Live on the edge for once.* "Thank you. I eat a lot, by the way."

A big smile from Luke. Encouraging. And he was going to tell me more. *Stuff.*

Did I want to hear more?

**\*\*\*\***

At home, I put my few groceries away, wandered up to my bedroom, and stood in the closet mulling over what I'd wear to a fish dinner. The black, skinny jeans and black T-shirt? The blue, straight jeans and fitted flowery sweater? Red flats? Or the cute silver flats?

So much trouble getting to know somebody all over again. If I canceled, I could put on my tatty shorts, pan fry the salmon, and read my book. Anyway, Luke had his nerve, inviting me to a huge home-cooked fish dinner and making a big deal out of it, right on the heels of making a big deal out of inviting me to dinner at a fancy restaurant in the first place.

Luke, who didn't bother to call after that first meet.

Resentment bristled. Even though we'd traded information that one time—and I remembered savoring the wine and drinking heartily—we'd have to do it again. The divorce, the kids, the job, and did he like it? Trying to figure out his ballpark income so I could report all that stuff to my friends, deciding sooner rather than later whether he was worth pursuing. Listening closely for red flag areas, like did he call the ex-wife nasty names, harbor resentments against his mother, family, co-workers. Did he rent or own, was the place a shit-house or was it too clean, too perfect? Like Frank, with his suits in plastic bags, the expensive, zippered kind, his shirts in little compartments in his closet, stretchers in his shoes. I hadn't seen such a sight since my grandfather's closet.

My mind switched from Frank back to Luke. The on-again, off-again girlfriend he'd mentioned and then apologized for mentioning.

That clinched it. Even though I had a few clues, I wanted to know why he never called. I would ask. Nothing to lose and it would be fun to watch him squirm. I sifted through my jean choices. No, no jeans.

Plus I had an idea. One thing I remembered was that Luke was a fun guy. It would be interesting to see if he'd go along.

The house was in Spring Glen, a few streets off Whitney. I turned right, then left, and my mind pulled me back. This could be one of the streets Noah had picked for park-and-peck pleasure. Left onto a dead end. Nice. I pulled into the driveway. The house was a sprawling cream, with deep Mediterranean-blue shutters and a thicket of maples at the side. Luke put in serious landscape time.

I slid out of the truck, grabbed my bag and the bottle of red I'd brought, and slammed the door. Luke maintained the opposite of a lawn. Red rock and a mixture of ground cover, ivy and that stuff that grows fast, multiplies. Little plants and shrubs in clumps, with two huge boulders as centerpieces, surrounded by grasses, the expensive kind. I could tell they were expensive because the depth of green varied from a deep forest to a pastel shade the color of mint chocolate chip ice cream.

A note was tacked to his front door. *Welcome Sunny. Come around the back.*

He was standing on the deck as I came around the

corner and he smiled, hoisted a long-handled fork in one hand, a giant spatula in the other. "Welcome. Climb on up." He motioned under the table where a gray dog with a silver muzzle lay. "This is Bertie. She'd shake your hand but she has a little trouble getting up these days. Bertie raised her head and thumped her tail as I mounted the steps to the deck.

"Hi Bertie. Hi Luke."

He wore a faded flowery shirt over shorts. Sandals. Nice legs. "You look terrific," he said. "Dressed up for me? I'm flattered." I'd worn my deep pink skirt and flat silver sandals. "Any trouble finding the place?" he asked.

"None." I handed him the bottle of wine. "It's nice here." The barbecue rested on a wraparound deck large enough for six or seven couples to foxtrot to a little Sinatra. Below us the yard stretched out, trees blocking any view of the houses behind Luke's property. What a difference in temperature a few dozen fifty-year-old maple and pine trees made. I could imagine napping or sipping lemonade on a sweltering day, barely feeling the heat.

He put down his tools and took the wine. "Have a seat, let me open this." He unwrapped the bottle and closed his eyes for a beat. "Ah, the French. Shall we? I mean is this for the here and now?" When I nodded, he wiped his hands on his apron. "A minute." He walked over to a side door. "I'll just get my opener."

Well, this was nice and oh, so relaxing. Being outside did it, none of the tension of being in a closed, more intimate space. Luke had candles planted in the ground every few feet. I slouched into the picnic chair, a solid, heavy wood. No lightweight plastic here—part of a set. Six chairs and a round table.

"We're on our way." Luke had two pots, one in each hand. The corkscrew, huge, like a piece of machinery, sat on one of the pots. He set them to the side of the grill, lifted the lid and put the pots on the grill to warm.

I eyed the grill. "Giant. That's more of a family thing."

"Yeah. I've got the space, so I figured what the hell." He placed his machinery-corkscrew on the bottle and pulled down.

"Fancy."

"Oh, this thing is great. A gift. Wouldn't ever buy one, not like this." The cork lifted out in one smooth movement. "See? I can't embarrass myself leaving cork in a bottle of superior French wine." He poured, handed me a glass. "Thank you for bringing this, very thoughtful."

"My pleasure."

"Mine too. I'm glad you decided to accept my invitation." He held up his glass. "A toast. To Stop and Shop and our fortuitous meeting."

We clinked. A little tremor of excitement. That was definitely a compliment.

"Very nice pinot noir." He looked at his sandals for a moment, hesitated, and stood watching me. "After I met you...I didn't go out with anyone else. I want you to know that."

"Oh." Well, another compliment, at least it sounded like a compliment. Was I supposed to be flattered that Luke didn't go out with anyone else after disappearing on me?

Other than the girlfriend, of course.

"Why did you ghost on me?"

We experienced a moment of silence that kept on ticking. I swigged my wine. This was suddenly turning into a two-glass conversation, and I didn't care if the awkward gaps made Luke tongue-tied and sweat. I could wait. I could wait the way Mark, who'd bashed my Jeep and tiled my bathroom could wait. And if my resentment showed, too bad.

"Ghosting?" he said finally, his voice heavy. He dug his heels into the deck and scooched his chair closer. "I never thought of it as ghosting." His mouth went crooked. "I think of ghosting as passive-aggressive, for the chickenshits in this world, and up until this minute, I didn't see myself as one of those. I'm an asshole."

More silence. For a moment, I wondered if there would even be a dinner tonight because of the rules, rules dictating a platter of banter be served with dinner.

I cracked a smile. "I can't disagree with your self-assessment."

That crooked mouth again, this time with the ends turned up in an attempt at a smile. "That was such a great evening," he said, "even though I remember talking crap, getting caught up in my theories about meeting someone new, discovering little things that bother you, on and on. The thing is, I liked you so much. Right away." He grabbed his wine and took a long sip, and Bertie came over and put her head on his knee. "I was so miserable."

What could I say? The resentment shifted to one side, as if making room. *He liked me right away? Funny way to show it.* I was softening. Not so fast. I wasn't getting sucked in, not yet.

"Why did you ghost?" *I won't let it go, will I?*

"I was still seeing her. Entangled would be a better word. It wasn't the right time."

Still I waited, refusing to fill the gap, even if he squirmed. I listened carefully between the lines.

"Back when we met, I thought of calling you or emailing. Texting seemed lame. What could I say? I've got this on-again, off-again thing I can't let go? Wait for me? So I did nothing. Shitty. It was shitty.

"I shouldn't have been dating. I wasn't ready. But if I had not been dating we wouldn't have met." He stared past me at Bertie, back on her doggie pad.

"It took a long time. I needed to be clean in my head. I went into therapy. I think I told you. That helped a hell of a lot. I still go, whenever I feel the need. And I hope you'll forgive me for...now it's different. I'm different."

I sipped and thought of all the toasts, the bottles of wine I had shared over the past year—less than a year—thought about how I didn't want to talk about the past, not tonight. I sat down.

He turned, yanked open the grill, and peered in. "I'll put the fish on in a bit." He pulled one of the chairs closer and sat opposite. "We can relax, have a few bites of shrimp." He leaned toward me, holding the wine. "This is spectacular."

"One of my favorites."

"Let's not talk relationships or marriages or divorces," I said. "Not now. No family or jobs either."

"Oh? Well...fine by me. Even though we talked about that stuff." He cleared his throat. "When we first met."

"Whatever we remember, well, we can't help that.

Of course that's fine."

"Okay."

I blinked. "Well, I don't mean you should be afraid to say what you want to say."

He took another sip of the wine. "I get it," he said. "Shall we say whatever comes out naturally is perfectly acceptable?"

"Shall we?" I was getting drunk on half a glass of wine. "Today my mom called and asked me if—"

"You mentioned your mom. Isn't she family?"

"Oops. I giggled. "Hoisted on my own petard." I raised my glass. "Here's to petards, whatever they may be."

"A petard is a case that contains an explosive used to break down a door or a gate or to breach a wall." He sat back and raised his glass.

"Petards aren't normally a topic of conversation."

"Depends on your circle." He sat back and raised his glass. "The name pinot noir is derived from the French words for pine and black, tightly clustered, cone-shaped bunches of fruit." He took a sip. "Medium bodied, not too dry, but certainly not sweet. In short, perfect. Chosen expressly for this meal." He put the glass down. "Be right back. I'm going for the shrimp. "

The flashback from our first meet rolled in, Luke hoisting his glass, cute-pattering about the flavor. Sure, a few shrimps. Soon would be good for a bit of food. I didn't want to appear fluff headed, a woman who couldn't hold her... Was wine liquor?

Luke would know. He would be a useful team member at a party game where you make up fake definitions, and everyone has to guess the real one. A couple of shrimps would fix me up good.

Chapter Twelve
Luke for dessert…

"I'll take another sliver."

"Sliver. Coming up." Luke put the salmon on my plate. The evening was rolling along, a soft marshmallow of an evening, unhurried. Small gaps in the conversation that didn't matter. I sat back, sighed, and sniffed the air. "Roses?" I raised my head. "Rose bushes?" A subtle cloud of fragrance.

Luke gestured with his thumb. "It's the candles. And a few rose bushes."

"Did I eat or did I eat?" I patted my stomach. That's when I realized how little I'd eaten since a breakfast of yogurt and blueberries.

He sat back and told me how he'd found his dog, Bertie, on the road. Crouching behind a shrub, shaking and shivering. A throw-away. "I don't believe in strays. *Stray* is a cover-up for the mean things people do to dogs when they don't want to face their responsibilities."

I told him about Pluto, and how I was going to Paris to visit for a few weeks, how I'd catch up with my friends and take Pluto for walks.

"Paris," he said. "I'd like to hear more. Another time."

He touched my shoulder, his fingers lingering for a moment. Heat spread from my shoulder in a wave down my chest to my belly.

"Not sure how you say mosquito in French but the candles are dying down and I'm feeling the pinch. Come, I'll make you comfortable inside." He stood, still holding his glass, pulled me up very gently, walked me to the back door and opened it, calling Bertie. I stepped into a dimly lit room with two huge couches and a fireplace. He had built a fire.

"A springtime fire," I said. A huge painting above the fireplace and bookshelves to the ceiling. More bookshelves than I'd seen in a long time.

His hands massaged my shoulders. "Yes." He was touching my neck. "Any excuse for a fire will do." He kissed me, a gentle touch, more of a brush with his lips.

"Nice. I've had quite a lot of wine and everything is so nice." I looked behind me at the couch and my eyes closed.

"Do you need a nap?" His mouth was moving on my neck so slowly I felt breathless. Did he mean a nap for two? Not yet, *not yet*. The kissing was going so hummingly, like a little hummingbird. Half my mind, the practical part, focused on cleaning up all the fishes, carrying in plates, and rinsing. The other half jumped up and down. This kissing was going well, and I knew it was going well because I felt the tingle of it all the way down my back to my toes.

"Ah, yes." He took my hand and led me to the couch, eased me down, careful to leave a cushion's space between us. He reached out, touched my face, so gentle, his hand lingering a few moments. "I couldn't stop thinking about you. That was a big clue. Everything in my big, dumb brain kept coming back to that."

I leaned away from him to get a better look at his face in the darkening room.

He swayed closer and there were kisses, the faintest of kisses, his voice soft and low. "I hope it's the right time for you. I hope you're not dating anyone, but I'm not asking any questions. Not yet."

More kisses, delicate as breath, slow, deliberate, until all thinking dissolved. *Enough.* I had thought and planned in the past, asked questions, analyzed, searched for red flags, discussed, telephoned, and emailed. This time I was doing what I felt like doing, and what I felt like doing was being kissed and doing some kissing back.

His hands on my neck, the bend of my arm, sweet kisses to my shoulders. In no hurry. He reached for my glass, handed it to me. We sipped and he told me how nervous he'd been about phoning to ask me out. And I told him I'd almost canceled for tonight.

He made a hurt face. "I didn't want to push you. In the store," he said.

"I thought you were stalking me."

"Stalking you, yes. Big game hunter. Couldn't let you get away."

"Don't you think we should at least rinse the dishes?"

"Not on your life. I'd much rather kiss than rinse dishes."

And so it went for the next three hours. Until we landed on his massive king-size bed, still in our clothes, his touch light, smooth on my thigh above the knee. He whispered about going on about salmon and tuna for so long he thought I'd laugh in his face and walk away. Cancel our Saturday date. "I needed to find a reason to keep you talking."

My insides turned over and embraced this man, my wariness and mistrust crumbling. What if I got hurt? All the clichés about men and the chase. Believe the actions, not the words. All of it galloped through my mind, and what surfaced was the part where I told myself to take a chance. I rolled onto him, kissed his neck. He moaned as my mouth moved along his jaw, my tongue flicking his ear, the tiniest hint, a sensitivity test. He moaned again, his hands moving down to my butt.

"I'm in no hurry," he said. "Eventually, I'd like to undress you."

That was slow, too, the undressing. First my top, his lips on my breasts, his tongue running down my stomach and around in circles. He pulled up my skirt, an inch at a time, a tease I could feel through my clothes. His hands moved on my inner thighs, brushing that little sensitive spot as if by mistake. And up again, then down my legs to the back of my knees as he rolled me over, undid my bra. His tongue found the small of my back, one hand going underneath my panties to cup my ass.

"I'm not good at talking dirty," he said. "But I'll make up for it." His voice was low, a gentle growl from back in his throat.

"You sound plenty dirty to me."

"Oh, I am," he said. "I'm a dirty, dirty—"

My giggling shut him up, and he kissed me. "Your skirt is hampering my style," and he removed it, swung it around in the air, let it fall on the floor.

\*\*\*\*

Where was I? I rolled over, blinked. Luke. Oh. Oh,

yes. *Oh, no.* I blinked again, saw a dresser, a chair, a lamp. No Luke. Charcoal gray, all shadows, although it seemed to be the next day. Luke had the kind of curtains that block the sunlight completely.

In the bathroom, I used my finger to brush my teeth, found cream for my face—Luke had Nivea and some exotic looking European stuff on a shelf. I blinked at the image of a woman with heavy lids in the mirror and tried to puff out my hair. The bathroom was huge, as big as my bedroom. I stared at the tub. Gray. You had to step up to get into it. A Jacuzzi. I eyed the controls, aware that the water would swirl and soothe, and I wanted that feeling of being massaged. I turned on the faucet, adjusted the temperature, and then locked the bathroom door. Didn't know the man, didn't want him popping in to check me out in the tub unless he had a mug of coffee in his hand. I climbed the steps, hunkered down in the tub, and contemplated my pink toenails. Surely, he wouldn't mind my taking a bath.

Later, wrapped in the fuzzy robe I found at the foot of the bed, I tracked Luke down in the kitchen, the skylight illuminating his unshaven face, a sweet face. I had done this edgy thing a while back, slept with a man I'd met once and then reconnected with at the fish counter in Stop and Shop. Over twenty-five years since my last one-night stand, and it seemed I was a sucker for a good fish dinner.

I stood looking at him from the doorway, and my face burned remembering what it had been like, what we had been like together. He slid close and put his arms around me.

"Early riser, and I didn't want to wake you." He hugged me harder. "Good, you found the robe."

"Whose is it?" I asked. "She's bigger than me," and I cringed inwardly, hearing myself.

"My daughter's. She won't mind."

*Whew.* This felt good, right somehow, relaxing against him, Luke holding me, stroking my back, in no hurry, no hurry at all. I could feel the scratchiness of his beard on my cheek.

"Coffee? I just made it. Did you have a good soak?"

"Yes, please. Coffee. Lots of it." I nodded. "Great soak." No matter what I said, I wouldn't say things like *I never do this, I never sleep with a man I've just met.* With luck there would be no relationship talk, no vertical-horizontal discussions, no tank theories.

"Be right back. Sit. Sip that coffee." He handed me an envelope. "Put this away for now. Save it to read when you get home, when you're in the mood."

"In the mood." He didn't say he would call me. "How in the mood?"

"Not in the mood exactly. Rested, ready and relaxed. Once you read it, you'll understand what I mean."

"Oh."

"Then call me. After."

"Okay." I sipped my coffee, wondering if I should hustle out of there. Lingering was not a good idea, and I'd come off as needy.

"Shall we have breakfast? Pancakes with fresh blueberries, the best buckwheat pancakes in the world, according to my daughter. When she was four. Or would you rather have an omelet? I've got peppers and a little ham I can dice, a little tomato. Or oatmeal? Steel-cut with the blueberries."

"It all sounds so good."

"Then we can take a walk. Either go to Sleeping Giant and do one of the trails. Or, if you have stuff to do, we'll take a shorter walk at the reservoir. What do you think?"

What was more awkward than the morning after when sleeping with a guy for the first time?

And this wasn't. Not at all.

"Pancakes, definitely," I said. "And tell me about your daughter."

\*\*\*\*

Breakfast went on for two hours of leisurely banter in between trading sections of *The Times,* chomping on Luke's stupendous pancakes with extra blueberries, and making out on the couch. In the middle of making out, we took breaks, and during one break I checked out the built-in bookcases lining the walls straddling either side of the fireplace.

"Built-ins. I love them, and I'm jealous you've got so many books." I ran a finger down the shelves, weighing and measuring in my mind. Everything from *A Tree Grows in Brooklyn* to Art Spiegelman. Luke had quite the collection. "They're not in alphabetical order."

"I'm not that anal."

"You've got Joyce Carol Oates and Norman Mailer side-by-side? Isn't that a little risky? I'm not sure they get along."

"Never heard a complaint from either one," Luke shot back, and I rushed over to fling myself on him, crumpling the Book section he was reading. "Help me, help me Rhonda," he sang out in a surprisingly good imitation of whichever Beach Boy had the falsetto. He flipped me over and attacked my neck, his lips blowing raspberries until I lay still and limp. Then he kissed me slowly, starting with the places on my neck where he'd raspberried me, traveling to my collar bone, and then up to my mouth.

We enjoyed some more quality time in Luke's bedroom.

By the time I extricated myself, it was too late for even a short walk with Luke. At home, I changed. Left the envelope on the kitchen table when I went to pick up Isabel, after school, for our girly afternoon out. The teacher on maternity leave was back, and this was my first day not working, a real bummer.

We tooled north on the highway, Isabel jabbering on about a new student from Crete who spoke four languages, while we headed for the Crystal Mall, an hour away. Shopping. Always the right thing to do after you've had rather spectacular sex with a man you're all mushy on. Though, I hadn't yet shared any of the more intimate details about Luke with Isabel.

My mind meandered over the turns the evening took, rolling here and there, reliving the high spots. There were many. His hands sliding down my arms, my neck, a man who understood the seductive power of slow. I shivered.

"Did you hear me?" said Isabel, reminding me she was right there in the car, and that imagining Luke's hands all over me with my best friend at my side was plain creepy.

"Yes, trying to concentrate here. Where do I turn off?" I thumbed the steering wheel audio control button. Thelonious Monk jumped out of the speakers, bringing me back to reality.

"Too loud," said Isabel, raising her voice over

Monk, "and we don't get off for another six miles."

Crystal Mall was huge, and the parking lot was empty, except for a cluster of cars near the entrance. My phone whistled as we headed for the entrance, and I pulled it from my bag, stopped and read the message. "It's from Dana. Listen to this. She wants to do our New York thing 'cause I won the stupid contest. Isn't that gracious? A weekend next month." I texted back the thumbs-up emoji.

"Nice, yes."

Yes, it would be nice, and maybe I was uptight about the contents of the envelope Luke had given me. I should have read it, not left it home on purpose. But I didn't want to involve Isabel, start a whole discussion when I didn't have any idea of what I might find.

We entered through the automatic door, ignored the huge multicolored mall map, and headed for H&M, the trendy teenage store.

"You get thirty minutes at H&M, because I couldn't squeeze my left tit into one of their little tops, and then we go to a normal store, where the clothes fit normal women."

"If your students could hear you now," I scolded, scoping out the store on a holistic level, the huge space arranged by color so the eye was pulled in, overwhelmed and overstimulated. "Dana calls H&M cheap and cheerful," I told Isabel. "The sort of place where you get an outfit for a Saturday night date."

"Yeah, for teeny-tiny people, who wear skirts skimming the *pupik*," Isabel sneered, using her grandmother's Yiddish word for belly button.

*I have a date for Saturday night. Don't I?* Luke hadn't mentioned anything about getting together for our Saturday night date. *Was Luke a one-night wonder?*

A woman in her thirties wearing a long brown skirt, and baggy beige shirt browsed the sale items. I gestured with my chin, and when Isabel didn't notice, I jabbed her with my elbow.

"Ow, cut that out. I bruise easily."

"Over there," I said in a low voice. "That woman is so young and look what she's wearing. I don't know if it's cheap, but it's definitely not cheerful. We can do better, can't we?" I guided Isabel over to a sale rack, and pulled out a red pencil skirt with a kick pleat. "Not too short for a woman my age, is it?"

"Not bad," Isabel said, fingering the material. "A little gem among all this little girl stuff. Try it on."

"Don't rush me. I've just started looking." Isabel was putting me on edge when we were here to have fun. I wanted to relax, but all I could think of, now that I had the one-night stand in my head was…would I see him again, or not?

My phone rang. Isabel gave me a look while I groped around in my bag.

"Look, I'll meet you at Express. Call me," and she was gone. I answered, but the call dropped. The area code wasn't familiar.

I took a circular route around the color-coded racks, grabbing a white sweater here, a fitted silver blouse there, wondering what Isabel had up her ass. So impatient. My phone rang again.

"Hello." I headed for a corner nook thinking I could crouch, not disturb anyone.

"Hello, I am calling Sunny Chanel. This is Janet Carbaugh with *The Latest Word*. Do you have a moment?"

"Sure." *The Latest Word*?

"You responded to a survey found on our *Latest Word* podcast, and I am following up with comments and interviews from women in their fifties and over, dating after a long hiatus. Do you recall participating?"

It took a fuzzy moment before I recalled contacting someone at the *Latest Word* podcast. "Oh, that was a while ago, three or four months?" Three or four months, a lifetime ago when it came to online dating.

"Yes, it generally takes some time to listen to responses and collate the material. Enjoyed your input. Articulate and savvy."

"Oh, thanks."

"May I ask some questions about your first date after a long-term marriage, subsequent dates, the process, and why you decided to try online dating? Your motivation, the challenges?"

"Sure." Out of the corner of my eye a yellow sleeveless blouse caught my attention. "I'm in a store right now, so it's a little difficult."

"I'm on deadline. Could you talk to me later in the day? My number is now on your phone. How about five-thirty?"

It was already four-thirty. We'd barely been here forty-five minutes. At this rate, she might as well interview me now. I pulled out a pen. That and my cell and lipstick were all that fit in my mini-bag. "Give me your name again, please." I wrote it on my hand.

"Five thirty today?" she said.

Speed-shopping was no fun, and we'd want to stop for dinner. What if Luke called? My kidneys tilted. "Seven. I can do seven." We'd have to race through the mall and eat in the car on the way home.

"You're using my name?"

"Yes, that was the agreement. Seven it is," and she hung up before I could ask when the podcast was airing.

\*\*\*\*

Isabel refused to eat in the car, so we ended up at the food court, our bags of goodies on a chair, plates of stir fry with extra veggies, white rice, and noodles in front of us. Isabel sawed through a spring roll with a plastic knife and gave me half while I opened the hot mustard and made a little mixture with the duck sauce. She dipped the spring roll in sauce and took a bite.

"Whoa, this mustard is hot." Her eyes watered.

"I slept with Luke last night."

Isabel made a little choking sound and covered her chest with a hand. "*The* Luke who ghosted? From before?"

"The same. I bumped into him at the supermarket." And I filled her in on everything I'd been hiding, from the phone calls when I was mooning over Noah, all the way up and through our bountiful breakfast and the making out. *He's a better kisser than Noah.* No, I didn't say that.

"When are you seeing him again?" she asked.

"I'm not sure."

Isabel went quiet.

"He gave me an envelope. I didn't open it."

"It's not money, is it?"

"Funny." My cell rang. I glanced at the number on the screen, not one I recognized. "Could be the reporter."

"Hello, is this Sunny?"

"Yes." I couldn't remember her name, the reporter.

"Janet Carbaugh. Do I have your permission to record this?"

"Yes, uh, I'm—we're in the food court at the mall, and my friend is with me." *She's recording this?* My shoulders tensed as I tried to remember why I'd wanted to do this. At the time, I'd been fascinated by internet dating and its workings, but now the reality of throwing my name and dating opinions out there in the public domain held little appeal.

"May I begin?"

"Ask away."

"As an over-fifty woman, are you looking for different qualities in an online date than when you were younger?"

Isabel poked me and mouthed *speaker*. I shook my head, trying to concentrate. "Well, I think I'm more accepting at this age. I don't have a long list of must-haves and demands."

"Do you feel it's more difficult dating at your age because men are looking to date younger women?" She put the emphasis on *younger*, in case I didn't catch her drift.

"You just turned fifty," hissed Isabel, who has super hearing, and how could I have forgotten? Her eyes held that warning look I knew well.

"Men who want to date younger women don't contact me, so I don't know." Isabel scrunched closer. "Do you think men want to date younger women?" I asked her.

"A few jerks, sure."

"My friend says a few jerks want to date younger women." To hell with it. I pressed speaker.

Raising her voice to be heard over the din of mall

traffic, Isabel said, "Ask her where she gets her information."

There was a pause before Janet asked, "Do you choose outfits that make you more competitive with younger women? When you're planning what to wear?"

Confused, I looked to Isabel, who shrugged.

"More competitive?" I said. "What does that mean?" My voice conveyed that ornery tone you get when you're doing someone a favor, and they insult you without even knowing it.

"More competitive," Janet said, "in the sense of formfitting, say, or sexy."

Isabel leaned toward me. Without lowering her voice, she asked, "How old is this interviewer anyway? Did she finish eighth grade?"

I turned my back to Isabel, clutched the phone. "Dress sexy, well, not on a first meet."

"Excuse me," said Janet. "I don't mean to offend your friend." A pause.

"Are we done?" I asked.

"Almost, just a little background now. Have you dated a lot of men? And do you consider yourself a cougar?"

Isabel catapulted out of her chair, came around and stood leaning down to speak directly into the phone. "You are insulting, and you're ignorant about women our age. You will not use the information from this interview, and if you don't agree—" The phone exchanged hands, floating into hers. "I want to speak to your supervisor, *now*. Unless you cancel this interview and delete the recording."

The word *supervisor* held all the nuance necessary to get action from Janet Carbaugh, who, it turned out, was happy to terminate the interview. Which was perfect, because I wanted more hot mustard with my spring roll.

On the drive home—with still no word from Luke—Isabel quizzed me on why I'd wanted to be interviewed. "What was that? Do you enjoy being talked down to by some young bitch reporter from some obscure podcast? If I had the time, I'd go online and write a review. That is irresponsible reportage."

"A review? Seriously?"

"Don't mock me when I'm trying to defend your honor."

"You'd take the time to write a review? You're worse than me. It was a crap interview. Super crap. Remember when we used to call everything super crap, whether it was good or bad?"

"The good old super crap days, I remember them well."

"I'm so glad we still haven't grown up," I said and reached over and squeezed Isabel's cheek.

"Keep your hands on the wheel."

But I could see her smile from the corner of my eye.

\*\*\*\*

Back home in the kitchen, I scooped peanut butter from the jar with a spoon and slapped it on a half slice of bread. That was it, no jelly, just a dry mini-sandwich I ate in four bites before logging on to my email.

There were a couple emails from the dating site, but nothing interesting, and I felt antsy, so I got busy. Got out the vacuum and sucked up dust balls and crumbs in the kitchen. Sprayed the counters with Windex, and rearranged the stuff in the freezer, long overdue.

Afterward, I sat on the couch and opened my e-reader, but didn't feel like searching for a new book. Because. Because there was that envelope sitting and waiting. My stomach gurgled and peanut butter reflux rolled up my throat.

A glass of wine was needed. Pinot noir to be precise, the antidote for reflux of any variety. I poured a generous glass and toasted myself, took a sip.

Was it normal to give a woman an envelope to open after you'd had this great time, fooled around, and then made love, and—

Wouldn't a normal man *call* the day after? A text would be the absolute minimum, better than nothing. I put the e-reader aside. This sucked, this not knowing, and I couldn't concentrate with the envelope floating at the edge, unopened.

Wait a minute. A text wasn't better than nothing; a text was pedestrian. Luke had given me instructions. Simple and clear. Told me to read whatever was in that envelope later, when I was in the mood.

*Once you read it, you'll understand what I mean.* Isn't that what he said? *Then call me. After.*

I rose from the couch, took the envelope, and cut it open with my kitchen scissors. The sickening peanut butter taste repeated but I toughed it out, pulled out a single sheet of paper and unfolded it.

A poem.

*The Dynamics of Chaos*

*You look at me and the current from your blink sets off chaos miles away for people who have never even seen your eyes, theirs plucked by the spinning of the wind.*

*You ask—have you ever undressed a woman whose skin smells as good as she looks? Have you ever breathed her in so deeply to unloose the soapstone lodged in her roots?*

*I say—do you know Australia's moving at the rate of your nails' growth? Will something so huge ever falter? As my foot pounds down, a tsunami hits Cuba's coast six months from now.*

Read it again, then slipped it back in the envelope, and propped it next to the lamp. In junior high, Peter Donovan had written a poem, more along the lines of a *roses are red* type of thing. He handed it to me in the cafeteria and scurried away looking embarrassed. I avoided him after that, later heard he transferred to a Catholic school to prepare for the priesthood. The priesthood. Isabel and I made jokes about how I'd been instrumental in steering him in the right direction. Well, it seemed funny in junior high.

This poem was different. This was an adult poem. Unfinished, perhaps a bit raw. I plucked the sheet of paper from the envelope, reread a key line.

*You ask—have you ever undressed a woman whose skin smells as good as she looks?*

Was he talking about me? I could ask, but that was the direct approach, and I had another idea. After another few sips of the pinot, I logged on to my email account.

*To: Luke*

*From: Sunny*

*Subject: no panties*

*I was thinking of kissing your neck and having you slip your hand up my leg, discovering all I was wearing was my garter belt and stockings, no panties. I'll have to try that. You'll have to try that, too.*

I stared at the email, my first dirty email ever, and therefore long overdue. *Luke's hand on my thigh.* The flesh there felt the weight of him.

One and a half nanoseconds after the panty email, Luke called.

****

The next night I wore the yellow blouse from H&M for ice cream with Luke.

I'd spent twenty minutes scrounging around for my favorite jeans, the weathered, not-too-tatty ones that flattered my ass.

Jeans, the yellow blouse, and cute sandals. Since I didn't want to invite him in yet, I ran down the steps as soon as his car appeared in the driveway.

"Hey, so glad to see you," he said when I slid in. He leaned over and cupped my chin, gave me a quick kiss. "Winward's?"

"Sounds good." This wasn't supposed to be awkward, but it was, a little.

He started to back out, looking over his shoulder, and instead, he stopped the car. "Let's do that over," and he pulled back up the driveway, unbuckled, and tilted toward me, his hand on the back of my head, the second kiss slow, meandering. "Now we can go. Winward's, you said?"

"Oh, yeah," I breathed, any trace of discomfiture gone. "It's the best."

"I've changed the plan for Saturday slightly. I'll tell you about it over ice cream. And I want your critique of my poem. You haven't said much, but I know what I can use to loosen you up. A sundae, gooey and disgusting," he said and pulled away from the house. "We'll share."

"Share? I want my own gooey sundae."

"I'm flexible," he said and headed up Whitney. We enjoyed a few minutes of comfortable silence. Until I didn't feel so comfortable. What was going on with us? Was it because we'd...well, that shouldn't embarrass us, but I couldn't remember the last time I'd had sex on a first date. In my twenties? Yes, and what was his name? Frederick. Who could forget a name like that? Frederick didn't like being called Fred; I knew because he told me. And why was I thinking of Frederick?

Luke pulled into the parking lot. "So, you did read the poem, didn't you? My poem?" We got out and stood for a moment taking in the pale-yellow splendor that is Winward's, an ice cream store that looked like it belonged on the block, as if a family lived here. He took my hand, but before we reached the door, Luke pulled me to the side and put his hands on my shoulders. "Look, I think we're both a little nervous. I want to put it out there that we're not...let's not..." he leaned in close to whisper, "not sleeping together again just yet. No worries, there's no agenda."

When I opened my mouth to respond, he put a finger over it gently. "That didn't come out right. I like you a lot, and want you to be comfortable. You seem on edge."

"I'm on edge all right. Drooling for the ice cream you promised me."

Inside at the counter, Luke didn't get a sundae after all. "Too much sugar isn't good for you," he said. "And by that, I mean me." He ordered a maple walnut cone, and I got coffee with chocolate chunks. We sat in a corner in the little annex, the window looking out at the parking lot.

"So. You read it?" Luke said, his tongue curling around the maple walnut. I took a nibble.

"Of course, I read it." A family of five bounced in with two kids under four, followed by three teenage girls in shorts and sandals. The little boy wandered over from the family, peered up at me, and reached out a chubby hand.

"Me," he said.

"Matthew, leave the lady—" His mother stepped over to scoop him up. "Sorry about that."

"He's a sweetheart," I said and turned back to Luke. "I have trouble with poetry." In the corner the teenagers howled, passed their phones around. A giant banana split sat in front of the trio, three long-handled spoons protruding like tools.

"Let's take our cones and finish them in the car. Quick, before they melt," and Luke grabbed my hand. Outside, the air was thick and starting to chill, the sky darkening. We scrambled inside Luke's car, balancing the cones.

"Whew, quiet at last." I sat back against the headrest, holding the cone out to make sure no drips reached my blouse.

"When you left, I didn't go out all day. I was afraid I'd miss your call. I figured you knew I was a crazy man. Writing a poem, that was bad. But giving it to you. Then it was nine at night and you hadn't called. I was about to phone you. And then I checked my email."

"Ut oh."

"No *ut oh* about it."

"We're talking about your poem," I said. It was one thing to send a dirty email, especially fortified by a glass of cabernet, and quite another to be reminded about it. "I'm intimidated," I said, crunching the cone. "Intimidated by poetry. I so seldom receive, of an afternoon, a poem."

"Of an afternoon, huh? Pity." Luke held his hand out for the napkin, rolled it into a ball and tossed it onto the back seat.

"So...when did you write it?"

"That morning, while I was waiting for you to make an appearance."

"I embarrassed myself, carrying on at the fish counter," I said out of nowhere, flashing back to the supermarket.

"It was very cute."

"Cute?" I shuddered. "You're joking."

"You were trying so hard to be helpful," he said.

"So." I thought of Luke behind me in the checkout. "You tracked me?"

"That was nothing. The hard part was inviting you to the barbecue. I kept expecting you to walk away. Then afterward, I didn't even know if you'd want to see me again." He stopped and looked at me. "Put on your seat belt. I'd like to take you somewhere. Okay?"

We were both quiet on the drive, and I didn't ask questions, not even when we ended up in East Haven at the beach parking lot with no other cars around. All the popular eateries along the road were closed, and the whole area was quiet, sounds coming from the gentle lapping of the waves, the moon a spec behind clouds. Luke cut the motor and turned toward me, tucking my hair behind my ear and making my skin tingle.

"Yesterday," he said, taking up where we'd left off in Winward's parking lot. "No, two days ago. When you were telling me about those fishes." He leaned in and kissed my neck. "All those fishes. Tuna." More little kisses. "Salmon." Kisses. "I knew you—"

"Don't remind me."

"Don't remind you? I'm reminding myself." He stopped the kissing, looked at me. "When you took off, I followed you. So we'd meet together at the checkout. And now I want to kiss you. Can I come over there?"

In one smooth move, while I balanced, my hand on the middle console, he slid over and wedged himself under me. I straddled him, and he ran his thumb over my shirt. "The other night?" he whispered. "You turned me on so much." He reached behind and slid his hands under my jeans in the back. "Maybe one day we can do it all again," he said kissing me. "What do you think? Would you like that?" He slipped the shoulder straps of my bra down, and planted kisses on my shoulder, first one side, then the other. He lifted his head to look at me.

"You are delicious," his voice raspy. A car pulled into the lot, its lights illuminating the car's interior. Police.

He pulled down my shirt. "If they catch us like this," he said, "they'll laugh and walk away. I couldn't stand being laughed at for making out in the car at my age." I hunched up, my hand on the door for balance as he slid over into the driver's seat. For a moment we watched the police car as it made a tour around the lot and exited. Then he turned back and took my hand.

"Would you like to come home with me?" he asked.

Chapter Thirteen
Lukie…

Luke parked in front of the garage, came around to my side of the car, and opened the door, offering a hand to help me out. "I wasn't sure you'd come home with me," he said, hugging me against his chest. "Ice cream and now this, how lucky does a guy get?"

I craned my neck to look up at him. "I love it when you wax corny."

"Corny? Don't have a corny bone anywhere." He leaned down and kissed my neck, tracing a path with his mouth up my cheek, making me glad I'd decided on my red thong and matching bra at the last minute. *I'm wearing this for myself,* yup, those were my very thoughts, a liar's thoughts.

"What I do well, though, is talk dirty," Luke said in my ear. This prompted a fit of the giggles, and he wrapped an arm around me as we walked up the path to the house.

"Say something dirty," I said, effecting a pseudo-posh British accent. "Prove you're a dirty, dirty man."

"Lukie?"

He spun around before I could even register the voice, coming from somewhere in the dark behind us where a woman stood, the streets lights reflecting off her pale hair, frizzy and wild, the kind of frizzy that is the exception to the frizz rule, and wild in a good way.

"Pamela? What are you...you shouldn't be here."

The hair framed a heart-shaped face, lips painted a deep dark color I couldn't make out at night but guessed was Joan Crawford red. It didn't matter. They were full and lush. Post-sex lips.

"Who says? You put me on ignore, don't answer my phone calls. How else do I get your attention?" Her gaze fastened on Luke as if I didn't exist. Not that I expected this woman—Pamela—to introduce herself.

"Please. This is not the time. Get in your car and go home."

"Not until you talk to me. Don't be mean, Lukie." Her voice took on a petulant tone, a weird combination of sexy-husky and pleading.

"Another time. We'll set up a time and place to meet," said Luke in a no-nonsense tone I'd never heard. "Not now. Can't you see—"

"Now. I need to talk now," her voice rising as she moved closer. She stood a mere foot from Luke, blocking our way. I stepped back.

"Give me a minute," Luke said, squeezing my hand.

"Aren't you gonna introduce us?" she said. Luke shook his head. A shiver rushed through me. This Pamela had her hands in her pockets, not the most reassuring sign that she wasn't out to rip my eyeballs from their sockets and throw them in the bushes.

Luke leaned closer and lowered his voice. "I've got no choice. I have to talk to her."

"I'm sorry, Lukie," said Pamela. "I didn't mean to come over here like this, but I miss you." Her hands came out in plain view and hung at her sides, her shoulders slumping. "A few months ago, you said you'd call me. You promised. Are you going back on your promise?"

*The old girlfriend, definitely.* I wandered over to the house next door to give Luke and Pamela some space and privacy. Lights shone from what looked like the living room, a family enjoying a quiet evening of reading or Netflix. Reruns of Roadrunner were better than this.

They talked in low voices for a few long moments. Pamela glanced my way once, tilting her body and watching me, but Luke's hand snaked to her shoulder, turning her to face him again. Their voices stayed in low murmur mode, too faint for me to decipher the words. Funny that when he mentioned her on that long-ago first meet, the whacko part hadn't been so obvious.

There is a moment during situations like this when you decide you've had enough. Not that I'd ever been witness to a stalker situation, and maybe this wasn't a real stalker thing. Maybe Pamela had dropped over for an ill-timed, friendly visit. Maybe she'd baked brownies and wanted to share, or her pet Mexican red-knee tarantula, the kind that lives up to thirty years, had run away from home, and she needed Luke's help tracking him down.

It didn't matter. The mood we'd built up in the car was lost, and nothing tonight would fix it, not with the Pamela baggage lingering on the sidewalk.

Luke joined me in front of the neighbor's, shaking his head. "I could give you the keys to the house so you could go inside while I..." His voice drained away to nothing, as if he were reconsidering this idea. "She doesn't want to leave just yet."

Pamela stood where he'd left her, knees bent in an

awkward pose, a sweater pulled around her slight frame. All in black, she blended into the bushes, a murky figure. Her pale hair shone, catching a few rays of moon glow, a good witch Glinda gone wrong.

And there was that petulant voice.

"What a mess. I'm so sorry," Luke said. "She did this once before, a month or so after we broke up for real, but I haven't seen or talked to her in seven or eight months." He bent down and whispered. "She could be off her meds. I'm not sure. She was pretty compliant about taking them, but who knows?"

*Off her meds, off her meds, off her meds,* ping-ponged in my brain. Glenn Close in that Michael Douglas movie. What was the name? *Fatal* something, with *fatal* being the key word. Here I was in the middle of the biggest movie cliché ever. The stalker ex-girlfriend off her meds.

He'd dated a woman who was now his personal stalker. Whatever that said about Luke, it wasn't a recommendation.

Look," and he leaned toward me, "I don't want to involve you in my problem here. I'll need to make a call or two—"

"I should go."

"Saturday. We're still on for tomorrow, aren't we?" Luke drew back to look at me.

Saturday. Our dinner date. There would be no spending time with Luke, not tonight, and who knew what would happen tomorrow. I'd been so looking forward to...well, to going home with Luke. Not that I'd thought of going home with him exactly. Okay, so I'd thought about it. A totally normal thought when you go out for ice cream and end up making out in the car at the beach with the waves crashing and the occasional foghorn in the distance. Or maybe that had been a police car honking.

"Lukie?"

"I have to deal with her. I'm sorry."

"I'll get an Uber," I said.

He looked confused, smacked a hand to his forehead. "So sorry, that's right, I picked you up, didn't I? I'll take you home. No problem." He jerked back, pulling his keys out of his pocket. "Wait in the car, Pamela, will you please?"

"Don't. I'll call an Uber. Not a big deal. You have plenty to handle here."

"Absolutely not. It'll just take a few—"

"I'll do Uber." My phone was already in my hands, and I was scrolling for the app.

He laid his hand on mine. "I'll order it, no worries. Please." I nodded and Luke pulled out his phone and swiped. "Be sure to text me when you get home, will you?"

Minutes passed, the three of us standing like zombies on the sidewalk, waiting for the Uber, Luke and I, arms touching, Pamela on the grass off to the side, her eyes focused on Luke. Behaving herself, so far. What would she do once my Uber sped me away? And what would Luke say to her? How would he phrase it, patiently explaining the obvious, that she didn't belong in front of his house? Or would he tell her to go the hell home? Call the cops? These were details that interested me.

On the other hand, I wanted so badly to be in my own bed. All the pent-up frustration and mistrust and doubt of the past months, starting with Mushroom Man, and then Frank and ugh, that ugly business with José, followed by Noah, the man who professed his infatuation right up until he dumped me…everything leading up to my big, big funk—all came to roost inside my head.

And then inexplicably, Luke had contacted me. His texts and emails during my worst days, the hours spent talking. If you added it all up, it was weeks, weeks getting to know him on the phone of all places—so unlike most men—because don't most guys hate talking on the phone?

Instead, Luke gave me hope that I'd emerge a better, stronger person from the mess I'd made of the whole dating thing. So kind, so understanding, holding nothing back, from his Twinkies and Ding Dongs habit to going the professional route with therapy. He wasn't embarrassed to let it hang out.

Oh, and the poem. Written for me.

"*Now it's different. I'm different,*" he'd said. I believed him.

Was it true? Had he changed?

I grabbed Luke by the hand and dragged him across the sidewalk to the neighbor's house so Pamela wouldn't be able to eavesdrop. She probably had highly tuned senses, like a Rottweiler. Besides, the driver would be here any minute. "Come with me."

"What?"

"Come with me in the Uber. Leave her here."

A strange expression crossed his face. Even in the dark I could tell he was thinking about it, had an eager, furtive look that disappeared as quickly as it appeared. He glanced over at Pamela, put his hands on my arms. "I'd be postponing the inevitable. I have to deal with her, and I want to get it over with."

A red van sailed around the corner, slowed in front of us, and stopped. The door opened, and a young man in a baseball cap stepped out. "Who's coming with me? Any luggage?"

Luke didn't even look his way. "You understand, don't you? His voice lifeless, shoulders sagging. His arms came around me, and for a moment I thought about pulling back—thought about Pamela and how she might react, what she might do. I stepped forward into his hug.

His chin burrowed into my neck. "I'd love nothing more than to be with you tonight." An endearing half-smile cracked his face as I ducked, loosening his gentle grip, and clambered into the van.

Pamela was already walking toward Luke as we started to leave.

\*\*\*\*

Five minutes after the driver dropped me off, I was on the highway hitting seventy-five, checking the rear-view mirror for cruising police cars. My brain whirled with the image of Pamela's blondness, her desperation, her *Lukie*, and I couldn't help but picture her on the lawn in front of his house looking up at Luke.

I almost missed the Guilford exit, swerved off at the last minute, hitting the shoulder, sending forth a shower of rocks and debris and making my chest thump.

The phone rang with Isabel's special ringtone. I thumbed the Bluetooth button.

"Got to talk to you." She sounded out of breath.

"Funny, but I'm almost at your house."

"What?" she said. "You're coming here?"

"Yeah, a last-minute thing."

"Okay, I'll be waiting outside."

*What's with the waiting outside?* Sure enough, when I drove up, windows open to catch the briny smell of the sea in Isabel's backyard, she was already nestled sideways onto the huge porch swing, her chin on her knees. Beyond the house, lights over the water on Long Island Sound blinked, the nighttime insects sounding their cries.

She sprinted down the porch stairs, a bottle of wine in one hand, a bag over her shoulder. "Let's go. I've got a nice bottle of pinot noir and some yummy snacks. We're having a pajama party."

"Now? Tonight?"

"I've got to get the hell out of here. Robert is being an old fart. Besides, I miss shooting the breeze, talking about books and movies, and going down memory lane. We haven't had a girls' night in a while. Can I ride with you? I've already started on the wine."

We headed out and, right before getting on the highway entrance, I sneaked a look at my phone. Nothing from Luke.

"How come you were in my neck of the woods anyway?" said Isabel.

Hesitation, a tell-tale sign Isabel picked up on. "A date with Luke. It didn't end well. Which is putting it mildly." I filled her in on the details, right down to my Uber exit from the scene. "His ex-girlfriend turned up at his house wanting to talk with him. What does that say?"

"She doesn't know her boundaries? She's off her meds? She wants his recipe for spinach linguini?" Isabel was in a strange mood. "By the way, is he a good cook? A man who can cook is a treasure forever."

"Be serious."

"What does it say?" Beside me, Isabel twitched, as if this conversation irritated her. "The guy has a little baggage, like any normal human."

"Think about it from my point of view," and I feigned patience I didn't feel. "I go out with him and he doesn't call. Then months later, he calls. Well, you know the rest and here I am letting my guard down and starting to trust him and boom. Pamela turns up. It makes me wonder, is this out of the blue, or has he been keeping in touch with her?" I was determined to get an opinion out of Isabel. "They could have been in contact, easily. Nowadays it's so simple."

"Things happen. Relationships aren't always smooth."

"That's all you've got? That's newsworthy, relationships aren't always smooth? I'm having second thoughts here, and you're not helping. I need logic."

"Logic. What's logical is to ask the man. All I can do is guess."

I pulled into my driveway, wondering if we'd get through this evening without carping at one another. Hard to admit, but Isabel had a point. And yes, I'd speak to Luke. When he called. And I didn't have control over when the man would call.

Isabel opened the door. Instead of getting out, she leaned back into the car.

"Give me a break with the analyzing and therapy thing. I'm fed up with my honey always being too busy and frazzled to spend time with me, and basically all we've got together are Sundays. This will be going on for the whole school year." She heaved a sigh that shook the car. "I don't mean to take it out on you. Let's go in and have that wine, and I'll vent more. Hell, I'll let you vent too."

Twenty minutes later, in our pajamas on the couch with wine and snacks, Isabel traded in her pissed off tone for a resigned one. "We're cooking dinner, he's taking calls and texting. Coming to bed with his laptop. His laptop, it's insane." She drained her glass and poured another. "So what good is living in a house on the beach if you don't have any free time? Although, in all honesty, how could he refuse that big a promotion? Two and a half thousand students is a hell of a lot of responsibility. And hormones. He loves it. But the reality isn't that much fun for me, and I'm a selfish bitch." She took a big gulp of wine.

"Yeah, two selfish bitches having wine." Isabel smiled and raised her glass, and I raised mine. "Look, no matter what you say, you're so lucky you're part of a couple. Roberto is a great guy, even if he's a little consumed at the moment."

"This is the first night I've spent away from Roberto since I moved in." She sat for a moment staring into space. "Talk to Luke," she said. Take one thing at a time."

"That makes sense. Of course, I will." I managed a smile.

Isabel swiveled her head, checking out the living room. "Your place is starting to come together. I love the couches, the old posters."

"Thanks." We sat lost in our own thoughts for a few minutes. "Well, it's almost eleven and—"

"You want to know what I honestly think?" Isabel said. "I'm thinking you gave Luke a second chance already, and it worked out. So, see it through. Don't drop him now just because his old girlfriend turns up."

I nodded, holding my breath. *Yes, it could be that easy.* "Then why hasn't he called? Or texted? A text— how easy is texting? You can do it in the bathroom for crap sake."

"In the bathroom? And why would he have to—oh, never mind. I'm sure he's got his reasons. Like it's past eleven and he doesn't want to come off weird, now there's a thought."

"True."

My cell rang and I grabbed it, squinted at the number, my vision blurry with wine and stress.

"Is it him?" Isabel asked. "Answer it. Who else would—"

"Not him. Not a number I recognize." I let it go to voicemail. *He's not calling, not tonight. Too much on his plate to deal with.* "Shall we call it a night?" I said. "I've got a few things I need to do." Isabel gave me a look, as if she wanted to say something, but the moment passed.

"You should call Roberto," I said. "Give *him* a break."

\*\*\*\*

After Isabel disappeared into the guest room and closed the door, I went straight to the computer. I couldn't help it. I had questions and Google had the answers. I typed "Woman stalking man."

My cell rang. The same number as before. A shard of irritation pricked. Didn't Luke realize this not calling or texting, the equivalent of the silent treatment, was driving me crazy? "I'm on pins and needles," my mom used to say. She probably still said it. "Pins and needles," I said out loud. "I'm on pins and needles, you *idjit*," pronouncing idiot with my special Brit accent, probably not authentic, but who cared? Luke was a lousy communicator, and I would tell him when I saw him.

At the thought of Luke, my mind went to dirty places. Fun dirty. This wasn't good, this *craving* Luke. Worse, it wasn't like Luke to ignore me, not the Luke I'd come to know better, the attentive Luke. Hadn't it been hours since I'd left them on the sidewalk in front of his house?

Google showed fifty million results for *woman stalking man*, and twenty-nine million for *women stalking men*, along with videos. One featured a woman who'd sent 65,000 texts to a man she dated once. Apparently, anyone can be a stalker, but most stalkers are men.

My phone rang again. I studied the number— definitely not a Paris call. So, who calls at almost midnight? A persistent person that was who. Deranged? Maybe Luke's ex got hold of my number. *Get a grip*, my brain shouted.

Oh, what the hell. "Hello." It came out like a croak.

"It's Luke, so don't hang up. Finally. I was afraid I'd wake you, then I thought you were out when you didn't answer."

"I'm up. What happened? This isn't your number."

"Can't find my phone. Do you believe it? I went out and bought a throwaway, then I had to hunt for your number. I thought first of coming over there, but considering the events earlier tonight, me coming knocking on your door is way too creepy." He breathed out, a long sigh. "You don't know how relieved I am."

"Is there a problem?" *Is she still there with him?* All charming and Lukie this and Lukie that so…no, no, I'm getting carried away again. I sound like the crazy lady who wears her nightgown to the supermarket.

"When can I see you? I'd rather explain in person."

"Please, tell me now." I tried to keep my voice calm, but the worry seeped in. If there was a problem, I wasn't waiting until tomorrow to get the bad news.

"Well, I talked to her. Ten or fifteen minutes. We were outside. So, that seemed to satisfy her because then she got into her car and left. No trouble. The thing is she has a boyfriend. See, she wants me to—I'd rather speak to you in person."

"What does she want?" My voice was hoarse.

"She wants us—wanted us—to remain friends."

And as soon as he said this, something rose in my chest. *See, see, things aren't so simple. You knew this would happen, whatever this is.*

"Remain friends? Are you friends now?" My voice cracked, and I felt that thing in my chest freeze and grow heavy.

"I told her no, that wasn't going to—I'm coming over there. I know it's late, but I have to see you. Five minutes, that's all. Now. Okay? I'm leaving, but I'm keeping you on the phone the whole time. Going outside, locking the front door." I heard rustling and a bump. "Going down the steps." The beep of the alarm. "Getting into the car." There was dead space, and then he was telling me he was turning the corner. "I'm on my way. Still there?"

"Yes, yes." From the guest room came the murmur of voices, Isabel talking to Roberto. "I'm hanging up now. I'll put the outside light on."

After shutting down the computer, I went into the bedroom and threw on jeans and a sweater over my pajamas, then checked my face in the mirror. I sat in a chair staring at my thumbs, wondering if Luke was a reliable guy. Because once a reliable guy, always a reliable guy. It was obvious Luke worked at becoming just that and…was still working on it. He wanted to be trustworthy.

I was crazy to judge him by that first blip of a date. That first date when I'd been so attracted, when we'd been so *in tune*, leaning toward one another like jazz musicians making it up as we went.

The doorbell rang, and I jumped as the guest room door flew open. Isabel stood in the middle of the hall in a sweatshirt over her pajamas looking around, startled, phone in hand. "Did I hear the doorbell? It can't be the doorbell. It's almost midnight."

"It's Luke." I smiled, a wide reassuring grin to signal this was a bit odd, yes, but all was under control. "Come meet him," and I opened the door. Behind me Isabel laughed, saying goodbye to Roberto.

He stood in jeans and a T-shirt, wearing a shaky smile.

"Get in here."

Luke entered, glanced at Isabel, and if he was surprised to see her, he hid it. I introduced them.

"Well, you two have had quite the evening, haven't you?" Isabel, ever the jokester.

"You could say that." Luke shook his head. We all stood looking at one another. Isabel blinked in the bright light, and gave a wary smile. Luke did his best to appear unruffled, but I sensed the nervous energy beneath his calm façade. Poor guy must have been plenty frustrated with me not answering my phone.

"So, how's Roberto?" I asked Isabel.

"Roberto is fine, and I'm going to bed. You two need your privacy. Nice to meet you, Luke."

"Stay a few minutes," I said, inflecting the short message with enough weight so she'd get that even a fifty-year-old woman wasn't immune to wanting the opinion of her good friend about the new guy she's dating.

"Luke? I wanted Isabel to meet you anyway. She's my oldest friend."

"She doesn't look very old to me, but I totally get that you want her to check me out." He stepped forward and hugged her. "Don't worry," he said, and she looked at me over the arm curled around her and mouthed *cute*.

"Watch out, though, I'm the guy with the misguided ex."

"Glad you stopped by," said Isabel, rearing back and looking up at him. "And by the way, we've got wine. I'll pour."

"Oh, God, yes please."

"Sit," and Isabel gestured to the couch.

"Luke and I took the love seat, and he reached for my hand. Isabel handed him the glass.

He took a long gulp. "Nice wine, too nice to glug, but I'm a bit stressed. Losing my cell was the topper."

"Hey," said Isabel. "I'm down with a good-looking guy coming to call at midnight, and you're a generous hugger. Do you cook?"

"Well, yes, indeed I do," and Luke's smile made my stomach jump.

"So," I said. "Is there still a problem or—"

"Okay, here's the story." His gaze drifted to Isabel

and he wrapped an arm around me, hugging me to his side. "So far, my ex-girlfriend isn't a stalker. Unless her surprise appearance at my house is repeated. Her new boyfriend? Who knows if he's got—"

"She has a boyfriend?" Isabel asked, her voice registering real surprise.

"She does. Although who knows if he's got the patience to deal with her issues. Sorry, but that's not my problem."

"What sort of issues?" I asked.

"She's on meds for anxiety disorder. I used to be good at talking her down, calming her. Sometimes she needed that...extra help. Not anymore. Can't do that." His voice took on a softer tone, as if he wanted to distance himself from the events of the evening. "I told her we can't be friends, or have contact of any kind. And we haven't been in contact, just so you know. The whole thing shook me up, and that's probably why I lost my phone." His gaze went from Isabel to me.

"Before you came, I googled stalkers," I blurted.

His hand froze in the air, his mouth opened and closed.

Isabel took this as her cue and stood. "It's been great meeting you, and I'm thrilled you're so open with the personal stuff. I mean that, Luke. Off to bed," and she was gone.

"Well, I don't blame you for getting a little wigged out." He turned on the couch to face me. "Find anything interesting?"

"A lot. Stuff about repetitive behavior, um texting and calling and—did she do that?"

"A couple times. I didn't respond."

We sat looking at one another, not a comfortable,

fuzzy feeling, not like in the restaurant when he'd kissed me at the table.

He ran his hand down my arm. "If I ever hear from her again, I'll tell you. You know by now I'm a sucker for you, right? Sunny? I get all corny because you're special to me, and I won't jeopardize what we have…our new relationship. I hope you'll begin to trust me. I want…I want the real thing with you. A relationship."

I scooched closer and laid my head on his chest, and he slid an arm around me, pulled me close. "I'm looking forward to tomorrow night. A normal evening with you. And now I am leaving. I promised five minutes, time's up."

"I can hardly keep my eyes open."

"So I see." He kissed the edge of my mouth, working his way down my neck and back up, released me, and was up and at the door. "Goodnight, sweet Sunny. Lock up."

Luke had guts coming over here after that visit from his ex. That counted for a lot.

Even so, I didn't dare think about what counted and what it all meant. I'd be like Scarlet O'Hara and think about it tomorrow.

Chapter Fourteen
Trattoria …

"So," said Isabel, tracing maps of France while I cut out little French cheeses and wrote their names on index cards. "You got the job offer at seven this morning? The phone call that woke me up?" Isabel yawned. We were sitting at the kitchen table prepping material, so I'd have lessons for my first day or two of class.

"Yeah, my supervisor sounding frantic. The teacher on maternity leave isn't coming back after all, so I get to finish out the rest of the school year with my twenty-two pseudo-Frenchies. Raging hormones and all that."

"Almost four months." Isabel pounded the table. "Best news ever. Okay, the maps and the cars—four different models—are done. Let me finish the Perrier, and I'll start on the olive oil. That's plenty. You'll have to get to school early to run off copies."

After the phone call, I'd driven downtown to Atticus, the restaurant-bookstore, for maple-frosting muffins and almond croissants. A sugar high to celebrate.

"I don't get why they called you at the last minute. Who the hell was covering your classes?"

"All I know is they were left in the lurch, and I didn't ask questions. This dropped in my lap." I reached for my muffin and took a bite. "Besides, I love the students."

We busied ourselves cutting and pasting the mock-ups. Isabel paused, held the scissors aloft. "What are you wearing?"

I looked up. "Wearing? When?"

"Tonight. Your dinner with Luke?" said Isabel.

"Don't remind me, I'm too keyed up."

"About the job?"

"No. Well, of course about the job. It's not that. I'm keyed up...the whole Luke thing has me keyed up." I capped the glue stick and folded my arms.

"Come on, the guy's a sweetheart. And the stalker thing isn't an issue. Unless you're making it into a big deal."

"So how do you decide if you can trust a man?" I said.

"What is this, eighth grade?" Isabel dunked a chunk of almond croissant in coffee and stuffed it in her mouth. "This is so good, and I'm so hungry."

"Didn't you have doubts? About Roberto? Wasn't he dating other women?"

"In the beginning. But it was too early for the let's-take-down-our-profiles talk."

"Luke and I haven't had that talk. Should I worry? Maybe we need that talk." A sliver of angst trickled down my belly.

"You don't get it, do you?"

"Get what?"

"I knew my ex better than he knew himself," Isabel said, giving a mocking laugh. "Knew when he was backing away before he did. The point is, Luke is...besotted. A word I never get to use, so I love using it now."

"You're serious?"

Isabel gave me a look, waving the scissors. "Wait a minute, there's something else going on here."

"There is?"

"You," she said. "You're holding a grudge. That's it."

"No, I'm not holding a grudge. That's ridiculous."

"Yes, you are. You're holding a grudge against Luke for not calling you back on that date about fifty million years ago, like in the Paleozoic period. Even though he's worked hard on—"

"What do you know about how hard he's worked?" *Was I holding a grudge?*

"I have excellent recall of minutiae as you well know, and I remember how heartbroken you were after one lousy date. He must have worked hard to get you to go out with him." She snorted.

"Now you're snorting?"

"You had sex," she said. "You must really like him." Accentuating the word *really*, making it into a low growl. Making it sound dirty.

Trying to stare her down didn't work, and I burst out laughing.

"It can't have been easy for him to call you after such a long break. And you are holding a grudge. I can feel it. Grudges aren't healthy." Her laser gaze leveled at me, Isabel stacked the maps in a neat pile and secured them with a paper clip. "These are done."

"It could happen again." This was Isabel, and I could tell her anything. "The backing off. Three months. Three months and men tend to back off. I read about it."

"Yeah, I know the feeling," Isabel said. "Trying to read into every little nuance. But you don't want to live your life that way, do you? Either being afraid to open your heart, or cutting a relationship off early so you won't get hurt. Not good either way."

I sighed, scooped up the maps and all the cut-outs, and put them in plastic bags for Monday. I straightened up and grabbed the markers and scissors. "Thanks. Takes a load off my mind."

Isabel tilted her head and looked at me. "Are you blind? The way Luke looks at you. He came over at midnight, for God's sake, to make sure you understood he was done with her. The stalker. In front of me...he told you—" She raked her hands through her hair making it puff up and out. "You are so frustrating."

What to say to this? I still wasn't sure where we stood, Luke and I. *Would I be a fool not to give him a chance?*

"Give him a chance," said Isabel, as if reading my mind. "Roberto's picking me up in half an hour, and I've nagged you enough about Luke, except to say Roberto isn't perfect either."

"Good." I felt a surge of possibility. The importance of imperfection was one of our private jokes, anyway.

"You never told me what you're wearing, so I'll tell you. No black."

"No black."

"Those sexy new peep-toes? Build your outfit around them."

"Wow." I took a long look at Isabel. "You're invested here."

"One last thing. About Luke."

"Yeah? What about Luke?" An inward groan. Isabel, so helpful, such a pain in the ass.

"He's hot. That's usually considered a good thing. You know that, don't you? Tell me you know that."

"Shut up. Shut up," I laughed, and flicked her arm with my finger.

"You're an idiot," she said and hugged me.

\*\*\*\*

I wouldn't let Luke pick me up, even though it was a little mean. I didn't want to be a sure thing, and having Luke drive was too intimate, potentially too intense. *Let him wonder how the night will turn out.* It was pointless anyway to guess how I'd feel about going home with Luke after dinner since I didn't yet know myself.

Maybe Isabel was right about that grudge after all.

The restaurant was Sofia's, a real *trattoria* in Fair Haven, one of those great old Italian places known for their slow-cooked tomato sauce, their homemade pasta, their three-page wine list and gigantic portions.

Wearing the hot pink crepe dress I'd found on the sale rack at Macy's, I felt spectacular. Sleeveless with a scoop neck, a perfect fit. I'd have paid full price because it made me feel *that* good.

And, yes, the sexy pink peep-toes.

The scent of garlic, oregano, and basil floated up from the tables near the podium, and the hostess spoke as if she recognized me. "Miss Chanel? Mr. Munroe is waiting for you."

Mr. Munroe wore a big fat smile as I walked toward him in all my pinkness. It was as if we were going back in time. Sure enough, he raised his glass in the air. "Join me, will you?" A corner of his mouth lifted. *He's doing this on purpose, waiting for me at the bar. Reminding me of our first meet.*

I stood close by his side, the better to tease him. "The next thing you're going to say is that your wine is redolent of—"

"Thought you couldn't pronounce that word."

"I've been working on it ever since...ever since you first used it."

He touched my arm and I fluttered. What I needed more than anything was to relax and let this evening unroll, not try to control anything.

"Would you like to try what I'm having? Zinfandel. Napa Cellars." His glance dropped to my dress. "You look beautiful. Did you wear that dress for me?"

Caught off guard by his teasing, I smiled, shifted my gaze to the bar.

"I enjoyed meeting Isabel, by the way." He signaled the waiter.

"She likes you, too."

"Come and sit by me. Remember the first time we met? Well, this is our do-over date. We're going to have a lovely evening—"

"Do you often use the word lovely?" I was feeling more at ease.

"Yes." He patted my hand. "When we're together."

Dinner passed in a haze of wine and talk and laughter. We shared the eggplant *caponata*, a goat cheese spread, and I had to stop Luke from ordering more appetizers. After that, pasta with sausage, swiss chard, and pine nuts for Luke, the chicken milanese with arugula salad for me. Way too much food.

"Spectacular," I said. Every pore in my body

hummed with contentment, and the wine was making a vital contribution to my feeling of well-being. My wayward thoughts were all directed toward Luke, imagining his hands slowly caressing my arms, his mouth on my neck. Yes, I'll admit, I'd popped into Victoria's Secret and splurged on hot pink panties and a matching lacy bra, my dirty little secret.

And yet I wouldn't let him pick me up tonight.

"So, if you'll pardon my jumping in at the deep end," Luke said, "I have this feeling you're leery of relationships crashing, and I totally get it. Why we fail at them is never straightforward. What's your take?"

"Why relationships fail? That's a serious topic." I paused, my fork impaling a rotini. "The usual." I put down the fork, lifted my wine glass and took a sip, eying Luke over the rim.

"What's the usual?" he said. "Mistrust, growing disgust, and lack of passion?" He dipped a chunk of bread into the *caponata*.

"Resentment, lack of respect, and boredom, right back at you," I said.

"You were married and bored?"

"So little in common. And Laurent wasn't interested in me. After all those years."

"I can't imagine," he said, leaning closer and touching my hand. "I'm enthralled. I want to discover—"

"Be real. We're having a serious discussion, and you're making fun of me." The waiter trotted over to refill the water glasses.

"Am not." Luke tilted his head. "What did you argue about? Or is this too maudlin a topic?"

The pasta was delicious, and I chewed slowly,

imitating Luke's unhurried way of responding. I thought about the question, pushed the plate a few inches toward Luke. "Want a taste?" He shook his head, pushed his plate closer, and I forked a little sausage. "For me it was resentment, the same arguments round and round. To Laurent, it was important to lay blame. Win the argument."

"Did he win?"

"No one wins." I sipped the wine, enjoying the buzz.

"What's the point then?" he said.

I put down my fork. "To be able to talk about how you feel about things and not be worried the person will—love you less. To be able to disagree. Ugly stuff. Even ugly stuff can come out and you get through it and agree to disagree." Luke focused on what I was saying, rarely interrupted. "No pouts. No passive-aggressive."

"Pout?" he said. "I got the silent treatment." He thought for a few seconds. "Two weeks I think. That was the longest."

"That's torture. The silent treatment," I said.

"Yes, and the sad thing is I remember the two weeks of silence, but I don't remember what we disagreed about."

"Yeah, I know what you mean."

"I blame myself. For the problems in the marriage." His voice grew softer, and I leaned forward to hear. "I'd get angry but not say anything to clear the air. That's not a good way to communicate. In my next relationship I want to do better."

*His next relationship.* Was he talking about me?

"So," and he took my hand, "this is all so new for

us, starting out. I want to get this right. I don't want any more *next* relationships."

"Oh," was all I said, and my chest squeezed with the effort to process the deeper meaning behind Luke's words. *I don't want any more next relationships.* Was he saying what I thought he was saying?

"Maybe it's too soon. Never mind. Aren't we having a splendid evening? Be truthful. You weren't relaxed before, but now you are, and it's partly due to my soothing personality. And the wine. Are you enjoying yourself? Because I am."

"Yes, yes I am, you silly," I giggled as he kissed my palm, and a shiver rushed up my arm straight to my nipples, which stood begging for attention. Under the table I crossed my legs.

"It's a bit early to tell you…this," he said and leaned in close, his lips touching my ear for an instant. Another shiver. "I like you an awful lot. As you may have guessed."

My instinct was to speak, but he shushed me. "No big confessions here, just stating the facts. No playing-hard-to-get games. So, here's the thing. We're more than halfway into our evening, and I'm putting some pressure on you." He lifted his glass and took a sip before going on.

"I want you in my life. I want to get to know you, and I hope you feel the same way. You know, spending time together…I'm looking forward to it. My daughter. She's great. You'll meet her. No rush. We'll take our time." He paused, his expression expectant and I opened my mouth, but Luke gave me a look and I shut it.

"Please." He leaned in and kissed me on the cheek,

took both my hands in his. "One more thing." When he was sure I wouldn't interrupt, he continued. "I will show you I'm that man—the man who's reliable, who wants to be with you, and who will have your back."

He gripped the back of my head ever so gently and kissed me on the lips, tasting of fresh oregano. "I adore you. I love being with you. And that's all I have to say on that subject. For now." He held onto my hands. "I bought you flowers. Daisies. I love daisies. They're wilting on my kitchen counter right now. I feel sad about that."

"Oh," I sighed.

"Right this minute, we have important decisions to make. Like what dessert to have, and whether to go for an after-dinner drink. Now, may I offer you a little more wine?"

I nodded and leaned toward him, inhaling his scent, and something shifted inside me.

\*\*\*\*

"Let me have your keys," Luke said, as I swayed unsteadily toward him. "Grab my arm."

"Here," I said, handing him my bag. "It's in the side zipper."

Luke unlocked the door and I wobbled inside, gripping his arm tightly. I'd gone past tipsy straight to drunk.

"Hey, watch it there." He reached out an arm to steady me.

I made a face to cover my embarrassment. Not only did Luke drive me home, he also had to escort me inside. My car was still at the restaurant.

"Come," and he guided me into the kitchen. "Nice built-in pantry you've got. Sit, I'll make us some coffee." I plunked down at the table as Luke opened the cupboard nearest the stove. "Coffee filters right where I thought. You keep your coffee in the freezer?"

"Yup." I was all fake-chipper, ignored the banging between my eyes, and forced a smiley face. "Dim the light, would you?" My vision was going squinty, and I held my head at an angle to minimize the nausea. The wine I'd joyfully inhaled at dinner had integrated unpleasantly with the pasta and sausage and chicken milanese. And wasn't there eggplant *caponata* and goat cheese somewhere in that mix? I'd eaten like a trucker and felt like a semi.

Elbows on the table to support my weight, I slumped as he moved around, filling and plugging in the kettle to boil water, measuring out the grounds for two cups, opening the cabinet doors to find the coffee cups. So much energy, how can he have so much energy? I wondered if he heard my gut gurgling.

"Yours is the *Never Give Up* mug, am I right? This summer, I think we should plan a grand tour of the Orlando theme parks because I'll get to scream with you on the rides."

"You're talking rides? At my age?" It came out like a squeak.

"I'm talking too much." He eyed me over his shoulder. "You think I'm nervous? I think I'm nervous. I totally lose my cool around you."

My stomach roiled. Luke turned around.

"Hey, you don't look so good." He handed me the mug of coffee. "Drink up, it'll help."

I looked down at the coffee as a sour taste rose in my throat. I swallowed. *No, this isn't happening.*

He sipped his coffee and we were quiet for a

minute, Luke looking around the kitchen at the new tile floor, the refrigerator magnets, my collection of old movie posters—Marlon Brando in *Sayonara*, Fred MacMurray in *Double Indemnity*, and the obscure French version of *The Adventures of Rabbi Jacob*. He rubbed a finger on the plank table.

"My car is still…"

A rumbling I could no longer ignore, the eggplant, chicken and goat cheese at war in my gut. "Excuse me," I said, steadying myself with my hands, the room spinning, I stumbled out of the kitchen.

"Hey, no worries," said Luke. "I'll take care of—"

In the hall, I put on speed, made it to the bathroom, slamming the door and getting on my knees, staring into the toilet bowl. It took a few seconds for it to come up, and I closed my eyes as my dinner, along with the Napa zinfandel hit the toilet. I waited, eyes squeezed shut, as the smell of what must have been goat cheese wafted up from the bowl.

I reached for the toilet paper and ripped off a piece, wiped my mouth, rolled to my side, and without looking, let the seat slam shut before I flushed. With my back against the tub for a few minutes, I breathed hard, hoping Luke wouldn't rap on the door and ask how I was doing.

Finally when I was sure barfing time was over, I hobbled to the sink and peered in the mirror. Huge mistake. I held a hand over my mouth and breathed on it hard to determine the level of my bad breath. Ten out of ten.

Where was my toothbrush? I reached for the toothpaste and squeezed it on my finger, stuck the finger in my mouth and moved it around. The headache was still there. Where was my washcloth? Was everything disappearing?

I pulled open the bottom drawer to grab a clean one, and the room swam, forcing me down to the tile floor again. I rested, wondering about Luke.

Was Luke still here? Probably not. The poor man had given up, gone home. My car...? Nothing I could do about that. Not tonight.

Crawling out of the bathroom on hands and knees, I reached the bed and braced against it for support. I clawed off the spread and got in, pulling the covers up.

Luke would have to fend for himself.

\*\*\*\*

I awoke with a jerk and rolled over in the darkness. It took me a few seconds to remember. Dinner with Luke. Wine with Luke. A lot of wine with Luke.

Throwing up. That I vividly remembered.

Oh, crap. I sat up to assess damages. Head on the achy side, but no throbbing. The plus side to vomiting, definitely. A few Tylenol would help. Weird. I wasn't wearing my shorty PJs. I fingered the material. Whoa, I'd worn my new crepe dress to bed.

Where was Luke? Probably gone since I'd deserted him. Too late to worry about his feelings, not until after I showered. By the time I finished scrubbing up and pulled on shorts and a T-shirt, there was a faint glint of light outside.

In the kitchen, the first thing to greet me was Luke's sports jacket on the back of the chair. My coffee cup sat in the drain along with another cup. It was coming back now, sitting here last night, Luke making coffee.

I moved into the hall and glanced toward the guest

room. Funny, the door was closed. I tried the handle and pushed. A sliver of light edged in from a corner of the blinds, enough so I could make him out in the bed. He slept with one arm curled around his head facing the window, fingers splayed on the pillow.

*Cute.* I wanted some of that cuteness. I stood a few seconds watching him, hoping this didn't count as stalking before I slid onto the bed trying not to breathe. Wait, what if I still had that stinky throw-up breath in spite of the brushing and the gargling? What if he didn't want me here? What if he had a meeting in the morning? Hold on, it wasn't a workday, and he'd asked me to spend the day with him.

Luke called out in his sleep. One word, a word I couldn't catch.

And then he opened his eyes and focused on me. And grinned. "Oh, my dream came true."

He reached for me, his arms crushing me to him, pulling me under the sheet, kissing my forehead, my cheek, my chin. "You're beautiful in the morning, you know? Are you feeling better? You feel so good, your body against mine, you're so warm, like a little heater."

We were kissing, deep kisses, and I could feel a hardness pressing into my leg.

"I love kissing you," I said.

He pulled back to look at me, a smile tugging a corner of his mouth. He kissed me again, slow and lazy. "A little birdie told me you had a good time last night."

"I'm so embarrassed—"

He stopped my words with a kiss. Then in one movement he raised himself over me, whispering, "Let's just ease off that little top so I can—"

He groaned. "No, leave it on. I don't want to rush

you. No, let's take it off. Is it all right if I take it off? I have to ask permission because—"

"Luke?"

"Yes, darling."

"Shut up."

\*\*\*\*

*Three Months Later...*

I poured the coffee. The old plank table was set with my new plates, a collection of mismatches in bright colors. The gouges and cracks from other families added to the charm of a table with history.

Luke sat watching while I stacked the fresh bagels on a sunshine yellow platter and put out the cheese Danish and blueberry and veggie cream cheese—all goodies he bought after our run this morning.

"What do you know about coyotes?" Luke forked a piece of omelet.

"What?" I said, helping myself to one each of the oranges and pears I'd cut up and served. I followed his eyes to *Prodigal Summer*, the Barbara Kingsolver novel I'd just finished. "Oh. Yes, I have new respect for coyotes. They're smart."

"I liked the old man. Feisty and scared."

"Me too, but I liked the old woman better. Feisty and not scared." I bit into a wedge of pear. After that there was Roald Dahl to talk about, Janet Evanovich— he'd never read her—and Anne Tyler and Jacqueline Susann.

He put his fork down. "Got to stop. Trying to watch what I eat." He chuckled. "Well, watching isn't the problem. Controlling I should say. I'm trying to control what I insert."

I nodded, took another pear wedge. "Aren't we

all."

"So. I'm thinking a trip to Orlando?"

Luke had brought up Orlando before, but I'd thought it was a passing idea.

"We'll go with Lily and her boyfriend, Bryan. I'll get a suite, full kitchen. They're terrific fun to be with," and off he went, reeling off names, how we couldn't miss this exhibition or that. And some rapids thing. "You won't believe the special effects," and here he leaned forward, running his hand along my shoulder. "We'll have a blast."

I cringed on the inside and managed a smile that probably came out more like a grimace. Lucky for me Luke was more absorbed in slathering his rosemary bagel with a thick coat of cream cheese to notice.

Three days of intimate coziness with two young people I didn't know, one of them his daughter, gave me the shivers.

*Lily and her boyfriend? Is he serious?*

I'd met Lily exactly twice, and our encounters were brief—once in the supermarket, and another time when she came for a run with Luke. We all had oatmeal afterward. Lily had taken down that bowl of oatmeal in two minutes flat, crunched the walnuts between her teeth like they were bubbles, washed everything down with cold, milky coffee, and she was on her way.

"Let me nail down the dates and text you," he said. "It'll be sticky hot, and the place will be mobbed, but that's all part of the fun."

"Yes, it sounds lovely." Lily was a lovely girl.

*It doesn't sound even remotely lovely.*

And it's not like we could bond over a quick bowl of oatmeal, anyway. A big bite of my Asiago bagel made me feel better for the moment. Luke was sweet, wanting me to meet his daughter, her boyfriend, be part of the family.

Rushing it a bit? Maybe, but trust was a big deal. And how could he trust me if I didn't admit to dating all those guys?

"I'm job hunting again. Check the listings every day."

"The long-term sub job won't be permanent?"

"Who knows?" My voice was flat.

I took another bite of bagel, and reached for the plate of pears. Luke grabbed my wrist. "Hey, what's going on?"

I sank back into the chair. "I don't know about this trip." I couldn't look at him.

"Oh?" He considered this, his eyes on me.

"I wanted to tell you...I meant to tell you all this sooner. What...it happened before we met. You should know that for the past four or five months I've been meeting men."

"Oh."

"It was a contest."

"What? A contest?" And his face broke into a grin. "Are you frigging joking?"

"Let me explain. Well, not explain exactly. I was helping a friend who was afraid of online dating."

I told him about Dana and the dating contest, and how it worked. "Only Dana met Jerry, and they hit it off on their first date, so she got to stop. Not me." Dropping my voice so he had to lean in to hear me. "So, I ended up meeting twenty-five guys."

"Wait, you *had* to meet twenty-five guys?"

"Um..." I wanted to tell him my friends egged me

on, but that wasn't true.

"Never mind. What's the prize?"

"Dana's taking me to New York for a weekend."

"Nice." He sat for a moment. "Was I one of the contestants?"

*Ut oh.*

"I never thought of the guys I met as—"

I stopped as he grinned, vaulted out of his seat and came behind me, squish-kissing my cheek, his lips stretching to the side of my mouth. My heart thudded a little.

Okay, so it thudded a lot.

"You're sadly easy to tease. Tell me, can you name them all? Did you take notes?" He dragged me into the living room and pushed me onto the couch.

"It's all a blur, and besides, I only dated guys named Bob." Now I was laughing.

"A blur, huh?"

It wasn't a blur, of course it wasn't a blur, and I stopped fidgeting, turned serious. "Do you get it?" I could no longer gloss over it, the whole dating thing. "Why I was doing all that dating?"

He pulled me onto his lap, and I buried my face in his neck. "You were looking for your special person," he said. "Everyone wants the same thing, you know."

"What do you mean? Everyone isn't the same." I rocked back to look at him, figure out if he was kidding. His expression was intent.

"We all want to be special and have a special person in our lives. That part is simple."

"Simple?"

"It's finding that person and the acceptance, those are the hard parts."

"Wow. You've thought about this."

"Yeah, and seeing my therapist helps. Now it's monthly. More often than an oil change. Keeps me honest."

"That's a good thing. Look," I said, "about the dating. Middle-aged people? It's hard to meet someone at this—at our age. I don't work in a place with available men."

"Ah," he said. "Well, I'm glad about that."

He deserved the dirty look I shot him. "My mother loved the contest idea so much she told all her friends and started texting with links to dating advice columns."

"Now you can tell her about me," and he put on a huge, exaggerated smile that made me smile too. He slid me off his lap, stood and peered out the window. "Let's take a hike today. Perfect day. Perfect for a hike on the Sleeping Giant and a picnic after. At the bottom, where they keep the picnic tables. See, I haven't told you, but I'm not a pedestrian guy when it comes to food, so it'll have to be a gourmet picnic."

"Luke. Believe me, I've noticed."

"Oh, of course. I'll figure out the food and you decide on the trail. I've got a map in my car. Blue is the toughest, keep that in mind. Am I nervous-babbling again?"

"You don't have a nervous bone in your body."

He slapped his head. "You've cut me to the bone. And now you've got me using clichés. This is bad, very bad."

"Don't blame me for your clichés."

"I blame you," he said. "For everything." And in one motion he reached over and pulled me close. "My plan for today, you like it?"

"I love your plan."

"My Orlando plan?" he asked.

I rubbed a finger across his cheek. "I'm coming around." A chance to get to know his daughter. It would be fine. And Luke didn't care about all the Bobs after all.

"There's more. You know that island, the clamming island I told you about long ago? I want us to go there together. This summer when I don't have courses to teach and you won't be working."

"I want to visit my friends in Paris. This summer."

"You're visiting, not moving?" he said.

"Just visiting."

"And you won't be gone too terribly long?" he said.

"Not terribly."

"We'll plan around your trip to visit with your friends." His fingers caught mine.

"My friends and my dog Pluto," I said. "He misses me, and I miss him, our long walks. And I'll have to see my ex-husband. He's not such a bad guy."

"Of course."

"He was instrumental in helping me secure this residence."

"Instrumental, huh?"

"Yes."

"You secured this residence?"

"You're making fun of me."

"Not at all. I love your formal mode of speech."

"Thank you."

We stood looking at one another in the middle of the living room, his arm around my waist. Outside, the day beckoned, and later we'd spend the evening together, stir frying, or we'd grab takeout. Whatever we did these days, we did mostly together. Sometimes with our families—his parents, my parents—which surprised the heck out of me.

"Twenty-five years ago," he said. I waited to see where this was going. "That's when I was in Paris. For pleasure. I'm not counting conferences."

Why was he telling me this?

"Paris," and he gave an exaggerated sigh meant to convey all sorts of…innuendo? "There's no place on earth like it."

My chest thudded a little. Was this a hint?

"What do you think about…"

His voice drifted off, and my chest thudded a little more. This was almost definitely a hint.

"Do you miss Paris?" It didn't hurt to ask. "It's a very addictive city and twenty-five years without pleasure is way too long." If he wasn't hinting, I was going out on a limb. Was it too soon? Our togetherness was still new. In three months, we'd spent one weekend away.

And every weekend together.

"It's been way too long," he said. "I could use a dose of Paris."

*A dose of Paris?* "Are you good with animals?"

"Excellent. Mothers and animals love me equally."

"Ex-husbands?" I'll admit to a little smirk.

"Not much experience there."

"Never mind. Some things you can't predict or control."

"Am I being too bold? Asking to come with you? Five days, the last five days of your trip?"

He took a breath, and I leaned against him, a full-body lean, listened to his chest rumbling as he talked.

"You need time with your friends. But the last leg of your trip, we'll stay in a hotel *ensemble*. That's French, by the way. And Pluto, get custody of him for those five days, and I'll make sure the hotel takes dogs."

*He wants to come to Paris with me.*

"Your friends, I'll meet your friends, and we'll dine well because it's Paris. When in doubt, you grab a baguette or one of those *croque monsieur* things. Am I pronouncing that right? Plus we'll—"

"How long have you been planning this?"

He drew back and looked down, put a finger under my chin, bent to kiss me.

"You mentioned it one day, wanting to go back for a visit. I've been thinking about it ever since. Wasn't sure you'd go for it." He was watching me, measuring my reaction, and that's how I knew.

Isabel had got it right that day, the morning after our pajama party. I remembered her exact words. "Luke is besotted. A word I never get to use, so I love using it now."

And maybe he was, and so was I.

"You and me in Paris? S'marvelous. *Merveilleux*."

"That's settled then, we're tripping to Paris," and he squeezed me to his chest. "More fun than humans should have." He bent and kissed me a smooch that went on for so long I thought we'd scrap the hiking plans.

"Woman," and he pulled back, "are you ready for a hike?"

In the kitchen, I pulled out two water bottles. "I'm

ready. All I have to do is put on my hiking boots. You?"

"Let's swing by my house and I'll grab mine." He stood looking at me, then came into the kitchen wearing his serious expression. No, on second thought, this was his fake-serious expression.

"I'll go hiking with you on one condition."

I waited.

"You'll put up with me if I can't keep my hands off you? Those steep rock formations on the blue trail? I gotta do some serious ass grabbing to push you up those boulders."

"Only on the way up?" I asked.

"You didn't let me finish." He came close and pulled me against him. "On the way down, too, like this, like I'm doing now."

"Oh. Some serious snogging—"

"British for kissing—I'll need to do that with frequency."

"Snogging, yes, it's mandatory."

"Snogging next week, and the month after, and…all the other months. At the gas station, the supermarket," he said.

"In dairy or in deli?" I asked.

"You're not taking me seriously."

"Sorry." My arms wrapped his neck like a muffler.

"In Orlando I can grab and kiss you on the top of the roller coaster?"

"Sure."

"In Paris. At the Eiffel Tower."

"It's a cliché, but sure."

"You'll help me with my French?"

"I'll help you with your French kissing."

"You'll smooch me good?"

"I will." My chest hummed with the silliness and the pure pleasure of planning future smooches.

"Promise?"

"Promise." *Oh, yes, this was such fun.*

"For how long?"

"For as long as it takes."

"Deal," he said. "I like going slowly."

"Lucky me."

"Me too. I'm the luckiest man alive."

"Yes, you are."

"Let's stay home tonight," Luke said, "cuddle with a pizza."

"Cuddle with a pizza?"

"You know what I mean," and he ruffled my ears.

"I do."

"I do, too."

## A Reading Group Guide to *Middle Age*ish

1. What about Sunny Chanel's starting over adventure, do you relate to and why? Why do you think Sunny reacts the way she does to Laurent's request for a separation near the beginning of the book?

2. Sunny starts over in many ways and has doubts about her ability to support herself and to connect with a man. How does she cope with and overcome these doubts?

3. Friendship is a theme of Middle Age*ish*. How do Sunny and her friends help one another?

4. What role does food play in Sunny's life and how does its importance shift as she makes her way as an independent woman?

5. Internet dating becomes a focus of Sunny's new life in the book. Why do you think she begins to date so soon after leaving her husband?

6. Would Sunny have begun online dating had Dana not challenged her with the "contest?" How are her expectations for a positive outcome realistic? How are they not?

7. Sunny tends to develop crushes on a few of the men she meets during her quest. Why do you think this is important to the story? How does it help define Sunny's character? Can you relate her online dating experiences to those of your own? If so, how?

8. When does Sunny begin to lose respect for Frank? Is there a particular event or a set of behaviors that cause her to think differently of him? Why does she say he smiled "liked a salesman?"

9. Noah is very dear to Sunny and she takes him seriously. What character traits in Noah is she drawn to? What in Noah's behavior causes her to doubt they will last as a couple?

10. Would she have continued dating Noah if he hadn't ended their relationship? Why or why not?

11. What do you think the confrontation between Sunny and Mark, the kid who hits and runs, tells the reader about how Sunny grows and changes in the novel? How does Mark change?

12. Sunny and Isabel have known one another since childhood. How do long-term friendships differ from newer friendships such as the one Sunny enjoys with Dana?

13. Sunny is attracted to Luke and yet he doesn't call her back, even after a successful and fun first date. Afterward, she is hard-pressed to trust him. What behavior and actions on his part make her change her mind?

14. Do you think Sunny would have started over if Laurent hadn't confronted her with his desire for a separation and divorce? Why or why not?

15. Would Sunny have continued to date Luke had Isabel not prodded her to give him a chance? What do your responses tell you about Sunny's character, and how she evolves in the novel?

## A word from the author…

I'll admit, my friends like to guess which stories in *Middle Age*ish are true, but I remind them it's all fiction, and I have a vivid imagination. I'm hoping you finished *Middle Age*ish with a smile on your face. If so, perhaps you'll consider leaving a review on Amazon, Goodreads, or at your favorite bookseller. Good reviews are like a hot fudge sundae to authors. We do a happy dance every time.

Meanwhile, check out my website to find the latest info on my next book, plus articles and book recommendations. And, of course, you can always find me on Facebook.

~

**Author Shirley Goldberg, a former ESL** and French teacher, has lived in Paris, Crete, and Casablanca. A writer and novelist who writes about relationships and starting over, like the main character in her novel, *Middle Age*ish, Shirley began dating late in life. Her website http://midagedating.com offers a humorous look into dating, and her friends like to guess which stories are true.

Thank you for purchasing
this publication of The Wild Rose Press, Inc.

For questions or more information
contact us at
info@thewildrosepress.com.

The Wild Rose Press, Inc.
www.thewildrosepress.com

CPSIA information can be obtained
at www.ICGtesting.com
Printed in the USA
BVHW060104240820
587115BV00003B/70

9 781509 232505